Sacred Lips

of the

Bronx

Douglas
Sadownick

St. Martin's Press
New York

Author's note: During my research into Yiddish orthography, I have found there are as many ways to transcribe dialect as there are Yiddish speakers. I hope I have not offended anyone. If I have, *zay mir moichl* or, then again, *zayt mir moichl,* or . . .

SACRED LIPS OF THE BRONX. Copyright © 1994 by Douglas Sadownick. All rights reserved. Printed in the United States of America. No part of this book may be used or reproduced in any manner whatsoever without written permission except in the case of brief quotations embodied in critical articles or reviews. For information, address St. Martin's Press, 175 Fifth Avenue, New York, N.Y. 10010.

Design by Jaye Zimet

Library of Congress Cataloging-in-Publication Data

Sadownick, Douglas.
   Sacred lips of the Bronx / Douglas Sadownick.
     p. cm.
   ISBN 0-312-13165-8
   1. Gay men—California—Los Angeles—Fiction. 2. Puerto Rican families—New York (N.Y.)—Fiction. 3. Bronx (New York, N.Y.)—Fiction. 4. Los Angeles (Calif.)—Fiction. I. Title.
PS3569.A263S23 1994
813'.54—dc20   94–1924
                                                         CIP

First Paperback Edition: June 1995

10 9 8 7 6 5 4 3 2 1

For Tim Miller

Acknowledgments

Nothing worthy of mention in my life has been possible without the help of teachers. I'd like to acknowledge Mitch Walker, Michael Callen, Mark Thompson, Lewis Segal, Arnie Kantrowitz, and Kit Rachlis. My editor, Michael Denneny, guided me to go all the way on the wacky vision I had for the book; he was nervy and brilliant. My agent, Charlotte Sheedy, gave fine literary advice and friendship. Thanks to the pals: David Román, Matt Silverstein, Steven Corbin, Jill Burnham, Robin Podolsky, and Luis Alfaro and my colleagues at the *L.A. Weekly* and at the 18th Street Arts Complex. I should like to acknowledge my ancestors. And my parents. And my students. Also my inspiring brother, Dan. Fran (Freydeleh) Chalin, cantorial assistant at Temple Beth Chayim Chadashim, helped me with the Yiddish, as did Dr. David Lieber, President Emeritus of the University of Judaism in Los Angeles. Marcus Kuiland Nazario helped with the Spanish, as did Alberto Sandoval. My friend Sandra Golvin, a poet and dyke mystic, read the first pages years ago and never lost faith in that crone Frieda. Above all, my boyfriend, Tim Miller, provided financial and emotional support, without which I could not have written this book.

Acknowledgments

Nothing worthy of mention in my life has been possible without the help of teachers. I'd like to acknowledge Mitch Walker, Michael Callen, Mark Thompson, Lewis Segal, Arnie Kantrowitz, and Kit Rachlis. My editor, Michael Denneny, guided me to go all the way on the wacky vision I had for the book; he was nervy and brilliant. My agent, Charlotte Sheedy, gave fine literary advice and friendship. Thanks to the pals: David Román, Matt Silverstein, Steven Corbin, Jill Burnham, Robin Podolsky, and Luis Alfaro and my colleagues at the *L.A. Weekly* and at the 18th Street Arts Complex. I should like to acknowledge my ancestors. And my parents. And my students. Also my inspiring brother, Dan. Fran (Freydeleh) Chalin, cantorial assistant at Temple Beth Chayim Chadashim, helped me with the Yiddish, as did Dr. David Lieber, President Emeritus of the University of Judaism in Los Angeles. Marcus Kuiland Nazario helped with the Spanish, as did Alberto Sandoval. My friend Sandra Golvin, a poet and dyke mystic, read the first pages years ago and never lost faith in that crone Frieda. Above all, my boyfriend, Tim Miller, provided financial and emotional support, without which I could not have written this book.

Preface

Way back when—as far back as the 1970s, even—you could walk like a person in the Bronx, blowing off the dope dealers and junkies on-the-rag with a squinty "fuck-with-me!" look in your left eye, and if a simple cruise got too Mission Impossible, a makeshift Bruce Lee kick *kapow* to the balls. Clunky, but you'd get your point across. Those were the days, like the song says. I had this cool hike, one that took you from the unkosher hot-dog stands near Yankee Stadium to Alexander's—the best (and cheapest) department store in the entire North Bronx—where you got your lousy egg creams and burnt-to-a-crisp grilled cheese sandwiches, but boy, did they hit the spot. You didn't have to be that outrageously lucky, or built like Mark Spitz even, to score. I mean, you just had to have the right line. "Got some smoke?"— that worked great. Another: "Hey man, whereju get yah Pro-Keds—at John's Bargain or something?" I mean, I hooked up with a lot of kids my own age that way. The best and most ambitious took me out for ice-cold Sankas and Diet Rites, then home to parentless, slipcovered, four-room apartments not far from the Bronx Botanical Gardens. In the spring, when you wanted to lose your cherry, you had the cherry blossoms going bananas like you;

in the fall, you had the paper-thin purple leaves making a forest-like mess all over the steps leading to the elevated IRT. Always you had the hot concrete under your feet. I resisted many a lonely come Saturday morning this way — Bronx-long bebops in my Converses, a suspicious twinge in my dungarees.

I'm telling you, I did plenty to cut loose from the trip that I was some nice Jewish kid with babbling Yiddish ancestors. I cruised the Grand Concourse like there was no tomorrow. Donna Summer was Queen one muggy summer and I went so far as to carry her gospel-raging voice on my shoulder in a two-ton black ghetto blaster. People looked at me like I was mental. I was of the streets — big-nosed and wiry, and yet there was something else: qualms about loud noises, chin-scratching, bookish pupils. I could count on uncanny reactions from kids smoking lazily on apartment stoops, eyeing me as I passed by: "Yo, faggot, where's yah dress?" or "Hey, man, cool music." One nice boy — his name was Franky — he struck up an authentic conversation. His mother called him Frankly Franky because, like he said, he called her "Martyr Mom." Me, he called "Mixed-up Mike." We'd get stoned out of our minds in the Loew's Theater on Fordham Road; afterward we'd neck like Jodie Foster and What's-His-Name? in urine-dripping stalls. Mr. F, which is what I called him, had red-stained hands and square tousles of hair; I thought he shined his muscles with car wax. Once, while his mother and stepdad were confessing at a Catholic church, he tried to slip his way into me. The tip impaled. I suggested he try again. But he said, "Man, I got a bitch who loves this thing better than you could ever." He took me out for a Dr. Pepper, and that was that. When he moved, I blamed myself.

I'm trying to remember the puzzle of things then, the flip-flops of heritage and boy-crazy seizures that drove me *loco, pendejo*, because the Bronx of my youth is dead-as-a-doornail now, over-run with crack babies, gang posses and tooth-spitting white people. But there's more: In a person's youth, a great moment of love comes, unexpected and irrepressible, like a fart, if you know what I mean. For me it was in a Chinese restaurant, over clotting egg foo yung. When the damp fortune cookie came, I was either too

stupid or too head-over-heels to crack it open like you were supposed to. There have been two such unread fortunes in my life.
I abandoned them as one closes the book on outdated figures
from Greek mythology: a Puerto Rican Zeus, a Jewish Athena.
All I see now is lips old and young. I go to kiss them and the
ethereal memories split, like I'm a cop or something, wrecking
the oncoming dope buzz for everyone, including myself.

I sometimes daydream that I was born into a Bronx body just
to pry these lips open to say what they once said, only this time,
damn guys, don't fucking turn away so fast! I have commuted
down the Cross Bronx Expressway in beat-up Chevvies, three-
speed bikes and drunken middle-of-the-night stomps just to rescue these lips from the ghost town that is now me — a Bronx no
one in his right mind would want to visit, let alone reside in. I
have come up not so dumb as you might think, but curious as to
why nature (or God or whoever it is!) made Jews, Puerto Ricans,
blacks, queer kids and other types. I mean, we could have all met
up in North Carolina — or Timbuktu, for that matter — but for the
purposes of our particular *karma schmarma* we lived in one ghetto
and then another. What a headache life can be! And what a worse
headache if you forget who gave you head and whose heart you
made ache. On with the story.

The Marriage

pike barks. He scampers to the door. The nails on his feet make sounds on the oak floor: *click, click, click* — like he's typing. I stop typing. Robert must be home. I look at my watch. It's dusk. I hear the fence door swing open, then slam shut. I get up to be with Spike. I look out our foyer window. Robert lumbers toward the porch like he's Bud, the teenage boy from "Father Knows Best." I open the front door. I see the sky, red-tinted from the setting sun. "Hi," I say. Robert walks in the house; he wipes his feet. I act as if I know nothing. Sand sails down Robert's back onto the floor. I want to apply the Dustbuster. I resist. I wait for the peck on the lips.

"Hey, Mikey," he says.

There's the peck.

He stands, looking at me like I'm not who I am. He brings his lips close. I expect him to break away after the first brush.

He doesn't.

"Robert!" I say, moving my eyeball toward the center of his flushed face. His refusal to let me go — it fills up the house, which smells of Venice Beach seaweed and Spike's moist dinner.

"Didn't know you'd be home, Mikeroo."

"Didn't know you'd be out."

He holds my hand. I almost forget what I'm supposed to be

worrying about. So does he, it seems. We might as well be scientist gorillas in *Planet of the Apes*.

He fiddles with the thermostat. He shuts the blinds. I want to make him think this through; I want to make myself think it through, but as usual, he's irresistible and what's worse, he knows it, or at least he acts like he does. He's trying to show me something he can't explain. His voice trails off: "Ah." He looks to my face.

He touches a hand between my left cheek and chin. I taste a hint of urine on his fingers, as if he's been cupping another man's testicles for the last few hours. I groan absurdly at his fingers touching my lips. All this ties Robert in, too. It's like he's reading me different now, seeing how far I will go. He wets his finger before touching my lips. Like he's about to turn a page of the *Los Angeles Times*.

There's a kiss that's not really a kiss but a skirmish. A trigger has been turned on inside him, and it's made him a little wild, that *go, don't go* voice. Now it's lips touching lips: low-pitched surfaces, nothing deeper than that. At least not yet. There's a new variation on a theme by Robert: teeth on gums, on corners, matched sets, then mix and match and then, boom, the elusive tongue makes a debut. *Hello, you don't know me, but I know you.* Flat and waspish, it's still a tongue — even if it does speak in monosyllables. Did I hear a moan? *No*, the tongue says, *I'm sorry*. The tongue retreats to its little cave: so shy.

Not so shy. Robert tackles me down to the carpet. The setting sun casts sullen figures in our house.

It's so dark: I can't see his stubble or angular jawbone or foolish smile. The gray shag carpeting smells of our dog's piss, dead fleas and dry fur. Robert dry-kisses my mouth like they do in 1940s movies. For years I never felt beautiful. I smell the stink of a stranger in his hair. With his left hand free, Robert unbuckles. He fumbles with my jeans. He wiggles out of his shorts. The sunset and its orange-blasted palette poking into our exhausted scene from a twisted fragment of the venetian blinds. Everything darkens. Robert turns over and lies on his stomach.

His body, a weighted mass of whiteboy muscle, moves softly.

He knows to just lie there, indicating the gravity of this position, and all the ambivalent power it suggests. I want him to ask me, "You like it?" I want to say "Yeah." But instead he says, "Yum." I stare into his face, chiseled like a pageboy's — the hair short and brownish black, the chin dotted with stubble.

His mouth opens, a signal for me that it's okay. I go on in. His body snaps into a kind of orchestrated chaos. I cover his mouth; our cries have been known to disturb our neighbors. I am not close. He is. It is unspoken, but constant: our safety, fear of poisons. I slip myself away from him. He grunts. We lie in a pool of light on the living room carpet — apart now. Robert puts his hand to my torso, as if to suggest a certain reciprocity. I pat his hand. *It's okay.* In a moment, he seems asleep. In the dark, he searches for my hand. Frantic. Like he can't go to sleep without it. I withhold my pinkie. He won't sleep. I give in.

———

I turn on the light to my room. It's white, assaultive. I see signs of life and lassitude: posters for AIDS demonstrations, pinups from postpunk porn magazines, books about political theater and theater as political spectacle, graduate school loan bills, unfiled press releases, a list of unanswered phone calls, the unread Sunday *New York Times*, car payments. I light a votive candle and shut off the artificial lights. Now: a red incandescence.

In sex clubs and porn houses, a beautiful man armored with muscle will become a totem for all the plain Janes. In my life, Robert is that magnet — no, more to the point, it's pictures of Robert. Robert is a performance artist. Robert is an AIDS activist. Robert is never just Robert. A photograph that catches the context of his sweaty bicep before it falls into the oblivion of memory: that's sex. A photograph that reveals Robert being Robert in the world, leading groups of men into arrest or applause: that's lights, camera, action — especially as the real Robert snores in the other room.

Shirt off, chest silver-pale with the sweat of exertion. Robert throws his shoulder and upper body into this explosion of emotion: *I'm beautiful, stop AIDS, have sex, be real free, get a cool haircut.*

Theater lights bake him as they must bake those men posing naked for cameras in *Stroke*. Robert speaks into a mike. The song Robert sings might as well be a U-2 ballad. His eyes flash up. Maybe some stranger will take this memory of Robert home and silently, while his lover is asleep and snoring, masturbate to the image of Robert being aware of being watched as Robert.

There's a brown mole under his nipple. A glimpse of pubic hair, an abdomen so snug it curves away from the hips and chest like it's plastered. The hair is washed with Ivory soap. As you kiss this stranger, your fingers work their way into this nest of Brillo; you think of Boy Scouts, students learning how to smoke, teenagers snickering, softball. Robert performs in San Diego, Kansas City, New York City, Atlanta, Austin, San Francisco, Houston, Buffalo, Paris, London, Sydney. Men put posters of him up in their closets. Teenagers write notes. Evangelicals scorn him on "Nightline." All this gives the grin a boyish sheen. Narcissus pleases with his remoteness.

There's a second photo. In the heyday of AIDS activism, ACT UP closed down buildings. This time it's the Federal Building in Los Angeles or New York or Washington, D.C. — one of those places. Robert-the-Artist has written a manifesto for Robert-the-Activist. *We want more money, we want more respect, we want to stop burying our friends.* The crowd cheers. Robert is a member of the affinity group — The L.A. Raiders. The Gang of Ten plops itself down by the building's entrance. Robert sits center stage. Leather jacket, ACT UP T-shirt reading, ACTION = LIFE, whistles, eyes staring into the shields and gloves and badges of a city's riot police. A standoff a moment before war. Arjuna without all the doubts.

A fist gets raised; curses at the police. An emotional life as layered as anyone's emotional life, only this one is being played out for the cameras. *"Help us, we're dying,"* Robert screams to the public.

The crowd cums in appreciation.

My hand reaches for the Kleenex to wipe the goo off the photo. I insert the photo back in the file marked "personal." The smell of the burning wick calls out to me: rest. Failure.

I stumble into bed. I touch Robert, his taut buttocks, hushed and unassuming, as I fall off to sleep, chasing the porn movie of

Robert as much as I can before my own dreams chase me else-
where.

———

At the beach, a high society forms around the sunset. Grey-haired
hippies who live in boardwalk tenements on Venice Beach or old
ladies who sit alone in Santa Monica rent-controlled apartments
or Latino homeboys from Boyle Heights at the beach to smooch
with their girlfriends and get away from the dissing—they all
shuffle down to the surf to watch the sun set into the Pacific.
Surfers treat the sunset like a pagan god. It's as if each twilight
could bring about the end of the world, a change of heart, or a
new relationship. It's dead quiet, save for a clumsy whiteboy
skateboarder singing like Madonna in a boy-toy belt, or a tipsy
Vietnam vet playing John Coltrane on a little phonograph he
plugs into an outlet by the pizza place. Colors get teased out from
clouds: blotched violets, layered purples and azure flares.

Along the Santa Monica bike path you find a concrete stoop.
It runs, as a mini-cliff, for miles. The curvaceous slab acts as a
resting place for strollers and sunset watchers. Like a bench, it's
only two feet high. I call it "The Great Wall of Santa Monica."
People sit there, getting as close to Asia as they can before the
burnt-red sunlight slips from the hemisphere. The wind blows a
heated damp wind. You can smell so much: the offshore drilling;
the sewage that flows westbound from the streets of Los Angeles
into the bay; the dope people smoke near the ocean as it gets
safely darkened; the incense the crystal peddlers burn at the
boardwalk.

The quiet intensity cuts you off from the past.

I am on my early evening run. I sprint. Past the tarot-card
readers. Past the black guy in a white turban who plays electric
guitar. Past the midget amputee who sings for nickels and dimes.
Past the crack babies, the homeless, the schizos, the Crips and
their finger signs. It's a blur, but I think I see him. Third day in
a row now. On a run sometimes you hear thoughts—quotes-of-
the-day, such as: "I'll be at the demonstration today," or "I won't
be home for dinner," or "I'll give you a progress report when I

get back home." I'm pretty sure it's him. I slow up—feeling a wooden stiffness in my legs. Can it be him? His fingers folding into the vague form of another young man's hand? I don't dare stop.

From what I can pick up, the other guy is light skinned and ardent—a boy. Other associations come to mind: WASP, less than six inches, squeaky clean, a way with art history, post-Kennedy. The two sit on the Santa Monica stoop, partly obscured by the green benches and debris used by people who have nowhere else to sleep. I continue on my run. The scene of two lovers-to-be vanishes in that cinematic spinning runners and drunks and writers live for.

I thud to a stop. Venice Beach *turistas* glare at me, just in case I am one of those mimes who might imitate their Kansas City step.

I think of walking over to the two men, taking off my headphones, tapping the-man-who-could-be-Robert on the shoulder and saying, "Fancy meeting you here."

I don't.

I might be wrong.

What if it's not Robert?

What if it is?

I head on home, sweating like a pig, catching a chill in the dusk winds. Robert said he'd be late tonight. He said he'd be attending the demonstration. *No*, he didn't intend on being arrested, *but you never know*. I wish I had gone, but the weekly newspaper I write for, *The Angeleno*, wouldn't assign me another AIDS story. I'm trying to make a name for myself. Who knows, maybe Robert has called in from the demonstration? Or perhaps Ann-the-Leading-Activist called to say Robert got arrested. Robert needs bail; Robert needs Mikey; Robert needs dinner. I run home.

I arrive at our lovers' nest. Spike, who buys the home-sweet-home hype, chases his tail in a fit of muttlike bliss. I pat him, serve him three scoops of Science Diet dog chow, fill his ceramic Snoopy water bowl.

No messages.

The sun sets. Spike and I sit outside on the porch to watch the sky tarnish into reddish penumbras.

When Robert comes home, about three hours later, he greets me with a song: "Do You Know the Way to San Jose?" He retreats into the shower like a naked pinup star. I have boiled four cups of water for two cups of brown rice, and steamed a few sprigs of broccoli. I set out the Franciscan red-flower ware his mother gave us. I arrange the table with seltzer water, spinach salad, olive oil, balsamic vinegar and a dozen wild daisies Robert grows in the front garden. I turn off the lights in the house and light two candles set in a wax-coated brass candelabra for the table. Robert emerges from the steamy bathroom, beads of dampness around the back of his arms and calves. Spike licks the calves. "Drink up, Spikey-Poo." Robert wraps a white bath towel around his waist. He grins at the food and takes his place at the table, pulling out a wobbly wooden chair with a surgical screech. He's ravenous. "Yum," he says, burrowing his face in the steam rising up from his plate. He shakes a bottle of tamari over his rice as if a fire were blazing on it. He spoons the mush into his mouth like he's a kid with a carton of Breyer's. When he is done, he looks at me in his grateful but noncommittal way. If I didn't know any better, I'd guess he was falling in love with me.

"I still have this headache," I say.

"It's been months," he says, burping so loud even the dog lifts his ears. "Did you take aspirin?"

I show him the bottle of Advil. I turn it upside down. It is empty.

"Mikey, stop worrying," he says, worrying a little.

"It's a nice piece of advice. For some reason I haven't yet figured out, it doesn't work."

"You don't have AIDS. I promise."

"How do you know?"

"I *don't* know."

The house turns dark. The light from the candles casts Robert's face in shadow. Our house is large enough for us to have a tiny bedroom plus our own separate rooms, so when the inside grows dark, the shadows appear, and you don't know from whose neck of the woods they come. Shadows annoy Robert. For his sake, I turn on the fluorescent light over the kitchen sink. While I'm there, I do two or three yogurt-caked dishes. I do not break any over Robert's head. Robert remains in his chair, trying to get my attention by making faces. Lips pucker. Eyelashes bat. Cheeks puff out. He gives up, sighing loudly enough for Spike to gallop over. Robert moves away from the table, making skidding sounds. I grimace: I mopped yesterday. Unbelievable: the dishes remain intact. A few show cracks. Dirt has seeped into their ceramic veins. Robert walks into his own room. I hear him turn on his computer; it's four years old and hums like a metal fan. I take one yellowed plate and toss it in the air. I catch it.

"I saw the most amazing sunset tonight," I say from the kitchen.

"Aw," he says. "Too bad I missed it."

"Robbie, it was so fucking romantic!"

"Really?" he says. "Stayed late at the demonstration, Mikey-Moo. Police really roughed us up. We could have used your expert reportage."

"Any arrests?"

No answer.

I turn off the water, even though there are five more dishes in the sink. Zucchini and snow-pea cuttings clog the drain. I steady myself at the grimy sink. I try one more time.

"Any arrests?"

The question makes me feel dirty—like I'm fishing. I dunk my hands in the sink. I don't give a fuck about dishpan hands. I find another bottle of aspirin. The throbbing ache at the top right point on my forehead is growing more localized, but less splitting. I go into my room. It looks barren—filled with papers, notices of demonstrations and photographs of people getting arrested, including Robert. Shit, I have forgotten to put that photo away. I scan it for incriminating stains.

Robert walks into my room, just as I slide the photo into a stack of unopened bills, his eyes darting around the four walls like Inspector Clouseau.

"Why do you always do the dishes when we finish dinner?" he asks.

"Do you suggest a better time to do them?"

"Wouldn't it be nice to talk?"

I look at him.

He looks back, his dark, short hair and sunburnt face giving him a beach-bum *je-ne-sais-quoi*.

"I didn't know you wanted to talk."

He says nothing.

"Would you like to talk now?"

"It looks like you're on deadline."

"I kinda am."

"Uh-huh."

"I'm writing about the demonstration," I say, looking at his crotch, a tactic I have picked up from watching him watch other boys. He shifts his position. "It's too bad there weren't more people there," I add.

He blushes. He looks as if he is about to run. Then he stands his ground.

"Gosh, Mikey, I didn't know you were there. Man-oh-Manischewitz. I mean, we could've driven home together." He shakes his head, as if clearing it. And then: "I thought you said you weren't going to the demonstration."

"Got a last-minute assignment."

"Oh."

"I looked for you," I say. "But you were probably inside the Federal Building by the time I got there. Being a hero and all."

"Well, a man's got to do what a man's got to do," he says.

"And some men are very single-minded."

He smiles bravely. That's my Robert: big on modesty, forget irony. I continue: "I'm really sorry I missed your fight for justice. You know how much I get off on watching you stand up to the law."

"That's my Mickey," he says, brushing my face lightly with his hand. "Late as usual. I forgive you."

"I wasn't as late as you think."

"Huh?"

"I mean, you got into the Federal Building so fast. You were ahead of schedule."

"Uh-huh," he says. "Well, good luck with the story." He turns his head, as if about to leave. Then he pops in once again, a shy look of confusion and even fear on his face. "I'll be turning in pretty early." I nod and stare into the blank screen as if Robert weren't there. He pushes one more thought: "I be sleeping alone so much lately. I kinda lonely."

I suppress a gag. I just say, "I work best at night, when you sleep." He leaves the room, closing the door softly behind him. So polite, that Robert.

I slam-shut the door. I hear him muttering to Spike: "Tell Mikey I miss him." I turn off my computer and put my head down on the desk. It occurs to me to go run into his room and huddle in his arms and say: "Can we stop this?" But I don't know what *this* is. I hear him kiss the dog goodnight — "What a good dog, Spikey-Poo" — and turn off the stereo, then all the lights in the house: click, click, click. I hear the down comforter being shaken out and the pillows pounded into rounded places. The pages of a book — *The Rise and Fall of the Third Reich* — being turned. A few belches. A polite fart. A giggle or a hurrumph or a sigh or all of the above as a page gets turned. Then the book falling to the bed. Then a falling-asleep snore (very cute). Then a wake-up snore (very crude). Then one last chance: "Come to bed, Mickerooney," his voice slurred with sleepiness. My heart opens in a forgiving moment. His voice. But I delay. Then it is too late. The house grows dark, as it always does when Robert enters into the other world. I feel alone, frightened of the dark, and of what Robert sees when I'm not there.

Next thing I know, it's dawn. I am lying on the little futon in my office. Someone has come in to throw a blanket over me. A cup of hot coffee steams on my desk. I turn on my side and go back to sleep.

———

The sun pours into the house through the open windows. The white polyester-mix curtains, bought at Sears, are pulled back like tight corsets. I get the feeling that the roof has been peeled off the cottage. There are seagulls sleeping next door in a parking lot. Who's to say they won't land inside and shit over our books: my Freud collection, his Will Durant. Every blind is pulled open, too. There are three windows in the kitchen alone; two in the adjoining living room, and then one huge windowed door leading out to the back garden. It's so bright. Has there been an atomic blast?

Robert is busy at the stove, dancing with a spatula. The dog is inspired, too, following Robert with a wagging tail. Robert hoots seeing me. Spike mimics him. Woof. I point to the burning toast. Robert is shirtless. "Spikey will eat it." Around his waist is a beige Mickey Mouse apron.

"Is today Christmas or something?" I ask, blowing the ashen air in front of my face. I rub my head. I try to piece together the dreams: an old woman, the cracked concrete around the corner of the Bronx Botanical Gardens.

"Pancakes!" Robert announces, as if he's won the Nobel Prize. "Robert's Famous Amos pancakes."

"What did I do to deserve this?"

"You don't have to talk," he says. "Your job is to eat and drink. I won't inflict myself on you till you're up and at 'em."

"Famous last words. Hey, watch the butter. I need to lose another five."

"Mikey, this is getting out of hand. This is becoming anorexia. This is becoming scary. Have you ever considered UA?"

"UA?"

"Undereaters Anonymous."

Robert's specialty is blue-corn pancakes. He makes them with bananas, apples, walnuts—and what he calls "WASP TLC," which to my mind is a little like "WASP soul": you need to spend ten years with it before you develop the acquired taste. I sink my fork into the layers of blue corn and fruit. He smiles like he's in training to be someone's boyfriend.

"I am not used to you waiting on me," I say.

"Eat," he says. "Ya look skinny."

He hovers over me, watching every move.

"It's good," I say. "Really."

He takes a dainty seat. I look for the front page. But he just keeps looking at me. I want to reward him. But it reminds me of what he once was not, and I have a hard time forgiving him for his elusiveness, even though it was almost ten years ago. I dig into my pancakes, caked in layers of butter and honey and yogurt.

"You know, it's fun making you breakfast," Robert says. "It's like feeding a savage beast. I should do it more often."

My eyes catch the front page article in the *L.A. Times*. The subject: another experimental AIDS drug the Food and Drug Administration has approved only five years after everyone is using it. The thought triggers a worry: will I need to use it?

Robert shifts the newspaper a little on the table, so that it's at an angle from me. I shift it back. He shifts it again. He whispers mockingly, "I wish you loved me as much as you love your newspaper."

"What's with you?" I ask. "You're giving me a headache."

He takes the paper away. It's so Robert: this ability to shift gears from wounded inner child to wounded Mussolini.

"I've noticed you've been acting more Jewish lately," he says. I put my fork down and stare at him. "Are you going crazy?"

"Nah."

"What, then?"

"Just more observant."

"What is that supposed to mean?"

"It means you're becoming more you."

I look around the kitchen. My impulse is to take the plates, pancakes, honey, yogurt, coffee, newspaper, milk dish, orange-juice carton, butter knife, planters, vases, porn magazines, bills and sweep them onto the floor. The dishes are very Mission Viejo and would make an elaborate design on the black-and-white-tiled kitchen floor, which I notice hasn't been swept or cleaned since I got on my hands and knees last month. I stare into my pancakes.

Robert glowers. "I said you're acting more Jewish, not that you were getting lazier or fatter or more annoying."

I glower back. "Don't you see?"

He doesn't. On the stereo, Michael Callen's "Love Don't Need a Reason" plays.

"See what?" he asks.

"See what?" I mutter.

"Mickey . . . ?"

"We had an agreement," I say. "And now you're breaking it."

"We never wrote it up or anything. In fact, this is the first time we're discussing it."

There is some soul-searching silence as we eat. I grab for the calendar section in the *L.A. Times*. Robert studies an article inside the front section. He is a fast reader. When he is done, he hands me the section. I scrape the remaining butter from the last remaining pancake. There is a full-page article in the *L.A. Times* about Holocaust survivors who sell knishes on Fairfax Avenue. I turn to page two. Robert turns it back to page one. I shove the newspaper toward him, and in the process knock one of the dishes off the table.

I scramble to pick up the pieces. He grabs my hand hard and holds it. Lifting my palm to his lips, he says, "Mickey, I married you because you were a Jew."

It has the ring of a Barry Manilow song. I jerk to move my hand away, but he is stronger and reacts by pulling me closer. The best retort I can come up with is this: "I married you because you let me forget I was one." Very "General Hospital."

This comment changes his expression from giddy pleasure to defeat. He lets my hand go.

"Anyway, we're not married," he grumbles.

"Not in the eyes of the law," I add. "But the eyes of God — now, that's a different story."

"You wanna talk about God?" he asks, pissed.

"No, not particularly."

"Tell me what you know about God. I mean, I would really like to know."

"Don't push it," I say. "You know as well as I."

I drink my coffee, which is too weak. Robert has no sense about grinds, measurements and aroma.

I go back to the paper. He sits still. Another article. He shifts in his seat. He's not done.

"You've been talking in your sleep," Robert says.

He pulls his chair from the table so that it makes a skidding sound. I put the newspaper down. The dog wanders over and rests his narrow muzzle on my cold knees. I push him away; Spike looks bewildered, as he always does before one of us slugs the other.

"You're lying," I say.

"Why would I lie about a thing like that?"

"I don't know," I say. "Have you been lying much lately?"

He gets up from his chair. "I don't know why you're being this way," he says, whining. "I'll never make you breakfast again."

"I didn't ask you to make me breakfast."

Then he's off—slowly moving away from the table and out of sight. In a moment, he is in his room, shutting the door.

His absence hits me hard, like a person who runs into an airplane so fast he hasn't given you a hug. ("Wouldn't it be terrible if the airplane crashes," you wonder to yourself.)

"What did I say in my sleep?" I ask, feeling the plane take a nosedive. I ask the question again, loudly, so it travels from the kitchen to Robert's room, where I presume he's stalking.

From Robert's room, I hear this: "I don't know, it was in another language. Sounded vaguely German."

Silence.

The airplane crashes.

———

Robert gardens, his fingers blackened with manure and mud and desertlike sagebrush which seems to grow near the ocean. I walk outside our little white cottage to watch him weed. He's crouched—like a bird surveying its nest. He digs into the silty beach ground with a spoon and a shovel—intent on keeping cuttings safe and laid out prettily on a stone. I count ten little plants laid out in even patterns.

Robert is obsessed with how things grow. Some of the cuttings are only an inch or two tall. Others are nearly a foot. His way with plants speaks to an inner delicacy. The shovel hits a rock, and he touches the rock as if he's hurt it. The plants, little green babies, curl into the air like just-born kittens. He addresses them: "Now, little babies, we're going to stick you back in the ground where you come from." There's a kind of synthesis of opposites here in his activity. The shoveling is haphazard, fast and aggressive. He unearths Spike's shit, bones as well as trappings from Robert's compost: tea bags, orange rinds, intact pizza crust. The treatment of the small plants is studied, calm and dainty. The ground near the beach is both rocky and crumbly at the same time — more silt than anything else.

At some point, Robert notices me watching, and smiles that Katharine Hepburn smile of his. I always expect him to say, "Oh, dahling." He says, "Mickey, Mookey." Then he starts telling me stories he seems to have made up about the history of tomatoes, ice plant and snails. Tomatoes were considered poison by native people, devil's food. Ice plant was used as a way to keep humans off sacred roads. Snails were considered angels in disguise. He hates killing the snails, but kill them he must. The murdering lets the plants and vegetables thrive, which in turn help to provide him and me with nourishment: our dinner tonight, for instance.

"So you mean something dies so something else might live," I say. I approach him so that my crotch hovers nearby his bent form.

"You could say that," he says.

I tell him that I am going to be away all day. I have to interview an AIDS activist, arrange a photo shoot and attend a fund-raiser for a new AIDS hospice in South Central L.A. I'm going to take the beat-up 1982 Nissan rather than the gray-and-black '69 VW we also share. I won't be home till dinner.

"I'll miss you, Mikey," he says, smashing a snail with his fist.

I look into his brown eyes to see if he means it. He mistakes my look, which is pure suspicion, for pure desire.

"Michael," he says, exaggerating a certain raspiness in his voice.

"What?"

He lurches upward and grabs my crotch a little too hard, like he's been studying the move. I gasp, feeling put-upon, yet curious. He stands. He covers my mouth with his hand. This is a new Robert—the one who can't get enough of me. My eyes must register surprise, shock, alarm, hesitation and now, yes, a touch of craving.

"I love feeling your dick through your pants," he says. And then, with a grin and a sniffle, he asks, "I'm learning, aren't I?" He gets distracted by an itch on his nose.

"You sure are," I say. Enough is enough, though. I notice that he's poking out from his black shorts. They are ragged; he cut them down from old jeans.

"The neighbors," I say.

"They can't see," he says, fondling himself dumbly.

I try pulling away. This isn't the plan.

"I want you in me," he says. "See," he whispers, noticing my momentary dilemma. "All surprises."

In a moment, he has slid his shorts down to his knees, and one leg is free. This is unfair. His ass is mounded like a melon cake in my mind; every ounce of love I have ever felt for him resides there. The safe deposit is never depleted.

He falls like Camille to earth. I follow him.

"Put it in me," he whispers conspiratorially, spitting in his hand.

My arms cradle his muscular back. One of his hands helps to point my way toward him. He rams himself onto me, impaling himself.

"Not so fast," I caution.

"I don't want you to be late," he whispers.

There is a silent maneuvering along the garden stones that suggests we are going too fast. He wants his torso here—no, there; no, there. An inch or two to one side, then the other. No, back where we were. Okay. No, not okay. The head is angled to the right, the butt to the left, the arms notched like so above his neck. That doesn't work, either. I rest. He closes his eyes.

His head rests on my shoulder. A breeze comes direct from the South Pacific. *"You will meet a stranger . . . "* I wonder if I'm wrong about my suspicions. He is flaccid. How sweet. Enough for now, I think. I am wrong. He touches himself, then shimmies a bit. It's his *Look, Mom, I'm flying* dance. A delicate sway here, sway there. It's all in the spine. The little ballet has been known to arouse me even in my most spent condition. And in a moment, we are back where we were, his athletic body tensed as if about to crack.

"You want it so bad, huh?" I ask him.

"Yeah, sure," he says, not quite at ease.

"Then open up," I say.

That first comment will usually break the first layer of cool between us. It's the way we let ourselves forget we are Mickey and Robert. Michael the commentator, the Howard Cosell of sex. I dab spit on my finger and say, "I am dabbing a little spit on my finger." I apply it to Robert's asshole and say, "I am applying this to your asshole."

Lately, very little passes — not even a sigh from the guy at bat — without recitation. I say, "I am making you all wet."

Usually he says, " . . . all wet . . . ?" But this time he breaks into a little smile. "Not too loud," he says. "The neighbors."

So I whisper: "Okay . . . I'm putting it in."

"Oh, okay."

He smiles like a kid: "It's the word game," he says, mocking the game a little.

"I'm fucking you," I say, mocking his cuteness a little.

He moans, as if on cue.

"You like it, doncha?"

He moans a little louder, a little less as if on cue.

"Say it," I say. "Tell me how much you like it."

He moans; the cue is now the same as spontaneity.

"Say it," I say.

I haven't changed position. I'm just holding myself inside. He is playing a bit with himself. I want it to go to his head. It's my power. His is his beauty.

"I like it," he whispers, just like a beauty.

"Say it!" I say, shoving. The action often detonates his word inhibitor.

"I like it. . . . "

More shoving. "Tell me how much you like it in your . . . "

"I like it in my . . . "

"Tell me . . . in your . . . "

"I like it in my . . . "

I surprise myself: "In your pussy."

"Huh?"

"You heard me. In your —"

"In my pussy?"

Hearing his own voice mouth unspoken words elicits a strange reaction in him. Like he's shed ten years, and in the process has become the street urchin I first met. He's coming, letting loose, and just as he spurts out stuff, he lets out a scream: "In my pussy, I like it in my *pussy* . . . in my *pussy!*"

I try covering his mouth, but it's too late. Like a firecracker that has too many fuses, he's exploding in my arms — rocking and rolling and sputtering the words "pussy" and "wow" and "you made me." I hold him tight, fucking him during what seems like longer than the entire time we've been together: years and years. I want to whisper, "The neighbors," but I don't dare stop and instead whisper, "Let it out."

We lie in silence. I am running late. I make a gesture to rise and leave him lying in the garden. "Don't go," he says.

"I have to."

I peel off the condom and make a gesture to toss it in the depths of the garden, where the bamboo grows so high that even Spike won't venture into it.

"No, not there," Robert calls out from his resting place. "It's not biodegradable."

I pack my red knapsack. I leave a message on the phone machine that I can be reached at *The Angeleno*. I pat Spike, who is curled up in a ball. Arrange my papers in piles, articles I am writing. One is about a split among AIDS activists; another is about black AIDS agencies. One concerns lesbian militants; another is about closeted celebrities. My life disappears in each piece. I turn off my computer.

Outside, I continue the charade. I kiss Robert good-bye; he has returned to his weeding. The kiss is dry. His hands are dirty: muddy fingers pointed in the air like a Hindu god: Vishnu, waving me on. I spray some of his garden water on the Nissan's smog-stained windows, check the water and coolant in the crusty black radiator. I wave; Robert doesn't see.

I drive a few blocks, slowly—as if I'm a quickly aging person with cataracts. When I'm sure no one can see, I make a U-turn—and then head back toward home. I park on a deserted street, nearby a rotting Venice Beach canal where the ducks and homeless sleep at night. I am, after all, a journalist. Lurking around other people's dirt is my middle name, especially if the dirt is my business.

I walk home quietly.

I slink around the back of the house, where a vacant bungalow separates our house from the beach parking lot. I arrive at the side door of the house. I creep like a criminal toward a corner. I've counted on the fact that Spike would sense my presence. I throw two or three doggie-bone fragments toward the back of the house. Spike gallops toward them in his canine way.

I creep indoors, all the while making sure that Robert is still gardening. He sings to Spike, "Found an old piece of pizza, hey Spikey-Poo?" I eye the walk-in closet situated between the living room and the dining room. I've selected this closet because of the gaudy French doors the previous tenants installed. The chipped beige wood is so unsightly that we shoved our highbacked couch in front. I don't think we've opened that closet more than once or twice in the two years we've lived in this bungalow. I move the couch a bit; it's on wheels. I open the French doors. Wafts of

mothballs and mildew seep out. Yesterday I had moved the boo-
gie-boards and family albums to one side so that I could make a
seat for myself in the center, with old winter coats, tablecloths,
sleeping bags and flannel pajamas. The seat is just as I left it. I
tumble into the cushy garments. I shimmy the couch back toward
the closet. Finally I shut the french doors from the inside. Very
"Get Smart." I'm inside the closet.

I get comfortable. Thank God, it's a cool day at the beach.
My heart has quieted down, rounded out into a rare tranquility.
The plan will work. I sense my own drowsiness. I nod off.

———

I hear sounds. Robert is giving someone a tour of his garden:
tomatoes, mint and (ha, ha, ha) ten-inch green zucchinis. I detect
a man's voice—Robert's age, no, younger. The two edge their
way closer and closer into the living room where I'm hiding. I
recognize Robert's voice, although something about it seems
strange: shy and adolescent, as if his voice is cracking to prove
its puberty.

"Hey, Marty, wanna beer?"

"Hey, Marty, come and look at my dead snails."

"Hey, Marty, you like living in Hollywood?"

Marty follows Robert into the living room. They sit down on
the couch that leans against the closet door. The door shakes.
"Hmm," Robert says. "I wonder why this door seems ajar." He
pushes it closed firmly. I lean on my knees so I can see.

"So what the fuck did you say you do, dude? You're an
artist—fucking A."

"I'm a performer. Actually, I'm what they call a 'performance
artist.'"

"Oh, I know you—you're kinda fuckin' famous."

"You're kinda famous yourself."

"Hey, whaddaya mean?"

"You know what I mean."

"Hey, don't touch the material."

"I'll touch whatever I want."

Much laughter—giggles, too.

"I hear you have a boyfriend. That's too sweet. Whatcha doing with me?"

"Oh, I love him, and everything. He just doesn't put out."

"Bummer."

"It's kinda like the ten-year itch."

"I hear you. Are you guys gonna do divorce court?"

"Oh, nah, we would never dream of breaking up."

"Well, then, I donno about today, dude. I respect the sanctity of home and hearth, you know."

"Well, Marty, maybe I can be talked out of it."

More giggles—laughter, too.

I am looking through a crack in the french doors. It's hard to get a full picture through the slats, filled as they are with dust. One of the Western world's most beautiful men is thumbing through my Proust collection on my couch. I've never seen a surfer wannabe with such wannabe Italian features: dark sideburns, sculpted, firm pectorals and a fleshy kind of waist, arranged like a sash over his girded hips. In a Platonic sense, Absolute Health. Which makes me feel only more potentially ill. All his exercise apparently pays off. The guy sports a naughty sideways glint in his eye. He even has the audacity to smoke a cigarette in our house. I watch him take one out of a pack of Marlboros. Robert has the audacity to light it for him. With the cigarette barely lit and inhaled, Robert is mauling the poor boy. *Robert, take it easy.*

"Got an ashtray?" Marty asks.

Robert stops and gets a coffee saucer from the kitchen. "My mother's Melmac," I want to scream.

The guy ditches his cigarette and says to Robert, "Hey, seems like you haven't gotten any nookie in years."

"Haven't."

"Poor dude," Marty says, opening his mouth wide for Robert. They tongue-kiss. I expect Robert to break away.

Ten minutes have elapsed, and I hear the sounds of slurping tongues.

"Wow!" this Marty says. "You're some expert kisser. You sure you ain't fucking Mediterranean or something."

"Well, my boyfriend's Jewish."

"Fuck, invite him over."

"Nah. He wouldn't be into it. He's dealing with some pretty intense AIDS paranoia."

"Join the fucking club."

"I think he probably thinks I gave it to him."

"Didju?"

"I don't know."

"Are you telling me you guys ain't been tested yet? Is that what you're trying to tell me?"

"I don't know *what* I'm trying to tell you."

Marty picks a strand of hair from his mouth. "On that note," he says, zooming in on Robert for the close-up, "let's kiss. At least kissing won't fucking kill us."

The two collapse to the floor, in a fit of urgent wrestling. Robert lies above Marty. They play with tongues on lips, as if this foreplay was the be-all and end-all of their sexual palette. Robert lifts Marty's T-shirt up from his arms, revealing a creamy, soft layer of skin pulled tight over layers of muscles and delicate bone structure.

There are some muffled sixty-nine sounds, and I find myself reaching to the remote control for the fast forward on our VCR. Robert fondles his way into Marty's tight black jeans—ripped in a hundred different places, but still somehow jeans. Up till now the moans have been predictable. Now the two seem to have touched voltages in each other.

"You have a condom?" Robert asks in a whisper, as if he thought someone were overhearing.

"Hey, a boy always comes prepared, right?"

I've always wanted to watch Robert fuck another boy. We discussed it: me the voyeur, him the actor. Of course, it's never happened. Now my presence feels like a Gnostic secret: palpable to Robert, I guessed, but only in the secret crevices of his head.

"Oh," Marty offers, his eyes turning moist. "Oh! Dude, you got the groove."

"Yeah," Robert adds.

I watch Robert dab a little spit on his finger. "I am dabbing a little spit on your asshole," he says. I watch him apply it to Marty's asshole. "I am applying some of this to your asshole."

"Your boyfriend's a lucky man, boss."

"And you're going to be a lucky boy."

Robert excuses himself to find Vaseline. By now I can see Marty's face: magenta from all the biting and kissing—and flushed like a marathon runner's. He plays with himself dumbly to keep hard. Once or twice I think I see him wink at me.

Robert returns. He treats Marty with a certain affectionate insolence. Marty lies on the floor. Robert kneels down next to him. They both smile, but do nothing. Marty angles his neck toward Robert's lips and Robert pushes him away, then grabs Marty by the neck and gently raises him to his lips. They kiss. Both are worshiping. Robert pushes Marty away. This little dance—*stay away, come close*—gets repeated over and over again. I think to myself: wouldn't it be funny to try this little semaphore on Robert and see how he reacts?

With Marty, Robert has met his match: another whiteboy who is quiet in bed. Robert's face suggests a determination to crack a certain mirror. Robert plays with himself.

"You want this?" he asks, referring to his dick but not quite daring to have the savoir faire to glance down at it.

Marty nods.

"C'mon, Marty."

Marty nods again.

"Say it."

Silence.

Robert spreads Marty's legs gently. He then straddles him, with Marty's head lurching back in an affected gesture of rapture. Maybe it isn't so affected. I watch Robert's naked buttocks shake a little in fear.

"You want this dick in you."

"Ye . . . "

"Do you?"

"Yeah . . . "

"Then say it."

"Yesssss . . . "

"Say it, say: 'I want it in me.' Okay?"

"Okay."

"Okay!"

"Um . . . I want it in me." (Not all that convincing.)

By now, Robert is rocking over Marty's body. Their connection is all about possibility, but they are not there yet. It could go so many ways: big brother/little brother; fuck buddy; unrequited love on either's part; master/slave (if either of them were equipped to play such games); lovers; boyfriends; sacred intimates; coupled warriors; cheap tricks. Both men seem to be doing quite a bit of questioning through their grunts — eliciting sounds of adjustment and pleasure and discomfort. Robert is trying to loosen Marty up with affectionate kisses. Marty seems to be sweating.

"Are you sure you are up for this?" Robert asks, completely himself, self-conscious and kind.

Marty jerks his head toward the ceiling to suggest: don't break this. He mouths words like a mantra. "I want it in me." But it's clear neither he nor Robert believes them.

"You want it where?"

"In me."

"Where?"

"Inside — in."

"Where?"

"In. In."

"You want it in your ass?"

"Um, in my, you know."

Every victory seems to mean a little more pleasure for Robert, who then pulls out of Marty and turns Marty on his stomach — to Marty's protestations. Marty is talked out of his protestations.

Robert tries something new. "Say you want it in your pussy."

"Huh?"

"Say that's where you want it."

Robert stops moving. He blinks while holding Marty's hair. "Say it."

"Say what?"

"Say you want it where I told you you want it."

"I don't get it"

"Yes, you do. Jesus . . . "

"I want it in my pussy . . . is that right?"

"Say it."

It takes a while, but by now Marty has gotten the hang of being fucked the Michael way. Robert holds him. Marty breathes. Robert caresses his hair. Marty breathes. Robert moves a little. Marty breathes. Robert moves. Marty breathes. Then Marty raises his ass in the air while propping his brown-tanned body on all fours. (I see that his hull is blotched by sunburn and skin peeling.) Robert has lost his restraint. Both are pressed together, with Robert murmuring quietly in Marty's ear and with Marty murmuring back. I can't hear.

I don't have to strain very long. Robert holds Marty by the shoulders and then pushes in as hard as I have seen Robert do anything. Marty grabs his center and then lets it go, then grabs himself with both hands, then falls to the bed. By now he is gurgling, shouting: "I want it in my *pussy*. In my *pussy*. In *my pussy, dude!*" Spike barks.

Just then there is a knock at the door. Robert freaks.

"Oh, shit! What if that's Mickey? *Omigod!*"

I recognize the voice at the door; it's our elderly neighbor, Mrs. Weinberger. She complains when I play Miles Davis's "Someday My Prince Will Come" loudly, or whenever Robert and I fight, or when Spike gets lonely and howls.

"I don't know what you boys are doing in there, but that is the second time we have heard that nonsense, and we have a family, you know. My mother is trying to sleep."

Robert falls back into Marty's arms—relieved. I stick a sock in my mouth to keep from laughing.

When the two retreat into the kitchen to indulge in some postcoital rice and vegetables—the dish I made for Robert last night—I slink out of the closet and tiptoe to the car. I have a story to write.

———

When I arrive home, Robert has made dinner.

"You're really into a cooking binge these days," I say. "Too bad, I was all set for a little brown rice."

"Spike ate the leftovers."

"He must have been really hungry. I made a ton."

"Yeah, I guess."

Spike throws his rear end against my leg. I go to pat him, but he scampers over to his bowl, his sign language for *Daddy, I hungry.* I approach the twenty-five-pound bag of healthy dog food. Spike vocalizes: *ahhh wow-ahhh.* It must be a three-scoop day.

The bowl brims with salty brown chunks. Spike peers up, drooling. "Okay," I say. Spike dives in; there's the crunch-filled, breathing-in, wolfing-down opera I associate with dinnertime.

I give Robert a domestic kiss. He gives me one back.

"Your face looks a little flushed," I say.

"Ya think?"

"Yeah, it look like you've been a little hot tramp all day . . ."

"Ever since our garden romp."

I hover over him as he cuts up garlic in cumbersome clumps. "Ever hear of 'mincing?' " I ask.

"I hate that word—almost as much as I hate snoops."

"Has anyone been snooping on us?" I ask.

"I don't know, have they?"

His eyes reveal no subtext. He scours the pan in which I sautéed the vegetables.

"I wish you would use hotter water," he says. "I gotta go over everything you clean."

"Remember the time you ate only pizza?" I ask. "We never did any dishes. I gained a million pounds."

"I didn't."

"Thanks for rubbing it in."

Our laughter trails off. I look around the kitchen, filled with iron pans, hanging garlic, baskets, flyers for performance-art events, Spike food, Spike drool and Polaroid pictures of turkeys I have cooked for dozens of Thanksgivings and Christmases. There are snapshots of the friends who gathered around the turkeys: John Drummond, Mark Ruffino, Rob Moore, mostly men, some of whom I have loved secretly, from a marital distance.

"Do you ever think of seeing different people?" I say. "I mean, of falling in love with other people?"

"Have you met someone?" he shoots back. "Because if you have, you should tell me right now and get it over with."

I think about the right way to proceed. If I reveal that I know what I know, everything might collapse from internal pressure. Like Eve taking a bite of the first apple. Like God poking his head through the clouds and saying, "Yoohoo." Like the end of the movie fading in at the beginning.

"I would think of having more affairs," I say, "but I'm worried about our health."

"What does our health have to do with anything?" Robert asks. "Besides, if we had taken the test years ago, Mickey, we would be a lot less freaked now."

That is Robert's line: We had our chance with HIV. It was in 1986, when the test was available and local AIDS groups suggested gay men take the test. We procrastinated. Now it feels too late. The drugs suck. No one knows what causes it.

Robert has another worry. "You remember Mark Ruffino, John Drummond's boyfriend? He took that test, got the result and died six months later."

I'd like to drop the subject now, but Robert can be a dog with a bone.

"That test kills people," he adds. "You just gotta fucking have safe sex and eat right and ride the waves."

Now he's talking like Marty.

"Thanks for the *fuckin'* prognosis, Dr. Humphreys . . . I mean, hang ten and everything."

Robert stares me down. Like, what the fuck is going on?

He regains his train of thought: "Aren't you the one who writes all the time about safe sex? Don't you believe in safe sex?"

"Sure," I say. "It's just that it only occurred to me a few years ago that we should not be coming in each other's asshole."

"We didn't know any better. We thought monogamy was safe sex."

"Fools."

"Fools-in-love."

"I'm worried that we may be getting sick," I say.

Robert dries the dishes.

"And then it would be too late to do anything about it," I continue.

Robert puts down the knife he's drying.

"And that you would leave me. And I would die alone," I add.

Robert stares into the sink.

"Why do you have these worries?" Robert asks, staring into the sink. "We're both as fit as fiddles." He makes a muscle. "See?"

I touch his arm.

"The headaches," I say. "They've been coming again."

"Oh," he says.

A year ago, a migraine exploded. We called an ambulance. By the time we got to the hospital, the throbbing ebbed.

"They are *just* headaches, doncha think?" I ask.

He holds me close, so close I can smell Marty's cigarettes. "You have been working hard, you know?" he reassures me.

"I guess."

"You have, Mickey."

"You're right."

"Of course I'm right."

"Mickey, let it go," he says, whispering. "Just let it go."

"You mean, that you came in my ass hundreds of times. Even though I begged you to wear a condom."

"You didn't trust me. That hurt."

"Not as much as AIDS. I hear that AIDS hurts like a bitch."

"It was 1981, '82 —"

"And '83, '84 —"

"We didn't know any better."

"I knew better."

The nonsensical dialogue goes on. I don't disrupt it because Robert holds on. His arms encircle my torso in an arc of delicacy and remorse.

"I'm sorry about that time," he says. "I think we're okay."

"It was ten years ago. Feels so long."

We stand still for a record-breaking ten minutes, Robert's head resting on my shoulder.

"Do you realize that you've never held me before like this?" I ask.

"What are you talking about?"

"I just feel like you never hold me."

"What are you talking about?"

He tries to pull away, but I don't let him. I hold his arms. I pull him close. I rub my chest into his, which makes him smile in surprise. I pull away, abruptly.

"See?" I say. "There are degrees in a hug. Like in a Richter scale, or a thermometer or a rating system or a roll book —"

"Why do you have to do this?"

k. d. lang cries in the background.

"Okay," he says, trying to go for a hug again. "Okay. We'll take the test."

I let him take hold of me. I fight my urge to pull away, just as I know he is fighting his own.

Then comes the shocker.

"Mikey," he says. "Whatever the results, don't leave me."

"What?"

"And no cheating," he adds. "I won't stand for it."

"Robbie?"

He lets a tear out.

"I mean," he continues, "if you fall for someone, just tell me. Whatever you do, don't keep it from me."

"Rob? Where's all this coming from?"

"Promise?"

"Okay. Okay. I promise."

He holds on to me for so long, I wonder whether we've changed places.

———

I take the Nissan to the Century Plaza Hotel. The Tammany Hall of the Southland. The stage for Vietnam antiwar demonstrations and LAPD beatings. The tower buildings boast clear windows, clean concrete, compact parking lots leading you to tiers of newly bought BMWs and Porsches. Workaholics slave at agencies with famous acronyms: CAA, ICM.

At night, the streets are as vacant as a gold-rush town after the rush. Cars swish by; lone agents walk Wilshire after locking a deal. Only the Century City Triplex across the street from the hotel vibrates. People love movies, including *Potemkin*, and will go anywhere to see them.

I have nothing against Century City or its noted hotel. I love a good landmark and a good bloodbath. I'm doing my best to stay calm. After all, the Century City Hotel is Republican territory. Tonight, ex-Presidents will break bread—and necks—to raise money for the GOP.

My car rattles so loudly I can't hear the Spanish AM radio. The traffic isn't bad until Bergdorf's. Then it's like a parking lot on Santa Monica Boulevard. Polite L.A. drivers never honk; these days, fewer are polite. I give the horn a shove. A police car tailgates me. He passes, keeping his eye on the real prize: two hundred gay activists a mile or so east, at the border between Beverly Hills and Los Angeles. I turn up my radio to see who's covering the demonstration. The only radio station the Nissan gets is *kabla-ee-oo*, the Mexican station. *"Andale, pues, we are going to hear some Mexico City rock 'n' roll."*

An approaching motorcade smothers my Juan Gabriel ballad: "You Don't Love Me Like I Love You." First I see five, then ten, then twenty motorcycles—roaring in and out of the right and left lanes. Twenty additional officers sit astride horses down the street. I turn off the radio. I hear the whistles, the high-pitched jittery cries. I am getting close. One of the cruising cops looks in my window. The cop revs off—to the noise, to the whistles, to the pariahs. His smirk suggests he knows I'm one of them. Is he, too?

My heart quickens. I go for my trusty reporter's notebook, which is lying on the passenger's seat. It's white and narrow. I look out the window and see a cluster of last-minute shoppers. By their looks, they mistake the growing din for an approaching parade. *Santa's reindeer midsummer? An unannounced white sale? Barbra Streisand and her son window-shopping on Rodeo Drive?* I wonder with them. *What is it?* I try to put myself in their Gucci shoes. One young curly-haired boy pulls on the sleeve of a white-haired hobbled woman. His grandmother? The woman wears rabbit. Her Eastern European beak face betrays terror. *What could it be?*

The traffic loosens for a moment. A shirtless teenager stands outside the entrance to the sock store. I know he's rich by the sandals, the Rolex, the cotton athletic socks. Shouldn't I buy Robert a pair? I see the blinking neon lights: SOCK 'EM TO YA. The boy—he's nineteen? He lights a cigarette. Is he waiting for his mother? His girlfriend? Me? I watch him inhale. He swings his focus to me. He whispers a word. "Fag." What do I need with a pair of fifteen-dollar socks?

I turn on Wilshire and then, like a drumroll, I hear it: "Fight AIDS. Fight AIDS. Fight AIDS." The sound of human rage draws you in. I turn into a parking lot. "How long you gonna be?" a Mexican parking attendant—an old man—asks. "An hour, at least," I say, taking the green receipt. "All night, at most." I zip up my leather jacket. With no natural resources save for polite plots of seasonal grass, the locale roars with the wind. Hollow land; hollow times; hollow sound in the breeze. No wonder those matrons wear fur in May.

The Century Plaza Hotel sits by itself, this semicircular tower of glass and chrome. In front is a circular plot of grass and a fountain. That's where the activists have pitched tents and their media tables and their troops. A steep incline from Olympic leads you to the hotel. It's blocked by barricades, police cars and men in suits talking into walkie-talkies.

I bypass the barricades. I take a secret route near Avenue of the Stars. I notice a black man who seems to be suffering from Tourette syndrome, walking fast. His arms jerk; his lips spew out "fuck" and "shit" and "Mary, you cheated on me." A white couple run across the street, avoiding a run-in. Silly. The man wouldn't hurt a fly, or a liberal. It's John. Tonight he's memorizing lines.

"John Drummond!" I say, loud enough to distract the actor.

"I mean, Tahar. You and your black ass is scaring the poor, in-nocent Century City white folk."

He stops in his tracks, sighs at seeing me. He walks across the street in boot-stomping steps, looking out for speeding Honda Accords. "Kaplan," John says. He plants a soft kiss on my lips. Two women carrying purple shopping bags shoot us wide-eyed glances.

"I *knew* your husband would be here," John says. "But I'd never have guessed that *The Angeleno* would lower itself and cover an AIDS demonstration."

"Anything's possible, John," I say, "especially after a little spray paint."

John eyeballs me. I'm not supposed to know that John planned a demonstration against my newspaper when *The Angeleno* dropped my AIDS column. I'm not sure why he arranged the action. I've never been a hero to these activists.

He blows the subject off. "Do you know what *this* particular demonstration is about, Mr. Kaplan?"

I explain that a certain Republican congressman, sponsoring a bill that would make it a crime for people with AIDS to have sex, is hosting a fund-raiser for another Republican known to be undergoing investigation for making sexual advances to his sec-retary.

"It's a chance for them to deflect attention to the real sex scandal," I say. "And a chance for us to yell and scream into the cameras and convince ourselves we are doing something to stop AIDS."

"So it's like that, Mr. Reporter? You know for some people, AIDS activism is a matter of life and death."

"I'm sorry."

"No, you're not."

I change the subject: "How is your poetry, John—Tahar, whatever the fuck your name is?"

John smiles. "Not bad. The only problem is that I had to be hit with a terminal disease to write like my life depended on it."

"You don't have a terminal disease," I say. "You have HIV. We don't even know if that causes AIDS."

"Who you talking to, boy?"

Six months ago, John buried his lover Mark.

We are now a block from the Century Plaza Hotel. I do a quick head count: about three hundred activists have gathered. Not bad. I see faces and behavior I recognize: Ann-the-Leading-Activist whose black hair swirls in the Century City wind; Jose, the quota Latino, his hands clapping in an early chant; Sue Canelli, the straight secretary from *The Angeleno* who shows up at all the AIDS and prochoice demos, chain-smoking. I can make out the banners: "ALL PEOPLE WITH AIDS ARE INNOCENT," and "TEST DRUGS, NOT PEOPLE." The sound of whistles, screams and police bullhorns work wonders for my migraine.

"I'm bored," I admit to John.

John stops. He grabs me. "Wait," he says softly. "Just wait."

We walk over to a concrete stoop. Two policemen jog past us, ignoring us. He looks at me and shakes his head. "Mike," he murmurs. "You can call me John or Tahar. I don't care. The name 'Tahar' . . . it's just an actor thing. I'm worried about you."

"I like the name 'Tahar,'" I say. "John is normal. 'Tahar' has a voodoo-ish, magical ring to it."

"What do you know from magic?"

"I know a few card tricks."

"I have a few card tricks of my own. You should come over the house sometime."

The last time I was in Tahar's house? A year and a half ago. He called me. He mentioned something about leaving TV — being made to. He asked that I help organize a meeting of writers to talk over the tyranny of politically correct speech in a culturally pluralistic time. We called ourselves *Fuck PC and Fuck Me*. In a few months, *FUCK* evolved. John raised enough money to start a newspaper, *Queer Blacktress*.

I volunteered now and then for *Blacktress*, writing articles for no pay on subjects for which no one else would publish me. He'd call: "Mikey, it's your secret admirer." I never took Tahar seriously. He'd call only when he needed something. Once he whispered: "Your husband doesn't know how beautiful you are, leave him and be my white slave boy."

I'd snort: "Tahar you can't fuck your own sister — that's incest."

"Incest is best," he'd say.

Tahar didn't know: secretly I had fantasized about him and his voice. At first, when I heard the dish on John, I was appalled. He was defensive: "You can't pay the rent by publishing a black queer magazine." Word had gotten around: In the '70s, John had been the wunderkind of Folsom Street. "I'm the sweetest sadist you'll ever know," I once heard him growl on the phone. "One hundred fifty in. Two hundred out." He didn't know I was listening.

"Have you ever seen so many queers at this corner in your life, dollface?" Tahar asks, zipping open the vomit-green Gold's Gym bag he often hauls with him. Usually one finds a gym belt inside — gloves, Gatorade. Today: a blond wig.

Tahar, who doesn't suffer fools lightly, gets to act the fool's part at AIDS demonstrations. He takes on the persona of a character the media has made almost as famous (although not as reputable) as Robert's: "Tahar, the black bitch with AIDS."

I've always seen the Tahar-in-John as a class act, a way to pull down the tough-guy pedestal erected by too many TV auditions. "Tahar gives John humanity," Robert says. But John has all the humanity he needs. Last year, news of his HIV status caught on in The Industry; fans connected Tahar's nelly face with John's stoic gangster's look. "I'm getting a new makeup artist," he quipped. John was no joker. He came out in an *L.A. Times* interview. Overnight, Tahar became a Hollywood pariah, a man full of doubts and debts. That was when the name Tahar caught on.

Tahar puts on the Dolly Parton wig. Presto. "Where is that photographer of yours?" Tahar asks, snapping fingers indelicately in my face. "That white bitch is never around when I need him." Tahar removes his leather coat, revealing a pink-and-purple sash. The crowd roars. I try not to get too distracted by Tahar's dress, ripped to expose his Athletic Club cleavage. Tahar catches me looking, and exacerbates the tear near his chest. In a moment, he stomps off in the middle of Wilshire Boulevard, his high heels clip-clopping. Stunned motorists stall. "Eddie Murphy fucked me!" he screams. "I should have been in that movie."

The demonstration has begun. Two ACT-UP banners, SI-LENCE=DEATH and ACTION=LIFE, get raised from two different rooftops. The sun sets and a purplish lavender color rings the horizon. The signs broadcast desperation. Three women in furs run across the street to taxis. Cars speed off. Police run. I watch Tahar and Ann-the-Leading-Activist chase the three young women, slapping ACTION=LIFE stickers over the women's backs. Five police motorcycles make ominous U-turns off Wilshire. Ta-har and Ann sneak back into the crowd.

I look for Robert.

I scan the crowd for my photographer, who is usually on time. I see two hack reporters I know from the *L.A. Times* near the media desk. Tahar and another fellow in a tattered pin-striped suit hand out press packets. Ann's current squeeze, Cynthia, as-sists. Ann wears her black hair in wild curls. This activist loves her buttons—and pedigree: DYKES AGAINST AIDS; BLACK BELTS AGAINST AIDS; PEDIATRICIANS AGAINST AIDS; BISEXUALS AGAINST AIDS. She nods at me, pointing abruptly to a press kit, as in "Why don't you take one and get out of my face?" I know Ann: she doesn't like me.

I regard the press table, my heart beating, approaching the suited man, his hair slicked back like he's out on a date, or a photo shoot. A cigarette dangles from his lip. Is the man assisting . . . Marty?

I had seen Marty only in bits and pieces, what the slats through the french doors would reveal, a brazen beefcake sepa-rated by parallel lines. I think now: maybe the slats covered up layers of unsightly cellulite and a face that made men bark. They didn't.

"Hi," I say to Marty. He ignores me, handing a kit to a Valley reporter. "My name's Marty Augustine," he chirps to the *Times* journalist. "Press officer extraordinaire." The sallow, closeted writer is known for skewering radicals.

More Marty: "Call me morning, noon or night. But whatever you do, call me."

Well, Marty, selling your ass to the ruling class?

Meeting someone you know who doesn't know you is a gift of irony from the gods. It's not unlike the way you memorize Tom Cruise's looks for a decade, or jerk off to his *Top Gun* pecs when they are revealed on the cover of *Rolling Stone,* and then bump into the celebrity at Builders' Emporium. "Do you know where the lawn mowers are?" he once asked me. It's him, but it's not him. The charm of cinematic reality has been pulled back by the genuine intimacy of life. Today Marty boasts the wet look in his brunette curls.

Marty sees me staring at him.

"Wassup, doc?"

"The wet look is dead," I say.

"Excuse me?"

"I prefer you with less gel," I say.

"What is your media affiliation?"

"Marty, *Mar*-tttyyy boy," Tahar chides. "That's Michael Kaplan."

"Michael who?" Marty yawns, scratching his neck.

I stick my face near the boy's. "I cover the gay beat for *The Angeleno.*"

"So."

"I've written about these demonstrations ever since they started."

"Wanna medal?"

Tahar mutters, "The young have no respect."

Marty turns his attention to a cameraman in a mohawk, who is taping the show for a heavy metal–band video. The man shoots Marty a look.

"Peace," Marty calls out, adding a dozen syllables to the word. The cameraman blushes.

I'm pissed that the man Robert is seeing has the gall to flirt with a straight cameraman.

"Marty."

"Yeah."

"That cameraman is straight," I say.

"Not after last night, he ain't."

Tahar whispers in my ear: "You're getting some bad shade from this homeboy. Quit while you're ahead."

I pull out the big guns. "Marty?"

"Yeah."

"I'm also Robert's boyfriend."

"Robert who?"

Tahar purses his lips and in his this-has-gone-too-far manner, clearing his voice: "The rumor is that you and Robert is *good* friends."

"Fuck rumors."

"I know something else I'd like to fuck," Tahar murmurs.

"It takes two to tango," Marty says. "And my dance card is filled for the time being."

Tahar pulls me aside. "I don't like that Marty," he says. "Ooh. I don't like him one bit. I don't care how dedicated an activist he is." Tahar wears his hair in dreadlocks. His body, which fills out his dress, is cut in delicate angles near his ribs and hips. But it's his throat that one notices; Tahar's Adam's apple gallops. I see his eyes, bloodshot and impatient. I wonder at the impatient part: Does it chase people away?

"Honey, when was the last time someone told you you are pretty?"

I look at the melee, which is growing.

"What?"

"You heard . . . "

"What?"

Then pandemonium: whistles blowing, drums pounding, leather boots shuffling, crowd movements — the sky falling to earth, a circus tent collapsing. Marty waves at Tahar, snapping in the direction of the raucous, as if to say, "Get yourself over there, dude." Tahar stands by me, as if he's worried he won't see me again. "Say your prayers," Tahar says.

Someone calls out to me; it is my photographer: heavyset, cranky and ready for work. "What do you want, group stuff or some arrests? . . . C'mon, the show's on the road."

I hear this: "Police maneuver." And then "Military maneuver, the fuckers!" And then a scream. "She's been hit!" And a drum.

Or is it the drum falling? Or sticks falling? "Goddamn mutha-fuckers . . . ." And this: "Hey, wait a minute." And then a chorus of "*No violence, no violence . . .* the whole world is watching!" From a microphone: "You are advised to get off the streets. Anyone found on the streets will be subject to arrest." About fifty activists, including Marty, have formed a line in the streets. Hands over hands. Voices over voices. Fists. A chant has begun. "Two, four, six, eight, what Republican slime do we really hate?" They must hire a new chant writer.

"No wonder the media no longer covers these anymore," I say to Tahar. "We've seen this all before."

Tahar snaps, "I don't think we've seen this before." Tahar points. Officers on horseback appear from the north and south corners of the Century Plaza Hotel.

I see Robert. He looks disoriented, in the way a movie star looks disoriented when you catch him looking at you. A small crowd of male admirers circles him. An African-American woman waves her hand to Tahar: It's time.

"Good-bye Mike," Tahar says. "Watch us well."

I head over to an LAPD officer and ask about the horses (there are at least two dozen of them) and the riot gear (all those truncheons!) and the parade permit (apparently ACT UP says it secured one, but the police say the activists haven't). About the question of a City Hall investigation about the police violence last week? ("Don't know, sir, you'll have to call the department.") About the inevitability of more violence? ("Absolutely not.") About why the activists have been demonstrating so much? ("They want their rights.") About allegations of department ho-mophobia? ("There is no discrimination in the department, sir.") Happy to be working, I wander around.

Ann-the-Leading-Activist runs over to me. A clove cigarette dangles from her lips. A red sash wrapped over her left shoulder signals she's a "legal observer." She grabs my coat.

"What the fuck are you doing talking to the cops? People are getting arrested."

"Ann."

I remove her hand from my coat.

"We need witnesses. We need our people watching—over there!"

"Ann, I'm a reporter."

"Your boyfriend is getting beat up by the police. Why don't you try and report that?"

A group has formed around Ann and me. I hear one activist mutter, "Police spy."

I move through the throng, parting it a little. People know me. They wink and sneer. Ann has exaggerated. No one is getting beaten up—yet. The police form one rigid line, the activists another, like a medieval combat before it begins.

"Look, it's the guy who says he's a reporter," Marty announces. He jabs Robert in the side with his leather-clad elbow. "What a dweeb!"

Someone calls for a "kiss-in!"

Marty and Robert kiss, no wooden slats this time. I smell their bodies, the distinct odors of perspiration and leather. Marty sticks his tongue in Robert's mouth, and Robert does everything to discourage him. Marty pushes onward—ha, ha.

I open my reporter's notebook and jot down my name.

Robert sees. "Mickey-Mackey," he cries.

The line is rushed by the police: a sideswipe, quick and surgical. A stampede of twenty or thirty cops on horseback, wielding wooden truncheons, clear the line of activists. Activists fall over each other. Others push forward. I am in the middle. "No violence!" Ann screams. Drops of blood splatter to the sidewalk. Horses whinny. Marty throws a placard at "the fuzz." That makes the police crazy.

"Remember Rodney King!" Tahar yells. Marty has been struck. Robert crouches over him. Achilles to Patroclus.

"Move him!" Ann screams.

The police return. I think about fleeing to the press area.

Another impulse occurs to me. "Let's take the street," I say to Ann in a voice I don't recognize. "It will distract the police."

"Good idea, Mr. Reporter."

She and I form a circle in the street; a dozen others join us. We sit, halting rush-hour traffic. Horns blast. There are a few sympathetic fists from some cars. My heart races. The police warn us through a loudspeaker that if we do not disperse in the next minute, we risk being arrested. Policemen, some on horseback, some on foot, encircle us. Activists shout, "Shame! Shame! Shame!" The contingent of cops has situated itself so that we can't retreat beyond the wall of defense made by horses and black and white cop cars.

Ann and I hold hands. "I'm frightened," she says.

There is an opening between two female officers. From the street, I see Robert glaring. Marty hangs onto him. Robert tries to wiggle free, but he's lodged between bodies. He gesticulates toward us, or rather toward Ann.

"What?" Ann asks, her voice hoarse.

Robert grabs a bullhorn from a legal observer. "Mike's never been arrested," he announces.

Ann looks at me. "Well, dear. It's too late. Just don't tell them anything about yourself. Don't be disrespectful. When they handcuff you, hold your hands like this, so they don't cut off circulation." She clasps her wrists together, birds of paradise.

Robert's square face is contorted in a tight rectangle: eyes squinting, hands by his lips to make his voice carry, hair crazy in the wind. Horses close in on us.

I think I feel Tahar's hand on my shoulder. It is warm, and full of possibilities. How did he get through the horses?

"Hi, Tahar."

Then: Cossacks. Strange voices. The sound of whips.

And then the strident sound of a young voice and an old one mingled together, as in a kind of wailing jazz: *Ikh bin a yunge meydl un mayn harts tut mir vey. Ikh bin Gekumen dir tsu lernen. Farges nisht vos Ikh hob dir ongezogt.*

———

I wake up in a strange house. Ann's scratchy doctor's voice and clove cigarettes tell me I'm at her place. In her bookcase an odd assortment: Carl Jung, Kate Millett, Stephen King, pharmacology texts. Indian-print cottons everywhere. I see antique tables and activist brochures.

"I think we should get him to the hospital," Tahar says.

I fall back to sleep.

Later I feel a hand on my face. "Anybody home?"

"Tahar . . . ?"

"We thought we lost you in there for a while."

"In there?"

"Ann said it was just a shiner. Robert said you had no insurance."

"Hi, Mikey," says Robert. He looks tired. Once, when Spike had a stomach operation, Robert slept solidly for one week.

How did I land here? Robert tries to tell the story. I was hit in the head, then pulled off by Ann before the arrests. Ann, a resident intern at the University of Southern California, predicts my swelling will go down in seventy-two hours. Ann was hit, too, on her back. There is talk of a lawsuit against the LAPD.

I fainted when I was hit? Had some kind of fit? Marty has the information.

I find myself dozing. Later, Tahar sits in a rickety wicker chair to the right side of the bed. He fiddles with ragged strands of cotton from the comforter.

"I felt you near me," I say.

"Hmm?"

"When the horses came."

"Oh?"

"Yeah. I felt your hand . . . ."

"Just rest."

People come close. "He'll be as good as new in a day or two," says Ann. To Robert. "Give him these Motrin."

Marty throws in his two cents: "Did you see him after the police hit him. He was like that girl in *Poltergeist*." Tahar shushes Marty. Gone are the wig, the dress. Tahar's leather jacket hangs on his chair, covered now in dozens of activist stickers.

Later, the sun sets. Tahar stirs me.

"Mike," he says. "The others have stepped out into Ann's garden so we can talk."

"Oh."

"Mike, I have to ask you a question."

"Tahar."

"Who is Frieda?"

"Who is who?"

"Frieda. You kept saying 'Frieda.' "

"Frieda who?"

Tahar grabs a piece of paper from Ann's night table and writes something down on it with a tiny pencil. The pencil point breaks, so he goes for the pink highlighter, the kind Ann makes lists with. I watch Tahar look at the paper, then look at me, then look at the paper again. He blinks his eyes, dispelling the ambivalence. He hands me the piece of paper. In the living room, someone plays Mary Williamson's gospel rendition of "You're Just Too Good to Be True."

The piece of paper says "Dr. Myron Smith."

"I see him," Tahar says.

"For what?"

"For what do you think?"

Apparently, he thinks I know.

Tahar gets up and leaves.

———

Robert and I get home a few minutes before midnight. We drive the Nissan slowly. We share the same quiet superstitions. *If you make it out of a riot alive, drive home like your life depends on it.* He holds my hand until we get on the freeway. He concentrates on his driving, his long face shadowed by the headlights of passing cars.

Once at our place, you can hear the sounds of foghorns out at sea. There's mist everywhere and an excessive amount of bungalow dampness. I had put some clothes out on the line yesterday; they'll never dry now. "It's wonderful, isn't it, Mikeroo?" Robert asks. "So good for the transplants."

In the house, Robert collapses on the bed. Spike is a wreck, running from the foyer to the kitchen. He can't decide what's more important: eating, peeing, crying? I escort Spike to his favorite telephone pole and then stand sentry with him as he peruses the street he thinks he owns. He throws his head against my leg. *Thank God you're home. I've been worrying.*

Robert is sprawled on the bed, his legs dangling off the edge. His body smells like musky air and other people's cigarettes. I tidy up: papers, Spike's bones, tea bags. Robert, who is not a snorer, snores in an abrupt intake. The jolt wakes him. "You want me to put ice in your pack?" he asks. He's asleep again. I take off his shoes and pants. I persuade him to roll under the covers. I turn off the living room and kitchen lights.

I go into my room. I keep one file cabinet locked. I had stashed hundreds of relics there when we moved to the beach five years ago. I find the key and slide open the drawer. There is one photograph of my grandmother, a sepia-toned snapshot from 1955. She's sitting on a floral-patterned couch. Her brown-grey hair is tousled; she is heavily compact, not obese. A silk dress hangs peasantlike over her body. She wears clear wire-rimmed glasses. A prayer book rests on her lap.

I pad back to bed. Robert's there, out. Whenever he goes to sleep without me, his body spreads out, like he's lost. I sneak under the covers. The bed feels cold. I try to decide between huddling up against Robert or curling up against the dirty wall. Before I can settle on a choice, I am fast asleep.

Frieda
And the
Angel of
Death

———

The year I began escorting my grandmother to synagogue was the year I began dreaming of another boy's lips.

Even my parents noticed.

"It's not the Sabbath, Michael," my mother said, as I changed from a Patti Smith T-shirt to a double-breasted aqua-blue sports coat I had picked up at the Salvation Army. "What does a boy your age want with an old lady?"

My grandmother Frieda (pronounced *Freyda*) was said to be going through some kind of "breakdown" at the age of seventy-eight, so they all worried. Frieda had always been pious—and ignored. But when my grandfather Isaac died, she grew lax in following some of their more firmly cherished Jewish commandments. That's when she became the talk of our Bronx neighborhood. *"Vos iz mit Freydele?"* the remaining old Jews wondered, using the Yiddish diminutive for my grandmother's name.

If a butter dish touched a piece of roasted meat in the refrigerator, for example, Frieda didn't go overboard scouring the plate three times in scalding salt water. When the Day of Atonement came around during the first of the fall breezes, and she felt light-headed from a morning of fasting, she helped herself to a piece of carrot boiled in onion broth. Then she downed a mug of buttermilk in three or four hearty gulps. "God doesn't want me to die from hunger," she said, patting away a coating of creamy saliva from her old-lady's mustache. She used the corner of her white cotton tablecloth as if it were a napkin.

This behavior confused family members.

"I hated some of those customs," my father confessed to me one Saturday afternoon when he spied his mother-in-law waiting for a bus to Fordham Road on the holy Day of Rest. She was wearing her one fancy outfit: a black gabardine dress and silver-lined shawl. "But it's a crime to see them all go."

There were other infractions. On the afternoons during which Frieda was growing more and more lonely and forgotten, she could be found chatting with six or seven black ladies in her cluttered living room. Thelma, Mildred, Lucretia — I knew their names. They were engaged in making Frieda into a Jehovah's Witness and spread their *Watchtower* journals all over Frieda's 1940s coffee table like vacation brochures. My grandmother nodded over Lipton tea with them for hours, stringing them along about Jesus, just for the company. "Stupid *schvartzes*," she'd mutter the moment they'd leave.

And once I spotted her frail form sitting off to the side in a local coffee shop, ordering a BLT in her thick Polish accent. "Holt da mayo, please," she said to a doll-faced Italian waiter. I watched her for a half-hour from the L-shaped counter where you got your salt pretzels and malteds. When her lunch arrived, she peeled a slice of bacon from the triple-decker and regarded it as if it were a dollar bill she discovered in her sandwich. Frieda took a hungry bite and chewed greedily, but something kept her from swallowing. She pulled a strand of fatty gristle from her mouth and deposited the saliva-meat daintily in her lipsticked napkin. *Pfh.* She shook her head. I could see her thinking, *Such a big production to eat fried fat; who needs it?* Then she pushed the triple-decker aside as if the sight alone galled her gallbladder.

But, with all this, she never stopped going to synagogue. In fact, she began visiting the one-story, brown-brick building as much as three times a day, usually right after meals. Hung above the brass-lined doors, in reddish-gray clay, was the synagogue's official name: "B'nai El." Once you stepped inside, the never-mopped pine floors, red-brick walls and dusty, stained-glass windows made you feel as if you had barged into an old lady's living room just after she kicked the bucket. Mostly everyone called this synagogue "the Jerome Avenue shul." You were supposed to feel at home here, what with all the red carpets and "How's-by-you?" pats on the back.

I remember entering the synagogue with Frieda for the first time that year. There was a sudden brush with acute nostalgia. Four years before, I had been the shul's last bar mitzvah triumph. I sang the old Hebrew tunes like a pro; the rabbi lifted the Torah scrolls like they do in *Goodbye, Columbus*; the crowd stood without its usual moaning and groaning; Frieda and Isaac smiled to each other from across the sanctuary, like maybe they'd quit bickering. After that day, like most kids, I stopped attending 7:00 A.M. services religiously. What had happened to my devotion to the old ways? Now I was seventeen. The inescapable awkwardness of my bent posture, light olive skin, crooked nose and fleshy cheeks had made me into an object of intense interest to those who were either lighter or darker than me. I had what guys from New Jersey or Lower Manhattan called "a Bronx look." I didn't have to be in a room of half-blind Jews to feel special anymore. But it was so womblike and tranquil inside, and I felt a loyalty to Frieda's shul, especially the more I found myself drawn to riffraff.

It was a below-freezing day in January and many streets were trapped under intricate layers of ice, slush, salt and animal waste. (Frieda, who had refused to remain at home nodding off at Art Linkletter on the black-and-white TV, took toddler steps. I held her by her tiny elbows, wrapped in thick layers of wool.) I got a shock touching the brass knobs to the mahogany doors leading into the shul. I got another jolt once inside when I touched the metal bar holding the yellow prayer shawls, smelling faintly of urine. "Such a pretty boy, *Freydele*," the old congregants said to my grandmother when they saw me flinch. I heard whispers: "*A gutn yid*." "A good Jew." "God bless . . . " They beamed wide-eyed, like the well-dressed relations in *Rosemary's Baby*. As if pain were your sacred initiation here.

"Sit down, and pray to God, Mickey," my grandmother told me, her bloodshot gaze shifting from the smiles of her half-blind, half-deaf friends to the scene of screaming fire engines outside on a nearby Bronx street. "Before the whole world God forbid burns down."

Something was burning down.

You could smell the soot in the crisp air on the way to worship. The shul was located a block or two from Yankee Stadium, a few steps from the elevated IRT train on Jerome Avenue — the Lexington Woodlawn line, to be exact. It also was across the street from what was reputed to be one of the Bronx's finest network of basketball courts. That winter, only a lone crew of five or six Puerto Rican athletes dared challenge the bracing Bronx winds to shoot expert hoops. They burned newspapers, coffee cups and milk cartons in New York City garbage cans to keep their hands warm.

"Hey, it's the chump . . . "

"The one from high school . . . "

"Hey, brain!"

I was the youngest person at the Jerome Avenue shul. At first I would find myself disdainful of the archaic Yiddish that hung in the air like Havana cigar smoke, Old Spice after-shave and hair nets. But Frieda had picked up something about me that no one else had. My high school life was crowded with yearbook associates, theater rehearsals and honor-roll wannabes. My family was heaped high with aunts who spied on each other's adulterous shenanigans from nearby beauty parlors, phoning one another to *kibitz* over the weather — (God forbid they should be accused of *loshn horra*, Yiddish for "evil gossip"). My family was full of uncles who owned Bronx automotive stores and talked dollars and cents whenever you walked by (the 1968 Mustang I threatened to put a down payment on they dismissed as a "goddamn lemon not worth wasting your mother's hard-earned money on," but the Honda Civic — "Now, there's a car, and for you, kid, no tax"). But it wasn't enough. "It's in your face," Frieda once said. "Come sit with me in the shul. It will ease you."

"Okay," I said.

I told myself that I would accompany her because it gave me an excuse to walk past those Puerto Rican basketball players. Their improvised lay-ups, schizo dribbles and psyched-out passes impressed even Frieda, who winced at them. On the first hint of a thaw, they removed their windbreakers and sweated hard. When I closed my eyes in the shul during the passages in which the old rabbi muttered himself into a hard-to-shake trance, I'd see their curvy backs and wild forearms spiraling up and down in the air, and my breath would quicken, dartlike. Seeing this, Frieda would say, "Mikey, you have so much feeling for God."

I had seen these guys even before Frieda began taking me to shul. Sometimes they killed time over at Jerome Avenue, near the stores underneath the elevated trains. They leaned against the iron-girded green pillars that held up the tracks, iced with pigeon shit. They had just moved to our neighborhood and didn't know anyone. My father would curse them out from our kitchen window: "Goddamn spics" or "Go to goddamn hell."

I'd sit in English class, answering an easy question about Shakespeare, and imagine myself having been raised with a tight washboard stomach and thin purple lips. I secretly took up smoking (no menthols, please) just to see how the thickened, yellow puffs would trail out of my lips when I licked them wet. I felt a little as if I were going crazy, like Frieda. I began talking to myself in the pidgin Spanish I picked up on the streets. "*Te quiero* like you wouldn't believe." Or "*Pendejo*, suck my fucking *culo*."

It got so bad that I'd leave chess club early and hang around the dilapidated Jerome Avenue newsstands waiting for the roving teenagers to show up so that I could act like I didn't know them. They always showed up, too. Their gold-and-black Giants T-shirts, damp from basketball sweat and Gatorade, sticking to their flat bodies. I'd page through the *Village Voice* and catch a glimpse of them talking loud, and I'd feel lonely. It was a little like going to the movies by yourself. Here's one scene: two of the more hyper guys run into a narrow bodega and buy 7-Ups and exotic coconut drinks before heading home, a mere stop or two from here. And another: I stare down at the asphalt, and then lift my head up fast, catching sight of an angled, quivering muscle on the back of a shirtless teenager—he's turning away from the wind to light a half-smoked cigarette. Meanwhile, another boy—the quiet one—listens for the distant sound of an oncoming train.

Then: all five scamper up the forty or so stairs, two or three at a time, to the train platform, running into an open car door just as it's ready to shimmy close once and for all. They kick each other in the ass like Latino Harpos. Thump a basketball in front of a black lady's sleeping face. Scream out the train window: "*I'm going to throw up in your face.*" Collapse into graffiti-covered seats. They were bound for neighborhoods where they spoke only Spanish. Seeing them go, I'd feel lonely.

I picked up the quiet one's name: Hector.

"Hey, Hector! can't you play no basketball?"

"Hey, Hector! where'd you learn how to dribble, from your sister?"

"Hey, Hector! don't you eat, man?"

Hector was so thin. Sometimes I thought he was inhumanly two-dimensional. That one day he would turn to one side or the other and disappear into the sky, like one of Frieda's secret demons. That he felt good about being empty inside, so that he could run around the basketball court and feel both feather-light and numb in case he made a mistake. He had green-veiny skin that was discolored in snowflake designs near his shoulders. You could see the beige polka dots trailing up from his biceps because he cut his T-shirts into shreds, making them into ragged tank tops. Maybe he liked showing off his disfigurement. Maybe he liked the way it was laid over his musculature like a doily. He was such an eccentric beauty, who knows? I couldn't keep my eyes off him.

"Whatcha looking at?" his pal, a heavyset black Puerto Rican guy once barked at me after their basketball game.

"I'm not looking at nobody."

"Shit . . ."

It must have been obvious. Hector turned around, slowly— ghostlike. It was the first time I saw his entire face. It was oval- shaped, like a teaspoon, with a caffeine stain at his lips. He looked at me like I was a detraction from his full-time job, which was sweating and heading home. And being thin. He turned away.

The whole group of six knew a chump when they saw one and occasionally yelled, "hey, whitey," or "yo, faggot," or "bitch," or "kiss my *pinga*," when they saw one of us Jewish kids on the street trying too hard to come off as smart and good-natured. I always wanted to say something, but words stuck in my throat like they do in a dream. I felt terrible. I worried that Mrs. Minelli or Mr. McPhee, walking home from the butcher with brown-paper bundles of bloody chopped meat, had witnessed my being called a girl. "Move out the way, sonny," I remember Mr. McPhee saying. To him, it was just noise. Goyim. Niggers. Kikes. Eyetalians. He hated us all. We all made too much noise.

Once I ducked into a card and tobacco store when Hector caught me looking at him under the train tracks; a moment later, I saw him buying his mother an oversized birthday card. Another time, I stared at him when he was alone in front of a mailbox, and he looked right through me, blowing his nose in his fingers and then shaking the snot out on the street.

One afternoon after school, just as the late-spring humidity came like a blast furnace to the Bronx, he and his friends saw me and yelled, "Hey, you."

My humiliation was a kind of jump-start past my shyness, and I shouted back, "Hey, you." A few Italian ladies, walking home from the fish market, stared at me like they had heard a terrible joke.

The Puerto Ricans were laughing. "Hey, you!" one of those guys said, his hysterics claiming something inside me, like a forceps or a fishhook or a secret shot of my father's Seagram's Seven. "Hey, you! Hey, you! *Hey you!*"

Hector just looked. Everyone's sweat was evaporating from his body; I thought I saw a mirage through the smoky city heat: Hector walking over to me — his thin arms and legs filling up my entire vision. But he was just standing still.

"Hey, you! Hey, you! *Hey, you!*"

Eventually, a couple of friends from calculus class spotted me alone. They came over and yelled.

"Hey, you, Puerto Ricans!"

"Hey, you, Jews!"

One of the most irritating things you could do in The Bronx in those days was to call someone by his ethnic identity. It hurt like hell, but not enough to cause a riot. At this very moment, Frieda appeared, as if from nowhere. I didn't see her approach, but I felt her warm, pulpy fingers on my hand.

"Hey . . . you . . . "

"Grandma!"

"You are becoming a hoodlum?"

I shook my head, but her mind was already off somewhere. I took her hand and we walked toward the synagogue. In the distance, I heard the guttural cries and the assorted Bronx accents: "Heeey yyyyyoooo." I wanted to tell her something — that I was lonely, that those boys had called me names, but she shook her head. "Pray to God," she said. "You have the fire of the Evil One in your eyes."

So I went with her.

As a child, I paid special attention to Frieda's tales of the Evil One. ("He is quiet, like an angel," she'd whisper, "but swoops down at night . . . and gets you, and hits you on the face . . . !") The way she held me in her arms and kissed me! — I'll never forget that. These tales from the dark side seemed to unhinge my mother, who made a point of calling Frieda into the kitchen: "Ma, help me with the brisket, will ya?" And as I grew older — eleven, twelve, thirteen — I went to synagogue with Frieda and Isaac and watched the old man weep during the meditational standing prayer. "Your grandpa is one good Jew," Philip, the rabbi's son, said as I began preparations for my bar mitzvah. "Like almost the best." Like Frieda, the rabbi was getting infirm and a little crazy, so Philip began taking over on Saturdays. And when I was rehearsing the ancient tunes two, sometimes three days a week, I made Philip cry with emotion. Philip: he was a revered basketball player on Sundays, a seminary student every other day. He'd teach me the singsong chants in cut-offs, smelling like the asphalt. The aloof rabbi — a German refugee — seemed stirred by the progress I made in my renditions.

But my parents saw it as a sign of imbalance to keep up such practices after the bar mitzvah was over. "Are you normal?" my mother asked me as I persisted in praying in synagogue on the Sabbath. "Normal kids play ball on the weekends."

The rabbi's son whispered in my ear, "Keep with it. It's in your blood."

But it was not healthy. "There's no future in this," my mother said. "When you get married, then you can go and pray in shul like an old man."

These were the days when the Bronx was changing, and the change was having a strange effect on all of us.

Frieda and Isaac moved here in 1946. It's where they raised a family of five boys, four girls and twenty grandchildren. Frieda spoke a Polish Yiddish and went to market on 167th Street, a full day's experience back then, considering how many Jewish stores you had to browse through (bookstores, dairy markets, religious books and clothing retailers, butchers, bakeries, pawn-shops — never mind Frieda's and Isaac's tailor shop). Now those places were either burnt up or selling food we weren't allowed to eat. That's where my parents, brother, aunts, uncles and cousins lived in fear and resentment. In five years, our neighborhood shifted from blue-collar Jewish, Italian and Irish old-timers to poor Puerto Ricans and blacks. In our little courtyard you could hear the melodies; Zero Mostel from Mrs. Kaffel's kitchen, Mach-ito from Mr. Candelario's, Barbra Streisand from me.

The competing sounds drove me crazy. In my dreams I would hear the mambo and see Hector's pencil-thin lips. He'd be dancing with his basketball in one hand and a Coca-Cola in the other. I would wake up in the middle of a hot summer night with an erection, unable to go back to sleep, the bedsheets soaked through. Murmuring, "bitch," or *"pinga,"* I'd relieve myself, thinking of Hector and the way the soda pop made his lips shine like shellac.

One Saturday afternoon, the daydreams got out of hand. I wished I could go to synagogue, but that was out of the question. My parents, seeing some quiet but profound change in me, had prohibited too many visits with Frieda. "She's a witch," my mother would say of her own mother. "I always suspected it, and now I know it." Playing baseball with friends was suicidal; I couldn't catch the ball. So I just turned on a metal fan in the bedroom I shared with my brother and read Jacqueline Susann novels. But my mother played the Broadway recording of *Fiddler on the Roof* so many times that the album began to skip. Next door, a kid was blasting Santana's "You Got to Change Your Evil Ways." I ran out of the house — "I'll be back for dinner" — and reached Jerome Avenue. I took the subway down to Times Square, as I had many times that year.

I know now that the scenes in those theaters were no different from the shadows I saw in my head when I sat alone in synagogue and closed my eyes. Truth be told, I saw many of the same things in my mind's eye: men who smelled like my father's Chesterfields and whiskey; the reflection from a switchblade I once saw in the dark; the Puerto Rican kids who zoomed in on my nose like I was a long-lost Mediterranean; the Italian boys who called out "momma" as they came on your sneakers; the cigarettes I was too fearful to inhale; the hours in the dark away from my father's golf games and my mother's voice: "Turn off the golf game!"; the heavyset men who hunted me down like I was a stupid, starved animal who didn't know how to say no (I did not know how to say no).

I had memories of hours spent sitting alone in a broken seat watching anal intercourse on the torn-up movie screen. These memories came easy to me as I sat on a velvet-covered bench in synagogue listening to the monotonous singsong of the rabbi. Both places were stuffy, half-empty and secretive. In the theater, I'd wash the crusts of dried cum off my jeans and just-sprouting stomach hairs; in the shul, I'd scrub the stink of saliva-heavy kisses off my cheek and forehead. Neither place had soap. In the theater, I'd sleep and recall being held by Frieda when both she and I were younger. In the shul, I'd dream, too; Torah scrolls opening up, the words becoming big human lips — both Philip's and Hector's. (They both said very sacrilegious things.)

At home, in my parents' bathroom, I read *Portnoy's Complaint* and thought, "How polite." Sure, I knew I had to be very careful.

I feared bumping into my mother or one of her sisters on my way out of the theater. I wore a Yankees cap over my face. It was all a tense experiment. But there was more, too. These secrets were buried in me like a stripper's sense of self-respect. I knew I wanted love. And a boy's lips. Things you couldn't find in Times Square or synagogue.

Frieda was becoming all love, which was why she was so dangerous to my parents and their world. "I wake up in the morning and see the Angel of Death," she confided in me. "And, Michael, he has your face." But she was not frightened. So I decided not to be either. I kept a change of shul clothes at her house. I'd lie to my mother, running out of the house with a catcher's mitt or a hockey stick or a basketball or a bathing suit or a soccer ball, screaming: "Um, see ya . . . " But I was really bound for Frieda's house. We'd walk under the Jerome Avenue el to get to the shul, and see those basketball players.

"Hey, Hector," they yelled. "Here's your girlfriend walking by."

But, after a time, they stopped yelling. The sight of a young man helping an older woman conjured up something familial in them. They respected respect, it seemed.

"*Mira*, there's that *hombre* again."

"That old lady . . . she's a witch, man."

"No, man, that's his *abuela!*"

"*Shalom*," they screamed. "*Shalomy.*"

Frieda would just smile and hold my hand.

I began to know Frieda for real when I walked with her through the decaying Bronx streets to shul; the folds of flesh near her palm, so loosely wrinkled you could almost feel direct bone; the quiet sighs she took when we waited for the 168th Street light to turn green; the memories she entertained now of her mother, now dead, whom she had left behind sixty years ago in Poland, and who taught her to listen to her own heart; the secret potions, amulets and incantations she picked up from superstitious Poles, and now resorted to more and more. Just like I began to know Hector and Hector's guys for real; their odd loneliness among each other as they traveled two miles from their ghettos to play at our better-appointed basketball courts; the fear of the Jews and their holidays I saw in their eyes; the boredom that sometimes overtook them in the midst of an endless game.

———

Men cannot sit with women in Orthodox synagogues, so Frieda and I parted ways once we entered the little shul. The rabbi was immobile and stick-thin, but his voice still shook the chandeliers. It blasted: "God, oh merciful One, holy, holy, holy!" The old men who were already seated would gesture for me to come, sit down, and they'd wrestle each other to be the ones to show me the place in the prayer book. "Here." "No, here!" Frieda had many friends herself, but she preferred listening alone. From the lacy, wrought-iron partition that kept the aging men from the aging women, I watched my old grandmother shake softly in her seat, her droopy eyes closed, her lipsticked lips mouthing the ancient words by heart.

It was on a fall Saturday afternoon—a year after I had been escorting Frieda to shul—that I understood why I thought so much of Hector here.

On cold afternoons, I'd see him. When the weather got warmer, I saw him. When I began going to shul with Frieda on Saturday mornings, and then on weekday evenings, I'd cross paths with him. That summer, I worked in a deli, cooking kosher franks on a grill full-time to make pocket money for college. If I were energetic, I'd get up early and walk with Frieda to the morning service. I'd linger in the hushed sanctuary only for a few minutes; I needed coffee and some time to get ready for work. It would be very early—7:00 A.M. to be exact. (It wasn't uncommon to see the basketball courts start filling up by then. If you were an athlete during a New York City summer, you had to get up early to get your practice in; by noon, you'd fry.) As my morning routine with Frieda became a pattern, I'd see Hector on the Jerome Avenue streets at the crack of dawn, too.

Sometimes he'd be dribbling a lone basketball. Other times, he'd be paging through the pages of a *Playboy* or *Sports Illustrated* or *Redbook* magazine near the very newsstand I used to watch him from. As the weeks and then months passed, our eyes would meet, then bolt away. By the time the October breezes began turning the leaves on the city's oak and birch trees purple, orange and red, we were on Bronx speaking terms.

"Yo."

"Yo."

I might have kept walking, but I slowed down, as if it occurred to me that it was finally time to buy a magazine. It was cool and dewy still, a morning breeze sending the smell of percolating coffee and burnt white toast from the greasy spoon across the street. I felt lonely and acutely hungry looking at Hector as his eyes trailed across words on a page. I could smell the scent of Dial soap from his body, which seemed less sculpted than I had imagined from viewing him from afar. It was just a body, sharply carved and unpredictably pitched to one side or the other, depending on how his feet were planted on the concrete. I had looked at him so many times in so many different ways over the past year — sometimes in clandestine glimpses with Frieda; other times in defiant fast stares — that I had forgotten the difference between secrecy and reckless boldness. When it came to watching Hector, they both seemed the same.

When he turned to me, I saw his lips, framed by little flares of peach-fuzz, quivering. Then he picked up another magazine.

"You a Jewboy?"

I stared at him.

"You go with your old grandmother to church?"

"It's not church . . . "

"Jewboy," he said, smiling.

"Puerto Rican," I said back.

He nodded, matter-of-factly.

"Right," he said.

"Right," I echoed.

He snorted. I opened my mouth, as if about to laugh (a Bronx gesture, if there ever was one). "Yeah," I said. That seemed a little stupid, or even ill-mannered, but it came out of my mouth like a prayer, and felt good. I said it again: "Yeah." It was a big step. I think I moved my hand, as if to acknowledge this. He held his small brown fist to his side, like I'd better be careful. What was amazing? That we were talking. That he could both act dangerous and be dangerous, could act vulnerable and be vulnerable. These four directions played on his lips.

"Jew," he said, dispassionately. He gave me a look, as if to say: we have these lines.

"PR," I said.

I looked at his magazine: on the cover was a famous Puerto Rican pitcher.

He saw me looking.

"I got a subscription," he said. A few beats of silence. Then: "... a stack at home."

Cautious signals played on his eyes. My hands shook a little in the morning breeze.

———

Upstairs at his three-room apartment, two subway stops away, his mother looked a lot like mine. She balanced an unlit cigarette in her tight, cracked lips. She was a compact woman, with a youthful urgency and light-brown, discolored skin, like Hector's. Hector and I sat at the orange-and-white Formica kitchen table, covered in peach-colored, plastic place mats. She served us espresso and little cubes of sugar-iced yellow cake on a paper plate.

"He goes with his *abuela* to church," he told his mother, who nodded.

"Very nice," she said, like she couldn't be bothered. Then she left the kitchen.

"Jew."

"PR."

We both drank our coffees.

In his room, a few minutes later. The plaster-cracked walls were covered with pictures of Jesus and Joe Namath and Roger Daltrey and some Latin-looking keyboard player I didn't recognize. There were Catholic comic books and neatly written homework assignments on white loose-leaf paper piled near eleventh-grade textbooks and ratty spiral notebooks. He showed me some drawings and then his homework, pieces of paper on which bold

As and Bs had been inscribed in red ink. I was conscious of him watching me. There were more tours. I was conscious of Hector shutting his bedroom door with the help of his flat back. After some additional tours around stacks of *Sports Illustrated* and assorted seashells collected from "the clean beaches of Puerto Rico," he pushed me. By accident, I fell onto his linoleum floor, which smelled of Mr. Clean. By accident, he did, too. He lay his thin marionette arms casually over mine. It was more of a slow, motionless cascade than anything else. I was conscious of his fingertips searching for skin, like the feet of an upside-down insect, scrambling for the ground.

"What did you call me?" he asked, making believe he was holding me down against my will, locking fingers into mine.

"What did you call me?" I asked back, making believe I was getting aggressive. He held my fingers too tightly.

And although I felt the breath from his mouth pressing on my neck, and though I heard the words, "I called you a Jew, Jew," I didn't dare let myself give into him for fear that he would tell his friends. I stayed still, in one rigid posture, my body unable to rest itself on the floor and take in this curious predicament. Instead, I focused on the shock of a wish that was no longer just deferred, and the sense that Hector's moist breath on my neck may have meant one thing to me and a different thing to him.

It was a new place, just as shul and the theater had once been new; and, sensing this, I felt my neck release itself fully into the gravity of his tiny room. We lay there for a few minutes. Some strands of oily black hair rested in my face. It made my nose itch, but I didn't dare move to scratch. Nothing happened. The world of men had before been a mix of tactile boredom leading up to shattering appetites. Now: the smell of skin and a hint of mutual loneliness. Had all this been ordained by the forces of a Bronx in flux: the thud of a basketball, the cracked voice of a rabbi? I heard the thud in my head, and it hurt. It was a way of staying focused on the immediate problem: Now what? To my right I saw his bed frame and the dust balls beneath it. To my left was the bedroom door, against which his sneakered feet were jimmied.

I saw a look of wild despair in his eyes. "You like it?" he asked, his voice shaking, his eyes dark with shame.

"I don't know," I whispered, amazed to find myself unable to talk. My lips moved, but no words came out. I found myself uncontrollably — imperceptibly — caressing the skin in between his T-shirt and the black leather belt holding up his shorts. I felt goose bumps trailing up and down his side, where my fingers were.

"What the fuck do you do in that church?" he asked me, speaking into my neck through sweaty tangles of black split ends.

"The same thing you do in yours."

"Nah," he said, starting to stir. He shifted his weight and pushed his face away from my neck in a jolting arc, heading upward. He propped his left elbow up on the floor and balanced the left side of his face on it. It was clumsy, but fast and effective — like the way he dribbled a basketball. When he was done, his lips were positioned maybe a foot and a half from mine.

"What do you do in there?" he asked, staring.

I understood that he thought I carried magic amulets in my pocket, that I drummed up spells to make him follow me. He thought I was a demon, just as Frieda taught me to believe that he was one.

"We pray for you PRs to go away."

He smacked my face. "Well, we ain't going nowhere."

The blow was not expected. My face stung in a million places, even though he had not hit me hard. His soft palm really just dusted the right side of my profile. I had never been slapped like that, a dusting. I would have wrested myself from his grasp, except that suddenly my hands had been freed. You learn things sometimes by learning and not thinking. Like a witch sensing her magic in old age. Or a rabbi closing his eyes and seeing the end of his history and the beginning of something new and twisted up. I smacked him back, mimicking the action of the palm touching his right profile, much in the way you pat a dog's back. He clenched his lips when I said, "We pray for you PRs to drop dead."

He smacked me again, saying nothing.

I hit him again — not too hard, but hard enough. He made believe he lost balance and fell a little to his side. "Whew!" he said, scratching an eye. When he regained his position, he made a scrambling motion with his bony legs that said with a certain unspoken insolence, "move your legs." I did, making a V shape. I felt his crotch sink into mine.

"We want you Jews to drop dead," he said. This time he used a lighter touch, more of a brush than a smack.

"Then this place would really be a dump," I said, copying his style, but hitting the opposite side of his face, with a different hand. I had two hands free; he had only one.

His breath began to quicken. His eyes moved about in their sockets: little bloodshot marbles inset in Indian sockets. "*Coño,*" he said. The way he bit his lip, and allowed himself to slide into this new person now, made him seem superreal. As I had seen Frieda in the street after prayers at her synagogue. I was aroused. I moved myself away from my sharp zipper, inserting a quick hand in my pants. I knew that he knew. He lifted his weight up and allowed his eyes to scan down to my crotch, seemingly blasé, the way he would look when a basketball circled around the hoop a dozen times before it eventually shook itself through.

Then he buried his face again in my neck so that I couldn't see his lips. His voice was muffled. He was afraid to say it: "faggot." He pressed down hard on the word.

There had been moments in synagogue when I would feel tortured — out of it. Mr. Bluestein was incontinent. Mrs. Levine gave me the Evil Eye without fail. At such times, a prayer would seize up on my lips and I would find myself entertaining a strong impulse to murder Mrs. Levine and Mr. Bluestein. If I really went with the prayer to the next step — a repetition; a deep-throated tremor — a humble, riddled love of my people might flood over me. Strange, a simple prayer calling up an agonizing river like this.

"I hate the way you Jews pray."

"I hate the way you PRs ruin our neighborhoods."

And then: a blackout. Him grabbing me on my back, my fingertips on his wet, bony neck. His crotch swirling in place above mine like a hard and furious flapping of wings—was it the Angel of Death beating off? And then, when the light came back, a bucking of youthful abandon. A curl in the torso, the necks ready to crack out of line. Pants stayed on, half-on; shirts shriveled half-off. A spinning by the lips, some saliva sputtering from a hurried kiss you could confuse with a spit. What was going on? Two kids rubbing against each other? This time there was no underwear in the way, no escaping the fact. Still, so fast. Salty and strange tasting the sweat produced by disguised rapture. We lay frozen.

When I heard Hector's father come home and lumber into the toilet, I left the house. (How did I know it was his father? The banging of the doors, the drunken belching, the deep-throated cursing—that's how many Bronx fathers acted when they came home from work in those days.) My heart pounded numbly in my chest as I took the subway home.

When I got off the train, late for work, I spotted Frieda walking back from synagogue. Her shuffling gait looked more strained than ever. I felt ashamed to see her. She touched her fingers to my forehead and said, "God bless you." I walked her home. Her black leather shoes left a trail of marks on the concrete.

The next day, when I called on her to go to synagogue (and confess my fears and guilt), she was dead, her little form curled up in the dirty cotton sheets.

———

I have tried to remember the scene in different ways over the years, but the only real memory I have is of holding her hand. Then dropping it suddenly. It was cold and hard. Then a certain cloying shame. Could I not be more courageous with my grandmother? I was frightened to look out the window, for fear of seeing the Angel of Death flapping its notorious black wings like a B-movie zombie. For the first time in a year, I felt defenseless. I would have to call my mother, a thought that made me even more defensive and wary. She'd take over. "What were you doing over there?" she'd ask. I thought I should take my outfits and Frieda's stones and amulets—things she had showed me in secret — and toss them into the incinerator. But I was afraid to leave the body alone.

I walked toward the window and looked out. I still felt confused about what had happened with Hector, and now more antsy by a thought that occurred to me as Frieda's body got colder and colder: For one year, I was a true Jew. I had lived as Frieda's people had lived for centuries in forests and slums, their darkened lives turning around and around because the passion of love kept them alive. Now it would all be a memory. The faculties of my heart were ebbing as Frieda's soul sailed up to the Master of the Universe. I had no will to pursue this course alone. It would take me ten years to remember what she had taught.

Outside, a million people populated our streets, and most of them were not white. Out of their mouths you could hear so many languages, even with the window closed: Spanish, Spanglish, Italian, blue-collar white, ethnic English, Black English, Sicilian, Armenian, Greek, Creole, Pentecostal ravings. Buses lumbered by — destined for points farther south. Mothers were calling after their kids. Jilted lovers sat on car hoods, waiting for dates, mouthing their own quiet prayers of brokenheartedness. Drunken husbands screamed at their wives in front of the children. It was a cloudy day.

I wanted to say a prayer over the body. Anything. Frieda's name. Or Hector's. Yesterday, all that would have been second nature. Now, no. I looked at the filthy glass and saw a reflection of my face, the place where Hector had hit. In a minute, it would be time to call my mother. For now, I looked out the window. I saw two different versions of the Bronx: the scene outside Frieda's window and the spot on my face Hector had dusted with his hand. At one point, if I squinted hard, I could see both at once. Then all I could see was an image of myself squinting.

Analyzing the Situation

r. Myron Smith's office is located in Hollywood, across the street from Grauman's Chinese Theater. Tour buses line the streets from Frederick's of Hollywood to McDonald's, coughing out enough tank tops and spandexes to cast a Miller Lite commercial, which is what is being filmed across the street. I circle the block on which the office is located three times.

It's Orange Drive. In 1920 it was an orange grove. I know: the head doctor will say I am resisting. Who do I have to blame for this trip? John Drummond — alias Tahar. Wasn't it he who had given me the head doctor's number after my concussion? True to form, I promptly misplaced the scrap.

Later, when I was complaining about nightmares, Tahar wrote the number down on an AIDS flyer yet again. We were sitting on a park bench in West Hollywood after an ACT UP meeting, dissing Ann-the-Leading-Activist for her affair with a male model from Chippendale's. "I got tea on her," he said, handing out flyers for the next demonstration. "I fucked her model. He has an eensy weensy . . . " We laughed, distracting two teen hustlers.

I looked at the number Tahar had given me. I read the name scrawled alongside it. "Doctor?" I asked.

"For your head," Tahar said. I thought Tahar was referring to my migraine, which hadn't gone away. He pointed to my heart. "Who do you think I am?" I snapped. "The Tin Man?" I was touched despite all the pop cultural references I could wedge between Tahar and me. Tahar swooped into my orbit and dusted my lips with his own. He pulled back quickly. Thief. The teens went, "Oooh." I laughed, turning from Tahar so he wouldn't see how much he got away with.

———

I didn't mean to call. But I'd drive my car, and I'd see this one migrant worker — the one with the crusted eyes. The skinny man's smile weakened my resolve — or, rather, his wife's did. He wore a cowboy hat. She sported a pink and blue apron over her jeans. Elia: that's what he called her. Elia sold oranges on La Brea Avenue. Her young face: brown like wood, stained with sweat. "*Quieres* oranges?" she'd ask. In her eyes I saw phobias. Did she worry about the INS? The children? The drivers? SIDA? Once, I was about to turn left at the turn signal at La Brea, after purchasing a plastic bag of dried, tasteless oranges, when her mouth opened in a sigh, then a smile: "Don't drive so fast," she said, in accented English. "An orange a day keeps the *demonios* away."

I could have taken the freeway. I could have done without her and her *demonios*. But during the afternoons, one dodged the clotted freeways baking hard under the desert sun as one steered clear of the IRT during a Manhattan rush hour. Besides, I liked seeing people more than I liked seeing cars. In L.A., pedestrians are a low class. They consist of veterans, winos, Spanglish ravers and Anglo nuts resentful from all the noise. Pedestrians give lip to each other and the passing cars, especially "the Beamers." Those who resort to the Rapid Transit Department's bus system curse each other out for being so poor so as not to own a Pinto. *Not even a pinto,* ese? *Get a life.* The devout take to the streets too, screaming to Christ Our Lord in front of brown, gated cottages south of the Santa Monica Freeway.

Nowadays, there's no escape. More and more people sell oranges. Fewer buy them. Driving north from Venice Boulevard, heading at a snail's pace toward La Brea, you get dragged by the now famous tourist sights of South Central: Jiffy Lube, 7-Elevens, mini-malls and Thrifties — all scarred and razed from the fires and eruptions of the Los Angeles riots. *"Remember Rodney King"* goes the graffiti, as political as the tagging goes around here. The real revolutionaries get deported. In their place: sightseers. They eat up the natural wonders like cotton candy or rock cocaine, but never oranges, especially after they've done Universal Studios, Disneyland, and Elvis at the Wax Museum. Out-of-town families from the Show-Me State carpool to Venice Boulevard, borrowing their aunt's pit bull for good measure. The children buy cardboard 35mm cameras — the disposable kind. Blond boys and girls with lollipop lips pose near grated, abandoned liquor stores. I'm surprised they don't ask the migrant worker and his wife to pose with them and their dog as they examine an orange they don't intend to buy.

It's hard to live after the riots. I'd like to know what the shrink will say about *that*. Mostly, I want to ask him about the fruit woman. Just yesterday, she gave me a dry orange for free, which was no bargain. I couldn't help but recall a few things, such as how my grandmother Frieda ate them. A year or two before her death, she bought oranges by the dozens. She'd peel off every segment of rind in a flawless act of precision. Then, as if she were eating an apple, she'd take a bite. Projectiles of juice splattered everywhere — on the floor, her face, my hands. Frieda would laugh and continue eating until her face smelled like a grove.

When I watched Elia peel the orange in precisely the same way, her eyes fluttering and her mouth making the sound, *"ooooommmmmmm,"* I knew it was time to step on the gas. As I screeched off, a bit out of breath, I thought I heard the woman, in her Mexican tongue, refer to me as a *schmegegee*, the Yiddish word for "fool."

It was then I called Dr. Myron.

The phone conversation with the shrink had been predictably irritating. "I don't exactly know who you are or why I am calling," I said.

And, right on cue, he answered, "I think you know exactly why you're calling."

I should have hung up. Instead, I asked about price and scheduling and before he could answer I interrupted and said I didn't have much money and even less time. He suggested I let him respond. I hated the movie *The Prince of Tides* and told him so. He suggested he wouldn't come on to me, even if I paid him. He chuckled. I felt ill. He suggested we have an initial meeting before I jumped to conclusions. I told him I was ready to jump out the window.

———

Now the receptionist, a heavyset bald man who could have auditioned for *La Cage aux Folles*, suggests I take a seat.

"Should I be filling out any forms?" I ask.

The receptionist shakes his head daintily. He turns back to his conversation. I can't make out anything but "IRS," "he took an ad out," and "slipcovers, could you die?" Within seconds, the doctor is in. Or, rather, he stands at the threshold of his office. I get up from my seat to shake his hand, but he's apparently not into handshakes. He opens the door to his office and says: "C'mon in. I just got done with my last victim."

What a difference from the persona dished up on the phone! White around the temples, Myron boasts a full head of black hair. He is young. He's more masculine-looking than his psycho telephone voice led me to believe. Biceps are palpable, if modest. Collarbone juts out from denim shirt. Eyes show off a tricky brightness—and yet something shy. Have I seen him at the gym? At the Meat Rack? He is a little eccentric—vulnerable, even. No, not at the Meat Rack. "I've been admiring your work for years," he says, extending his hand in a limp handshake. "It's a pleasure to meet you."

"The pleasure is all mine," I mutter.

I expected him to be wearing a lab coat or a suit jacket, but he sports Gap gear all over his lean body. Over the loosely buttoned shirt he wears a red quartz crystal, which hangs from a leather loop. I had expected an intellectual.

"Are you one of those New Age-y people?" I ask, sitting down in a leather chair. It squeaks as if a fart-toy lurks below.

"I'm more into the Dark Age."

"Good line."

"You think I'm fooling?"

I shrug; I have nothing to lose, so I laugh. He does too, a little abruptly for me. It breaks the ice, but then he dismisses the jovial touch and stares me down.

"You're a psychiatrist," I remark, nervous all over again. "That means you're also an M.D.?"

He nods and continues to look at me. I look away and notice the three or four requisite college and graduate degrees hung in wooden frames. There are other objects: a fish tank and little sculpted images of what look like Indian gods. Shiva? Kali? Ganesha? What do I know from Hindu? I notice Kabuki and Noh masks, and hundreds of toy soldiers; half of them are red, the other green, lined up in formations against each other. There's G.I. Joe, and Barbie and Ken. Above the dioramas are paintings and drawings. You could call them mandalas. Colors swarm in triangles and circles of psychological hysteria. There are also images of naked men tucked in secret corners of bookcases. Next to Myron Smith's chair is a desk on which a photo rests. His lover? I look closer: a naked man in a dog collar.

Myron sits still, like a Buddha. I look around. There is a minute or two of awkward nothingness in which I feel embarrassed for being alive.

"Before we get too far into the analysis," he says, "I have to ask you a difficult question."

"In the first session?"

"Ready?"

"I guess."

He takes a deep breath, then shoots: "How will you pay for this?"

I'm appalled.

"It's a joke," he says, giggling like an urchin. "To break the ice. Everyone takes their analysis so seriously."

"I can't imagine why."

"I'll take between fifty and ninety, depending on what you can afford."

"Fifty."

"Then fifty it is."

I stare at the angels in the fish tank. They look aggressive for angels.

"So what brings you here?"

"I think I'm going crazy."

He looks at me and nods. He whispers, "Congratulations." He nods some more. Already this nodding is getting on my nerves. I can't decide whether to look at him or look away, so I look at him and then away. For someone so unassuming, he is making me feel self-conscious. It's how dogs must feel when you stare back at their dullness, drooping your lips in that zombie cuteness photographers die for. I try to jolt my head into wakefulness, but something in me feels weighted down. I can't remember why I ought to feel this way. Myron Smith's face wrinkles near his beard, and his jawbones strike me as almost Satanic. If I saw him in a bar, would I cruise him?

"I presume you're a gay man," I say.

He jots something down in his spiral green notebook. "You presume correctly."

More silence. More nodding.

"Your nodding is driving me crazy."

He smiles. "I'm just doing what you're doing. I'm 'mirroring.' " In case English is my second language, he repeats himself: "*Mirr ... orrrr ... innng.*"

I'm about to leave. I have a mirror at home. I can nod into it all I want for free.

"Don't you think it's disturbing that I may be going crazy?" I ask. "You said, 'congratulations' when I told you."

He writes some more, like a child who has just figured out the answers to the test questions and has only five minutes before the bell rings.

"Should I be disturbed?" he asks. "You don't look like someone who is going crazy to me."

I'd like to hit him.

Despite my growing hatred of the thin man with the nervous smile, the truth:

"I hear voices."

Done. I bite my lip. Odd; Myron's face changes. My hatred of him—it blows off. I take a breath; the back of the chair feels wet. Myron grabs his notebook in two hands and shuts it. He looks at the closed notebook, then at me. His face has transformed; it's cast in a feeling. Compassion?

"Voices," he says, enunciating. "Voices." He wets his lips. "Hmmm," he says, puzzled. "May I ask what kind of voices?"

"A woman's voice."

"A woman's voice?" he says, repeating my tone again, syllable by syllable. I think he has discovered a trace of Bronx in my speech. He gives the "oi" diphthong an extra bounce. I had spent so many years neutering this sound. Has it come back?

"I think I feel her. It's like a weight. Flesh and blood."

"Is that so?"

"She won't leave me."

"Oh, dear. Do you want her to leave?"

I look at him. I had expected Myron Smith to chase me out of the office, or to call up the guards from a mental institution and have me escorted into Bellevue, or Willowbrook, or the L.A. equivalent. I had not thought I would have this conversation with anyone. I had not had it with myself. In the last few months, I had felt a gnawing pain in my skull. The voices confirmed suspicions: *Invasion of the Body Snatchers* and Freddy Kruger—you haven't seen anything yet.

"Do you want her to leave?"

His voice has taken on a quiet calm.

"No," I manage to say.

———

It's a lie what they say about L.A. Everyone *does not* drive. The intersection of Hollywood Boulevard and Highland Avenue teems with America's carless masses. Street hustlers hitch rides. Hundreds of white-trash blue-collar types take the bus, their *USA Today*s all rolled up in aggressive cones, ready for Fido—and the missus. A roundish man looking like Charles Bukowski reading Charles Bukowski sits on a bench waiting for the Pomona express. "It's a fucking hour late," he says to me, as if I've lived in Pomona all my life.

A young man with Irish red hair dyed green lifts a bass fiddle onto an RTD bus that's heading for the Valley, via Hollywood Boulevard. The fiddler is slightly overweight and out of breath. He seems to know how to angle the instrument through tight spots. "I got it," he says over and over again. But he doesn't have it. The fiddle is jammed. The strings make a low, buzzing sound. He sighs and shrugs his shoulders. The drone doesn't end; it enters my mind and melds with my headache. I would like to get close to the fiddle, to see what makes it drone. I'm thirsty; I'd like some orange juice. There's a health-food store ten blocks away; they have a juicer. Maybe I'll take the bus there. But: paralysis. Will the drone drive me crazy?

Fifty people stand behind the musician, dazed and thirsty. They push mildly against the jazzer so the bus driver knows that the tone deaf deserve fair treatment, too.

"I gotta be somewhere," a black woman cries out.

"Bitch," mutters the musician, "I got to, too." His white pants, soiled at his haunches, slip down to his ass; his red-and-white boxers show through. The woman and the musician look related, not by skin color, but by the eyes: deep and annoyed.

"Faggot," the woman says under her voice. "Get a real job at the Postal Service."

Now the bus driver, a skinny black man with a pencil-thin mustache and greying temples, sighs. "Can we all get along?" he asks.

The crowd stops its pushing. The old black woman sees me and shrugs her shoulders. "Live and let live," she adds, as if she's thought better of it.

The sun beats down on the group — not a breeze in sight, or a cooling palm tree swaying in the desert wind. The bus driver continues to work with the red-haired musician, so determined in a kidlike way. "We ain't gonna get this baby on," the older man says.

The black woman watches, curious and cranky. She could be

anywhere from forty to sixty; her wavy hair drops down to her shoulders; it's speckled with gray, voluptuous. Creases by her lip double onto themselves. She frowns. "What the fuck!" she says, pushing past the crowd toward the musician. "Move outta my way."

The bus driver worries. "Can we all get along?" he has the nerve to ask again.

"Shut up with that shit!" the woman pleads. She taps the bassist on the shoulder. He steps back, afraid. She shakes her finger, as in: *No, don't be afraid.* "Push it this way," she says, stooping down, slipping the bottom at an angle in the door, like a shoe saleslady. The bass slides in the bus as if it were made to ride the RTD.

"See," she says, exonerated. "You gotta ask for help in this world. You can't be doing all your shit alone."

The musician shakes his head at her, like she's talking Swahili. "C'mon," the bus driver whines, "we can't go nowhere forever." Passengers file on.

Out of an impulsive urge, I step on the bus. I'm thirsty. I have oranges in mind.

"How much?" I ask.

"What?"

The driver looks at me strangely, his open brown eyes red and watery with smog and squinting fear. I see the baseball bat near his seat. I see him glance at it.

"Just get on," he says, jutting his head. By the twisted — shot here, shot there — look on his face, I get the impression that he is terrorized. White people asking how much the bus costs! What the fuck: it's the CIA. The KKK. Worse, a liberal. His eyes lock into mine. What does he see there? "There's a window seat back there," he snaps. "Next to the old woman, the one who don't mind her business never."

He's referring to the musician's helper.

The bus kicks into gear, turns. I grab hold of a metal bar near a seat so I won't fall down. I stumble to the back of the bus. The old woman sees me and grimaces, barely moving her legs enough for me to wriggle over her callused knees and sit down.

The plastic glass is scratched; you can hardly see through to the T-shirt stores and peep-show emporiums on Hollywood Boulevard. The graffiti on the window says, "L.A. is a disease." Buildings burned during the Rodney King insurrection have been boarded up with plywood.

"Don't pay that no mind," the black woman says. I can't tell whether she is talking about the graffiti or the disaster outside.

I smell a rancid smell: dead rats? My nose twitches. The old woman reaches into her pocketbook and extracts a half-eaten Big Mac. Ketchup drips onto my lap. "Ah, shit!" she says, cleaning up the dollops with her two fingers.

The smell makes me sick.

"Young man," she says, her voice giving off a Texas accent. "Where you heading?"

"Excuse me?"

She offers me a bite from her grey hamburger.

"You need something," she says.

I demur.

I think: How did I end up here?

In L.A., a Zen of Western absurdity passes over the eyes of pedestrians. *How the fuck did I end up in this dump?* It's even worse for those behind the wheel, lodged in steel compartments on stalled freeways. It's as if every Eden-like moment here reveals its own ugly truth: the West is haunted, the palm trees house rats, the people are poor, the gunshots heard in broad daylight are headed for your gated windows.

I look again at the black woman, now done with her hamburger. She burps. "Boy," she says, "could I use a Pepsi." I see her lips mouthing silent words, her head shaking slightly in her seat. A silver cross dangles from her neck; it trembles against her dress. She turns to me — slowly. Her face looks changed, crinkles of skin moving into place, plates in the earth.

"*Azoy sheyn,*" she says.

I look at her, dazzled.

The bus jolts, as if it's hit someone. "What the fuck!" the musician screams, his instrument having crashed against a sleeping school kid. The woman's eyes stay on me.

"Such a good-looking boy," she says, translating. Her accent: thick, Yiddish-sounding. Perhaps it's the vague light, entering in through the dirty window by the lines of the graffiti. Her lips redden. A ketchup-coated finger rises toward my forehead. "God bless you," she says.

"Hold it!" I yell out to the bus driver. I get up from my seat and, pushing past the standing people, make way to leave the bus.

I hear the woman mutter to me as I leave, *"Shmegegee."*

———

I find a telephone booth and call Tahar. My hands shake as I let my fingers punch out his number. My headache has returned, on its way to its metallic migraine hell.

"Tahar," I say. "Thank God you're home."

"Mike?"

"Just saw your witch doctor. Thanks a million."

"Mike. Your voice. You okay?"

"Yeah, fine, Tahar. Couldn't be better."

"Did he pull the dog-bone trick on you?"

"Huh?"

There is a pause on the other line that lets me relax into a feeling I had been fighting: not fear, but impatience. Tahar knows something — something about the bus ride, the black woman, the oranges. I'm not sure he knows precisely; it's delicate. In the quiet of my nighttime fantasy, I have intuited something I never dared let myself understand fully: Tahar's warm embrace would cast away doubts, just as a man's hand brushes dust from a car surface. His cruelty would rescue me from fear.

"Mikey, you sure you're okay?"

"Yeah. Sure. My body feels funny — tingly."

"Tingly?"

"Yeah, tingly — like it needs to go to the gym or something. You got a hot tub?"

"A hot tub?"

"Yeah. Or a bath. How about a tub?"

"A tub?"

"You know, something you take a bath in?"

"I know very well what a tub is."

"Tahar, you have no reason to be snippy. I won't ask you to get in the tub with me."

"Mike . . ."

"Yeah . . ."

"Look, if you're flirting with me, I'd advise you to think twice before you get yourself in some, well, hot water."

We take a moment to laugh.

Tahar breaks off. I'm the only one laughing now.

Tahar breaks into the revelry: "Meet me at Cantor's in fifteen."

"Tahar," I say, trying to get a grip. "Wait . . . I can't stand their food — dairy. Yick."

"Then order a burger."

"Tahar!"

He hangs up.

Thanks, Tahar. I need red meat like I need a hole in my head or another bus ride, which I have to take to get back to my car.

I call Robert and speak to his machine: "I might not be home till one or two in the morning. Another deadline. Don't wait up for me, hon. How about Robert's Famous Amos pancakes tomorrow morning?"

I head out toward Cantor's. Or, rather, I hop on a passing RTD bus, hoping it's the one that will spirit me back to my car. Thank God it's empty.

———

I drive up to the restaurant, located in what is known as "Kosher Canyon." I pull into its parking lot.

"Two dollars!" yells a woman driver ahead of me in a Long Island accent. "*Chutzpah.* Highway robbery."

I honk my horn. "C'mon, lady!" I yell out. "Just pay the goddamn two bucks." These people bring out the worst in me. It's one of the few places in L.A. where you're obligated to feign impatience. I pay the fee. I see Tahar's jeep, parked among five other jeeps. The grey tin contraption is older than every other one in the parking lot. A collage of happy Jews living in a world

of diversity with other Jews—liberals, Hasids, old women, Israelis, Moroccans, New Yorkers, old farts, Miami Beach widows, single sexual compulsives, punkers—adorns the side of the building. Very Yeshiva meets Chagall.

Inside, the place stinks of air conditioning and chopped liver. An assembly of Yemenites crowd the dessert counter, stealing cookie crumbs from the sample plate. "God forbid a white Jewish person should want rugelach," I find myself saying. One young man kisses his dark girlfriend with a delicacy that tells me they are in love and it will never last. A woman who could be his mother—she's tall, thin and black as coal—yelps: "Safi, wait till the wedding." It looks as if this couple hasn't waited for anything. Safi ignores her, kissing the bride-to-be so long that the crowd forgets about stealing cookies. (A new plate has arrived.) The pawed woman breaks away and cackles, joking in a language I've never heard.

The Russian woman in a white apron who runs the bakery rolls her eyes. "Next," she says.

I see Tahar. He's seated in the back, chain-eating pickles, absorbed in *Daily Variety*. There's the trademark: a gold and black bandanna tied tight above his head. An earring in the shape of a cross dangling from his ear. Few know what I know: a precious diamond is inset at Jesus' crotch.

"Is that your friend?" the waitress asks. It would be a mistake to call her fat, even though she must weigh nearly two hundred pounds. Everything about her looks compacted, muscular, including her eyelids—adorned by dripping mascara and fake lashes. Her hair is so blond it's yellow. Roots show through. For a moment, I get the impression that she looks just like my grandmother in her younger years—her forties—long before I was born.

I nod.

"Correct me if I'm wrong. But is he Denzel Washington, the movie star?"

I nod.

"Is that a diamond in Jesus' . . . "

I nod.

"Oy vey is mir," she says, running off. "I gotta tell Sylvia, she'll have a shit fit."

By the time I approach the table, the restaurant has brought a bottle of California champagne to Denzel's table.

"They think you're a star," I say. "Don't disabuse them."

"I wouldn't dream of it. Let's give them a show."

He puckers his lips. I do, too. On cue, we kiss: quick smack. I pull away. Nope, not so fast. Tahar grabs my face with his dry fingers; he presses closer. His tongue makes a certain indolent way inside my mouth. His thumb caresses my neck. His breath tastes like kasha, sweet and grainy. At first, I thought he was a card. Now I think he's a bulldozer.

The waitress comes by with a menu.

"Don't let *me* interrupt," the blondie proclaims in a deep voice. "I mean, a lot of my friends are. Can I have your auto-graph?"

Tahar scribbles some scrawl on the menu, putting finishing touches on the "D" and "W."

"Cheeseburger," Tahar says, handing the menu back to the large women with his soap-actor-out-of-a-job grin.

"Same," I add.

"Not very kosher," the woman says to me, shaking her head. And then modeling her own waistline: "And not very slimming either, if you know what I mean."

"Okay, okay," I say. "Chicken soup."

"Better."

She grabs the menus and leaves. "So, doll," Tahar drawls, "how be your first session with Miss Myron?"

"I don't know."

"Did he make you crawl on the floor and bark?"

"No!"

"Michael, for a radical you are *so* conservative. I think a little barking would suit Miss Thing. She takes your career so seri-ously."

I take an exasperated breath. Tahar isn't smiling, but looking inquiringly into my face, my eyes, as if he's trying to see whether or not he made a mistake. In a moment, I see that's just my paranoia. He's looking to see if I think I made a mistake.

I say in a quiet voice, "I had a dream that Robert and I were looking in a refrigerator."

"Maybe you boys was hungry."

"That's exactly what Dr. Myron said."

"So what's the problem?"

"The refrigerator was empty."

"Oh, that *is* a problem."

Our food comes. "They was outta fresh matzo balls," the waitress says. "I tasted what they had. It'll give you gallbladder. So I brought you your hamburger in the end." She looks at me. "Enjoy," she adds, turning on her heels before I can absorb the information.

I look at our dishes. Blood pours from mine.

"I should have told her well done," I complain.

"A little blood won't kill you. Did you expect the refrigerator to be full, Mike?"

"Dr. Myron said the refrigerator stood for our psyche. But I didn't tell him the truth. It wasn't a refrigerator, it was a freezer."

Tahar shivers into his swallow. "You Jewboys do love to work a good dream. Thank God I was raised a Baptist. Wasn't that Jacob something of a dreamer? I think he was gay, too, all that wrestling. Doing the nasty with angels. Shame on him."

"I can't eat this." I push the hamburger away.

"I'll take it home. So—you going to see Miss Myron again?"

"Don't think so."

"Oh."

"He's so confrontational."

"Myron?"

"Yeah. He talks too much about 'my shadow this,' 'my shadow that.' If I wanted shadows, I could stand in the sun."

"Michael—"

"I feel worse, not better. I want to feel better."

Tahar takes my hands and raises his voice. "Maybe you're not supposed to feel better," Tahar barks.

"Yeah!" a postpunk punk in purple hair and a white dinner jacket at an adjacent table interjects.

"Tahar . . . "

"Maybe you're supposed to feel really bad — and then deal with it."

"Deal with it," the waitress echoes, combing her blond hair with her greasy fingers.

"That's what you get for waiting so long. You didn't go to the mountain. So the mountain has come to you."

I drop my fork into the plate. "A Sermon on the Mount I don't need in Cantor's."

The waitress laughs so hard she almost falls. She gets my joke. Too bad Tahar doesn't.

He picks up my fork and grabs it tightly in his hands. "What is it that you need?" he asks. "Do you know?" He asks so loud, even our waitress puts a finger to her fatty lips.

"Yeah, man," the punk asks. "Do you know?"

"I think so," I say, looking right into Tahar's eyes. "I think I'm beginning to know."

"Well, then," Tahar sighs.

"Well, then," the waitress chimes in.

"Well then," I say. "Let's get the hell out of here."

"My sentiments exactly, homeboy," Tahar says.

"Denzel, dude!" the punk rallies as we pay the tab. "Way to go, dude."

"Thanks, boys," the waitress adds, picking up her three-dollar tip. And then to Tahar: "Keep up the good work. Your performance in *Malcolm X* literally gave me multiple orgasms."

Tahar makes a black-power sign with his fist. The waitress makes one, too. "By any means necessary," they both say, at the same time. I hear forks dropping, sharp intakes of breath.

———

In the Nissan, driving alone toward Tahar's home, watching the palm trees get dusted by the late-afternoon marine breeze. John lives only a block or two away from Cantor's. But the restaurant's lot closes at night, and I don't know what my lot has in store for me. Tahar cruises a few feet ahead. Why did he take his car today? He is one of millions of people who has two cars and yet walks miles to Denny's, auditions and ACT UP meetings. "It's good for my T cells," he once told me. "If it weren't for my doctor, friends and career, I'd move back to New York, where I have no doctor, no career and all my friends are dead. But at least people walk there. It's just that I don't know any of them."

Tahar loves to make me laugh, but lately he's seemed so sullen, especially around me. It occurs to me that he might have driven to the restaurant to keep himself separate. It is the etiquette in L.A. to give people rides to their cars, especially after dining, even if they parked mere feet away. With this in mind, I would have been compelled to give Tahar a lift back to his home. Apparently, he wanted to avoid the quandary. Did he want to save himself from the predicament of suggesting something I might not be ready for as we parted at his front door? For years, I had voiced curiosity about his room "out back." For years, he flirted with the curiosity: "I'd love to give you a tour of my room 'out back.'" The chiding had stopped recently. I know my eyes told a story: that I wanted to tell a story. I would have to say as much. I couldn't—yet. You can knock car culture all you want, but it works wonders for asserting boundaries in a world filled with the dysfunctionally ambivalent.

Tahar's house is his own, bought with family money and the profits made from a pre-activist life acting on "The Cosby Show" and gang movies playing crack addicts and drill sergeants. Located on a quiet block where old white trash, Mexican families and ancient Hollywood elite all live in disharmony together, "*Le Cottage*," pronounced in a faux French accent, is one of the few Victorian homes remaining in Los Angeles. It is adorned with a front and back porch, two terraces, innumerable fireplaces and enough wood bookshelves, floors and portals to sell out a Lemon Pledge factory.

"You can park in the driveway," Tahar calls out to me from the driver's window, before heading in himself.

Tahar digs his key into the doors without looking at me. I walk into Tahar's house. I see four votive candles, situated in four places in his oak-paneled living room. I know Tahar's place: it's sparse, yet comfortable. Chrome bookcases offset the mahogany furniture and hardwood floors. A red *moderne* couch and accompanying love seats come from his old lover; so do the hutches.

The odd thing about Tahar's place: it's plantless, save for one sickly aloe vera clipping Tahar tends. When Mark-the-Lover died, so did the flora.

I walk about and see the grief Tahar lives with. Mark Ruffino died six months ago. The living room is covered in pictures of the young man, an Italian guy from Bensonhurst who helped found the local chapter of ACT UP/LA. The two were together five years. The eight-by-tens are very *Turning Point*. There's Tahar, bare chested and "militant" at a Gay Pride march in San Francisco, kissing Mark. There the two are, lounging off the coast of Mykonos on a kayak. And there's my favorite: the mixed-marriage couple feasting on ribs; it's Christmas Eve at Tahar's house in Jersey City. Tahar's mother, a thin woman with flushed, inset cheeks, has one bony arm over Tahar, another over Mark. Her smirk says, "Mess with my boys, and I'll deck you."

"Would you mind taking off your shoes?" Tahar asks. "Just got the floors waxed."

"No problem."

I scan the photos hung above his baroque mantel while wrestling off my boots. "Mark was a warrior," I say. "I'll never forget the time he climbed a flagpole in Washington and hung the SILENCE=DEATH banner across the roof of the FDA."

"He was a character. He dead now."

I cough.

"I've been meaning to take them photos down," Tahar says. "Time to move on."

"Tahar," I chide. "He was your lover."

"I know who he was."

It occurs to me that this tête-à-tête isn't happening.

"Maybe I should be going?" I say. "I mean, it's so dark in here, and everything."

"Scared of the dark?"

I sigh. "As a matter of fact, I am."

Tahar sits down and rubs his face in his hands. "Mike," he sighs. "You sure you up for this? I mean, you just had your first session with a shrink. Don't you think that maybe one psychotrip a day is enough? I mean, you and I are friends. Friends shouldn't—"

"Do you have any water?"

"Water?"

"You know, H-two-O."

Tahar blinks. "I'm sorry. Water? I'll get some water. Evian or Perrier?"

"Tap, it's so French."

Tahar goes to fetch some Perrier—and a bottle of California Chardonnay. I turn on a little desk lamp. His house is spacious, its five rooms feathered out from the broad living room. Floors and ceilings broadcast elegant mahogany door frames, a rickety porch, intricate cornicework, awnings. The wood shields the house from the sun. Eudora Welty could live here. The plaster moldings of seraphs around the perimeter of the living room pull whatever is left of Hollywood Boulevard from your pores. You can calm down at Tahar's.

An awkward shyness overcomes me as he returns. I watch him dig into the corkscrew.

"I haven't done this since Mark died," says Tahar. "I'm a little rusty."

He hands me the bottle, and rather than bother with reapplying the corkscrew, I just push the cork down into the wine.

"You got glasses?" I ask. He points to the kitchen. I pad into the room where a fluorescent light leaks through the french doors. When I return with two goblets, I see Tahar standing in a corner, perusing *The Leatherman's Handbook*. I clear my throat to let him know I'm back. He ditches the book deep in the shelf.

Tahar broods into his own silhouette now. The outline of his tight, pumped-up chest can be seen from his T-shirt.

"You look fucking great," I say, pouring the wine.

"Don't even try it, Mike. Don't even. You have yourself a nice, stable boyfriend. And if that's not enough, Robert's a friend of mine. I don't want to get mixed up in family business I'll regret. Please, do yourself and me a favor, okay?"

He sits down again.

"Tahar. Do you want me to go?"

"No," he says. "Of course not."

"I should go."

I head toward my shoes.

"Mike, wait!"

Now everything seems to have lightened, if just a bit. "Look," Tahar says. "I've done some thinking about this over the years. I mean, I've had teachers. There is information out there, you know."

I nod patiently.

He stops dead in his tracks.

"You have no idea what I am saying, right? What *am* I saying? I don't want to sound pompous, but I've paid my dues. I guess I'm sounding pompous. What I'm saying is that I can offer you something. Yeah, I'd like to offer you something, as a friend. Like the way one friend teaches another how to play basketball, or how to bake a cake."

"Tahar. What *are* you talking about?"

He stares at me, stifling a tight twist in his square chin by opening and closing his mouth.

"I'm a little slow," I say.

"You can say that again."

"So speak to me in English," I add.

"You don't know why you're here. Do you?"

"I called you, right?"

"Mike. Look. I'll do this for you, Mike. Like a friend does another a favor. As long as we're clear on that?"

"I get what you're saying. It just sounds a little cold to me."

"It's not cold, just clear."

"Maybe."

"Trust me."

"Okay," I say. "But let me ask you a question. What's in it for you?"

He blinks. "Good question," he says. "No wonder you're a

journalist. What's in it for me, huh?" On further reflection, he adds, "I guess you could say 'friendship.' "

I look at him hard. "I thought we were already friends," I say, eyeing him.

"Real friends share secrets," he advises. "And we really haven't done that yet, have we?"

"You can say we've gossiped now and again."

He laughs. "Yeah, but I'm talking *real* secrets. The kind you really don't want anyone but your best friend to know."

"Not even your lover?" I ask.

"Certainly not your lover."

He claps his hands, his entire attitude virtually changed. The clap makes me nervous, yet curious, too. "Now that we've handled that," Tahar announces, "how about a bath?"

"A bath?"

"I give all my clients a bath first. Why not do the same for a friend?"

———

The sound of running water soothes. I sit in the living room, waiting. Candles placed in corners shed a dim Catholic glow. Tahar returns, dressed in tight blue jeans and a black leather vest. He looks ten years younger, like the upstart Langston Hughes that Tahar immodestly compares himself to. He brushes the hair on his chest with a lazy, absented graze with his knuckles. I haven't seen Tahar like this: exclusively masculine.

"Take off your clothes," he says.

I don't. Tahar looks at me—or rather, he looks me over. He smiles, as a cook or a hunter smiles to himself when the game is behaving as one had hoped it would—for now. His countenance changes. He approaches. He takes his hand and moves it around the layer of air above my face and chest. His right palm lands on my top button. He undoes me, one button at a time. The shirt dips open, tails out. He must see the goose bumps. He blows on them. Fruitful, they multiply. Tahar pulls off the shirt. He walks behind me. I know not to move. I feel him, a half-naked man whose mind I don't really know. From behind, he grabs firmly.

My back vertebrae crack. He doesn't seem to let up on the pressure. Paranoid thoughts seize me.

"Hey!" I say.

"Breathe."

"I believe I am already breathing."

"Like you mean it."

He's right. The breathing sets off something inside me, like a whirlpool or a dull fan. I sweat.

He walks me into the bathroom and escorts me to the tub, now full. I put a finger in: it's scalding.

"Too hot," I say.

"Get in."

I dangle one foot in, then quickly extract it.

"Breathe," he adds. "It's just hot water you're getting yourself into." Then he smiles; he's getting to use his sick puns on one of his sick friends. The prospect delights him.

In a moment, I'm in. Something in my upper back, like a bird, flutters in my spine when I sink into the clear, steaming tub. Then out my head, like when clogged water in your ear goes pop.

"Do you do this with all your clients?"

He splashes me with water. "No," he says, a wicked smile on his lips. He grabs my hair, which is wet with sweat, and starts to pull hard. "Only for the ones I love." And with that he slides me down in the tub and dunks me.

My eyes open underwater in an early flare-up of panic. I send a signal that I need air, and the hand holding me down lifts me up.

"I'm not going to kill you," he says.

Am I supposed to feel calmed?

Tahar takes the orange sponge and dips it in the water. He rings the excess moisture out on my scalp and chest. "For a skinny boy, you have a pretty chest," he says, like Tahar. Then with a heavier tone: "I want you to stop this crazy dieting. I mean, a little meat won't kill you." Tahar takes the sponge and drenches my face. The soap smells like apricots.

"My witch gramma makes this soap in Atlanta," he says. "It has healing properties."

"I'm not that gullible."

"I'm telling you the truth."

John Coltrane plays on the CD.

"I can't remember the last time I had such a romantic evening," I say.

"Oh, save the sentimentality for Robert. I told you, Mike, this isn't about romance."

"You and your New Age boundaries."

"They come in handy, believe me."

Robert and I have never showered together, let alone sat together for an hour near a tub. The phone would ring, or I would get a chill, or feel self-conscious about being too fat for Robert.

"Comparisons are odious," Tahar says.

"Are you reading my mind?"

"I am a mind reader."

"A witch."

"A devil." A wink, a guffaw, a stare. "Let's get you out of here," he says. "You came here for a reason, right?"

"I guess."

"You guess?"

Tahar dries me off with a large red-and-purple beach towel. Every part of my body is swept by rough, impatient hands. Again the stranger. I shiver. The mystery of my naked body being held by a man I thought was a friend. His towering black muscular form overpowering me. Me sliding into fear, like an animal who suspects he's being sacrificed to the gods. What has become of my reason?

Tahar ushers me into his living room. He pours wine in clear drinking glasses. The *moderne* couch is covered in tapestries — red, white and black arrows. Mark bought the blankets when the two of them went to New Mexico last year. I remember the postcard sent from Santa Fe, Mark's handwriting illegible. Tahar throws a couch pillow on the floor. I sit on one. Tahar sits on another pillow, opposite me, cross-legged. His jeans grip; he unbuttons his crotch buttons. He lights a candle in between us, then some incense. Nearby, a mahogany coffee table offers a tiny drawer near the floor. Tahar opens it by pulling on its brass latch. His eyes dart in the dark. With his thumb and forefinger, he lifts up a small wooden pipe and sets it down on his lap. With the same dexterity, he fingers a plastic bag. Then a small, thin black box of matches. In a moment, the air is filled with smoke.

He shifts himself closer.

"So let's talk," he says.

"Yeah."

"We could just chat and relax. Or we can — go somewhere."

"Go somewhere? You mean, to another room?"

"No." Tahar looks down at the pipe, smoldering.

Tahar takes his hands and puts them on my face. He plants his lips on mine. Then he pulls away, his hands still on my face. I see his pupils.

"Do you want to go on a trip?"

"A trip? Sure."

"Will you let me take you?"

"Yeah. Sure. Why not?"

"Then check in with your spirit guides."

"What?"

"In other words, communicate with your Higher Power," Tahar adds, with a touch of exasperation.

"Tahar. I'm a New Yorker. My higher power is *The New York Times*."

He laughs. "Then think of your ancestors, doll. Surely you have some of them."

"I suppose."

He chuckles again. Tahar reaches for the coffee-table drawer again. He pulls out a deck of cards, a tarot deck. Looking carefully at me, then at the deck, he shuffles the cards three times. He sets the deck on the carpet between us. He nods to me.

"Pick a card."

I do.

"Look at the card."

I do.

"Don't be frightened."

I am.

The card says: The Fool. A rogue wearing a blue robe and a pointed hat. His eyes reveal the double-edged irony of Lear's sidekick. The fool boasts a bent nose.

"Don't look so long."

Okay.

"Lay the card on the floor between us."

Okay.

Tahar laughs.

Okay.

Joke over. Or begun.

Tahar makes a fist with his hand, then relaxes it. He does this several times before grabbing me by the neck. The hands on my upper shoulder feel warm, and then threatening. My eyes open in fear.

"Fool—"

"Tahar . . . "

"Get on your knees!"

"Tahar, I can't."

"You little shit! On your knees."

I giggle. I bite my lip so as to stop, but another giggle erupts.

Tahar slaps me. Not hard, but hard enough to sting me out of my fear of looking foolish. My face goes to the right, locked in place. I can't move it, can't look at Tahar, can't focus on the Keith Haring collage across the way. I feel hurt, small, angry—and unreasonably horny. I regard Tahar with disdain; how could he do this to me? "You fucker," I say, as if it occurs to me who Tahar is.

He grabs my crotch.

"Aw, little Mikey's upset—and hard."

"Fuck you!"

Tahar shoves me down on the floor. I trip on my own balance and fall.

"I'm 'sir' to you. Okay, boy?"

I crouch.

"Now get on your knees, boy. And answer when you're spoke to."

I stay crouched.

Tahar kicks me, lightly. Who does he think I am? A broken appliance?

A fool.

He strips the terry-cloth robe off me: "Give me this piece of shit." Then he kneels down in front of me and caresses my face. In his real voice, as if as an aside to the audience: "Mikey, if you don't let go, it won't work. Okay? Now, c'mon, be a big boy and get on your knees."

I get on my knees. Tahar fetches the bag he brought out from his bedroom earlier. He extracts what looks like a dog dish. And a leather dog collar. He holds it lovingly, as if it's a piece of Mark's body.

"This is a very special collar," he says. "Only people who I love wear this one. So wear it with pride, boy. Okay?"

"Okay."

"Okay?" He raises his hand, as if about to slap me again.

"I'm sorry. I mean yes."

"Yes?"

I snicker. The whole game is foolish.

He slaps me. I hold my face in my hands, to keep it all in one piece.

"This is not a game, Mike. This is your life. This is about respect. This is how things get fucked up. This is about spirit. Do you read me? Or is the evening over?"

"I understand, sir."

Tahar pushes the dog collar hard in my face. He makes me smell it, the hint of Crisco in the soft black leather. "I can see this is going to be a tough one," he says. "An all-nighter. Glad I ate my Wheaties—never mind my AZT—this morning."

Then he puts the dog collar on.

He raises me up and walks me to the mirror.

"Now you're a little doggie. How do you look, little doggie?"

"Good, sir. Thank you, sir." I've read enough porn to be catching on. "I really mean it, *sir!*"

Tahar walks me into a room, a large walk-in closet that is beyond his bedroom. I see a ten-foot-long wooden cross. Attached to it are ropes and chains, about two dozen of them, neatly tied and arranged on both the right and left sides.

"This is usually the scariest part," he says in his Tahar voice, as he binds my legs and arms to the cross. "It's not the pain, which isn't pain at all. It's about being immobile. Most control queens can't stand it. It's exactly what their mothers did to their fathers."

I entertain thoughts. In tomorrow's newspaper: "Hack gay journalist hacked to death." I almost laugh, but bite my lip for fear of risking Tahar's wrath. My heart beats fast. Sweat gathers at my brow. Tahar takes a towel and wipes my face off. I'm sweating again. He puts his hand on my heart. He kisses my lips. His lips taste sweet. No tongue or open mouth, just the dry lips. He kisses me again. I lose count. I moan into the lost count. The moan touches him: Dr. Frankenstein. Now Tahar, his hard, curved chest exposed by his leather vest, is my only protector. I am nothing to myself. Tahar picks up a glass of water and makes me sip some. He see terror in my eyes.

"Why do you want to hurt me?" I ask.

"I don't want to hurt you," he whispers. "I want to torture you."

Guffaws.

I smile, despite myself.

My front is tied to the cross, a crisscrossing of white rope, human basket weaving. I see myself in the mirror. My back is open to him. I feel his fingers trail down my spine and then up to my bare shoulders. It's all tender. His nails dig in. He caresses again, soft, too soft. He gets to my butt. His nails scrape hard at the surfaces.

"Ouch!"

"Ouch, what?"

"Ouch, sir?"

"You're getting the swing of it, pretty boy."

"Thank you, sir."

"Fool."

Then he returns to feather-light caresses, up and down my spine. Playing into the rhythm of the opposing sensation, my dick sails up in the air. Tahar sees. He touches my dick, then slaps. "Nice," he says, in his sick, puzzling voice. "Jewish salami." I feel him fingering my buttocks, which makes me nervous. I don't allow anyone down there. He sees me tense. He slaps my butt.

"Relax!"

Then he gives light whacks. Five to ten. I breathe heavy, and sweat. It's feeling a little cruel, not the smacks, but the setup. With friends like this, who needs Himmler? I look Tahar in his eyes; I'm still hard.

"You're dripping," he says.

He kisses me; the tongue makes a showing. Soft and prancing. I sigh into its darting play on my gums and teeth.

"Say 'Thank you, sir.' "

"Thank you, sir. *Sir!*"

"One 'sir' is enough."

"Yes, sir."

"I've always wanted you, Mikey," he says, "so much so — you have no idea. Funny that you would come to me in this way."

I open my mouth to say something. He covers my mouth with his hand.

"Now listen up, whiteboy. This is not about pain for pain's sake. If something hurts you too much, just say stop, okay? And we'll stop. But also see how far you can go, okay? Let yourself relax into it; see it all as medicine. So look, you have two jobs. One: breathe. Deep breaths in, nice soft ones out. Two: scream. You can scream in this room. It's fucking soundproof, the wonders of egg cartons. But think of your screams as, well, you know, sacred. I mean, don't shit them out, but see if you can make them come from your heart, not your throat, if you know what I mean."

I don't know what he means. He touches my chest. He closes his eyes and quivers a little, as if he's winging this whole thing, worried I'll figure that out. I feel how Spike must feel — the dog's emotions dependent on his master's.

"I won't blindfold you," Tahar says, regaining his composure. "But I will ask you to close your eyes. And in your mind's eye, see a path. And the more you go, fly down that path. If you stay focused, you will fly."

I worry that my legs and arms are tied too tightly for me to live, let alone fly.

Tahar takes a stick from a black bag. The black bag has appeared from behind the cross. It's a piece of bamboo. He taps the bamboo on my shoulders, then up and down my back, then on my butt, then down my legs, the fast stinging like cups of coffee on a sleeping body.

"Breathe," he says.

I follow his direction. He steps around me, in the back. I turn my head to see. He pushes my head against the cross.

"You are a little pushy bottom," he says. "When the fuck you going to grow up, fool?"

Next, a paddle: black, leather and very Phi Beta Gamma. He applies the leather in rhythmic strokes. It's aural, percussive. I start to congratulate myself and chastise myself at the same time for worrying so much over my obsession with this scene with Tahar. No big deal.

Tahar smacks. I shout.

"That's nothing, Mike. Don't fucking grip. Don't fucking tighten. Let the pain seep into your body like a drug, okay? I'm telling you, it is a drug. Your body produces painkillers. Let the body do what it will do."

He builds up the paddling again, more drumming: one, two, three; one, two, three. A waltz of sorts. With one hand he applies the leather paddle; with the other, he taps my chest area, to remind me about that heart thing. He orders, "Breathe." The paddling builds. The music played on the CD is Space Age crap, Vangelis: psychedelic horns and a few Diamanda Galas–styled shrieks. I'm not sure if it's the women on the CD or me. Tahar shouts, "Let it happen." I sing out.

Our own little opera.

It all clicks—or disconnects. I can't be sure. I feel dizzy. Tahar pounds. A thud, a slam, a cry. A certain glimmer in his eye. Whose eye? The mirror shows all. Slam! Or Unslam! A bomb or photo album stuck open, its commercial glue has been slammed, smacked and undone. The photos stream up, slow motion. A camera catches the footage and plays it back on a screen.

I see images, but can't put faces together with names. I'm falling down — up, really — ready to crash on Tahar's floor, when I realize that I'm chained to his cross. Are we having an earthquake? Is the entire building falling down?

"Is it shaking?" I ask.

"Yes, it's shaking."

Tahar holds me from behind. This time, I'm falling, skydiving.

"Is it the big one?"

"No, I don't think so. But maybe."

Then: a net or a hammock. A swinging or a rocking. No, I'm mistaken. It's Tahar. He holds me in his sweaty, hairy arms from behind. Swaying.

He serves water. He snaps fingers in my face.

"This isn't going to be as hard as I thought," Tahar says.

"Great, sir."

"We're just beginning, boy."

"Yes, sir."

"Good boy."

Tahar extracts a new item. I can hear it. I can't see. I rest my head against the cross, seeing my sweat pour down on the wood.

Tahar steps in front of me and shows me what he has; it's a whip.

"Bad boys must get whipped."

"Yes, sir."

"And you've been bad, haven't you?"

"Very bad — I think."

"Do you want to tell me what you've done wrong?"

"Yes, sir." I have to think. "Handing in an assignment late?"

"That's bad, but not *very* bad. What have you done that is *very* bad?"

"I can't remember."

"Exactly."

"Huh?"

"You can't remember."

"Right."

"You have forgotten. And that is why you are a very bad boy."

Tahar takes the whip in his hand. He shakes out strands, the marionette arms. Dainty black ribbons. He throws his hand up in the air. He's serving a volleyball. He slices the whip hard against the floor. It makes a sound: *thwack!* He repeats this loud show three times. *Thwack.*

"It straightens out the strands," he says.

I hear the boot-clopping steps. He's behind; I can't see. So Buddhist: imagine what's in back of your head. I hear Tahar close against me; he's in my ear. From behind, his two hands seem raised above my head. They descend, holding the whip taut. He tightens the whip across my face, my nose. I breathe in the smell of leather, beating with the soul of a dead being.

Tahar chokes me.

"You are now going to get the massage of your life," Tahar says, pulling the whip away from my neck enough so that I can breathe.

The thuds on my back feel massagelike. Tahar is right. It's a soufflé, a warm shower. The whipping increases; I don't flinch. Tahar is right. The body adjusts; it hungers. A runner knows. The difference between punishing the body and rewarding it. A thin black line.

Tahar travels down. I have developed a rhythm with him.

"Talk to me with your spine."

Tahar is right. Breath steadies the body's reaction to the pain, an anchor as one's knees weaken.

The hard ones come. I cry out.

"Good," he whispers. "See the path. Go there."

He lets up for a moment. Then he increases the flight pattern.

"Jew," he mutters. "You are a dirty Jew."

I am shocked. I don't want to go there.

"Jew," he says again. "You have sinned against your God. The God of Abraham. Isaac. And Jacob. And Frieda. Who you have forgotten like you have forgotten yourself."

The whip slashes into my ass. I cry out: "Oh, God!"

"Good," Tahar bellows. "Atone, Jew. Your people are dying all around you. Atone!"

The photo album again. In the sky again. Spewing pages and snapshots all over me. Snapping heads, crying eyes; elevated trains. Chicken Little. Images are encrusted, moistened by tears. Whose tears? I feel covered in it. Overbearing fragrance. Images turn and twist in the sky like Dorothy's house. An airplane crashing from midair. The boat leaving from the Balkans, a steamer. I see them: Mother. Father. Frieda. Hector. Robert. Me. Tahar. Russians. Then nothing. The black space of a black mirror.

And this cry: "Oh, God!" Words I don't recognize.

The whipping stops. Has the crying? I don't know. Tahar holds me. He says "Let it go."

A scream. A torrent of sin and sacrifice emerging in the form of a twin brother, relative to the Angel of Death, who has come from the North. I see an image of myself looking out the Bronx window: a good boy. I see the flapping of wings; precious vessels, young bodies smashed against a subway car. Boys roughhousing in the crisp winter sunlight of the Bronx Botanical Gardens, then losing each other down paths chalked in snow.

———

I feel Tahar rubbing my chest, as if he's trying to fit my heart back in its cavern like a bypass surgeon. His warmth thaws the puzzle a bit.

I settle down.

"I think we've taken our trip for tonight," he says, kissing me on the lips. "I'm going to take you down. Scene over."

Tahar undoes me. He helps me walk to the living room. Can I put one foot in front of the other? I sit on his couch, still. For almost thirty minutes, I don't move. I see an image of a face, embedded in a blaze, mouth open in a flaming, southern roar. Is it a shadow of mine?

I scratch my head and say, "Thank you."

Tahar smiles. "The pleasure, as they say, was all mine."

———

Tahar suggests some tea, and we talk about tea for a moment or two. When he's gone to boil the water, I see the tarot deck lying on the coffee table. I take a card. There's a fighter holding a shield and an arrow. Did Tahar put that there? I put the card back.

Tahar and I sip our chamomile.

"You were really beautiful up there," he says, caressing the lines in my palm.

"Really? At times, I felt so yucky."

"That's what I mean. I think watching a man let go is one of the most beautiful things. I mean, how often do we get a chance, never mind a fuckin' invitation, to let go? It's too bad."

"I guess that was what knit you and Mark together?"

Tahar sighs. "This leather routine is more a remnant of my old San Francisco days," he says. "With the more psychological stuff I've done with Myron, well, I've tried to give the leather thing—um, you could call it, for lack of a better word, a technology—a new, added dimension. You can say a healing touch. But no, Mark and I never played like that. Never. He never even liked me to talk about it." Tahar clucks his tongue at me. "Don't look so goddamn shocked, child. You and Robert aren't exactly Siamese twins, if you know what I mean."

"But I thought you were the perfect couple. You looked so great together."

"As you well know, Mike. Sometimes looking the part is the best way to grow apart."

"I see."

Tahar looks sad, distant and spent from all his efforts.

"And speaking of partings, you have a boyfriend to attend to," he continues. He rises from the couch. He takes my hand. I fetch my shoes. Tahar walks me to the door. I want to talk about the cards, the last one, the photos on the floor, the touch. But all that comes out is: "John, whew. What a fucking trip."

He smiles. "You going to be okay?" he asks. "I mean, you had a big day today."

"Yeah. Sure. I'll be fine."

"Now I want you to call me tomorrow. I mean, the day after, sometimes it's hard to live with yourself. No, never mind, I'll call

you. But do yourself a favor? Take a breath before you do anything rash. Sometimes when you start to open up Pandora's box,
it spins out."

"Nah, Tahar, I feel pretty calm and collected now."

"Cool. That's how you should feel."

I walk out the door, the streets of Hollywood filled with the
smell of night-blooming jasmine. "Mike," he calls out. "Remember
what I said. About the friendship thing. You'll remember what I
said?"

"Of course I'll remember."

Tahar winks. I wave good-bye and head toward my car.

————

I drive toward the beach, speeding like a demon on the dark,
deserted Santa Monica Freeway. At the tail end of the freeway,
I hear foghorns.

At home, Spike is hysterical. *Where have you been?* He is so
upset, I have to put my bag down and cuddle him; the cuddles
make him whine as if I've stepped on his tail. *Daddy, love can hurt
when you're a dog.* I don't want the cradling and crying to wake
Robert. Spike has peed all over the kitchen floor. Didn't Robert
take him out? I escort him outside. I feel like I'll have to explain
my lateness to Robert. I won't be able to remove my shirt for a
week.

I notice that Robert's VW isn't in the lot.

I walk into the house. The bed, which hadn't been made in
days, is empty. Robert's not at home.

I check the clock: 2:00 A.M.

I check the bed: empty.

I check my phone machine.

There is a chatty message from my editor at *The Angeleno*,
Larry Ravin. Another from Ann-the-Leading-Activist. Nothing
from Robert. I wonder: He's probably visiting a friend, another
performance artist. I decide to sit up in bed, lights on. I peruse
a book Robert bought for me: *The Jews: History's Pariah Class*. The
writer talks about the cult of prostitution in the First Temple.

They didn't teach you that in Hebrew school. I fall asleep with the book in my hands. When I stir, it's 5:00 A.M.

So unlike Robert.

At 7:00 A.M. I call Ann-the-Leading-Activist.

"No, Mikey," she says through an annoyed yawn. "I haven't heard a peep from Robert."

I call Marty.

"Who?" he coughs out from his sleep. He, too, hasn't heard from Robert. "I wished I had, though," he adds. I hear him light a cigarette. Good-bye.

At noon, it occurs to me to call the police. My editor, Larry Ravin, phones. He has demands: "Let's go over your piece word by word."

"Anything you say, boss."

"You up for this?" he asks. "You sound distracted."

"Robert seems to have disappeared."

Larry, who is straight, knows about gay men. "They are not to be trusted," he mutters. But he also knows Robert. "Robert's not like all those queens." This, he adds, "offers cause for pause."

We edit the piece anyway. I answer every call waiting. No Robert.

Spike and I play catch for two minutes. Spike is like a cat when it comes to fetch; he'd rather eat. I let him jump on me; we tussle on the grass Robert has just planted. Spike slobbers over my face with licks of gratitude. His fur, however, makes me itch. Allergic though I may be, I can't bear to push him off. That's when I catch his scent. My dog smells funny, like Grey Flannel. I take a whiff again. My dog has Marty all over him.

At three in the afternoon, I call Ann again. I ask for Marty's address. Like any good activist, she offers information with trepidation. "I mean, you called him already," she advises, "and he said he hadn't seen Robert."

I answer pertly, "I don't believe him."

She laughs in the phone. "So what are you going to do, big boy? Bop him on the head when you catch Robert in his arms? I mean, it *is* a free country."

"I don't expect a melodrama," I say. "I just want peace of mind."

She gives me the address. "Now, be calm," she counsels. I get in my car and drive like an emergency case to Hollywood, not far from Tahar's house: 308 Selma, a little tan cottage adjacent to the Hollywood Freeway.

I pull up. I open a rusty gate. The front porch has been sprayed with maroon graffiti. I step on weeds. Two beer cans and one Pepsi bottle adorn the yard. I approach the front of the house. The gated windows are filthy. I see into the living room–slash-kitchen. It is a bachelor's mess: clothes, porn magazines and dirty dishes. I see a SILENCE=DEATH poster. I see a black-and-white photo of Marty in a demonstration; shirtless, holding his crotch like he's Marky Mark.

I make my way into the backyard, bushwhacking through the weeds into the concrete path that leads to the back of the cottage. I hear the whirl of the freeway.

There they are, sunning themselves, asleep in each other's arms. They lie naked, face-to-face, on a makeshift deck area, made with wood chips and bamboo. A plywood fence offers privacy, as do tall weeds and one dying olive tree. I can't imagine how Robert, with his green thumb, can bear a moment without pruning. I pull a few tumbleweeds.

"You hear something?" Marty asks.

I freeze.

"Nah," Robert answers. "It's just the wind."

Marty has another question: "You ever do this with What's-His-Name? Just lay around and do nothing?"

Robert stirs again, rubbing his fingers on Marty's too-tight chest. "His name is Michael. But no. Not really. Not anymore."

"Don't you miss it? I mean, this is heaven."

Robert smiles. From my perch, I detect a touch of sadness in his smile. "Come to think of it," Robert says, "I love Mikey-Moo because he works so hard. He's so dedicated to making the homophobic planet safe for little young snotty queers like you. I really look up to him for that. So should you."

"Sounds like a workaholic to me."

"It's good to believe in something. A little workaholism won't kill you."

"Maybe you and I should get back to work," Marty says, planting his hand on Robert's crotch. Robert smiles and puts Marty's hand back on Marty's side of the blanket.

"I want you to be nicer about Mikey," Robert says, looking a little confused, nervous. "I mean, he's still my boyfriend, you know?"

Marty turns on his side, pouting. I get the appeal; he's Robert's younger self, whistle clean and baby-like.

"I thought you said you were in love," Marty whines.

"I am," Robert protests.

"I mean, with me."

"Marty," Robert chastises, pressing his stomach against Marty's hard back.

Despite myself, I sigh over their beauty.

I see Robert angle himself toward Marty provocatively. "No," Marty moans. "It needs a goddamn rest. I have goddamn human functions I need to perform there." Marty takes Robert's hand and brings it to his mouth. He closes his eyes and kisses.

"I'll wait for you," Marty whispers. "I'll do whatever I have to."

"Will you be nice to Mikey?"

No answer. They fall back to sleep.

The snores provide me with my cue: Kick ass!

———

I can't. More Hamlet than Othello, I get in my Nissan and drive off. I entertain a flashback: the look on Robert's face as he slept with the child Marty. Eyes closed over lids, softly. Mouth open at the center. Arms over Marty, Robert's cute stuffed animal. The worms, the dry grass, the winds, the birds. I had never seen Robert look so relaxed: open and brazen. Had I not given that to him in all our years together? What a loss for him.

And for me.

I have to get out of the car. I pull over, in South Central. My head. My head. There is the thud again, a migraine. Before last night, it had been so long since I cried like a child: a whooping-cough hiccup of a cry that is dry like cotton. Here we go again. I see the card. I thought I would never see it again.

Fool.

Hector

and

Family

Values

———

rieda's funeral took our minds off the fact that she had died. The Jewish custom of sitting *shiva* to mourn for the departed — coupled with the chore of feeding all the sitters dying from hunger and heartbreak — provided our family with a project big enough to distract us from the fact that Frieda wouldn't be sitting and eating, too. My mother could be heard hollering, "Hey, Ma, give us a hand here with the chopped liver, will ya? We gotta feed a hundred." Then she'd think twice, sigh and mash the two dozen hard-boiled eggs herself. I stayed home from high school for two weeks to help out. Distant relations from California, Israel and Newark poured into our narrow four-room apartment, the senile and the shrewd alike. So did their chicken livers and playing cards, never mind the "tsk, tsk, tsk-ing" and never-ending nose blowing that seem to follow a good Jewish cry. There was no place to sit down in peace, let alone fantasize about a Puerto Rican kid who ejaculated in his dungarees while you defamed his people (and he yours).

Like I said, Jewish mourning is a sit-down affair. The suddenly observant family convenes on cardboard boxes for a week, telling bad jokes, noshing and complaining about how uncomfortable the boxes are. Of course, not everyone's buttocks are made for grieving. Aunt Sylvia, who hadn't spoke to Frieda in a decade, was mourning on the down-stuffed silver couch. "The best mother in the world," she could be heard saying in between swallows of cashew nuts and drags on Pall Malls. Uncle Lou led the room twice a day in the prayer for the dead; it was standing room only. My cousins, ex-hippies who hadn't made the transition to the Jimmy Carter era, monopolized the bathroom. They got stoned on bad hash and tried to turn me on. My mother wasted her breath debating them: Hadn't the Democrats sold the Jews down the river? My father chimed in: Wasn't the goddamn neighborhood getting blacker by the day? Our house was such an opera of *"oy"* this and *"oy"* that that I couldn't hear myself think. I forgot to notice how Hector had come and gone. When there is thunder but no rain, you forget you saw the sky ever sharpen in neon colors.

The bathrooms in my high school were famous for being places to go if you wanted to get high or beat up. I swore I'd never see the inside of those sweet-smelling hellholes. But during the period of mourning, when one ate and drank for two (the dead and the living), I found myself walking around in the afternoons feeling as bloated as one of my shuffleboard-playing uncles from Miami.

A few days after Frieda's burial, the situation grew desperate. I had no choice but to run into the "drugstore" located on the deserted fifth floor, my anatomy almost protruding from my faded tan corduroys. The fifth floor — that's where my Shakespeare class was. Only nerds and drug addicts climbed the 374 stairs. Once in the men's room, I saw an empty stall and scooted into it. I assured myself I had a private moment and released what felt like a year's worth of Gatorade, Hawaiian Punch and instant coffee. I stood still for a minute or two, shivering with pleasure.

"Yo, wassup?"

I looked up and saw a head peeking out from the adjacent stall.

"Hector!"

He disappeared, jumping off the toilet onto the floor. I heard noises: a belt buckling, a book shutting, the toilet flushing, his Converses shuffling. His head poked through underneath the par-

Hector
and
Family
Values

——

tition between our stalls, then his whole body squirming through: a Bronx limbo dance. He stood beside me, his awkward elbows and knees moving in place here and there. Both of us just pissed — numbly. One thing I have to say about Hector; if he had to pee, or do anything else that came to him naturally, like laugh or snort or crack a joke, he just did it, no two ways about it. He zippered up his fly. He ran off. In his absence: a hint of Old Spice after-shave, the kind from the red box, the kind our fathers wore.

I had questions: what was Hector doing inside the "drug-store?" Why did he shuffle into the stall with me? Why did he split so fast?

Once outside our high school, I let the questions go. There were spring winds, and you could smell the magnolias and cherry blossoms creating hay fever all over the Bronx.

Inside, our school felt like a beige plaster jail. Outside it was more expansive. The building was surrounded by rusted wrought-iron gates and statues of people who ran for president but never won. Often the unexpected took place here, on a big flat brown block on the once-elegant boulevard known as the Grand Concourse. We were between the worlds: the torture of school life and the torture of home life, so for a moment we felt free. The few teenagers who wore ties loosened them; they had been to Catholic parochial school. Kids smoked Newports; they popped Lifesavers. The girls pried open compacts. Guys in grey jerseys from the baseball team parted company: the blacks in one direction, the Italian and Irish in the other. Teenage girls in Huk-a-Poos eyed both, but spoke to neither. If there was a date to be made, after some pretty nasty name calling and egg-salad throw-ing in the cafeteria, this stoop was the place. But this was not a dating year.

That's when I saw Hector, leaning against a rotted telephone pole. He was smoking. The fall winds blew his black hair in a strawlike bun above his head. His pal, Eliseo Martinez, waved curiously as he ran for the bus: *Hey, man, ain't you comin'?* Hector nodded his head but didn't move. The gasping bus left. Black teenage girls pushed smaller white freshmen. An Irish guy I knew from chemistry pulled up in a beat-up Chevrolet and picked up a gang from biology. Two aloof and painfully thin black girls from college English class talked William Blake to our emaciated teacher, known as "Twiggy." I watched Hector fight the wind.

I had no idea what to do, and out of stupidity, I would have walked home. My mother needed me. Mourning aunts and uncles were fighting life-and-death struggles over Anwar Sadat and Menachem Begin. What if I had followed my impulses? Maybe I would have fathered three children, all CPAs now. Maybe I would have lived nearby my greying parents and kept them company in old age, what with condos in Florida, saltless lox on Sunday mornings and doting grandchildren. Maybe I would have smoked tarless cigarettes and gained fifty steady pounds, but I would have had nice letters from insurance companies, a special "hello, how are you?" from my wife's aerobics teacher not to mention a running invitation to the guy's pinochle game.

What if?

All I know is that I walked toward Hector. He pointed his index finger at me like he was about to shoot me, just like my Uncle Morris would have done after a long-time-no-see. The gesture had a certain class to it: *I know you, you know me, get out of my face.* I had to smile. From the distance, I thought I saw Hector smiling. Memory might fail me here. It was windy, and like my grandmother Frieda used to say, it is hard to see in the wind.

"You hungry?" he asked, throwing the cigarette in the gutter.

———

At a coffee shop near the Woolworth's on Fordham Road, we talked a mile a minute. He told me about moving to the city from Puerto Rico ("Man, my mom got real tired of the fucking poverty down there") and about the memories he recalled ("She grew all these cool eensy-weensy flowers, I forget their goddamn names") and insisted that he would have been better off had his parents never left ("People don't act so fucking cold to you down there, like they gonna ice you or something") and his father would have been somebody ("Nobody drinks like a fucking fish down there — well, not so much"). He explained why his English was so good

("Fuck, I was born here and lived in the Bronx most of my life. I'm a fucking American, dontchu fucking forget it, whiteboy") and what had caused their departure ("My father lost his dumbass job in the sanitation department") and why his mother couldn't divorce his father ("He'd fucking murder her ass and then he'd come after me for talking bad behind his back"). When I told him about my grandmother, his eyes stopped buzzing. He had been fiddling with his cigarette without lighting it. Now he stopped.

"Oh, shit!"

I didn't know what window had been opened; I certainly had no idea how rarely it would open in the days to come. I felt the breezes. Not many. One, two. Hector snapped my hand with one of his fingers. He must have seen the wrestling. And the rain. Just a drizzle, but rain all the same.

"She was your *abuela*, man."

He tapped Morse code on my hand. The waitress, taking away the cold ketchup-laden burgers, lifted her thick eyebrows at the scene while she raced around our half-eaten meals. Then she was gone; so were our plates. The table looked empty. There were our hands. I don't know what was the bigger deal. That I missed Frieda? That Hector saw that I missed her? That men of a certain age could see things? That he was hungry? That we would eat later that afternoon? That people seemed to notice that we were asking questions in our head, questions neither they nor we had answers to? That rain was now coming in from the open window?

"I don't give a flying fuck what they think," he said. Both of us were frozen by this, our moment in the restaurant with the window wide open. It said: this is who we are. It said this to people who had come to eat a late lunch here and who were dealing with their own feelings of guilt and despair for possibly ruining their dinnertime appetite. It said: This is the window that can open.

Now the diners had something else to think about but their peculiar eating habits. Hector and I were holding hands in the coffee shop. Neither Hector nor I dared move, the feeling around the room was wrought with everyone's strange hunger, including our own.

———

We got to his house by bus, a choking, lurching, crowded albatross that took us deep into the "ghetto." Hector and I sat the whole way in silence. It was a mile from where I lived. There were five burnt-out apartment buildings, then ten. Then I stopped counting. Just blocks and blocks of emptiness: grey rubble, broken glass, Budweiser cans, one white dog scavenging. I saw a cluster of black kids throwing two-by-fours into a small fire. I saw a deserted Good Humor truck. I saw an old lady ducking the wind as she walked home. My grandmother had died; now I was going to a foreign land.

Hector's eyes were bloodshot, his face lined with a thin layer of soot. I had the image of him peeling off the molded filth at home, like the way my mother cleaned away Noxzema. The early winter light that filtered through the bus windows shadowed every existing crack and crevice on Hector's nose, jaw and eyebrows. Every time he looked at me, his breath quickened. Or maybe it was mine. I rose to give an old Puerto Rican lady a seat. I stood in front of him, holding onto one of the swaying metal handles. I felt his face lean up against my jacket.

It was dark in the lobby of his mailbox-less building, dark in the piss-smelling elevator, dark in the narrow green corridor. We walked shoulder to shoulder. He turned to the right, then left, then guided me to stop. We stood still. I heard a dozen-or-so keys jangle. I saw his hand fling into quick position, then into the master lock of the front door to his apartment.

No one was home. There were echoes in it, people's voices, Indian syllables from long ago. Next door, an old jazzer sang "A Christmas Song," in a sad, suave way. Upstairs, a man talked to God. He kept calling out, "God, please," and "God, you said. . . ."

A votive Jesus candle, already lit in Hector's room, spread a scarlet light around us.

"You want some H-two-O?"

I shook my head no. He walked to the kitchen and poured a glass anyway.

"You get high?"

I shook my head.

"What do you do?"

Hector took off his shirt. I was nervous, but intuitive: I wanted to get past this part. I wanted everything to feel as it did in the restaurant. I took off my shirt, even though I knew I'd feel skinny.

Hector approached and nervously put his lips on mine. So sudden. I had never kissed a guy I knew. I had kissed girls, and male strangers who were older than me and hungered for my saliva—like it was a drug. To lock lips with a boy you had just talked to? To press up against a boy who acted as if he knew and loved your grandmother? To want to devour breathless moans like they were M&Ms with someone you had just taken the bus with? I felt self-conscious. Hector put his tongue on my lips. The wet spasm: it was like receiving a knock on the head or a whiff of airplane glue or a sudden and uncalled-for football pass. I broke free.

"Hey, whassup?"

I fell onto the bed, like a person collapsing into himself after a dirty joke. I needed a moment to think. Hector folded his thin, soft-skinned body onto mine, confused.

"I'm not sure," I said.

"Not sure of what?"

"Not sure of I don't know what."

Lips found mine and tried to drum out the doubt. But he couldn't. Layers and layers of hungers and hesitations got fused together like an elixir with each touch—and from a buzz or a drone I thought I felt in the air. I had questions: What if your mother comes home? Do you believe in God? Will you go away? Is there a membership to this club? But he wasn't interested in questions. He kissed me like he had a right to; I thought I would die. One lip on my top lip, another lip on my button, his tongue dipping around my front tooth and then back toward my lip, his front tooth chipping at my lip. I couldn't stand the feel, a pressure as much as it was an opening.

"Wait a fuckin' minute," I said.

He tore away from the bed. He turned on the light, a purple and gold plaster ballerina with no lamp shade. I got the impression that this was how his father acted to his mother when she resisted him at night. Hector paced in the room and approached his desk. He opened a drawer, rifled a bit and withdrew a switchblade. I heard the walls scream. Hector opened the knife, then looked at it as one looks at a looking glass. He shrugged, smiling goofily. He closed the knife and threw it in the drawer, hollow and wooden. He lit the cigarette he had been playing with in the coffee shop. He eyed it, as if it were saying, "Hector, I told you so."

He blew the smoke out of his open mouth, as if talking back. He was not a born smoker, as some people are. In the brazen light, his body looked taut and mismatched; his hips jutted out from his butt, and phyllo layers of muscles crinkled around his ribcage, as they do in paintings where teenage boys are involved. I felt a new surge of desire.

I touched a rib.

"Get the hell off!"

"Hector . . . "

"Get off the material!"

He stared off into space.

"I didn't want to be the only one . . . "

"You're not," he said, shifting his head a little toward me.

I grabbed his shoulders and made him lie down. He resisted, but politely, reaching over the double bed in a long and swooping stretch toward the ashtray, to get rid of the cigarette. He reached into his tight pockets, extracted a tiny bottle of green Binaca, and treated himself to three quick shots. He was more pliable. He let me lay atop him for a minute and let me kiss his lips without kissing back. He closed his eyes.

"It's too much," he said.

How horrible.

He fell on the bed, clenched and ball-like. "It's just too much. It's just too much."

He was laughing at me.

I went to smack his shoulder with an open palm, but he somersaulted away. I went for him, but he ducked. His bed sheets tangled us; we were sweating. I grabbed him by his shoulders, and he rested his damp head in the crease between my shoulder and neck, snickering. A cackle erupted in me, too, then some snot: almost a sob, but not quite. We both laughed so hard we forgot the rules we seemed to learn at home about love being about sacrifice. We kissed and held each other in ways that suggested more contradiction: struggle and softness, snickering and moaning.

As quick as that simple ease came, it went. I felt him poking his way near my asshole (a strange feeling, since I still had my pants on; so did he). My old terror again. When I looked at him before in the fifth-floor men's room, I noticed he was not circumcised. I had hoped I would never have to see a foreskin face to face.

"Don't fight me," he said.

I stared.

He fumbled. I saw him holding himself. I didn't move, even though I wanted to turn away. It was too large, as far as I was concerned. (Later, that would turn out not to be the case.) His eyes were pointed at mine, determined not to let me look off to the side and off the hook.

"Let me in, baby," he whispered, poking himself again toward the entranceway.

"I never . . . " I said, hearing myself stammer.

He covered my mouth and shook his head. I understood. Hector was not a literal person. Hector would teach me much about words and intentions and actions, which is that they were not the same. Words were both places and names, things that made the heart feel as if it were the dick. Hector would not fuck me that day. Yet he would open up places, like a window opens up places.

So this was it: our first real time together as something other than strangers. Outside there were sirens, gunshots and barking dogs: mere backdrop sounds to us. Someone even asked us to shut the hell up. We never shut the window, which poured in sweet city breezes, asphalt and autumn leaves burning in parking lots. We breathed in the odors like panting dogs. Eventually we had our pants off. We rubbed our hard bellies together. We screamed out curse words. We slept on our bare, sticky stomachs, our snoring mouths face to bad-breath face. The wind from the open window cooled the sweat off our naked backs. Soon it got grey and cold. We covered ourselves up with his woolen blanket and although it itched here and there, I slept more deeply with this dead-to-the-world Hector than I ever had alone.

———

Overnight Hector became a beloved member of my family. He forgave us our bigotries and eating disorders in a Christian way none of us were capable of extending to each other. At my grandmother's funeral, for example, my mother jabbed my father in his ribs for weeping uncontrollably. "She was my mother," she snapped, "not yours. Give me a break." Only once in Little League history did a hardball float into my outfield glove extended nervously in the Bronx early-spring air. I spent so much time watching my father put his hands in front of his eyes, the ball, once caught, sunk immediately from my mitt to the concrete playing field. In the Bronx, men carried automatics under their windbreakers, drank bourbon in their Pontiacs and slept the day away in darkened garages. Wives laughed to their faces while the children copied each other's homework. Hector restored your faith in the Bronx male sex. The first time my mother met him she seemed mesmerized by his charms: rain-forest eyes, fake introversion and a sappy smile that looked through you to the nicer person inside.

Once, when no one was home, I invited Hector over to my house to teach him about the Jewish way of life. I showed him my prayer shawl, phylacteries and a silver-plated wine cup. He was under the distinct impression that a bar mitzvah was a blood-letting ritual in which a grown boy was circumcised before the standing-room-only congregation as the rabbi sang to Mary and the saints. When I exhibited the color photos of my overweight uncles and aunts dancing in an unruly semicircle like Rockettes, he seemed deeply disillusioned. "Where's all the blood?" he asked, turning the pages. "You guys probably took it out for posterity, to save face and shit."

That was the afternoon my mother met Hector. She slaved as a school secretary to our high-school principal and wásn't expected home for at least two hours. Surprise. She opened the lead front door with her ring of a hundred keys, gasping like a silent-screen star at the scene of the bar mitzvah albums circled around Hector like a Christmas wreath. I understood how the Rosenbergs must have felt, being tried for divulging critical state secrets. Had a Puerto Rican ever set foot in our house? Hector was light-skinned, and his accent didn't seem any more obtrusive than my mother's own. He enunciated so much, my mother later asked if Hector was English or something.

"Hector's my new friend."

"I see," she said.

She sat down on a kitchen stool we put next to the front door for the purpose of removing shoes during snowstorms. I kneeled next to her. She required help in removing her slush-coated boots, cemented to her tiny feet from the saunalike heat the New York City Board of Education subjected its minions to in the winter, lest they come down with pneumonia and sue. My mother eyed Hector, curious why he sat so still.

"Such a handsome boy," she said, a little disbelieving.

Hector extended his hand — formal for my mother's taste. She was used to kisses, hugs or, if worse came to worst, little inept waves from friends who saw her small, hunched frame from across the street but didn't want to engage in conversations about whether or not the algebra tutor really went to Harvard or was just lying to take advantage of the unsuspecting — and mathematically inept — Bronxites.

Hector broke the ice by grinning.

"How ya doin', Mrs. Kaplan?"

"Got a slight fever," she said. "But I'll live."

She was not too infirm to sit and chat in the kitchen. "How's about some Lipton tea?" she asked. I set the Pyrex pot to boil, then extracted three tea bags. I dropped each in three Melmac saucers. That's when Hector blurted out that I needed only a single bag.

"Three cups for the price of one," he insisted.

I watched my mother clap her hands, as if she had just had a word or two with Moses.

"Stick with this Hector," she said, cracking a smile. "He knows the value of a dollar."

———

These were the days when Puerto Ricans and Jews waged a ground war for the Bronx. I fretted that Hector and I would suffer casualties, namely each other. I cringed at the dinner my mother insisted she make for him; he touched a plate of chopped liver and said, "*Mira*, it looks like pig fat!" I worried the time Hector shoveled my mother's pepper steak in his mouth and burned his tongue, shouting, "*Oy the fuckin' vey.*" My mother didn't bat a fake eyelash. Later she pulled him aside to clean up his Yiddish: "*Oy vey.*" I glowered when Hector brought exotic produce to our house — overgrown, green bananalike fruits he called *platanos*. Layered with cheddar cheese, the "loaves" tasted so sweet that my father, mother and brother devoured two each. That incident ended fights about monopolizing the toilet. For weeks, no one had to go.

The last straw? Here's Hector lifting up his arm to dunk a sponge basketball into my brother's plastic basketball hoop, hung above his bed. Hector's skintight red T-shirt reveals two robust holes underneath each armpit. My mother insists he remove his shirt. She runs for her sewing kit. Hector and I share mystified looks as if Hector's own mother didn't know how to sew or buy clothes for her kids! We seem unhinged at how creamy brown Hector's bare torso looks amidst my family's olive pink sallowness. "Now you bring all your shirts over to me," she says, "and I'll mend them." She takes her sweet time darning, as if the presence of a brown-chested teenager reveals something precious and ghastly about her current financial condition.

Funny, but Hector scored me points. "Thank God he's palling it up with someone who knows how to dribble a goddamn ball," I heard my father whisper to my mother. "If I saw him play with one more Barbie doll, I'd put him out of his misery." It had been ten years since I played with Ken, but my father had a memory like an elephant.

"He's like a prince," my mother said another time at dinner when Hector sat up straight and quiet waiting for his Shake-n-Bake chicken. She talked about him as if he weren't there, which, in my family, was a sign of being loved. Hector nodded politely and downed three bowls of chicken soup. He was fond of my mother's matzo balls, which he called "golf balls," a play on my father's "gallbladder balls."

"You're gonna fatten me up, Mrs. Kaplan," he said, thinking the notion would tickle her.

"Now, don't put on too much baggage," she'd admonish. "I like my boys thin."

I saw Hector's mouth open — as if he were about to say, "So do I."

My older brother Stan, an accomplished musician, saw in Hector a kind of role model in the area of spiritual redemption. "Hector has soul," he'd tell me in a rare instance of communication. Stan was not gifted with the political compulsion to make our parents, or anyone else for that matter, like him. He saw it as a losing battle. At dinner, I grabbed the attention. Once I went on about which kids were going to the City University of New York and those, like me, who were bound for the Ivy League. My brother, accepted to Juilliard, had decided that CUNY cost our parents less. Weren't the best percussion teachers — *congeros*, he called them — hidden away in East Village studios anyway? Stan had made his peace with living at home so as not to be indebted to anyone but himself. But listening to me rave, he dug his knife into his minute steak with a fortitude even my mother's cuisine didn't require.

"Hey, bro, it's already dead," Hector said, making everyone laugh, including Stan.

There was a tradition in my family of being openhearted to a fault to my friends. Allan Gasspan was given a key to the apartment and went through the icebox like a starvation victim. My father took a keen interest in what "the guys" were up to: "That Mark Rothstein, he ever buy that balsa wood model airplane he was talking about?" After browsing for books on human sexuality at the Mosholu Park library, I'd return home to see one of my high-school nemeses watching "Eyewitness News" with my parents, whom I, too, had begun calling "Willie" and "Linda" since everyone else in the world seemed to.

Sally Greenspan, my junior-year sweetheart, debated the pros and cons of Israel's giving back the Sinai Desert to Egypt. Judy Levine, my senior-year girlfriend, taught Willie how to make oatmeal cookies with macadamia nuts, which Linda claimed tasted like "the food Hitler gave to the Jews." My mother found little fault with the Sallys and Judys of the Bronx. She brought up her complaints in quiet ways, as in notes tacked on to the refrigerator with magnets from Atlantic City. "That Sally really put on a few pounds," or "That Judy never shuts up."

She never wrote a memo about Hector.

In the mornings, Hector would come to our house so that we could take the city bus together to high school. My mother often prepared a cup of instant coffee for him. Hector drank it down fast despite its metallic bite. Picking up the phrases common among Jewish housewives, he'd say, "Bustelo this is not." Soon after, my mother purchased a canister of espresso coffee — instant. "A dollar more than Nescafé," she pointed out. He drank the brown-black muddy water only halfway, saying, "Mrs. Kaplan, no one makes instant coffee like you."

On Sundays, we'd go to the corner Chinese restaurant, where the air conditioning gave you a postnasal drip, but the noodles were free and greasy. Hector's favorite dish was chow mein. My father tried to get him to order more adventurous fare. "Kid," he'd say, "try something a little more fancy, like egg foo yung." But Hector stuck to what he knew. The scenario never changed:

My mother pays the bill, checking prices against the menu. Hector heads for the men's room, embarrassed by the miserliness but too polite to say so.

His behavior impressed my parents, who found Hector both exposed and proud. Truth be told, my friendship with Hector drew my family together. My father had a vehement hatred of Puerto Ricans. "Linda," he'd boast to my mother, "if I had a gun, I'd shoot them all." Yet he never bothered to censor himself around Hector. Hector was able to take the hatred impersonally. He must have heard the same thing about the Jews at his house, and he ignored it all.

I wasn't so gifted. "Hector's PR!" I'd say, the moment Hector left our house.

"Hector's an exception," my father would answer, before turning up the volume on his golf game. But as a result of Hector's visits, my father did modify his rages at my mother, who consequently quit some of her nagging.

"Can I get you a cup of Sanka, Linda?"

My mother would be darning his toll-collector socks, or cutting coupons for frozen pizza out of the newspaper, or writing her rich sister in Maryland snippy letters. I'd watch Linda struggle against the impulse to say my father made the worst Sanka in the Bronx. "Thanks, but no thanks, Willie," she'd just say.

The most powerful peace was between my brother and me. We talked about sex and romance, without naming names. We did so through vague anecdotes and words like "my date," "the person I'm seeing" (and, I have to admit, in one weak moment, "my fucking girlfriend"). His new girlfriend had a pussy that smelled of lavender. Hector liked to kiss for hours, and had a pussy (for that was what we called it) that smelled of talcum powder and sweat. Stan's girlfriend understood Stan's endless brooding and paralyzing loneliness the way Hector empathized with my phobias over sports and dread of public speaking. (Hector did not share the latter; he could never overcome the former.) With CIA-like dexterity, Stan and I parceled out intelligence that just a month ago would have been Top Secret. The two in-laws almost shared similar initials: Hector Gonzalez Rodriguez and

Helen Grant. Both were probably older: Hector by six months, Helen by three years. Both were—different. Helen, I began to understand through a clue here, a clue there, was black.

As always, Stan drummed lightly with brushes as he talked away, doing his best to stay grounded in real-life particulars instead of the foggy glaze he got in his eyes when he used sticks or, more lately, his hands. By the standards of those days, his kit was not conventional. It included congas, triangles, tin cans, timbals and vibraharps. "Let me hear that one again," I'd say, soaking up the bebop percussion that had been the unconscious backdrop to my childhood. I ached to hear the rhythms I had blocked out. A simple *ratatat* evolved into a blizzard of African patterns, unassuming drumrolls, the *kling klong* of a tin can, a thumping bass drum. I told Stan that he was "not good, but great." The compliment, deferred for a Bronx eternity, touched a chord. For days I thought I saw him singing to himself.

The harmony brushed off on my gruff father, who began to take an interest in our quiet dialogues behind closed doors. "Your mother says you're studying," my father said once, when spying us from a crack in the bedroom door. "But it sounds like you're talking about girls?" We let him in on the closeness—as much as we could. He taught us the games we never learned, like poker and hearts. We took his wit and wisdom to heart—and with a tongue in cheek, responding to his anecdotes with his own idioms, like "You don't say," or "Win some, lose some." (Our favorite we saved for when he read us the riot act for not being nicer to Linda: "Monkey see, monkey do.") We loathed my father's unfiltered cigarette smoke. We tolerated the nicotine air for the thrill of betting. "I'll raise ya," my father would say over his cards. It sounded like a dare, but to me it was more of a promise that had been deferred.

I shared these vignettes with Hector, who smiled to himself with a certain poise. Home-fucking-run. In the evenings, he'd drop in to watch the Yankees or the Giants with "your *papi*" (Hector's word) in the "red" room. My father painted his model airplanes there and the furniture emanated a scarlet aura my

mother insisted caused her hemorrhoids, headaches and hay fever.

"Who ya rooting for, Mr. Kaplan?"

"The Mets," he said, applying some spit to a remnant of a
rag. "I'm a loyal schmuck."

"You know, the Mets suck. But they got the best pitcher in
the National League."

"You can say that again."

"The best pitcher . . . "

And so on.

At the third or fourth inning, I'd excuse myself to get my
chemistry homework done. Hector would pad into my room after
me to whisk through his social studies. First, he'd wrestle me to
my bed. He'd kiss me everywhere but on my lips just to torment
me while quoting my father's analysis for the Mets' losing streak,
batting averages, and most-valuable-player status, word for word.
It was just like Hector that he saw no inconsistency between
tolerating my dad's litany and, moments later, biting my neck. It
showed a certain sense: that he could get away with crossing a
secret border between men if he also kept the incongruent border
open between all men.

"Yah father!" Hector once rhapsodized while holding my
torso with both hands like they do in '40s movies. I saw that he
was getting something elusive out of this. He befriended a kid
who didn't want to buy drugs from him. He knew a family that
saw in him the simplicity of spirit they hungered for in themselves. My father called it "having a happy-go-lucky kid around."

Hector called it "the curse of love."

———

The more time I spent with Hector, the more time I couldn't bear
to be without him. For a time, I got up an hour or two early to meet him before school. "Where you going so goddamn
early, kiddo?" my father once asked, himself reputed to be the
early riser in the family.

"I got gym practice," I answered.

"You're the scholar in the family," he responded. Then he let it go. That morning, Hector and I necked like teenage kids in my building's stairwell. We were happy to breathe on each other. He nibbled my ear and held my face the way I saw jocks hold the faces of their girlfriends. I let him do so against my better judgment because the control he exerted sent druglike rushes through my circulatory system. Once I almost fainted from the push-and-pull of ownership.

The next day we tried the McDonald's restrooms. It was after school, and we had each devoured two Big Macs and one large Coke with ice. We had to pee at the same time and thought nothing of following each other into the men's room. But while we emptied our bladders, laughing over the "bastid who gave us the fucking hard time with the extra ketchup," we kissed by jutting the tips out of our mouths and then delicately sensing the other person's taste buds. It aroused us so completely that our dicks stood straight in the air—as we urinated! The trajectory of our piss hit the wall rather than the toilet bowl; the stuff splashed our pants. We were both so taken by our tongue experiments, and amused by the mess we were making, that we didn't mind the taboo we were breaking against urine. When he put a thumb in my mouth moments before we exploded, I tasted how already wet his fingers were. Was he testing me? The acidic fetor in my mouth brought me to an almost unbearable ecstatic state, which he exploited by covering my mouth with his stinky palm. Both of us shivered and shook so violently we almost fell down on the filthy floor. I never told him this, but that action wed me more to Hector than any ceremony could have done. "Nothing your body makes is bad," Hector said. "That's the truth, okay?" We walked quietly home under the elevated train tracks by Jerome Avenue, passing the newsstands and basketball courts where I had spied Hector a year ago.

And then afterward: his father's sedan when his father left his car keys on the family's kitchen table after a twelve-hour day as the manager of the Macy's shoe department. We resorted to this suede-cracked place more and more, especially at night. Hector did not have a license, but he knew how to drive and thought nothing of jetting us to Van Cortlandt Park whenever we wanted to smell the just-mowed lawns.

"Get the fuck on in," he'd say on a whim.

The sedan was a place for intermittent hibernating, the only place where we could "sleep together." We were careful not to jeopardize this secret place by giving in to cravings. Many less-discreet guys and girls had been busted by the police. At most, we held hands and stared out the window.

"What's going to happen to us, Mikey?"

"Who the fuck knows? We're almost eighteen."

With Hector, I never indulged in verbal romanticism. Once I told him I wanted to marry him. He hit me in the face and said, "Don't act like a girl." Now I think he regretted my reticence.

Our bodies were never reticent. I recall us holding hands while rummaging through the school library stacks, rubbing our lips delicately against each other's for twenty minutes until we both came with kittenlike pants. We blew air in each other's mouths. We calibrated the breaths the way musicians do when playing sweet love songs. Our musical bridge often came in the form of turning away from each other to steady ourselves. Then we'd make invisible smoke circles in each other's throats. His basketball-breath had an intoxicating shiver to it.

Then there was the time when we grabbed each other's crotches in an empty locker room, The harder we tugged, the more attuned to ticklish sensation our dicks got. Over a period of ten minutes, we yanked more and more, gauging plateaus by the gravelly moans each of us made when we seemed to hit a wall. At one point, I felt I was losing my testicles; I began to black out from the pain. That's when I came—like a thunderstorm, this time the lightning following the roaring cracks in the distance. Hector covered my mouth with his free palm; by accident, I bit it. *"Puta barata!"* he muttered. Then he put my hand to his mouth and came himself in his green gym shorts. " 'Ey, Mike," he said, this mystic Stan Laurel, "another fine mess we got ourselves into." He scooped the jism from his stomach like a yolk that had missed the cookie batter. Instead of throwing the goo in the trash can, he licked it up. I was too stunned to resist when he provided me with my first taste of what Hector called "little baby Hectors."

I had never been particularly oriented to certain parts of my body: nipples, asshole, the spaces between the asshole and the balls. Hector showed me all about them. Through the delicate use of his forefinger, he'd wake up areas like the nipples with a drip of spit and fortitude. "It's like an old, creaky engine," he said. "You got to give it some oil." My flat brown nipples began to stand up on end as if I had just emerged from a swimming pool on a cool day. Hector had a theory that, on a man, the nipples were the place God put the skin that he couldn't fit on the dick. Hector called it "the theory of three dicks," and by applications of breath and at first barely perceptible caresses, he confirmed his theory to me.

He was not so lucky in other areas. The first time he ever so lightly fingered my asshole, I nearly jumped off his bed, screaming so loud his mother had to ask, "Hector, *qué pasó?*" For some cultural reason, I suppose, I had a pathological distaste for that area in my body, and up until that time felt ridiculously unclean if I couldn't shower and shampoo after a bowel movement. Hector, who usually would laugh at my little obstinacies, found himself impatient with what he called "your crazy mixed-up ethnic fears." Before I could put on my shorts, he cornered me in his room, half-nelsoned me down to his linoleum floor, and straddled my arms with his bony knees and legs. I could have screamed. I could have bolted up. I could have bit his hand. By the same token, I didn't give in easily.

"Hector, man," I insisted. "Cut that shit out."

"No way."

"*Yes* way."

To his credit, Hector didn't edge himself farther inside me than my opening was willing to allow him. In twenty minutes, I guessed he had two fingers inside. But who, after all, was counting? He relaxed his own position and lay next to me. For the first time, I felt as if I were breathing from other parts of my body beside my nostrils. I relaxed into the visceral tundra of sensation. Something in my chest seemed to pop—not so much from the pressure in my ass, but in the release of pressure in my lungs.

That is when, I think, Hector inserted his third and final finger. I cried. I was embarrassed. He was tickled. "Now," he said, vibrating his fingers inside, "you are a man."

"What are you, my fucking rabbi?"

Afterward, Hector let himself go with me, astounded at how far away we could fly together. "Damn, we're fucking animals," he'd say.

"Birds," I'd answer.

He liked to kiss with two different parts of his body. His mouth; his ass. There was one time when he just lay on the bed in his humid apartment like a penitent. His eyes were focused on nothing in particular and his arms stiffly held his legs up in the air — as if he were a woman in the last of her labor throes. Releasing one hand, he grabbed my head by my curly brown locks. I was to meet his baby face to face. "Clean it," he'd say. Every dainty lick I gave him — barely perceptible at first — sent him into paroxysms of quick shivers. I gagged at first at the taste and fervor that emerged from him, tunnel heat smelling of bananas and sweet greenery. Soon I breathed it in like one breathes in fine cooking: the smells of cuisine in the air making you feel both nauseous and hungry at the same time.

We were very technical about our next proceedings. Sunday mornings, that's when his entire building evacuated for mass. (Hector's father demanded church attendance at least once a month, which is all he could stomach himself.) A white cotton sheet covered Hector's bed. We showered. He avoided breakfast. We kissed and rubbed our bodies together until we felt we couldn't hold back anymore.

"Let's try it another day, Hector," I suggested, content to be with Hector without fear of his mother singing hymns or little sister knocking on the door and then running off.

"No, Miguel," he said. "We have to get through this." (He called me Miguel whenever he wanted me to be especially sweet and caring to him.)

"What if someone catches us? Will they call us 'maricón'?"

Hector rolled his eyes for about a minute. "We got to expand your Spanish vocabulary. It's so fucking limited."

I attempted to be as gentle with him as he was with me, testing his puckered tightness with a finger coated in saliva. Hector lay on his back. "Just put the goddamn thing in," he whispered. "You would not believe it, man, but it feels better than a goddamn, pointy finger." I had so many strange memories around insertion. Sally had been a virgin intent on ending her suffering among her friends. She touched herself with her fingers, guiding me that way. When I spotted blood on my mother's sheet afterward, I thought I had killed her. It took me weeks to regain my honor around her. Forget my erection.

Now I was wilting again. Hector was a street magician when it came to my inner motor. "You gonna put that uglee thing in my PR ass, or what?" he asked.

I tried to go slow, but my gentility irritated Hector. "Just push it in, man!" he barked. So I did. "*Ay!*" He screamed so loud, I was grateful no one seemed home in the entire neighborhood. "That's Grade A fucking Jewish meat," he grumbled, "Hebrew-fucking-National." He told me to stay the hell put. When he regained his breath, he said, "Okay." I felt sloppy, uncomfortable, and concerned about injury. I tried to adjust myself—I had been balancing my body weight by holding my arms out as in a sustained push-up, facing him from above. Now I sank in. I grabbed his shoulders from behind his back. I felt something give in him. He held his head, as if dizzy or outside himself. I began to thrust for my own pleasure. "Oh, man," he whimpered, lost and deep. "Ffff . . . " I shoved. I think it must have hurt. He bit his knuckle and then, with his hands, held my shoulders, as if to block me from going too far too fast. Then, like a rubber band snapping, he thrashed into the bed sheets and pillows, then clenched his ribs and abdominal muscles, then let out a percussive "Ah . . . ah . . . ah." I felt the jism, but couldn't see it. I blacked out, a gushing inside him and me both, little bolts of light near my eyelids. I pulled out accidentally before finishing, burying myself in the sheets near his thigh, to release the rest. Holding each other, we let out a billowing moan that seemed to go on for a minute. High off that breath, we giggled, immobile.

In the end, we were not big fuckers. We detected a secret,

infantile practice I have never since created with another. I'd lie on top of Hector. Or he'd lie above me. Our two naked bodies, virtually identical in sensation and size, if not in tension and bone arrangement, created a magical abrasion that fought and collaborated with the laws of gravity. We'd rub until we stopped feeling as if we were rubbing. We made sure that not one spot on the skin could be exposed to anything but another boy's. The stifling, heated meshing drove us insane. We'd lock fingers. We'd crease our chins into each other's necks, muttering "Rub me," or "Yeah, man" or "Pretty fucking bird." We'd wait until the other had caught up, and then, like two birds of a feather, we'd fly off inside our heads, gasping into each other's ligamented shoulder, calling each other's name should one bird circle off into oblivion without the other and lose his way back.

———

One day, Stan stopped drumming on the drum he brought with him into the living room after dinner and asked me, "You on drugs or what?"

"What?"

"I know who it is."

"How do you know?"

"Whaddaya think, I was born yesterday?"

My brother looked like me, only stockier. His jet black hair rose above his head in stiff, hysterical curls that he tamed by shaving off his hair, crew-cut style. This made him look a bit like a skinhead—an anomaly back in 1977, when guys were still wearing their ratty hair down to their shoulders, or in Afros that rose like upside-down cakes above their foreheads. He had gotten a bad rap in our high school; Stan made it a point of honor not to talk to white people. He was two years older than me—nineteen and a half—yet he seemed to waver between an ancient quietness and an infantile weirdness.

My brother scanned my face, allowing our eyes to meet, even as he kept up his staccato spasm on the conga. I don't think we had ever looked each other in the eyes before. I thought of dismissing him, and of turning to the two life-sized bar mitzvah portraits of us two hanging right above his head as proof of the level of unconscious acceptance of our fates, but I saw how much of an invitation to his life he was giving. He turned his focus back to his instrument, fluorescent blue, speckled with silver pellets. When the telephone rang in the kitchen, he stopped — frozen.

"You waiting for a call?" I asked.

"Yeah, just like you."

"I feel like you're snooping on me."

"Nonsense."

Our mother, oblivious to all this, grabbed the receiver before the second ring, and sang with as much Bronx embellishment as she could muster: "Haellllooooeeeiu. . . . "

She walked into the living room, her hands covered in yellow rubber gloves.

"You're dripping," Stan said.

"It was Hector."

Stan returned to his drumming. I think he shrugged his shoulders, as if to say, *Let her deal with one phone call at a time.* My mother took Stan's gesture to mean "So what?" It wasn't "So what?" to her. She explained that Hector and his father had a fight about college, whether or not to go, which one to go to, and that Hector didn't elaborate further. Had Hector revealed so much in two minutes? I suppose she was fitting the details of her boys' own struggles with their father into Hector's predicament. I knew that Hector fought with his father, but their crisis focused more on the present than the future. I hadn't heard of any ultimatums. She apparently knew more.

My mother sounded not just upset but outside herself, like it took someone beside her boys — but the same age as her boys — to remind her who she really was: a mother, with a good mother's heart, who knew how to referee, and occasionally provoke, the ongoing war between old men and young boys.

"I told him he could sleep here tonight," she said, removing her gloves.

"Coming along, aren't we?" Stan said.

"He's such a sweet boy."

"Even for a PR," Stan added.

"I didn't say that."

"But you were thinking it."

"Was not," she said. Playfully, she threw one of her rubber gloves at him.

He threw it back. Less playful. Had she not caught it, the wet rubber glove would have hit her in the face.

All my life, I saw my mother look at Stan as if she was questioning whether or not he was her biological son. He didn't have the talkiness associated with the Kaplans — or the overeating, screaming and sleepwalking. All of us had thin faces, wavy brown hair and olive skin that made us all seem handsome to ourselves, even in the midst of clinical self-hatred. Everyone but Stan sported Semitic noses. His was tiny, but the facial creases were puffy.

"Stan?" my mother said.

"Yeah."

Stan's look said, *I see you — so what?* She turned away, looking at me as if for protection. I struggled for neutrality. She sighed. Her tender curved shoulders now constricted into her neck, giving her the look of a Bronx quarterback.

"Stannie-boy."

Stan returned to his drumming. My mother shivered. I wanted to comfort her. She found a nest in her swirls of frosted hair and scratched. She retreated to the kitchen. The business of the macaroni-and-cheese dinner, and Hector's appearance at it, distracted her, I suppose.

Stan lifted his hands up and then conjured a drumroll. He bore down on the drum skin with a concentration no one in our family had taught him. I thought I saw bolts of blue, sparkling light leap from his hands as they do in pictures of Gene Krupa in which two hands become two hundred in a slow-speed photograph.

"I know all about it, Mike," he said. "So don't try and pull a fast one on me — or yourself."

I saw that he was not so much accepting me, as preparing the way for him. We were, after all, the same grandchildren of

Frieda. Although I suppose he did not miss her the way I did, I know she came to him at night, too, like a bee spreading pollen, in the field of memory that was our common dream.

———

My brother was to become a famous jazz drummer—a player of the mambo as well as complex fusion beats. He was already something of a star in the neighborhood with his Latin-style rhythms. "*Chico!*" Mrs. Rodriguez would call out to him. "*Tu música es muy buenísima!*" By day, he would play baseball with his friends from high school. He was a splendid technical pitcher. I used to come by the concrete playing field to watch his arms swell up as he cranked up for a curveball. His nose would curve up, too, and I had to be careful not to laugh.

But by night, after he finished his college sociology homework, a thick silence would descend on him, especially on hot summer nights. Friends phoned after dinner—Greg Goldstein, Sandy Pinksy. Stan would take the phone from my mother and make polite conversation—"No shit? You fucked Arlene Silverstein doggy style?"—and then would get off.

My mother dried dishes, making believe she wasn't listening.

"You didn't want to go to the movies with Greg?" she'd ask. "He's such a nice boy."

"He fucked Arlene doggy style. Very nice."

She'd try to reach him. "Stannie-boy," she'd say. "Can I get you a cold drink? An ice-cream pop?"

"So I get heart disease like everyone else in this family?"

He'd be off somewhere.

There was a beat outside, and it seemed to drive my brother out of his mind. There would be Tito Puente and Pancho Sanchez; the screaming cries of trumpets and trombones and the improvisation of the soul. But more than anything else, it was the percussion beat. It seemed to live in his heart. Ray Barretto: That was not a name you heard a lot in Jewish houses. But my brother made us learn it. My mother and father complied, both because there were a little worried about him, and because they were growing scared. Stan began to walk with a gait that was not in our racial genes: It cried out "black." My parents watched it like they watched his drum playing. It was beyond them, protected by a dark charm they didn't dare touch if they wanted to remain in one piece.

———

At first Stan began secretly to take his conga down to the crowded streets at night. He'd wait till my father had finished the last of his veal cutlet and sauerkraut and my mother was on the phone for an hour about community school-board elections. ("Elaine has more power than that black bitch Shirley. But Shirley has the principal wrapped around her finger.") Stan would say he was going out with Greg Goldstein to a school dance. The hustle was big that year and everyone, including my brother, worked hard to learn it. But while my parents wrangled at the dessert table over whether to buy a dishwasher or wait till they moved (they never moved), he'd sneak his conga out the door. I'd watch my brother blow us off. I wanted to go with him, help him carry his drum, and maybe meet up with Hector, who was then teaching me how to smoke cigarettes. ("Just don't get fucking addicted," he'd caution. "Be like me: I'm *not* what you call an 'addictive personality.' ") I felt the loneliness of my parents' after-dinner philosophical discussions which never touched on a philosophy outside the Bronx. I couldn't desert them before dessert.

"Mickey," Stan once called to me. "Let them go. Just let them the hell go."

"What are you fucking talking about?"

He raised his eyebrows and walked close to me. I thought I smelled the odor of my father's Budweiser on his breath.

"How do we do it?"

"Do what?"

"Live here."

"What's wrong with here?"

"Mickey . . ."

"What?"

"What's wrong with here?"

I looked at him and screamed. "What's going on with *you?*"

When he asked the next question, I felt a punch in my lower abdomen: "You feel like you know things before they happen?"

"What the fuck?"

We stood in the corridor between our bedroom and the living room, from where the hostage crisis was unraveling on TV.

"Go bring Mom and Dad into the living room to look over the bar mitzvah pictures."

I walked into the kitchen and interrupted my parents' awe at the Shah of Iran's wealth.

"He needed three swimming pools?" my mother asked. "One wasn't enough?"

"Hey," I said. "Wanna look at some pictures?"

In a moment, my mother had cleared the kitchen table and I extracted the two bar mitzvah albums out from the pressed-wood bookcase and dusted them off.

"Jesus Christ!" my father bellowed as we started into my album. "I looked like a million bucks back then."

"That suit cost me a million bucks," my mother chimed in.

"Ahhh, it wasn't so goddamn expensive. Besides, I looked like a million bucks in it."

"You did. I have to admit it."

"Money well spent."

"I went bargain basement for my gown."

Meanwhile my brother spirited his conga out the door.

———

By August, my parents and I had exhausted every photo album in the house. It was so hot in our five-room apartment, that we had to open every window in the house, even the ones my father had painted shut by accident last year.

"I think I'm dying from heat exhaustion!" my mother sighed, her fingers caked in white paint chips. "You could have killed us with that paint job."

"If you weren't so cheap, we could have hired professionals."

"If you weren't so bad at making a living, we could have *been* professionals."

There was so much noise on the streets I couldn't hear my

parents show their love by fighting. Firecrackers. M-80s. Garbage cans toppling. Voices raised up in song. "What the hell?" my father wondered. "The Fourth of July all over again in August?" We decided to go for a walk to see what the commotion was.

Outside, my parents waved to neighborhood acquaintances sitting on chaise lounges and fold-out chairs.

"It's like the old country," my mother said.

"They didn't have PRs in the old country," my father countered.

My mother bowed down to an old Jewish woman who could have been Frieda's sister, except that she aspired to being a walking fashion plate, what with her scarves, pendants and costume jewelry. The woman turned on her hearing aid as my mother asked in Yiddish, "What's going on in the neighborhood?"

"The *goyim*," the woman answered. "They're blowing the world up. We'll be dead any minute now."

My mother snorted and took my father's hand. Old men played cards. I watched one bald-headed, brown man bluff. Old ladies in blue-and-white cotton housedresses were talking; an ancient women in a red wig fanned herself. The Jewish matrons were as obese as the Puerto Rican ones, and as noisy. They sat in separate cliques mere feet from one another. You heard the usual Yiddish: *Ikh bin farklempt,* which to my mind always sounded like the same complaint: *Oh, why-oh-why do I live?* (It had been Frieda's favorite.) The Spanish went the same: *Díos mío!* this, and *Díos mío!* that. The clipped opera of a heart complaint; the muddy repetition of a worry. For a minute, I thought I would die from this chorus of disappointment. I wondered if it sent some of the old women into subtle but incessant orgasms.

That's when we heard the music.

"Sounds like a goddamn bar mitzvah band," my father said.

"I never heard such *beuuuutiful* music on these streets," my mother commented. "Only fire engines and kids screaming at their nice parents for no reason."

My father touched my shoulder. "Get a load of that," he said, referring to the TV news team and the van parked in front of us.

"The last time they had TV cameras up here was when the hippies was marching."

"Must have been ten years ago," my mother said. "Remember, I always said that war was wrong."

"Those good-for-nothings almost burnt the goddamn neighborhood down."

"They had a right. It was their country, too."

"I *fought* for my country."

"That was another time, another war, Willie."

"I know all goddamn about it. I draw the line at burning down the neighborhood."

"We watched them from out the window," I said, trying to change the subject. "Remember all those drums. That's when you and mom bought Stan his first drum."

"He used to hit plates," my father added. "It drove me crazy."

"That's why we got him a drum," explained my mother.

"It still drives me crazy."

The closer we got, the more my heart thudded with the excitement of recognition. Cutting through the sound of trumpet blasts and clarinet trills was a drumbeat so edgy and percussive that it sent my body into the rushes I felt whenever Hector was around. At such times, everything in my life would melt into silvery metallic trills. Hector chalked it up to the Yoruba spirits his grandparents worshiped. Those demons and angels in our midst must have been making time-and-a-half in overtime. My parents and I reached the city block where the music was coming from. The drumming intensified.

"*Oye,* give him some elbow room," someone shouted. "It's the solo of his goddamn life."

My parents saw.

"Oh, sugar."

"Jesus fucking Christ!"

My brother sat on a stool, an unlit cigarette dangling from his upper lip. He was surrounded by men, all horn players, all Latin. Summer sweat poured off their faces; their skin blazed against the orange sheen of the city streetlights. My brother was shirtless. Everyone cheered Stan as if they knew him better than we did.

"Go, *compadre*. Send it home to your maker. The one who you brought down to earth for tonight's performance."

Standing off to the side of the band was Hector. Next to him sat his mother, whom I had met briefly the first time I spent time at Hector's house. Holding her hand on another chaise lounge was a curly-haired, big-bellied man, puffing on a Cuban cigar. The man snapped his fingers in time. I saw him glance every now and then at Hector, then back at the band, then at me, whom he did not know. Hector put a cigarette in his mouth. I watched Hector's father take it from his mouth and throw it to the sidewalk. Hector picked it up and stuck the stub back in his Marlboro box.

Just then my brother set his hands on his conga as if they had been flung into a spell. He hit the skins so hard I thought they would split open. Then he caressed the sides of the congas lightly. The change in dynamic set the crowd into thankful hysterics. My brother resorted to a schizophrenic mix of hard and soft licks that, to me, showed how much melody there was in rhythm.

"Send it home, Israel."

When my brother ended his solo, his face and hair were wet with sweat and the soot that emerged like exhaust from the all-night pizza stand. The crowd clapped so hard, I mistook it for thunder. Tenements echoed sounds. Just then my brother saw my parents' faces. He ditched the cigarette and rose quickly, as if about to explain.

My father walked over, his face beaming anxious pride.

"Not bad, huh?" Willie said, referring more to the crowd's acclaim than the music.

"Hey, Stan!" I tried to say.

That's when a TV news reporter approached my father with this question: "Are *you* the father of the Jewish mambo whiz?"

"I suppose I am," my father stammered.

"You bet he is," Linda chimed in, eating up the camera's

attention. "Me, I don't know the two from Adam. But if you ask me, the talent he gets from the mother. The looks, as you can see, from the father."

——————

That night I fantasized that Hector's mother invited our family up to their five-room apartment, just four blocks from the concert, to watch the exchange on Hector's family's new color TV. I don't know how it quite happened in my imagination, but Hector's mother and my mother had both been officers in the Parents' and Teachers' Association. Being Jewish and Puerto Rican, they kept a polite distance. They went in for different styles: Linda wore a light blue and white patterned skirt. Maria chose loose Calvin Klein black jeans. But sweating outside together in the Bronx summer night, with Linda the mother of an apparent new celebrity, Maria and Linda found themselves catching up on quite a bit.

"Linda," Maria cried out. "Is that your son?"

"Like the day is long."

"You must be so proud."

"You must be so hot in those pants. Don't you people believe in culottes?"

Before too long, we were all sitting around Maria's Formica kitchen table, the same faded coal-black color as our own. The adults on one end sipped coffees; the teenagers on the other downed ice-filled vanilla sodas and airy squares of yellow sponge cake. "This tastes like Jewish cake," my father whispered in my ear, when he got up to use the bathroom. "Dry as shit." Hector's two older brothers were not at home, but his older sister, Elena, entertained us with jokes she memorized from Johnny Carson. One my parents especially loved: "Harry Truman, you know, the ex-President, he goes up to Golda Meir and says, 'You can have any two generals I got. MacArthur? Patton? Which honcho will it be?' Golda answers, 'General Electric and General Motors.'"

Linda died from rib-splitting laughter. Hector and I laughed more from her laughter than the joke, which we had heard from Elena a million times before and never really got. Our heads collided into each other's shoulders from the giddiness of it all.

"I had no idea our sons were so close," Maria said to my mother, after she caught her breath. "What a good influence for my Hector."

"Nah," my father said. "It's the other way around. Mikey was on the verge of playing with dolls before."

My mother smacked my father in the head.

Their attention turned to the TV. "Eyewitness News" was almost over. Disappointing. Had they decided not to run the "Jewish mambo whiz" story after all? That's when the newscaster introduced my brother. "The greatest conga player in the Bronx . . . a Jewish boy known for his rhythm . . . a nineteen-and-a-half-year-old urchin of the downtown jazz clubs."

"Clubs?" my mother asked.

There was my brother, playing his conga like a possessed person. The crowd egged him on as it did in life. The cigarette dangled from his lip as it did in life. "Go, Israel," the crowd roared, as it did in life. My father stammered on TV as he did in life. My mother responded with her mix of pride and "Who-Taught-You-Everything-You-Know?" panache as she did in life.

When the TV spot was over, my parents froze in their seats, dumbstruck.

"You got yourself a class act, Israel," Hector's father said. "*Muy bien.* You can make a lot of money for your mother and father."

"And brother," Hector added. "Don't forget the brother."

"I wouldn't, *mijo.*" My father gave Roderigo — that was Hector's father's name — a Bronx pat on the back. "I wish I had a goddamn cigar," my father said, offering Roderigo instead a cigarette.

My mother wasn't buying it. "Israel!" she said. "I gave you a proper American name: Stan."

"Stan is a nice name," Maria agreed.

"I picked it out," my mother added.

"Hey," Hector interjected. "Why don't you change your name

to 'Stan Israel?' I hear a lot of Puerto Rican people with that name."

"Over my dead body," my mother chimed in.

"Anybody wanna play poker?" my father asked. My brother, who was a humble person, as well as a superb cardplayer, jumped at the chance. Roderigo found a new deck of cards and an un-opened bottle of tequila. My mother, forcing a yawn, kicked my father under the kitchen table. I saw him kick her back.

I followed Hector into his tiny private room. We crowded into a corner. He unbuttoned his plaid cotton shirt and took my hand and laid in on his skinny chest. I felt his heart beat, even though I worried. "Just for a minute," he said.

We heard the voices talking about the card game. My mother suggested my father bluff. But that was not his style. "Willie," Roderigo said. "You're some player, *hombre*. You want to form a card game, jes?"

"Jes."

———

In a few days, it was hard to walk down the Grand Concourse without someone screaming at me, "Hey, ain't you Israel's brother, that wild Jewish mambo whiz?"

My brother seemed undaunted by his new publicity. "I gotta keep studying, man," he'd say, talking about drum rhythms, the way the cosmic-setting ones elude you. He started apprenticing under a professional *congero* in Manhattan. The ancient drummer wore necklaces of red and black wooden beads; he smelled of musk oil and a strange bitter herb. His brown face creased into itself with frowns like Stan's. The day I visited the master in a spacious, but bare apartment on the Lower East Side, he hardly spoke; he just nodded *"bueno"* now and then.

After school, Stan would take the subway down to East 11th Street and Avenue D, where the drug pushers began to know him as Israel. Stan never told my mother how dangerous the deserted apartments and crowded alleys were.

"Mickey," he'd say in those days, his voice hushed, his eyes squinting under tremulous brows. "Whatcha gonna do?"

"What are you talking about?"

"Mickey. Don't beat around the bush. Or the dick, as the case may be." He'd laugh, like Frieda did during her last days.

I noticed a masculine new sharpness to his features, as if he had saved up money from his fifty-dollar-a-week work-study library job and gotten a face-lift on the sly. It was the look of someone who had woken up to the dream about himself. Stan took more time with his shaving. One day I saw him folding and refolding a polyester plaid shirt our mother had bought us for Chanukah. My family downplayed the behavior; it was so unrecognizable. But when I heard a woman's giddy scream come from my bedroom, I knew the masquerade was over. My mother had found a bottle of Brut in the bottom corner of my brother's underwear drawer. She called my father and me in to witness her discovery. We examined the bottle as if it were an Egyptian aphrodisiac, or the Rosetta stone.

"You think it's love?" she asked. "A girl?"

"It's the music," I said.

My mother was not stupid, and my father was intuitive enough to read into her darting eyes. She took out her wallet and began laying five-dollar bills on the table in three neat rows.

"I'm not *that* cheap," I said.

She fished for twenties.

"Is she white or black?" she asked.

All the money in the world couldn't tell her what she already knew. I collected the crisp bills, took a sniff and returned them to her housedress.

"You owe me," I said.

"Like hell I do."

She walked out. My father, not used to seeing his wife speechless, touched my shoulder.

My mother may have been conservative, but she was not a monster. All her life she had lived among black people. When necessary, she became their friend. Her boss, the high-school vice-principal, was a black woman. So was the rental manager who lived in the building. When I was eight, my best friend had been a brain named Reggie; he was black. Together we read the

Bobbsey Twins aloud to our parents, which they hated. Together we went to Little League games, which we hated. Together the two women fought their two husbands: Why was it not necessary that Reggie and Mikey be subjected to jeers in the outfield? The men were as macho as they were in need of male bonding between themselves. So we played ball. Before the Williamsons moved to Long Island, my mother invited the couple over for meat loaf. Already the Williamsons couldn't be bothered; the husband, wearing his grey pin-striped suit to eat mashed potatoes on Passover plates (our only china), left early to make business calls. "Call from here," Linda said. "We won't listen." He demurred. Linda shed more than a tear when the moving truck came, I think more because she was being left behind than anything else.

Later that night, my mother approached Stan, who was listening to John Coltrane on headphones. How petite she looked, sitting on the toy chest that separated Stan's twin bed from mine. She wasted no time with pleasantries. In this regard, Stan was cut from her cloth.

"Why don't you invite the girl over?" she asked.

Stan removed his headphones. "Will you be nice to her?"

"Would I invite her over to be vicious to her?"

Stan resumed wearing his headphones. "She's a black girl."

"So? The world's not perfect."

"When the time's right," Stan said, measuring his words, turning up the volume on his ghetto blaster so that we heard the crazy sax riffs from Stan's ear.

My mother looked plaintively at Stan, her brown Eastern European eyes rippling into yet another wrinkle.

"Don't wait too long now."

"But before six months is up," he added, as if that were any consolation.

———

Stan was right. The charm of love was about to wear off.

Hector had decided that we were seeing too much of each other; he didn't call me back for one entire day. (The next day he arrived at my house with a cracked voice and a dozen roses;

I told my mother they were for her.) Another time, he came on my face and I felt a little down about that. But then he let me try it on him, and we never bothered with that activity again. There was the time Hector flirted with one of the guys at a party he took me to in Spanish Harlem. I knew no one and spoke only pidgin Spanish. Everyone there was very effeminate, except for the guy who lived in the apartment, this short-haired, creamy-colored, tough-acting guitar player Hector seemed sweet on. Hector grabbed me hard by the neck and pushed into the guy's bedroom. For some reason, Hector wanted me to witness the guy shooting up, his muscular arms lined up and down like a sculpture with rippling veins. I saw the junkie's face transform into a beautifully racked stillness. It bothered me. I had supposed that such chemical warmth in the body was produced solely by the effects of love. I walked out and took the subway home at two in the morning. I waited an hour for that train; it broke down in the South Bronx, a stop or two before home, and I had to walk the rest of the way. The next day I made Hector beg on his hands and knees for forgiveness.

"So whatcha gonna be?" he asked, once he got to his feet and felt regret for what he must have seen as his too-wimpy surrender. "A nice Jewish boy all your fucking life?"

"I can live a good fucking life without watching people around me become heroin addicts."

"Ah, c'mon! You never wanted to try it once?"

"Mind your own fucking beeswax."

"I rest my case."

"Stoop!"

"Now you're talking like me."

"Nah."

There were hurdles to get through. When I woke in his bed around that time, during an afternoon nap when no one was home, I felt his smooth, lightly muscled arms around me. They clutched me as if I were a teddy bear. I thought: "I'm being clung to by a future matinee idol." That was intimidating. I regarded his limbs: crisp brown branches around me. His wrists were adorned by the erratic ligaments lining them. Curves and canyons, they were mysteries to me. Sure, I had played around with the bars in gym class, and even spent six months once on the school swim team just as my chest hair was growing in. What with all us Italians and Jews and blacks, there wasn't one smooth-skinned guy among us. But no matter how hard I tried, I never achieved the easy dialogue between body and will that seemed to come as second nature to Hector.

As we saw each other more and more, I felt guilty about drinking sweat and kisses from his body like a baby drinking formula. My blood felt cooked, and inside I worried I was dying. We kissed for so many hours one day that all his smells and tastes — cigarettes, *plátanos*, Coca-Cola and God knows what kind of dope — coated the inside of my mouth like a Popsicle that numbs your tongue in the heat of the summer. My fingers tingled. Odd circles of sensation rose up and down my stomach and spine like a yo-yo that had been tied too tight for too long. I grew a little more talkative for a few days, punctuating my speech with "man," and "be like that," and "psss." For a week I altered my pronunciation altogether and instead of "that's," said "thass," and instead of "you're," I said "yah." Yet all taken together, none of that terrified me as much as the fact that I began to grow obsessed with this terror, addicted to it like the way one gets addicted to horror movies or porn movies or both. I couldn't think of anything but Hector's body and how he sat when naked. I hoped Hector would never suggest shooting up with him. It formed my greatest fear and most puzzling thrill.

Some force must have been watching over me in those days to keep me from cracking up. Once, I remember waking up in a fit. It was not yet dawn in the Bronx, but the trucks, buses and paperboys had begun cranking up the city for its first stretch of urban activity. My brother snored. My father had already left for work on the tolls. In my dreams I had heard my mother sing "Sunrise, Sunset," in the shower. Later, in my sleep, I heard Linda rummage through her closet for a plaid dress and a beige blouse. I heard her walk in our bedroom, lay a kiss on my brother's forehead and then mine before shoving off to work. But that wasn't what woke me up for real. What had stirred me? Was it even human?

The sensation was akin to falling off a cliff in one's dreams. I thought I heard a light tap at the door. Like most doors in the Bronx, ours was solid metal. Every time someone knocked on it, a host of police locks, bolts and knobs shook in place. It didn't take much to think someone was always at the door; if we had a dog, it would have been barking continuously. (Dogs were prohibited where we lived.) Now it felt as if something—what could it be?—wanted in.

The horrible alien sound at the door was followed by something more human and consoling. I startled, out of bed. I got up and looked through the peephole. There was Hector, turning his face to the right and left as if about to cross the street, looking as if he'd seen a ghost himself. I opened the door.

"Hector!"

"Did you hear it, too?"

"Man . . ."

We were terrified.

"Let's do our English homework," Hector suggested.

"Okay."

After an hour of quiet writing in pencil and underlining quotations in yellow highlighter, my hand traveled under his shirt, lightly skirting his lower back, crawling up and down his gnarly vertebrae as if they were the bass notes on a piano.

"Silver and gold will vanish away, but a good education will never decay," Hector said, quoting Linda Kaplan.

His back was discolored much like his shoulders; it was just as taut. Touching it made blood rush to my head and my crotch so fast I felt hungry in my middle; a sucking in, a carnivorous sensation. In a moment I felt his back pushing up against my hand.

"Mmmmmm," he said. "Takes your mind off the fear, huh, Mikey?"

"What are you talking about?"

"My body."

I pulled back. "Is there something you're not telling me?"

"What?" he asked, a strange tightness in his throat. "You think we're just hanging out 'cause we got so much in fucking common?"

"Well, excuse me."

"You're excused."

A moment of reflection from me: "I guess you're right."

"Of course I'm right."

"Well," I said, pushing the matter. "What the fuck are you going to do about it?"

"What a dumb-ass question," he answered, snorting. "I'm here, ain't I?"

"Well," I added, turning over. "Don't look to me to reform you. I'm turning bad myself."

"Oh, no, you're not. You, *compa'*, are going to make it with flying colors."

"Don't be so fucking sure."

That was how we gave signals. Long before either of us learned the art of holding back and the power of love to hurt, we had perfected another kind of language which said, more often than not, "You can trust me." I'm not quite sure how it happened, but in moments such as this, we would fold into each other as if we were porn-star infants. We'd suckle each other's lips and fingers and whine like starved babies, waking up to a bottomless pit of hunger and darkness that would have destroyed normal kids — mutilated them, even — had something else not been watching over them like a charm.

Something was watching over us.

At first I thought it was the innate athleticism in our bones that wrapped its thighs and wings around us. A suckling sensation; home free, yet caught in the Bronx granite like nailed-down furniture. Then I thought I saw an image of a woman projected across the double windows in my room. At first I dismissed the 3-D cinema. But then Hector startled. "Do you see it?" he asked. I was about to forget his crazy outburst, chalk it up to the way love drove us both crazy, when this time Hector jumped out from the bed, the color leaving his face.

"Old lady!" he said, aghast.

"Omigod."

We clutched each other like kids do when the horror movie has gotten more scary than they had bargained for.

"I'm gonna puke."

"You smell something?"

"Miguel, what . . . ?"

"I know her!"

I sat up in bed, transfixed, revolted. Awed, I turned my head into Hector's arms. He didn't dare look. Me neither. It seemed hours might pass. We wiped the sweat off, feeling the brush of a winter chill on our bare backs. Finally we got up the courage to look around. It seemed the room almost went concave on itself, as if an air vacuum had been created, or a can of spray paint exploded.

The vision had disappeared.

"This means something," Hector said, crossing himself. He collapsed on the bed. "Oh, shit! I mean, oh, Mary!"

"Are you crying, Hector?"

"No fucking way, Miguel. Are you?"

Outside sirens screamed. We peered out my window. Fire engines collected at the dilapidated six-story tenement across the street. Smoke and flames jutted out from the roof.

"Fucking shit!"

"The fucking world is burning down."

We collapsed into the bed, huddling under the covers like kids scared of the dark. The play of images in our heads with those outside confused us and knocked us out. We fell asleep, as if drugged, because we thought we were already sleeping.

When we woke up, it seemed as if we had dreamed a foolish dream.

An L.A. Riot

———

saw both Tahar and Myron Smith twice a week, after work. On Tuesdays and Fridays, I'd leave *The Angeleno* early. I'd cruise through the bodega-cluttered streets of Silver Lake, where the *Angeleno* office is located, to the bombed-out tenements of post-riot Hollywood, where Dr. Myron can afford to see clients. After shaking Myron's sweaty palm, "So long, good-bye," I'd race the few blocks to Tahar's house in the dilapidated Nissan. Tahar provided the brandy to Myron's mental repast. I required balanced meals. Lights out. Candles flickering. Photo albums snapping open in the wooden beams of Tahar's house. I remembered the jazz that came from the desert of my heart. I heard the call: *STANNNNN-ley!!!!* Years ago, Frieda asked if I was becoming a hoodlum. I saw welts. They could have been the plastic tips on drumsticks; Frieda's fingertips. I wore a shirt to bed.

Robert saw.

"Spikey-Poo and I missed you," Robert sang after I had arrived home late one evening. We had made a date to clean the house together. Robert had gotten a head start. The toilet had been scoured clean. Spike was flea-dipped. A year's worth of piled-up newspapers, glass bottles and plastic bottles had been recycled. "We never spend any time together anymore," Robert whined.

I wanted to say, "That's because you're fucking Marty on a regular basis." I wasn't sure that was exactly true. I was afraid, actually, that it was false. I was wary of Robert's motives: that Robert wanted me to beg him to stop seeing Marty. I knew Robert. If he did my bidding, then I'd have to do his.

"You know," he said, as he microwaved the overcooked chicken he had made for our dinner, "I think we should vow to be monogamous."

He set the brown rice on the table as well as two cans of sweating Budweiser.

"I mean, you work so hard and you're gone so much," he continued. "I think we should become more devoted."

I poured the foaming beer into two clear glasses.

"I'll make the vow if you will," I said.

He put his hand on my shoulder. I felt the nervous buzz from his fingertips. From across the street, a neighbor blasted Sting's "If I Ever Lose My Faith in You."

"You're such a horny motherfucker these days," I say.

"When you turn on the spigot," he said, musing more to himself than to me, "you have more for everyone."

"Robbie," I said. "How generous of you."

He bent down to kiss me hard in his hard way. For years, I wanted softness. Now I'd miss the teeth, the muscles near the jaws. I smelled Marty's Marlboros in his mouth; the singe made me crazy with jealousy. But here I was, pawing Robert as if he were a stranger, which, to me, he was.

We wrestled each other to the floor.

"Hey," he whispered between licks of my ear. "We didn't decide."

I slipped off my shirt. I pulled his off him.

"We should decide," he moaned, losing his mind.

In a moment it was all over; the sex, the reprieve, the repartee, the vow about making a vow. When I left for work, he was sleeping the sex off like a doll. After driving around the block, I realized I had left my notes for an article at home. I opened the door and detected Robert's whispery voice on the phone.

"Marty, cut me some slack," I heard through Robert's closed

door. "Can't you just hang loose for a while. No, I'm not leaving Mikey. What was that? You want to do what to my what?"

I paged through the notes, realizing they were immaterial.

———

One night, soon afterward, I arrive home late from work. I had called from *The Angeleno*: "Robbie, you're on your own for dinner. How about milk and cookies at ten tonight?" I race home, with milk and Fig Newtons from the 7-Eleven, to get to Robert by ten sharp. No Robert. I check my phone machine. No Robert. Spike dances with his tail. *Daddy. I alone all day. Hungie.* I make a Pollo Loco burrito for myself from leftovers while preparing Spike's favorite dish: Science Diet with chicken skins and two-day-old coleslaw. No Robert. I make Spike sit before devouring. Spike drools, pointing his muzzle toward me like an old, toothless man. We both eat our way into oblivion. No Robert. I fall asleep in my jeans and ACT UP Clean Needles Now T-shirt. A siren awakens me. I look at the rectangular digital clock: middle of the night. I check my phone machine again. No Robert. At dawn, I turn away from the wall to Robert's side of the bed. An empty space there. I check my phone machine one more time. No Robert.

I get in the Nissan. I drive fast to Hollywood, 308 Selma, the tan cottage next to the 101.

I pull up, as I had done before. I don't bother knocking, as I hadn't before. I opened a rusty gate, as before. I see that the front porch had been sprayed with more white, blue and maroon graffiti than before. I step on more trash than before. I quietly open and shut the new gate as before. I see the filthy windows, as before.

I jiggle the door. And I see, as before, what I need to see. There they are, in Marty's filthy bedroom, in each other's arms.

"You hear something?" Marty asks.

I freeze.

"Nah," goes Robert. "It's just the wind."

Marty has another question: "You ever do this with what's-his-name, just lay around and do nothing?"

Robert stirs again, rubbing his fingers on Marty's too-tight chest. "Nah. Not really. Not anymore."

"Don't you miss it? I mean, this is heaven."

I'm inside. I touch Marty's shoulder with my pointer finger, then bend down to rouse him more fully. I set him vertical, pulling him up off the bed. The look on his face startles; he seems happy to see me. Marty stands at least as tall as me; but he is more pumped up in his chest and thighs. I steady him; after all, he was dead asleep a moment ago. Then, with all my might, I hit him in his face — forehead, really. A boxer I'm not. But something tells me that a boy like Marty can take it in his face. I whack him again. He slips off from his bearing, then hard to the ground. I watch as little drops of blood trickle from him to the floor of his bedroom.

"Marty!" Robert shouts, looking at his fallen lover. "Marty!"

Robert bends down. And that's that. I just split, get in my car and zip off with a *Boyz 'n the Hood* squeal.

———

The *Angeleno* offices are located in Silver Lake, where Robert and I lived years ago. We tended a bamboo-cluttered backyard twice the size of the interior which Spike converted to his own men's room. The land near our house was swampy from the creek and arid from the desert heat. Robert would call in the middle of deadlines and sing on the phone, "Come home, it's nookie time." Home was walking distance. I enraged many an editor that way.

The receptionist, Sue Canelli, smiles when she sees me. Now, this is unlike her. Sue's a dye-job, blond bombshell of an actress whose career was sunk by McCarthy. Now she writes turgid prose for *The Nation* about toxic-waste dumps and answers the phone at *The Angeleno*. She despises the younger staffers, especially their haircuts.

"Our hero!" she cries when she sees me now, lighting a Carlton, while another still smolders. "I knew you'd come around someday and become a human being."

"Hi, Canelli."

"Objective journalism, schmubjective journalism, that's what I have always said."

Canelli jumps out from her swivel seat, balancing her cigarette on her receptionist's table, which is just an extension of her ashtray. She gives me a hug. For days, I'll smell like a tobacco picker. Three or four members of the staff, who walk by to retrieve their mail, stare in disbelief; just yesterday I had gotten a deeply elaborate haircut. Very faux Crips, with a racing line down the sides of my head.

"Canelli's just like every other American," Shirley announces. Shirley's the youngest staff writer in the office. Shirley's so center left she's right. "You got to get your picture in the paper to rate."

"What?" I ask.

"Nice haircut," Canelli barks at Shirley.

Shirley lives with her parents in Sherman Oaks and is on the prowl for a Straight Jewish Male husband, what she calls "an SJM."

"Come to your senses yet about the opposite sex?" Shirley asks. "Imagine how happy I could make your mother as a SJW."

"I haven't spoken to my mother in years."

"Don't you think she deserves better?"

"Good question. I'll bring it up with my therapist."

Shirley has me in the palm of her hand. "Why don't you send your mother a copy of the *L.A. Times*, the one with your picture on the cover of the metro section."

"The what?"

She eyes me while rummaging through the metro section. "*Voilà*," she says, snapping the paper open. On the front page: a picture of myself getting beaten up by the LAPD. The caption reads: "Journalist takes a stand by sitting down in the street."

"What some people won't do to get their names in the paper." Shirley huffs.

"That demonstration took place a month ago."

"Old news is better than no news."

Then in a conspiratorial whisper, like she's doing me a favor, "The boss killed your piece on the demonstration."

"Fuck!"

"Don't listen to her," Canelli says. "She wouldn't know suffering if it came begging at her door."

Canelli hands me my messages, and in hushed tones: "They've been calling all day for you."

"Who's 'they'?"

"Reporters. Activists. Politicians. You name it."

"What?"

"People are looking for new leaders. You have a certain charisma, kid."

"For a GJM," barks Shirley from the corridor.

———

I walk into Larry Ravin's office.

"Larry . . . I'm sorry—"

"Sorry? We're all proud of you."

"Shirley says you killed the piece?"

Larry picks his eyes off a thick manuscript he's reading, acting a little like a cliché of a newspaper editor.

"Since when do you pay attention to Shirley? We killed the article because it's not relevant anymore. Too objective."

"Too objective? I thought that's what you wanted. Isn't that why you hired Shirley?"

"Are you hung up on Shirley? I yearn for balance. And you're going to be Shirley's balance."

"As long as I don't have to be her boyfriend."

We chuckle politely. Larry continues, "Everyone knows you've crossed a line. I don't care why you did it. The point is you did. I'm not so sure that makes great writing, but it makes a good read. The point is, we want you to write about the entire politics of objectivity and subjectivity in a series of cover stories. Like 'How to Remain Distant at the End of the Twentieth Century'?"

"It's a little self-helpish."

"In the first person."

"Huh?"

"We'd think it'd make a great exposé. Get into the person-
alities, the sexual intrigue, the politics."

"My boyfriend is one of the lead players in ACT UP."

"Write about him. Be honest. Get yourself in trouble jour-
nalistically. Break every rule about newspaper writing: you can
even sleep with the people you interview —"

"Larry!"

"You can do it, right?"

Before I can answer, Larry gives me a boy-to-boy embrace.
He reminds me of those white liberals who smile at every black
child they see on Santa Monica Boulevard, only to go home and
bark at teenage maids in Brentwood.

———

There's a pizza joint down the street, painted red and green,
tucked away in a fluorescent mini-mall. The Pasadena pizza rates
as Times Square stuff: crisp crust, gluey cheese and enough
grease to resurrect childhood acne. A well-kept secret in Los Angeles. The dive is often packed with homesick New Yorkers reading Susan Sontag and the local varsity crew from the high school
down the block. The tribes don't mix. The dweebs stick their
heads in the *Village Voice* while the freshly showered jocks snicker.
I order a calzone and a ginger ale. Not exactly diet food, but
what self-respecting Pulitzer winner-to-be cares about a waistline?

The pizza maker, Carmine Luzzi, is also the pizzeria owner.
His hair shines black like India ink. His muscles round into themselves like ornaments tucked under his skin. A Brooklynite, he's
tanned by recent afternoons lazing in the California sun with his
wife and two baby girls. He smokes like Gary Cooper does in
movies about Manhattan. Quick, abrupt intakes.

"No fucking salad today, dude?" he asks.

"Nah, I'm celebrating."

"Fuck, what's the occasion?"

"Job promotion."

"Shit, cool!"

"How's the wife and kids?"

"Ann's going back to college. The kids are as healthy as goddamn horses."

"Knock on Formica," I sigh, knocking on Carmine's Formica.

Carmine smiles, right lip creased up in a smirk, lower lip wide and gooey. He always pours me an additional Diet Coke, or slips me an extra slice of pizza — free. Then he'll sit down with me and ask questions about writing or the weather or the racial dilemma in Venice, like; "They close off the beach to swimmers after the fucking rain?" or "Heard a homeboy got it in the goddamn head on Ocean," or "For your information, there's a fucking accident on the Santa Monica Freeway, so take fucking Venice Boulevard, Jesus fucking Christ." It's as if he had nothing better to do than curse and monitor the California Highway Patrol on my behalf.

I watch him pour tomato sauce into a newly turned pizza crust. *Bella Luna.* "I'd be great in movies, right?" he says. Carmine and I are both from New York City boroughs. "You think we ever bumped into each other in the old days?" he asks.

He sits down with me. But the digital phone rings, and he bounces up to answer it.

I go back to my pizza, fantasizing about my Pulitzer.

Six high-school guys stumble in. The tiny pizza parlor roars with their testosterone. I watch the two lesbian poets sipping lemonade off in the corner hide their faces in their Annie Dillard.

"That fucking bitch," goes a jock's voice, sounding chemical, high. He's dark-haired and pale. "She thought she could get away with stuffing her titties."

A lot of unseemly guffaws.

"I told her if she didn't get silicone shots, I'd never fuck her again."

A reddish-haired guy in a torn tank top catches my eye. I linger on him a second too long, admiring his deltoids underneath the skintight red T-shirt that seems to show the mascot of his high school: a bull. I am not a paranoid person, but out of the corner of my eye I think I see a brunette guy seeing me seeing him. He's the group's apparent ringleader, looking a little like an overstarched Italian Tom Cruise.

"Hey," the brunette says to me. "That your picture in the newspaper?"

My mouth is full of pizza. I nod.

He tosses his head at his friends. "Hey, Chris," the brunette announces to his red-haired friend. "That guy's famous. His picture was in the newspaper."

"Tony," the red-haired guy murmurs, "take it easy."

I wave like Jackie Kennedy. Where *are* my white gloves? The group waves back, almost in unison, as if they've rehearsed how to respond to a First Lady. I return to my half-eaten pizza. I don't feel like taking them on a tour of the White House today. The china hasn't been stored, and they are, after all, bulls.

"Part of that gay group, right?" asks Tony.

I swallow the pizza too fast. "Actually, it's an AIDS group." Actually, *I'm* the bull.

Carmine puts down the telephone. I put down the pizza. The guys put me down. They giggle in a supernatural way, like they're vampires or Klingons or worse—jocks.

"So, you got AIDS?" Tony asks.

"Not that I know of," I say. "But you can't be too sure these days, you know."

"You a fag or something?"

My cheeks flush.

"Yeah, I am a fag. You one, too?"

I get up to introduce myself and watch myself offering a hand to Tony-the-brunette, like we've just finished lifting weights. I add, "Always glad to be a role model for a guy like you, Tony, a fellow homo."

"Hey, Tony, how the fuck this guy knows your name?" Chris asks.

Carmine snaps his fingers. He wants these guys "outta here," and he wants me to "sit the fuck down."

Tony has no answer.

"A fag in the pizza place," someone says. It's Chris, referring to Tony, not me. "He's probably breathing AIDS all over the place."

Poor Tony.

I step in, as crude as they are. "Don't ridicule your friend that way," I say to Chris. "I mean, your friend Tony has a lot of courage."

The group, in unison, vocalizes: "Ugh!"

I take Tony's hand. "I'm with you."

Tony pulls his hand away from me.

Carmine moves toward me. The group fumbling in the room, antsy, tripping.

"Let's get out of here," Tony says.

"No way, fag," Chris says.

No one leaves. Tony, fuming, revengeful, closing in. Carmine's red table overturned. Carmine pissed. Pizza, red-hot pepper, Diet Cokes, newspapers and my Pulitzer torn up, everywhere.

Chris heads toward me. He's raging: "Fag." I charge away. Chris goes after Tony, raging: "Fag." Carmine pushes me away, but for no reason. I'm not there anymore.

There's a jab, a block, a stumble. Somehow I've run out and returned—to watch. The brunette's body, let alone his fists, like windmills. Tony's gone nuts. I'm surrounded by a crowd. I am part of the crowd. The crowd laughs, but not at me—at Tony. No, at Chris. Carmine chases patrons out. "That red-haired guy's got a gun," a woman tells me, tucking books in her jacket, running. Tony decks Chris—in the jaw, a cuff on his face. Chris falls back, onto a table, sticking his flat palm behind him to cushion the fall. A claw lands on my chest, another on my left shoulder. I duck. Chris goes for Tony frontally and bingo: a jab in his jaw. Me? Who? What klutzes we all are. Out of control. Glass breaking.

Carmine shouting, "Fuck" and "Fuck shit" and "Mike, move out the fucking way." Tony and Chris now. They're at each other's throats, choking, spitting, hitting, stammering. It's been coming for years. Their friends shocked, then not so shocked.

"Kick his fucking ass, Chris."

"Beat the shit out of that bitch, Tony."

Two LAPD black-and-whites pull up into the mall. Chris and Tony and their harpies run off, disappearing into thin air.

———

Carmine and I fill out reports, give descriptions; use words like "hate crimes" and "provoked violence." Witnesses corroborate. The two cops, both African-American men in their twenties, voice muted concern. My eye's hit. An ambulance? Mustn't. I see ambulances in my dreams.

"C'mon," Carmine says the moment the black-and-whites pull away. He ushers me inside his store. I go to readjust fallen chairs, pick up paper plates.

"Nah," he says. "Leave that shit. I'll take care of it later."

We walk a few paces. Keys dangle. We dip underneath the counter separating the customers from the pizza makers. Toward the back bathrooms. I see another door through the cheap paneling. A secret door in the pizza place? Toward the back? Who knew? Carmine opens it. We walk through—the sound of hinges.

Then a little light, another door, then inside. Is this where Carmine and his family live? A three-bedroom '20s-styled L.A. bungalow.

"How much rent you pay for this place, Carmine?"

"I bought it with pizza."

Carmine turns on the lights. "Make yourself comfortable," he murmurs. Poor Carmine: so nervous? I wander. I notice leather couches, an extensive stereo system, plush blue-shag carpeting, dishwashers, dryers, microwaves, bread bakers, pictures of his blond wife and two daughters. The wife, Ann, comes by the pizza place now and then. A "snazzy" (as Carmine puts it) Italian-American woman with "a head on her shoulders," as Carmine says. She wants to be an accountant. Carmine disappears into the kitchen. I hear the automatic icemaker making automatic ice.

He returns, carrying a bowl of ice, a white towel, iodine and a tray filled with tea and chocolate raspberry cookies I assume Ann made before her trip. Carmine checks me out with a penlight. "I wanna see if you need to go to fucking Emergency," he says.

"I think intensive care would be more appropriate."

"Wiseguy."

"Not so wise. I nearly got myself killed."

"I'll give you some intensive care."

Carmine crouches over the glass table set in front of me and the couch. He rolls ice in the towel and tries to make neat ravioli out of it. He lifts the towel to my head. Ice cubes fall on my lap. I grab the towel. I redo the arrangement, emptying out half the ice, rolling the pack tight.

"You straight dudes got no style."

"Fucking wiseguy."

"You're all puns tonight, Carmine."

"Who's punning?"

I'd like to get home before my black eye goes down, to win a few sympathy points from Robert. But the Kaplan Curiosity Richter scale mounts to its all-time high: nine.

Carmine takes a place next to me on the couch. The Richter scale hits a ten. Carmine takes my temperature. "I only got fucking oral," he says. "That okay?" Carmine feels around in my scalp area to make sure "no bones is broken." Carmine pours me mint tea. Silenced by the thermometer, I look at his CD collection: Steely Dan, Grateful Dead, Guns 'n' Roses.

What an image: Carmine, the wiry, muscular tough guy serving crumpets, wearing an apron.

Carmine sits down and helps himself to one of Ann's soft cookies.

"Eat," he says, removing the thermometer. "You're normal," he says, eyeing the mercury.

"Normal? Don't be so sure."

He flashes his Pizza Man smile. "Didn't know you was gay," he says.

"Sherlock Holmes you're not."

He chokes on Ann's cookie.

"You think you act so gay?" he asks. "You don't act so gay."

First Carmine dotes on me with cookies and tea. Then he compliments me over and beyond the call of straight-man duty. I should get hit in the face more often.

"Well, Carmine," I say. "Gay men usually pick each other out. There's something in the eyes. Some call it 'gaydar.' "

"Nah . . ."

"It doesn't always work. But sometimes."

"You ever get real surprised?"

I look at Carmine. "Not too often."

He sees that I see. In truth, I don't see a thing.

"You got some surprises for me?" I ask.

"It's not what you think," he says.

"I don't think anything."

He smiles — a leer? "Oh, yeah?"

"Carmine," I say, getting up. "When I was eighteen years old, before I knew what 'gay' was, I didn't act this dumb. What are you trying to tell me? You're cute but not that cute."

"Don't fucking yell at me, man," he says.

"I'm not yelling."

"Yes, you are."

I stop pacing. My hand is shaking.

"Carmine. Please. I'm sorry if I was fucking yelling." Now I'm starting to talk like him.

"Okay, man. I forgive you."

I sit down, awed. Carmine chain-eats Ann's cookies. He catches himself crumbling white sugar on his apron. He stops chain-eating. He scrambles for a cigarette, but it seems he's all out.

"Shit," he stammers. "If I could only have done it over again."

"Hey. It's not the end of the world. We can go out and get more cigarettes."

"No, that's not it," he says.

"What is it?"

He takes a breath. He closes his eyes.

"I'm infected," he says.

I bring the teacup to my lips. I blow on the surface to cool it down. I see the ripples.

"They know?" I ask, pointing to the cookies.

"Yeah," he says. "Thank God, they're clean."

The cookies?

"Thank God," I say, not liking the "clean" word, but going along.

"You wanna tell me the story?" I ask.

He nods yes, but all he can do is drop his head to his chest. The humor has disappeared like a film from his eyes, like those pizzeria ruffians are back and they're after him, not me.

Carmine's hand slides over the couch and onto his hair. He's not a bad hair tousler. Then he goes to his neck. I pat his shoulder. The touch—simple as touches go—sends something off on him; electric, like it's been years since he's been so touched.

Carmine twists his neck. I imagine he is worried about getting sick, or abandoning his daughter prematurely, or the ambivalence he has about sitting alone with me.

I am wrong.

"I think I did infect someone," he says, settling into my hand. His voice is edgy, out of it. "About three years ago I was seeing this guy down the street. A nice guy. We talked. I didn't know better."

"What happened?"

"I ended it. He was falling in love."

"How tired."

"Oh, no, no, Mike. Me, too. I mean, he had a lover, I think, who he was trying to leave. The guy—he had a nice body. He made me laugh. Who knows? Maybe I was falling in love. I never saw him again."

"Oh."

"I never thought about it too much. Or I tried not to. Until I found out. Now I can't get him out of my mind."

"Oh."

I pause. What a cozy house Carmine has. Warm, inviting— full of transplanted New York City ethnic flavor. How strange that during all my time living in Silver Lake, before moving to Venice, I never knew that such a cottage existed. So many secrets.

That's when I ask Carmine: "His name by any chance—it wasn't Robert?"

"Yeah. How'd you know?"

"Just a wild guess."

It is a long car ride home from Pasadena to Venice—about twenty-five miles. With traffic, the trip takes an hour and a half. The sun sets in fiery jolts of color caused by smog. The Santa Monica Freeway takes you from the L.A. flats south of Hollywood to the Pacific Ocean. Traffic moves at a snail's pace. At the Fairfax exit, four miles from home, I get off. So jittery, I'm afraid for the freeway. I feel disease in my blood, Pizza Man–like brawls in my lungs and heart and brain. My concentration is off. Immune cells pump TB into each other, calling each other "Tony" and "Chris." I feel little HIVers in my teeth and toe jams fighting over marinara. I touch my head. Fever?

I see Robert's VW in the driveway.

The house is dark, save for a lone candle I lit about a week ago. It's a ghost house. No radio. No VCR. No Robert on the telephone. No vegetable pot pie from the health-food store in the oven. No singing in the shower. Nothing. Even Spike looks down. He welcomes me by not welcoming me, rare for Spike. Without yelping or sniffing, he just flops himself down in that little Spike curveball at my feet. During all this, no Robert.

"Robert."

A voice from inside the house: "Yeah."

I judge from his simpering voice that he is sitting on a chair in the kitchen. *Don't bother me, I'll sit in the dark.* I'm wrong. He's lying on the living room floor in the dark, which is an odd thing to do, considering that the rug is clotted with Spike's fleas and our unvacuumed pubic hairs.

"Where have you been?" he asks.

"Funny," I answer. "I was going to ask you the same question."

Now he gets up. He turns on the fluorescent light in the kitchen. Perry Mason, take a backseat.

"You almost broke Marty's jaw, I had to take him to the emergency room."

Almost. Damn!

More Robert: "It's so like you, Michael, to jump to conclusions."

"Jump to conclusions? Rob, I saw you sleeping together. You were wrapped in each other's arms. You never do that with me. You say you can't fall asleep like that."

"His best friend had just died from AIDS. He needed a shoulder to cry on."

"My heart goes out to him. But Robert, since when do we not come home to each other without communicating?"

"I called you two or three times. You weren't home. I didn't leave a message until the last time. Where the hell where *you*?"

"Robert. I checked the machine a hundred times. There was no phone message. I was worried to death! . . . "

"Are you accusing me of lying?"

"Robert, I checked the machine."

"Mikey. Don't be an asshole. I left you a message."

"Robert. *You're* being an asshole. I checked the machine."

"I left . . . "

"I checked . . . "

" . . . a message."

" . . . the machine."

"Damn!"

"Shit!"

He rises from the floor, wired with a strange new anger: "Well, this is really disgusting. My boyfriend, the guy I lived with for ten years, is accusing me of having some sordid sleazy affair."

"Well, if you put it that way."

With that Robert grabs me, a swooping up from behind my elbows. He holds my wrist. He's not used to hitting people.

"Well, if we're going to start lying to each other," I comment, "we might as well make good on the American family scene and start smacking each other around, too. I might get a hard-on for a change."

"Come here!" Robert barks, pulling me into my room. His grip on my elbow feels foreign, metallic. Robert the humanoid. He drags me into my room; then, feeling some resistance, he pushes me. "Hey," I say, mimicking Robert's favorite chant, "no violence. The whole world is watching."

The whole world is not. We stop at my answering machine.

"Push 'play,' " he says.

"Robert, this is ridiculous."

"Push 'play.' "

I won't.

"Push the fucker."

"No way."

So he does.

"Don't you think this is getting a little aggressive?" I ask.

"It's aggressive to be accused of lying."

There's the litany of messages once again: Larry Ravin, Shirley, Ann and then Robert:

"Hey, Mikey. It's Robert. About two in the morning. Where the hell are you? I'm with Marty. He called me. His best friend just died from AIDS and he's pretty distraught. He's like hearing voices and everything. So he needs some company. So I told him I'd stay to the morning. He'd love to see you, so if you get this message, hop on over. I love you." And then in the background, Marty's voice, completely cracked and believably distraught: "Tell Mikey, hey . . . I love ya, dude. . . . "

I'm confused and upset. I scoured the machine for a message like a junkie on his last dope leg. I had played and rewound, like a postmodern desperado, ten times.

Robert glowers at me, exonerated.

"I think you have some explaining to do," he says.

"I guess I do."

"I really think you owe me an apology."

"I guess I do."

Backed into a corner, once again. I start to cry. "I'm sorry," I stammer.

"It's a little late for . . . 'sorry.' "

I hate when Robert does that, mimicking my "sorry."

"Don't make fun of my 'sorry.' I'm trying to be sorry."

He does it again: "I'm 'sorry.' "

I cry harder, hoping to wear down Robert's enigmatic hardened WASP heart. When he's this angry, it takes a week of crying to soften the puzzle in him.

"Robbie . . ."

He stiffens. I go to touch him—a finger out, desperate. He pulls away.

"I was confused," I say. "I didn't know. I was worried."

"So you blame me."

"I said I was wrong. Let up."

Robert says nothing, his thin lips tightening into either disguised gleefulness or disgust with my emotional blackmail—I never know which it is. Why won't he say something? I'm about to descend into the nadir of sobbing—it's often been the way we break a fight—when it occurs to me that we have played this twisted crying game too many times.

I begin to see the game more clearly. I stop the pathetic psychodrama, the hair pulling. I stare him down.

I have it figured out: "You placed that message on my machine *after* I hit Marty, didn't you?"

"What?"

"You were caught, Robert. You were covering your ass."

Even in the dark, Robert's face looks flushed with injustice. I've never called him on anything like this before.

"Mikey, are you going crazy?"

"I may be. And it's about time."

"You're making me real nervous."

"You've been carrying on an affair with Marty for months. I saw you in April on the Venice boardwalk. You were sitting, holding hands. I saw you at the demonstration, the way you looked each other in the eyes. Robert, for ten years you and I have *never* looked each other in the eyes. I've experimented recently, to see if you could focus your gaze on me. You turn away every time. I see the way you brighten when Marty calls."

"You should get some help."

"Actually, now that you mention it, I am—and it's long overdue."

"Apparently. You really need some help."

"I'm not the only one who does."

"Speak for yourself."

"Can you actually stand here and say that you have never had sex with Marty before?"

"I thought you were the one who was big on extramarital affairs. You have been encouraging me. You called me vanilla."

"Answer the question."

"J.O. stuff. Once or twice. That's it."

"Robert. I saw you fuck him. In our very house."

"You're nuts!"

"Robert. I sat in the closet about two months ago. I watched you guys."

"You sat in the closet? I'm surprised you didn't hire a private eye or something."

"I didn't need to. You were so obvious. We hadn't had sex in six months, and then all of a sudden you and I have it twice, sometimes three times a day. I knew you were having an affair then."

"So why are you complaining?"

"I'm not complaining. I'm just telling you the truth. I saw you fuck Marty in our living room."

"You're nuts," he says. His face all twisted up, wrinkled in anger and concern.

"Are you telling me I'm lying?" I ask.

Robert shakes his head. He leaves my room and walks over to the closet in the living room. I follow, in the dark.

"Let's get to the bottom of this," he says.

He pulls away the couch that blocks the closet. It makes a scraping noise on the wooden floor. Robert opens and shuts the closet, amazed. Then, El Exigente, he places his finger along the slats.

"Mike. You couldn't see through these slats if you were an ant. They're glued together."

"Please!"

"You dreamed this all up. . . . "

"I saw you!"

"I have never fucked Marty. But I wouldn't blame myself if I did."

"What are you saying?"

"You haven't let me fuck you in the last seven years. It's a little bit hypocritical for you to deny me the right to fuck Marty and not put out yourself."

"You're changing the subject. Besides, I didn't let you fuck me for good reason."

"Oh, that alibi again."

"Do I have to refresh your memory. It was 1985. You wanted to fuck me. I asked you to use condoms. . . . "

"Mikey, cut it out!"

"You accused me of not trusting you. I, like an idiot, felt guilty, and let you fuck me repeatedly, in an unprotected manner—"

"Mikey, you're pushing me!"

"Then a very sick friend told us that, monogamous though we may be, we could be infecting each other, remember?"

"Mike!"

"Remember?"

"Mike!"

"And I personally believe that if there was any infecting going on, it was then, Rob."

"You did your share of fucking me, Mike."

"I never came in your ass. I always faked it."

"That's what you say."

"Now *you* are the one who is accusing me of lying."

"You've always made fucking sound so fucking clinical, fucking sinful."

"Well, it *is* clinical!"

"You know it's what I liked."

"The *only* thing you liked, Robert."

"Not true."

"Being so dick oriented as you are."

"Oh, and what the fuck are you, Mike? Mr. Polymorphously Perverse? I've never met anyone who had to take so many showers after sex. If I fucking *kissed* you, you had to take a fucking shower."

"You have always had a way of making me feel ugly, sexless."

"Your hang-ups, Mike, not mine."

"You made me feel ugly."

"You haven't always been what I'd call good in bed."

"Just because I never got into being fucked?"

"Well, Mike, I'm not the one who gained thirty-five pounds during our relationship."

"I lost it, didn't I?"

"Too much of it. Now you look like an AIDS patient."

"You see my point, Robert?"

Robert slams the closet door shut.

"It's simple, Mike. You don't like getting fucked."

"It's not simple, Robert. When there are two people, it's more complex than one person would like to believe. Two points of view and all?"

"All I know is that when I tried to call my boyfriend at two in the morning because a friend of mine was in serious psychological shape because we are all living in a goddamn crisis, you were not at home."

"Robert, neither were you—"

"You were not at home!"

"Robert . . ."

"Then you come to Marty's house unannounced, and break his jaw—"

"*Almost* break his jaw—"

"Then you accuse me of lying. It all seems a little hypocritical to me. Where were you at two in the morning?"

Silence.

"What the hell were you doing, Mr. Purity?"

I tell a white lie: "Getting whipped."

Robert sighs. "Mikey, it's not the time for joking."

"I'm not joking. Tahar did the honors."

"My friend John Drummond?"

"Your friend and mine."

Robert looks at me.

"It was nice to have sex with someone who doesn't giggle when he comes. I didn't have to hear the word 'yum' all night. And let me tell you, that was a relief."

"Shut up."

"Yum . . ."

"Shut up!"

"Yummy!"

Robert grabs me by the shoulders and throws me to the floor. I grab him by his hair and take him down with me. We tussle, at first forgetting that we're not being playful, then remembering. His arm pushes against my Adam's apple. I'm close to suffocation when I call out: "Carmine!"

Robert freezes.

"Carmine?" he says, as if asking himself a question.

"Your friend and mine," I say.

"What?" Robert asks.

"Carmine has AIDS," I say, lying. After all, Carmine just has HIV.

"What?"

"You heard me: AIDS. I hope I die before you just so you get to live with the guilt. *Fuck* all your yummy shit. You killed us!"

"Mikey!"

"It's on your head."

"Mikey!"

"Murderer!"

In a minute, I am punching him and he is blocking me with his hands. I scream, "Murder," gnashing my teeth. We draw blood through the resistance of fists. I grumble into a screech, "Blood. It's in our *blood*."

Robert retorts, "Shut up."

"Murderer!"

"Shut up! Shut up! *Shut up!*"

Spike-the-Torpedo dashes into the living room, like he does at night when he senses that Robert and I are either falling asleep or taking a short nap or easing into the cotton sheets to make love. In such cases, Spike's tongue hangs happily from his mouth, which is open, gulping in oxygen like it's love. He virtually runs to the little bed I keep for him in the living room, as if he realizes how wonderful it is to have several beds of his own, and circling one-and-a-half or two-and-a-half times, he dives down into his Spike-ball, falling right to sleep.

He looks much the same now: tongue out, mouth open, teeth showing. He is sniffing or sniffling—I can't tell. That frisky dog, darting from one of my legs, twisted around Robert's, to one of Robert's, then back to mine. He gauges each of our legs. Will he gouge? I want to warn Robert, and I see that he wants to warn me, but it's all fast, and Robert's in the middle of taking my curly hair in his hand and pulling it. I smack Robert's face. I hit Robert's face. Meanwhile, Spike's eyes are not his own—angry. He sees all.

Spike barks.

Robert shoves me in the chest with hard knuckles. I tumble away, then back toward Robert's head.

Spike barks again—a wolfish warning.

"Robert," I say, ready to alert. But he's so unwilling to hear me speak. I grab Robert by the neck to make him listen: *I am worried about Spike, about us.* But I'm greedy, and instead scream, *"Murderer."*

"Crazy!"

Foaming at the mouth, Spike sees all. More barking.

That's when I see my dog open his mouth in a roar. His lips shudder upward, as if he can't bear what he must now do. Spike's teeth are filthy, white and brown molars, plaque.

Spike is mad.

Running up at my leg, Spike sinks his teeth in my bare calf. I look down. I see: My dog's mouth opens into a canyon whose tunnel is pink and full of rage. My dog is biting me.

"Spike. Go lie down."

"Spike. *Stop it.*"

Nothing works. I push Spike away somehow, by a kicking or a twisting or a turning. "Go." But he's a dog or a wolf—or?— and he doesn't get pushed for long. Spike bites; Robert pushes. Spike bites Robert. I push. At first, Spike's a wimp next to two humans, but then his domestic reflex clicks off—off! for good!— and Spike becomes a kamikaze. I detach, watching myself feeling the wolfish pain: the pain of Spike turning on us after years of attention to his eating and shitting patterns, his whimpers at night, his dog giggles when Robert and I lumber into the house with a twenty-five-pound bag of doggie health food.

Robert picks up a broom and starts to beat our dog.

"Spike!"

Then Spike is after Robert. With a frantic jump, he lunges at his throat. Robert drops the broom. I grab the broom. Spike misses Robert's throat, as if on purpose. Somehow Robert and I connect. Without much eye contact, we grab two red bricks each, lying near the bookcase.

We raise them above our heads. One, two . . .

"Wait," I say.

We hold the bricks in the air—frozen. Not a move, not a fraction of an inch. Poised for murder.

Spike growls into silence. He curls up one and a half times and crouches on the floor.

We bring our hands down. Slowly. We place the bricks on the floor. Slowly.

"Good Spike," Robert whispers.

Spike closes his eyes. Slowly. Then he falls asleep, crouched in position, between Robert and me, standing guard.

———

"What an exciting dogfight," Myron Smith says. "Thank God— it's been such a boring day so far."

"Glad I can help out on a slow day."

"Thanks a million, Mike."

He nods in agreement.

"Am I nodding again?" I ask.

He nods in three quick jolts, then resumes the more monotonous nodding. I attempt to straighten myself into a more rigid position, and then he, too, sits up straight.

"After our last session," I continue, "I decided not to come back anymore."

"Why not?" He pouts.

"Well, for starters, I wanted a counselor, not a competitor. You seem a little aggressive."

"Oh," he says, going for his green spiral notebook, "do I?"

"Yes," I mutter. "You do."

"No?" Myron offers. "I'm just giving you what you give me; that's all. It's psyche that's trying to show you your own aggression."

"Please."

"Please, what?"

"My boyfriend is fooling around with the cutest guy I've ever seen in my life. Half of my community is dying. I'm depressed. I almost murdered my dog last night. I have headaches. I imagine a senile old woman is following me around in my dreams. I got whipped after our first session. I don't need aggression, I need understanding."

"You have that."

Myron tilts his head and regards me, eyes wide open. I imagine I see a tear collecting at both corners of his eyes, and I turn away.

I'm the one who's crying.

"Here's a Kleenex," Myron says, pointing to the small wooden coffee table to my right. I help myself to a tissue.

I narrate the rest of the Spike saga to Myron.

"So you slept together?" Myron asks.

"I tried to sleep in my own room," I explain, "but I couldn't. Partly because Spike kept scratching, walking between my room and the bedroom where Robert was. I was frightened Spike would bite me. So, at about four in the morning, I slipped into the bed next to Robert."

"I see."

"And fell right to sleep."

"I see."

"And when I woke up, his arms were around me."

"Spike's?"

"No. Robert's."

"How sweet."

I smile.

"So why are you here?" Myron's expression turns from hopeful to serious.

"Why am I here? I am here because . . . because I don't think I know Robert anymore."

"Anymore?"

"Okay. Maybe I never knew him."

"Now we're getting somewhere."

"Why are you pushing me?" I ask.

"Pushing . . . ?"

"I suppose you think I never knew myself."

"Well . . . "

"God! How arrogant. You and your fucking shadow!"

"Please do not use the Self's name in vain."

"Huh?"

"I have a rule in my office. You can do anything here; you can even shit on the furniture. But you can't use the Self's name in vain."

"What the fuck are you talking about?"

"I think we're shitting on the furniture now. I love it when my clients do that."

"I'm leaving."

"If you leave here, that's it. It's all over. You'll die."

"You're nuts."

"No, you're nuts," Myron says. He's calm, but his throat looks tight, as if he's reading from a script that somehow both moves and bores him. "Or, rather, you're not nuts enough. You're hollow in your nuttiness, wrapped around by it, but not embracing it, led around like a dog who doesn't know his own master. You dare to use the Self's name in vain. When was the last time you talked to God, you phony. You come in here and talk about your lover and your dog, and then you use the Self's name as a curse. If you leave here, you'll be cursed to walk the earth like a leper, a leper of feelings, a vampire, a vampire feeding off other men, with no soul of your own, chasing the secret of your life like a dog chases his own tail."

"I am paying you for a service," I say aghast.

"And not very much, I might add. I'm sick of these sliding scales."

Myron reaches in his pocket, extracting his wallet, fuming.

He extracts three hundred-dollar bills. He hands the roll of cash to me.

"Keep the change," he says.

"I'm going to report you," I say.

"Report me to whom? The gay P.C. fascist police?" He laughs.

"I'll write an article about you."

He laughs harder. "You'll be empty and hollow before you can write the first word."

Rage again: three times in one week. I storm out, the femmy receptionist scribbling in Myron's appointment book while chatting on the telephone. I rant and rave to the receptionist: "How irresponsible that asshole doctor is." But the receptionist ignores me and continues on with his telephone conversation. He picks up his bald head every now and then to lend an odd glance at Myron, who's followed me out to the waiting room, ranting and raving.

Myron continues, "If you leave here, it's over for you."

Since when do therapists curse their patients?

"Let me leave here in peace!" I scream.

"You'll be a shell. Fighting the truth. Every thing in your life will be a halfhearted attempt at life, self-sabotage."

A clay vase sits on the receptionist's desk. It's nearly three feet tall; images of Greek men in various stages of lewd conduct adorn it. With all my might, I throw my weight against the objet d'art. The vase topples over, crashing against the black-tiled floor, breaking into four compact fragments.

Ripples of shock surge through me: shock that I've destroyed a priceless object; shock that Myron angered me; shock that I seem so empty to Myron.

None of this shock compares to what my eyes see next. The vase contains items — things, morsels. What do I see? A hundred — two hundred — miniature dog bones? The kind you buy in bulk from the pet store? Can I believe my eyes?

The dog bones lie spread out on the floor.

Myron bends down calmly and reaches for one. He hands one to me.

"Welcome home, Mike."

I take the dog bone.

"The feelings," he says. "Hold them."

"Hm," is all I can manage.

"Spike is very powerful. How does it feel to let Spike out after all this time?"

I shake my head. "Spike?"

"Our time is up for this session," Myron says. He extends his hand. "But congratulations. I knew you'd pull through. Next week, same time?"

I take his hand, which is limp and sweaty, as if he's just passed a test of his own. I tuck my arms into my sides, like Mia Farrow in *Rosemary's Baby*. He says good-bye repeatedly, nervously—like Ruth Gordon. The receptionist, still on the phone, holds the receiver to his shoulder with his neck. He waves his fingertips ever so slightly with one hand. *Ta-ta.* I notice that the receptionist's free hand tries to conceal a jumbo-sized bottle of Elmer's Glue.

"Next week?" Myron asks a little sheepishly.

I nod. Myron retreats into his office.

I make to leave the waiting room. I close the door slowly, slowly enough to hear the receptionist's commentary to the other person on the other side of the receiver. "Doll," I hear the receptionist say. "We go through glue and dog bones in this office the way some therapists go through Kleenex." I stuff the dog bone into my pocket and shut the door to Myron's waiting room all the way.

———

"I feel like the other woman," Tahar says. I lie in his arms. His darkened house smells from a dinner of eggs, cilantro and toast. He has listened to my Myron Smith story. Tahar cracks up, pinching my cheeks. "Myron showed you your shadow," Tahar says, by way of an explanation. "He does that with all his precocious boys." Tahar's deep laughter begins to ease my fears that Myron is Satan and Tahar is his Prince of Darkness minion. I trust Tahar—or, more to the point, I trust his body, which has wrapped itself into mine, legs and arms akimbo in the living room. Now, Myron Smith seems more well-meaning, if impatient. "Impatient with all the gay men dying before they know who they are," Tahar adds.

"One manifesto a day, please."

Tahar shows me his own dog bone, a moldy little cracker, set like a trophy atop the fireplace's mantel. We laugh so hard it seems as if I understand what has taken place around my shrink and me. Truth is, I don't. The room is dark. I can see the hundreds of books lined up in the oak shelves Mark made before he got so sick. I see how Tahar and I must look to Mark's ghost: a tightly cuddled advertisement for race relations on a red art-deco couch.

The laughter dies down. Tahar's shirt comes off. His black jeans grip his waist as tightly as they do in ubiquitous Calvin Klein ads. No fat drops over his pants. Abdominal creases, hard and stiff, like beaten egg whites, hold the flesh in. Taut and extended: that's Tahar. Pulled; like a drum skin over his heart and liver and lungs. About to split from held-in tension. Who comforts him? I pat various areas: muscle, ligaments and flesh. I am intimidated by this delicacy, massaging little layers and points to make sure it's not makeup, pinching a tiny dot of skin as if it were a rash or a series of pimples on one's own body with which one grows obsessed. I compare Tahar's surfaces to Robert's. Robert's are thicker, Germanic — almost as smooth. I used to touch Robert's exteriors as if I were touching watercolor paper, the paper there to soak up the transparent moody purples, crazy reds and sun oranges I had to offer. But so rarely did we lie like this, merely touching.

Tea cups and saucers lie on the table; bits of crumpets half-eaten. The eggs harden into spoils. Clothes stay on. The hours pass in silence.

I had wanted to "debrief" the Myron incident with Tahar. I was resentful that Tahar turned me on to this Jungian moron, who wanted to turn me into a Jungian moron. How cultish: playing go-fish with my emotions. Werner Erhard and Marianne Williamson and Aimee Semple McPherson — and now Myron Smith! But talk seems cheap. We hold each other into the night.

It's dusk—burnt orange clouds in the east, a scarlet aura dimming into tonight's outdoor performance. Several hundred votive candles burn brightest here, in East Los Angeles. A hundred people mingle in front of the steps of a hospital—L.A. County U.S.C. Medical Center. From the 5 Freeway you see the hospital's white towers and large wooden windows, one of the tallest buildings in this, the poorest part of town. The barrio hospital, that's where the poor people get their shots, their casts, their last rites. It happens to be the largest hospital in the world. The two hundred steps leading up to the marble lobby are white and completely insurmountable by anyone with more than a 99-degree fever.

Over the last few months, AIDS activists have begun demonstrating here rather than at hotels hosting politicians. The health-care provider of last resort: that's L.A. County, that's this hospital. Five thousand AIDS patients rely on one tiny AIDS clinic. Arriving at 9:00 A.M. for chemotherapy, the skinny, sick people lounge on hardwood benches. Fluorescent white light blinds them. Nurses ignore them. If lucky, they eventually receive their poison in the hallways, vomiting blood, phlegm and saltines for the benefit of onlookers.

An outdoor rostrum has been set here by the activists. They plan a week-long vigil, and they require entertainment. The stage is set; it's black, slick and freshly painted. On either side, placards hold the blown-up photos of men and women who have died recently. There is Gregory Kayalis, a founder of ACT UP/LA, a handsome "media slut" in requisite long sideburns, distended biceps and an irregular crew cut. There's Tahar's Mark, Mark Ruffino. Another is Mary Lambert, a white lesbian who campaigned for better conditions for women in prisons. Her hair is blond, her pretty face covered in lesions.

Today, this kickoff to the vigil has the feel of a ghost dance—a ritual of a beaten tribe. The handful of spiritualists in the group join hands and "*om.*" I see Tahar among them. Most everyone else chain-smokes and stamps their feet in the chilly air, ignoring the annoying "God people" one can't help but find in the ranks of West Coast activists these days.

I sense a buzzing of disparate voices, and then annoying glares. I shrug my shoulders and wave to the few people I know intimately. There's Ann-the-Leading-Activist, her girlfriend Cynthia, Marty and Sue Canelli. "Our hero," Canelli says, approaching me with a Carlton blazing in her mouth. She attends demonstrations the way some people go to the movies.

"See Robert yet?" I ask, turning away before she spreads her nicotine breath all over my face.

"That creep," Canelli says. "Could he use a haircut!"

A tall woman in dyed green hair approaches. I worry she will attack me for my Gay White Male privilege; once she denounced my articles at a general body meeting of ACT UP not knowing I was there. She said I effectively "kept women from writing." I told her she was full of it and then left the room.

"My name is Lally," she says.

I look both ways before running.

She goes on: "I just want to thank you for your courage and your work."

I turn around, as if another Michael Kaplan stands behind me.

Marty approaches. "Hey, dude," he says. "Great picture in the paper —"

Ann-the-Leading-Activist runs over and slaps a kiss on my forehead. "I love you, you nut. Great article."

A few other people — some wearing nose rings, others in winter coats preparing for the nighttime desert chill about to descend on this place — circle around me. They want to touch me, as if I represent the kind of religious transformation activism seems capable of eliciting in boring people. I think back to my childhood, and the way the old men would follow the Torah around the room as the rabbi danced with it. By simply touching the parchment, they felt restored. Grace.

I turn away, toward the stage. I hear the "tap, tap, tap," on the microphone and the amplified clearing of phlegm. I associate these sounds with Robert. It *is* Robert. Robert will perform tonight. "A message to L.A. County, and the people with AIDS who survive the continuing war," he announces. Robert is the only person I know who can mouth those slogans and not appear as if he has an ax to grind. It's so Ronald Reagan. No wonder Robert has become so well-known.

Odd; Marty isn't paying attention to Robert. "Did you realize you'd become famous when you fought those horses?" Marty asks.

"Shhh . . . "

Ann talks over Robert's voice. "I hear rumors that you're going to write a major series of exposés on AIDS activists."

"Robert's about to perform, Ann!"

Tahar, who must have seen me in the middle of his *samadhi,* strides over.

"What are you doing here?" he asks. "Homie, I told you to rest. To stay away for a while."

"Tahar," I say, not moving my eyes away from the stage. "I had to hear him." I make the mistake of saying, "This is what I fell in love with ten years ago."

Tahar shakes his head. "You are a sick woman."

"Shhh," I say. "Robert's about to start."

Tahar mimics me: "Robert's about to start." He walks away.

Robert waits for the sound from the two large rented speakers to fill the plaza we're gathered in. It's Wagner; how Robert. Birgit Nilsson will sing "The Liebestod" from *Tristan and Isolde.* Can you imagine Nilsson's low-pitched diva voice quivering in the air above a smog-hazy L.A. night, no stars in the black sky? Robert lets the sounds sink into him. He closes his eyes, throws his head backward like Greta Garbo. Near me, there's an opera of voices interrupting Robert's opera. For years, I watched Robert perform to the aria of a love so supreme that it kills. I never thought it had anything to do with me.

"Mild und leise, wie er lächelt. . . . "

"I got fucked in the ass by a man for the first time that night."

"Mikey, you should be so proud of yourself . . . "

"Wie das Auge, hold er öffnet . . . "

"And the singer's voice took me up, up, up, to a despair bigger than my body that night . . . "

"Mikey, this is such a big break for you. . . . "

Robert sweats. The night grows cooler. Beneath Robert's leather jacket I see his bare torso. Two spotlights and two hundred candles highlight Robert's fleshy wonders.

Robert performs the way people do in rock concerts, craning his neck into a fit of orgasmic self-love, giving the crowd exactly what it wants, which is him getting high off them. He turns to the left; he turns to the right. He looks up; he looks down. A quandary of four directions: very Native American, very Bruce Springsteen. In this earnestness — "in the arms of lovers who were dying before me" — Robert falls into himself, the part of himself that I know is most real. That inner engine is the opposite of confidence, the opposite of fullness, but when it revs up, it fills up the empty places.

The Wagner aria launches into its layered crescendo, like a wave of German order, over and over and over into a release — a free-fall. Robert's nose crunches into his upper lip, his forehead creasing — such sadness in these prayers: "Let my people live."

"In dem wogenden Schwall."

"New lovers taking our place."

"Aren't you a media star now, Mike?"

"In des Welt-Atems."

" . . . the bodies piling up under the storm of discontent, my fear larger than my soul."

"Shouldn't you be home writing your Nobel?"

"Wehendem All . . . "

"My resolve to fight . . . our resolve to fight . . . "

"You've heard Robert do this one a million times . . . "

"You too, a traitor?"

"Wehendem All . . . "

"It's not wrong to touch . . . "

"How could Isolde have departed from this world?"

"Basil Schmasil."

"Do not scold me."

"Mikey, go home. It's Tahar. You've had a big day."

"Even in our last gasp . . ."

"Congratulations. *Nicht hate.*"

"*Verskinken.*"

"Not wrong to kiss. In our last embrace . . ."

"Will you profile me, Mike?"

"*Unbewsst* . . ."

"Not wrong to fuck . . ."

"Isn't Robert beautiful, Tahar? That's why I married him."

"*Höchste Lust!*"

"*Faithful friend.*"

"*Yingeleh* . . ."

"*Höchste Lust!*"

"In our last murmur of life. They lied to us!"

"*Höchste* . . ."

"They lied. . . ."

"*Deceit and madness. Tristan, where are you?*"

"Mikey, Robert lied. . . ."

"*Höchste Lust!*"

"They lied to *us!*"

"Robert lied to *you!*"

———

The music ends. The spotlights fade down, then up, then down:
then applause: *Go Israel, send it home to your maker.* Robert bows:
once, twice, then he runs offstage. He returns; the ovation builds.
Now: a standing ovation. Robert hates curtain calls. Sweat pours
down his face. His hair sags over his forehead, wet. From Robert,
the diplomatic: "Fight AIDS, fight back, ACT UP." From the
crowd, the chorus: "ACT UP!" I join in. Fists out, hand out-
stretched, voices hoarse.

Tahar stares at me. "Mikey, you've gone nuts?"

"He's so beautiful, Tahar."

All is forgiven. I run to the stage, ready to kiss Robert in
public. Pushing past bodies — Robert's fans. Forgiven. People see
me; they pat me on the back. They call me in a way I haven't
heard before — "Mikey, Mikey." All is . . . Robert stands a few

feet away. I want to grab Robert and whisper for only him to hear: "All is forgiven." I want to bear hug him like he's a new lover, causing a sensation for the cameras. All is forgiven. Robert bows. He does not see me. I'm close, closer still, like a character in a slow-motion dream, about to touch one's forgotten lover, when —

"Mikey, stop!"

It's Tahar.

"There's Marty," Tahar says. "Careful. Careful."

Tahar holds me back. Like an understudy, Marty emerges from the crowd and falls into Robert's extended arms. Robert, surprised, exhilarated, pulls Marty close into him. The two kiss. The crowd claps, a few hoots.

Tahar's right hand still clutches my left elbow. I pull him off me.

I walk away, toward my Nissan parked in the hospital back lot. I know, from the sound of the crowd, that the two men are still kissing. And, as I get in the car and turn on the cranky engine, I imagine the applause and the roars, although I can't hear the sounds above my loud car. And, as I drive away, I don't dare turn toward the stage, for fear that I might still see the two men kissing.

When I arrive home, Spike is lying in a ball.

I touch him.

"Spike."

He doesn't move.

Sacred
Lips of the
Bronx

———

ne night, during a hot-as-hell Indian summer in May, Hector's sister Elena announced to her immediate family that she was getting married to Carlos Enrique Lopez, her high-school squeeze. She was told promptly by her father, in epithet-driven Spanish, "Over my dead body." Okay, so Carlos was a mechanic. And truth was, Elena threatened to become a regular Dr. Alberta Einstein if she kept up with her straight As at Queens College, on her way, who knows, to Albert Einstein School of Medicine (located, by the way, in the Bronx). She deserved better than a grease monkey, or so everyone besides her (and Hector) thought. (Hector and Carlos passed as brothers by their dumb-ass routines on the basketball court. Hector: "Who falls out of a window faster, a Jew or a black?" Carlos: "Who cares?" Two points.)

A month or so later, Carlos declared that the local savings bank had provided him with a loan to open his own car-repair shop. "And why not?" Elena asked. Carlos owned a Bronx garden apartment, a 1975 Camaro, and more power tools than NASA. He had credit like you wouldn't believe. Elena's father relented when he saw RODRIGUEZ REPAIRS, located in the white ghetto known as Riverdale. News of Elena's good fortune spread throughout the ten-block radius surrounding Yankee Sta-

dium. It wasn't long before the Kaplans received an invitation to
the wedding.

My mother eyed the envelope as one regards a delicacy, a
Caribbean kiwi, let's say, or a Hawaiian mango, one that has
never been tasted, let alone held. You know the fruit ought to be
exotic, but part of you is worried about taking an impetuous bite.
Are those dainty pimples on the froggy skin normal? Will you
have to be rushed to emergency and have your stomach pumped?
With her pink fingernails, my mother sliced the letter open, zig-
zag, like she'd live a little.

The invitation looked no different from the cards my relatives
sent for weddings, graduations and bar mitzvahs. The Rodriguez
announcement stood out with its calligraphy and five-by-seven
photograph of the engaged couple. My father took one look at
the stick-thin Elena, her sharp nose and darkly lined eyebrows
offset by thick black curls, and fell in love at first sight. "Looks
just like you, dearie, in your younger years," he told my mother.

My mother caught one glance of Elena's pleated red dress
and put her fingers to her eyes, as if blinded by sunlight. She
went so far as to say: "They invited us because they think Jews
are made of money. Boy, were they barking up the wrong tree!"

A closer examination of the card melted her penny-pinching
heart. Hector's mother had written: "DEAR BELOVED KAP-
LAN FAMILY. GOD BE WITH YOU AND PLEASE, BY
ALL MEANS, BE OUR HONORED GUESTS. WE ARE
PUTTING YOU AT THE SAME TABLE WITH OUR JEW-
ISH SECOND COUSINS."

"Now," my mother said, "that's class."

Fishing in her fake-leather pocketbook for a tricolored Bic
pen, she improvised a response on the RSVP card: "We will not
be able to attend the wedding per se because my husband will be
having a root canal that morning, but we would be happy to
attend your daughter's celebration — with bells on." My mother
would have preferred impalement to setting foot in a Catholic
church. But she saw nothing wrong with appearing at the reception, taking place at a reputable Manhattan nightclub, called The
Latin Star.

"Linda," I cried.

"What?"

"We can't go!"

"Why not?"

Wasn't it obvious? We'd be the only people at The Latin Star who couldn't dance the samba and merengue. Sure, simplified versions of those steps prevailed at Jewish affairs. But the cha-cha-chas were played for the older generation, the Pall Mall–smoking, leisure-suited couples who cringed at our Crosby, Stills, Nash & Young (forget Freddie Mercury), as if it were Hitler's voice coming over the stereo speakers. We hated their *"Bei Mir Bist Du Sheyn";* they spat at our Queen. Now I felt bad: if only I knew the rumba.

"I refuse to go to that wedding not knowing how to dance the steps of the people," I said.

"So do yourself a favor and take some dance lessons."

"You'll part with your money?"

"I've always wanted my boys to know how to take a girl out dancing without embarrassing me in the process."

Taking the forty-five dollars in cold cash from Linda's hands, I saw that a more pressing problem had occurred to her. She must have heard from the Bronx grapevine that Stan would be playing congas along with a four-piece band at Elena's wedding reception. Oh, that *did* unhinge her. Judy and I would sign up for an eight-week class at Bronx Community College, but that solved absolutely nothing. Fate kept weird time these days; a Santana samba leaked into our house from a neighbor's lousy sound system. I watched my mother slump into a kitchen chair and stare off into space. Her time to relax, pray, scheme or buy earplugs. I could never tell which.

Hector and I had begun dating Dottie and Judy, respectively. I don't know how we managed it, but we spoke about the love we had "for the female race" while laying face-to-sweaty-face, our breath turning deep and expressive as our flatbed chests stuck together like two pieces of flypaper. We slouched on Hector's bedroom floor without shirts. Hector's mother used to scour the linoleum once a week with Mr. Clean, a job she abdicated to

Hector once she enrolled in Lehman College to become a dental hygienist. After Hector disinfected his floor, he'd call me over his house to "initiate" it. We could never neck without our sneakers on. Our kisses lacked a certain innate urban zest, almost as if, masquerading as surfers, we had forgotten our boards.

But the sneakers *did* make a mess. After the heat of passion had passed, and the floor felt sticky from sweat, spilled Coca-Cola and other assorted excretions, Hector would head for the mop and pail all over again. "Sit still on that goddamn bed," he'd admonish, "and don't you fucking move your ass an inch." I'd offer to help, but he'd dismiss me with a flick of his thin brown wrist. "I do it for my main man Jesus," he'd say. "He gets pissed if I don't carry my cross to bear." Afterward, we'd grab a slice of pizza and then cruise the streets separately for our friends.

I don't know how we kept our hands off each other when in public, but we did. You know the sight of a man and a woman drunk with craving? They embarrass everyone in Wal-Marts by being unable to concentrate on any fact of life besides the way their lover's fingertips feel on their skin. I could never understand such lack of discretion until I met Hector. Of course, he and I exercised great self-control when in malls, subway cars and triplexes. We didn't think it unfair. We didn't think about it. We did, however, try to give covert expression to the magnetism we felt anytime our bodies were within a few feet of one another. We did so through indelicate Muhammad Ali–styled punches; Harpo Marx–like kicks; you're-full-of-shit slaps on the face with both hands; and clumsy, pseudo-drunk walks in the street that had one or the other catch his friend before he fell to the filthy concrete. (Hector often made his body into a rigid sheet aiming, face first, toward the ground—like a toppling Tower of Pisa.) More than once I stepped in to save him from what I predicted would be a broken face. But on the occasions when either my timing was off or I was curious as to how he saved himself from a hard fall—after all, he was plummeting like a plate glass to the ground long before we had ever heard of each other—he did save himself through a suave use of palms and wrist action. "I got wrists like spark plugs," he'd say, meaning "shock absorbers" or maybe just "springs." I never bothered correcting him. I was in awe. He suffered no damage from such falls except for a dozen or so infinitesimally small vessels bursting where bone and cartilage met skin. "Don't worry about a little Grade-A blood, *mijo*," he'd tell me, licking drops of red-stained dirt up from his callused hands, "it's clean, man—no junk, no nothing." He once smeared blood on my fingertips, daring me to do the "taste test." I rolled my eyes and rubbed the grime off on my pants in a dismissive swipe. Later, however, when I returned home, I noticed traces left still in the grooves of my palm. I stuck my hand in my mouth and sucked. I stopped only when I felt my hand clean and tasteless. Did I panic? I think not. I do remember gargling for a half hour later on, but that impulse emerged more from a "you-can-never-be-too-careful" sense of dental hygiene than pangs of guilt. (My father later to my mother: "The Listerine I bought yesterday is half-empty. You think Mike's taken up smoking?")

During an episode of "All in the Family," I found myself chewing on myself until I drew blood from my thumb. My mother shot up from her TV-watching love seat, stormed into the kitchen, and, in a huff, tore into the icebox, rummaging for one of her frozen minute steaks. "Enough with this vegetarian nonsense," she barked at me as the meat sizzled on a frying pan. "Those crazy diets you and Hector go on. You know as well as I that you need a little animal blood in your system now and then."

(After I wolfed down my iron-fortified, ketchup-drenched flesh, I called Hector to quote Linda Kaplan word for word. We laughed so hard that my father peeked in the door to make sure I wasn't "asphyxiating or God-knows-what." How did Willie explain my hysteria to Linda? He said it came from my uncustomary ingestion of too-rare beef: "You know, Linda, all the hormones they put in these days . . . " Which only made me laugh harder—my father's accent, his "whore moans"—causing my stomach to contort in painful gasps which were matched, if not worsened, by Hector's horselike cackles on the other line. I had no choice but to hang up on a suffocating Hector in a gesture to save our lives.)

Despite the blood-brother business, Hector and I began going to the movies on Friday night with Judy and Dottie. We necked with them in Hector's father's brown round-hooded sedan. By ourselves we wouldn't have gone overboard pushing the double-dating issue, but for some reason, Dottie and Judy liked being thrown together. Judy was an avid reader of Betty Friedan, Gloria Steinem and Simone de Beauvoir and found Dottie's strong-minded street smarts, well, refreshing and inspiring. "I just wish she'd wear less perfume," she'd say. "Such a walking stereotype."

Dottie had her comments, too, which I picked up from Hector: "I'm gonna put that Jewish American Princess on a diet, before she's as fat as an unkosher pig."

Hector and I knew we were in for it when Dottie started to borrow some of Judy's thumbed-through textbooks. I know what Dottie did. She passed the tomes on to Hector, who inhaled them to "stay tuned-in to what the ladies want." ("The times they are a-changing," he'd tell me.) He'd then recycle the sociopolitical information in a language he knew Dottie could understand: Puerto Rican.

It wasn't long before Hector's father, searching for some spare (and kinky) pornography, hit upon *The Feminine Mystique* lying alongside *Pussy Come Home* under his son's bed. "You know what these bitches want," the older man screamed. "To cut our goddamn *huevos* off."

Hector claimed the books belonged to "Mike's bitch, Judy," which was, in fact, only a "white lie." A good thing, since Hector was a crummy liar, a fact Hector's father had sussed out years ago when a Clorets-smelling Hector said he had no clue where the old man's Cuban cigars disappeared to.

One night all four of us went to see the new hit movie, *The Turning Point*, starring Shirley MacLaine. The movie played at the now-defunct Loew's Theater on Fordham Road, from which we'd all soon be graduated. It bothered me to sit up front with Hector, as he steered his father's wobbly vehicle with one hand, sucking on a rolled-too-tight joint in the other. Judy and Dottie sat in the backseat, talking a mile a minute about Angela Davis, "reproductive rights" and "IUDs." Even the intermittent gropes I copped from the driver didn't console me. I hated the way the women presumed the "thick-in-the-skull" men would never understand anything they had to say about *Roe* v. *Wade*, forcing Hector and me into awkward silences during which we tried to eavesdrop like stupids.

"Shit," Dottie said, interrupting her train of thought. "I forgot my glasses."

"You can wear mine," Hector offered, trying to be a feminist.

"Not if we sit in the front row like you and Mikey do."

"You miss the whole movie if you sit in the back," he argued. "No fucking way," he added, really raising his voice so much I put my hand on the steering wheel. "I'm putting my foot down. We're sitting front-row or we ain't going."

"*Calmate, mijo,*" Dottie said, biting her tongue. "*No te preocupes.*"

"Sorry."

"Then, *mijo,* drive me back home a few blocks? *Tengo que...*"

Inhaling so deeply that ashes flew in his hair, Hector complied. True to form, Judy followed Dottie upstairs in the Bronx brownstone, leaving Hector and me alone for ten minutes.

"Mike," he said, saving the roach in an old case of Aspergum. "If we're going to take the girls out, we got to have them pay more attention to us. We the guys, and they should be acting more romantic, you know? *Fuck* Betty Friedan."

"Hector."

"*Fuck* her!"

When the women returned, I sat behind the driver's seat, fooling with the remaining Visine. The car idled; Hector spotted a runty dealer. Judy and Dottie looked confused by all the red eye and wheeling and dealing. Then Hector was running like a maniac across the street, dodging express buses and gypsy cab-drivers on 161st Street and one NYPD undercover Chevy, stuffing a Baggie in his dungaree jacket pocket. By then, I was sitting with a nail-biting Judy in the back.

"Get in," Hector said to Dottie. He turned the key and fled that neighborhood in a draw-attention-from-the-cops screech.

We drove in silence. I handed him ten dollars. He threw it back to me.

Dottie, annoyed by the new regulations, craned her dove's neck toward the backseat, toward Judy. "You know that Shirley MacLaine," she clucked. "I hear she's into the New Age."

"The new *what?*" Judy asked, leaning forward.

"You know, tranchannelers. Karman."

"You mean karma," Hector said.

"Dot's right," Judy said. "It's karman."

"Yeah, karman. Well, anyway, she's into life after death . . ."

"Wrong!" Hector blasted, slamming his fist on the dashboard. "It's karma, bitch."

Dottie turned away, staring straight ahead out the windshield.

Judy puckered her lips. "Excuse me," she said, "but what did you call her?"

"You heard me," Hector said.

"You're right I heard you," Judy stammered.

"Shut up, bitch," I barked at Judy. "He's right. You want to talk to Dottie, you go out with her on your own date."

We parked the car on a quiet tree-lined street between Jerome Avenue and Fordham Road. We expected coolness, but I saw how simple the evening had become through danger. The spring air invited us to take deep breaths and to smell the Bronx cherry blossoms. After the movie, Hector, taking his maze of shortcuts, drove us to the brink of the George Washington Bridge. We spoke like adults about cancer and morbidity. We got high off the five, six stars in the sky and from Hector's dope. Judy, who was branching out, couldn't stop cracking up. Dottie handed her a Motrin, and that only made us cackle more. I saw then that I wasn't anything but Hector's best friend, and that we made divisions that made sense but, in the end, divided nothing.

"It's funny with you guys," Dottie said as we drove her home to Mosholu Park. "It's like you're brothers. But Hector's Catholic, and Mike, you are Jewish."

"Christ killer." That was Hector.

"These two," Judy said. "It's like they're Siamese twins, connected at the neck or something."

"Or something," Dottie said.

"I once heard of twins who were inseparable," Judy mused. "When one guy got married, the other guy got married, too. Just so he and his brother could keep living together."

"Shit, that's incest!" Dottie declared.

"People do strange things, Dottie."

"Tell me about it."

"Do you think they shared the same bedroom?"

"You know, I wouldn't be the least bit surprised."

Hector and I gave each other mystified looks.

At the end of the night, Hector and I sat alone in his car. He drank a Yoo-Hoo and knocked his dungareed knee against mine to the beat of Marvin Gaye's "I Heard It Through the Grapevine." I sensed a hint of regret in his voice, the gravel tones of a guy who could have slept part of the night with his girlfriend but just didn't. I felt sympathy—not just for him, but for me, too. Judy didn't carry herself as lightly as Dottie. But her breasts popped out from her bra in a *ta-da!* manner, and the softness of her body soothed my anxieties in a way that Hector's pointy elbows and flattened kneecaps never did. Not that the softness could ever be confused with Hector's unremitting heat. It wasn't sexuality or even sensuality, but the mutuality of opposites that Judy gave.

"The night feels edgy with thoughts, Hector."

"Now you're starting to sound like me."

We slid our pants down, in a minimal way. I remember thinking about Judy's crotch, and how it revolted and intrigued me; I felt aimlessly for Hector's openness as it rested sweaty on the plastic driver's seat. I remember thinking about the discovery of Judy's clit and how it propped itself above her body like a sign on a freeway; I spread Hector open delicately, just a wee bit, for he was closed shut like a bank vault. I remember rummaging through those untidy folds of hers, shrouded by a forest of pubic hair, worried I would never find anything but more hair; I poked in and out of Hector. I remember fondling her breasts and finding her nipples and squeezing and squeezing until she screamed; I searched out Hector's nipples, unnaturally flat and thin; he howled *"ay!"* and I let go. I remember bringing my lips to Judy's salt-stained neck, grazing my lips against her rising tide of goose pimples, awed by the incessant waves of those little bumps; I smelled the perverse sweetness of Hector's neck, missing her ripe softness, oddly taken in, though, by the ligaments and lymph nodes that popped through the lines in his neck, braille for the blind.

I remember learning to tease her with a thumb and pinkie, watching the shudder in her eyes and wondering if there was something in Jewish girls that made the area down below feel hot and alive like a kitchen before a High Holy Day; now I could feel myself playing with Hector in unexpected ways, touching him more lightly than usual, like I would Judy, and then going hard, like I would Judy. Everything inside him was made transparent by the taut stretch of skin.

It wasn't a hermaphrodite's fantasy, but two different ways to be. There was no spurting wash of liquid, but an oozing out, not so messy. I had worried that I would never be able to hump a woman. But when the time came to do so, I craved the abnormality of curves. The rubbery feel of a clit on my lips could not compare to the wart on Hector, but it came in at a close second. I got the two mixed up. My tongue knew no reason. I closed my eyes and it felt pulled toward that which would pull it. What am I saying? It wasn't a matter of taste. In retrospect it was Hector, and the spell of the living body he gave. For when there is an abundance of love, it flows out, knowing no division. And the body cleaves; and the body can train the heart to go where it thinks it can't, and vice versa.

———

When the day of the wedding came, my mother and father set aside three hours to shower, shave, dress and check the radio for the weather. (You always checked the weather.) Hector had stopped by with a red bow tie for me to wear, but he had forgotten how to tie it. "Stoop!" he said, hitting his head with his hand. My father had forgotten too. Half-naked, freshly talced and whiskeyed, Willie stood in front of my mother's floor-length mirror folding the red cloth until it creased in a million places. "What the hell," he said, the sweat of anxiety beading up on his scalp, ruining his blow-dry. That's when I decided to resort to the clip-on. "We'll do red at Stan's wedding," I said. Suddenly we were running late. My mother modeled the green dress she bought but never wore for my bar mitzvah. She could never lose that last ten pounds.

"So," she asked, sucking in air. "What's the verdict?"

"It fits like a glove," my father said.

"A latex glove," she said. "I look two months pregnant."

"Three."

She ran to her bedroom. She emerged five minutes later in the looser fitting, gold polyester gown she wore for my brother's bar mitzvah.

"Now, that's an outfit," my father said.

"If you're giving a daughter away. No one wears gold these days. I feel overdressed."

"You'll be in good company."

The sartorial preparations for weddings and bar mitzvahs Jewish culture inflicts on its people! No matter how hard we tried, our clothes never seemed to transform our personas into the success stories we wished we were.

But, truth be told, my father stood tall, and, as Linda said, with "excellent posture." My mother moved her weight from one leg to the other vivaciously, "va-va-va-voom," as my father might comment under his breath. Both had unnaturally dark brown hair, dark eyebrows, contorted Roman-styled noses, and I-don't-believe-a-word-you're-saying panache, especially when they crossed their arms while smoking cigarettes. They didn't need clothes to stand out in a crowd. They didn't need money to have brothers and sisters in Armani cluster around them to ask, "How's by you?" (My mother's favorite retort while fingering one of her sister's Anne Klein blouses, "Fine, but if I had your cash cow, better. By the way, did you get it on sale?") But it was easy to confuse fabrication for the real thing. No wonder my parents' faces dropped to their chins whenever our Dodge Dart pulled up in front of a wedding hall.

Tonight's gala was no different, even though the walking-encyclopedia Judy accompanied us in the backseat, informing my parents about: the derivation of the merengue (it bearing resemblance to Spain's flamenco); the Puerto Rican manner of dropping the consonant "s" (as in *"estamos,"* pronounced *"ehtamo"*); why Puerto Rico wanted independence from the U.S. ("We exploit them. And they hate us for it." And from my chain-smoking, dry-lipped father: "Me, I'd pay them to secede from the Union.") During our nervous approach to The Latin Star, Willie took out his tortoiseshell cigarette case, Linda her tortoiseshell compact. *"You* look great, Mr. Kaplan," Judy said.

To which my mother replied, "What's your middle name, Judy? Tact?"

My brother could be seen arriving in a black beat-up van across the street, surrounded by a group of chain-smoking, tuxedo-clad, overweight men twice his age. I counted five amplifiers, one bass, three congas, two electronic keyboards and even an acoustic guitar. Who would play all this? The rented tux fitted my brother's muscular body a little too snugly in his shoulders, a little too loosely in his waist. He looked like a maternity case. "Oy!" my mother said, seeing him. "I raised him to wear red?"

My brother heaved a conga up high. He began a fast clip toward the back door of The Latin Star. A button that held his jacket together popped open. Either he didn't see us or was acting like he didn't.

Once inside The Latin Star, you felt blasted. The tried-but-true rumba beat of *"Guantanamera"* shook a person up. The horns and singer sounded so Big Band. Then we got it: excess was in. That meant so were we. Linda slipped off her spring windbreaker and exposed the gold jazz underneath. Her hems sailed off the floor. My father shed his Bogey-styled tan overcoat. All around were round tables covered in white linen and black and gold vases filled with roses and chrysanthemums. Lipsticked women and dark-haired men hovered near the oval-shaped dance floor like old people bracing themselves before a cold ocean dip. Soon they'd dive. Smoke clustered around chatty groups, young and old. You saw signs of celebration everywhere: napkins stained with lipstick; candles dripping wax on business cards in Spanish; coat jackets resting on chairs revealing white envelopes that said, "To the Bride and Groom — *¡Felicidades!*" Men surrounded my mother, almost all of them big-bellied and dressed in white tuxedos and red bow ties. They regarded her as a Hebraic-styled Madonna. A handsome dark-faced man bore an intense resemblance to Hector's father. "I'm the bride's uncle," he said, shaking my father's hand. "And· let me tell you, señor, you are a lucky husband to have such a beautiful wife."

"*Muchas gracias,*" my father said, attempting his best Spanish accent, cheery from his first whiskey sour. "But you can have her if you want. She's on sale."

"Be careful, Willie. Someone more sober than you may buy."

The music rang through the hall so loud it became physical, knocking your anxiety away the way a Bronx wind might topple the Yankees cap off your head. A trumpet whined. There was the banging on the conga skin; I knew the enraged thumping to be from my brother's hands. I caught a glimpse of Hector, his wiry body attenuated like a model-to-be in a tailored white tux. He escorted an ancient, dark woman to a place where a thin, middle-aged photographer in an El Greco–styled mustache took portraits. Hector made the woman sit still on a chair. He stood behind her in a variety of dignified poses, rolling his eyes at her complaints about his cigarette smoking, crappy Spanish, his poor attendance at Mass. In between flashes and forced smiles, Hector shook his right hand at me, as if to comment on my outfit — *muy caliente.* I think the photographer got that one, too. Afterward, Hector's mother, Maria, posed with Hector and his grandmother. The extended relatives gathered; always the old woman remained dead center. At the end, Hector's mother spotted my mother and me regarding the scene. For a moment, I thought she wore the same gold gown as my mother; up close I saw that it was a cotton-silk deal, stitched in a hundred places with a certain linen yarn that flaunted her curves and creases.

"Linda!" she screamed. "You stole my dress!"

"Oh, sugar!" my mother said, exasperated.

"If there was anyone who could, it's you."

Hector's father waddled over, tipsy. He shook my father's tipsy hand.

"Roderigo," my father said. "One helluva congratulation to you on the wedding of your beautiful daughter." My father handed Roderigo a box of Cuban cigars; it resembled the gold-lined box Hector had stolen from his father and had given to my father for Father's Day.

My mother took a deep, convoluted breath. "It's like a Jewish affair," she said. "The chicken fricassee and everything." Hector's mother clapped her hands; her sisters were arranging their kids in a photograph with the other ancient grandmother, the one who smiled more because, according to her daughter-in-law (Hector's mother), the old woman had to; she was less well-to-do. "Maria, Andela, Roberta, Monica, *venga aqui. Ouiero presentante a mi amiga Judía* . . ." A dozen Latinas, all my mother's age and size, surrounded Linda, clucking over her dress, mascara, and children, one of whom was starting up a percussion solo in a rendition of Tito Puente's "Ran Kan Kan."

"Our people of the Bronx have some rhythm, no?" Hector's father observed.

"And not just the Puerto Ricanos," Hector's mother said. "The Jewish people, too. Now, Columbus, he knew a few Jews in his day, no?"

My mother had never heard such nonsense in her life. Her eyes bulged open to show a suspension of belief. She was offered a piece of fried banana, which she declined.

"My people don't go in for shellfish," she said. "It says so in the Good Book."

"It's a banana, idiot," my father said. He savored the fried sweetness like he did all gourmet foods, with a smack of his lips. "It's not a goddamn shrimp."

"Willie," she said. "You know me and my ways, I won't eat *traif*, especially if it swims in the sea." She shook her head.

"*Traif*," she said to Hector's mother, "is the Jewish word for unclean food."

"It's washed," Hector insisted.

"More for me, then," Willie said, his mouth full.

A waiter circled the claque, doing his best to offer the crowd the dozen or so glasses of champagne he balanced not so well above his square padded shoulder. He was a year or two older than me; he wore a tight white apron around his tight black pants. Everyone was too busy drinking to drink. He now held the tray with two hands, annoyed. He jerked his head at me. I was taken aback by his hollow eyes; he needed help. No one budged. My mother helped herself to a glass. As did my father. "*Muy bueno,*" Willie said to the waiter, sipping. "*Me gusta la champagnyaaaa. . . .*"

"Come," Hector's mother said to my parents. "Let's go to your table."

My mother brought the cha-cha-cha from the piano player in her walk. My father took her hand. The room erupted in applause at the sight of them, crossing the dance floor. My mother jabbed my father hard in his ribs with her elbow. "Pull in your gut," she said. (Of course, the crowd clapped at every handsome couple who walked across the dance floor.)

I turned around, feeling stalked. It was the waiter. He seemed pulled toward the music just as Willie and Linda had. I stopped. I wanted to watch my brother from afar; Stan called up an effortless step-ball-chain, step-ball-chain of the wrists. The waiter hesitated also; he offered champagne to another waiter, who shook his head, irritated. I walked a few steps to the slick wooden dance floor. There was Judy, sitting at the table with Hector and Dottie. Her cleavage stood out firm in her padded bra. I turned toward the waiter. There he was again.

"*Te gusta la música?*" he asked me, looking aloof, his shaking lip betraying him. A stick-thin, near-death woman in a black dress took one sip from the glass of champagne he had served her and put it back on the waiter's tray.

"*Porqué no?*"

I saw Hector catch the dialogue from the corner of his eyes.

He kissed Dottie lightly on the cheek. He whispered. He pointed to the men's room, like he had to go real bad, or he'd explode right then and there and ruin the most important day in Elena's life. He'd be right back.

"*Hablas muy bien el español,*" the waiter said. "*Con un accento y todo? Como? Tienes un buen maestro?*"

"*Si. Tengo mucha suerte.*"

I helped myself to another of the waiter's champagnes.

By now, Hector stood a foot from my face. "If you're so fuckin' thirsty," Hector said, "why don't you fuckin' sit down at the table where you'll get served like a fuckin' person."

I felt tipsy from the champagne; the interchange went to my head. I winked at the waiter. "Thanks, man."

"Sure."

Blood raced to Hector's neck. Veins pulsed. He brooded— no, raged—a sight I had seen only in the basketball courts when a ball circled around and then in the hoop but then, by some act of neglectful providence, bounced out, losing him the game. He took his right palm and smacked the side of my head with it.

The waiter stepped back. "Whew," he said. "Take it easy, *hombre*. We was just talking."

"Yeah," I said.

"Get the fuck over there, Mr. Wise-Fucking-Ass," Hector said, gesturing to our table with his head—one quick neck-cracking jolt.

I turned to the waiter; there was a sudden look of apprehension in the young man's dark eyes. I walked to our china-laden table, where I saw Judy sitting, her back up straight and scholarly. Hector tailgated me, pushing. I had the impression that I'd never see the waiter again. That made me want to give it to Hector and call him a kiss-ass, two-timing, pushy-as-all-hell creep. But once seated, Hector smiled—forced and triumphant. He nodded to the guests at the table. Conversations stopped. It was not possible to ignore Hector, especially if he had been gone for a moment. Very well, then: We were under his guidance for the evening.

Hector turned to Dottie and blew in her ear until an army of goose bumps marched up her bare neck. Dottie shivered. That Hector! She blinked at Judy and me, as if trying to get her mind on something.

"Isn't Hector's sister absolutely, positively beautiful?" Dottie asked. "*Qué linda!*"

Judy put her hand over mine. Both of us felt anticipation about our debut; we had spent a half hour on the phone this morning discussing strategy.

"Tell us about the wedding," Judy said.

I couldn't pay attention. Hector was pouting. I felt myself to be sulking with him, a funny sensation considering what a good mood I was otherwise in. I felt very either/or. Either it was time to kill each other and call it (whatever "it" was) quits *or* call off the masquerade (whatever "masquerade" it was).

Hector snorted, like he got the conundrum.

"You got it?" I asked.

"Boy, do I got it."

"Not much gets by you."

"Not much."

During times we appeared together in public, a subtle-but-convincing field hummed in the air, as if a higher force had programmed our brains to know of each other's thoughts. Often the hum could be passed off as nothing more than intuition. Sometimes, though, the "buzz" signified much more, like a horrifying but invisible alien living alongside you.

About six months ago, for example, Hector and I bumped into each other at the Jerome Avenue Bowling Alley—he with his rowdy contingent, I with mine. We nodded and turned away to our groups, leading them as far away from each other as you could get in the dilapidated ten-lane joint. The place smelled of junkies, old men escaping their wives, and Alberto VO5 hair spray. Bowling was the one sport in the Bronx you could get away with playing even if you didn't know how to play. I was as lousy as they come. But I'm telling you, that night, I never bowled better. Greg Weinstein, a bulky, starting-to-bald member of the

high-school bowling team, nearly instigated a riot when it appeared I would beat him. But he was wrong to assume I was
competing against him. I was playing against Hector.

I could follow Hector's game, pin for pin, even though I
couldn't see him, couldn't see his scorecard or his silly green and
red shoes. Don't ask me how I followed his strikes and spares. I
just knew it when he hit ten pins, nine — clunk! clunk! He was
scoring that tonight — that's for sure. So was I.

"Man, are you on fucking steroids or something?" Greg
Weinstein asked.

Soon I saw Hector's skinny form bopping in his pseudo-placid
way to our lane.

"*Yo!*" he said to my friends.

Greg Weinstein ignored him.

Hector called me over to the soda machine. I bought us each
a Fanta.

"One of us has got to give in," he said. "The guys are looking
at me like I've seen the Holy Ghost or something. Fuck, I never
win."

I decided to lose. And for a time, life returned to normal.

Tonight the hum was back.

I had crossed a line a few moments before with the waiter
that had not been crossed before, and on his sister's wedding day!
I had flirted with another guy, a guy who, like *Boom!* saw something in my eyes, picked it out like radar as Hector had done. I
kicked Hector under the table. He scowled. Oh, shit. Hector
brushed away pissy moods like most people do away with a mos-
quito; he smacked it down with basketball or kissing or TV or a
Sidney Sheldon best-seller. I could count on my fingers the times
I recall him being "down" or, as he put it, *decaído*. "Hey, c'mon,"
I said, trying to get him to snap out of it. "Let's dance with the
girls."

"To this shit?" He was referring to the Jewish-styled Xavier
Cugat that the band was playing.

"Ah, why not?" I said. "It's music."

"I wouldn't be caught dead dancing to this *viejo* crap."

I looked up and saw my parents dancing waltzlike next to a few middle-aged couples.

I took Judy's hand and led her to the dance floor.

"*Mijo,*" he said, grabbing me by my free hand. "Do you know what you're doing?"

"Of course I do," I said. "Judy and I have been rehearsing for weeks."

"You've been what?" He broke into cackles. "Nah, don't tell me."

But his concern was too late. I pushed off of him.

In a moment, nearly two hundred people "oohed" and "aahed" at the sight of the jittery, pale teenage kids on the dance floor. The band started up an old-fashioned love lament, "*Oh Mi Amor.*"

The drum kit picked up tempo, and I took Judy in my thin nervous arms. I put my hand on her right hip and felt the fleshy softness of her body, contoured and intelligent to touch: quite sexy, if you ask me. She let me lead, even though, when it came to counting steps, she was the math whiz. Even now she whispered, "And-a-one, and-a-two," and then later, "Here's the turn around," and always in the middle, "Pay attention to the bridge — it's coming up." In class, I had been surprised to see her snap her fingers to the discreet congas she heard behind the singer's voice on the recording. When the time came for the conga solo to blast from the classroom's boom box, Judy's body flowed into some primal undulation, one that predated her addictions to calculus and feminism. The teacher clapped; she jumped. Oh, yes. "*Dance!*" she cried. "*¡Qué bailen los Judíos!*"

Our anorexic Latina teacher favored Judy and me because we were the only students she had had in years who weren't on Social Security. Not only that, we didn't have any preconceived steps in mind. Literally, we were putty in her hands. Señorita Angelita taught us over and over again her cardinal rules until we memorized them. She insisted: Let your partner go every now and then and just move. She admonished: Use your partner's arm like an invisible extension of your own body. She implored: Shake your hips during the approach and shake them again during the retreat. She implored: Enjoy, enjoy!

Señorita Angelita taught us well.

I never dug Judy so much as when she danced with me, for it was then that she smiled full throttle and forgave me my friendship with Hector. She seemed then not so much plump as vivacious; not so much judgmental as discerning; not so much lonely as openhearted. For that brief moment I saw her not in context of Hector and the Bronx (which is the only way she made sense to me), but just as herself. (To be fair to her, I hardly ever thought of Hector out of context to her.) For five short minutes that night, during Elena's wedding, we forgot the off-key ra-cha-cha of the singer. We forgot my mother and father dancing beside us, who, I knew, wondered if I ought to marry Judy or wait for something better (and less smart-mouthed) to come along. We forgot that these dances went out of fashion years ago.

We stepped to the right side — one, two, three — then the left — one, two, three; the horns blared. I dipped her backward slightly; the drummers drove their sticks into oblivion. I moved a hand to the right above her head and turned Judy like a doll; the crowd applauded. I took both her hands in mine, and we just shook a little to the left, then the right; the band played the bridge. *"O mi amor ... Te voy a enseñar a amarme ..."*

I saw Hector jump from his seat just as the alto whined. He held Dottie's reluctant hand.

Next thing, crowds of teenagers were crowding the dance floor. Judy and I laughed. The funny thing is, they danced the same way the old Latino people did: hands held, men leading, a Latin dip and dive to the hips and shoulders — except that the tempo was more "up." And the band, sensing the changing pulse and meter, segued from a ballad to pop, a sagging version of "Black Magic Woman," Yamaha keyboards and all.

"Man, I couldn't let you go on with that old island waltz shit," Hector said. "As your friend, I just couldn't."

It didn't matter to Judy and me. We felt glued to our spot, wiping a certain self-effacing embarrassment from our eyes with a downward glare. The electric guitar sizzled into its rubber band

of scales, forward and back to one sharp, one flat. The song went
into our backs, softening those curvatures. We dared not abandon
the lessons from our six-week Hispanic Ballroom Dance Class
even though Hector and his cohorts fused the semaphores of the
street with the gymnastics of rock 'n' roll. Their dancing synthesis
verged on calypso. I felt Hector grind his back against mine just
as I imagined him grinding his front into Dottie's.

I saw my brother emerge from the background to command
his solo. He let himself go. The keyboard man played simple
changes: D minor, G major, D minor. *"Mira!"* Elena called. The
wedding party had begun. Into a hysteria of percussive batteries
against all odds: Hector, Mikey, Judy, Dottie. From far away, I
saw that my brother had small, wild hands. I forgot he was my
brother because he had forgotten: his lips told the story, a lead-
in to the maddening rhythm that kept the real and only time in
his soul. I watched. I saw my mother and father disengage from
the dancing collective to stand to the side to watch him, too. I
saw my father grope for a chair, as if he had suddenly been over-
taken by cognitive dissonance: his son, not his son, the drummer
of these times. Too much. My mother stood still, her arms
crossed. I twirled Judy two or three times. Mascara dripped
down her face.

Dottie laughed, throwing her head to the side. Hector forgave
me, but only if I remained tuned in, eyes on his virtuosic hip
grinding, ready to catch his sweat should it have the nerve to fall
from his body. What a possessive muthafucka. The horns cried
out for mercy. "Who's that cat?" one of Elena's friends asked my
father, referring to Stan. Willie shrugged: "Who knows?"

We stopping dancing when the salmon dinner was served
along with side dishes of rice, yucca and plantains. The bride and
groom alone remained in the oval; drunken toasts were made to
them through the static-filled mike. My brother sat at my parents'
table. It seemed to annoy my mother that he did this as a favor
to her.

"So where's your girl? I thought she would be here."

"She didn't know nobody."

"She knew you."

"You see any black people here?"

"You know, I didn't give it a thought. But you're right, there are no *schvartzes* at this affair."

They picked at their flan. My mother took a forkful into her mouth, and then, as daintily as possible, retired the wet clump in her linen napkin. "Don't these people know from rugelach?"

"I'm going to invite Helen over," Stan said. "That cool by you?"

My mother nodded, affecting her Art Carney attitude. "Cool, man, cool."

"Is Friday good? Is that a good Friday?"

My mother: "What could be bad about Good Friday?"

The party continued. Feelings were hurt when Elena's old uncle, resurrecting business gripes, cursed Elena's father. Feelings were mended with gifts. The Kaplans gave theirs. Elena and Carlos left for a honeymoon in Atlantic City or Acapulco or both. Hector and I ate two helpings of yellow cake and drank bitter espresso, knowing we'd never sleep till dawn. My father made a fool of himself speaking bad Spanish to everyone, even the Jews.

But that's not really how it ended, is it?

Don't ask me to explain what happened after the last frenzied dance (before the band played "The Party's Over"). All I know is that suddenly, in the midst of *Oye Como Va*," all proceedings stopped: the music, the dancing, the drinking, the toasts. The habitués of The Latin Star simply froze — suspended animation or a bad "Twilight Zone" episode. I braced myself for Rod Serling. Or a black-magic woman.

A dark shadow rose from the dance floor. A pair of drumsticks knocked up against the rim of a bass drum. *Konk. Konk.* No one played. What was in the waiter's champagne? Hector, frozen stiff, seemed plugged in, too. "Man," he said. "You been smoking coke, or what?" I saw my grandmother, back from the dead. There was Frieda, wearing her one fancy dress, a blue cotton housedress deal. She walked to Stan and grabbed a speck of dust from the back of his ear. She sauntered to where my parents slumped and inserted the morsel she stole from Stan in the back of their ears.

That was the best she could do. She held out her hands. She tried to speak. English was always a second language to her; now it was a third. What did she have to say that was so pressing that she couldn't wait till our nighttime dreams or eventual deaths? I couldn't tell. She walked over to me to lay a kiss on my forehead. Her eyes revealed the sign of what I thought of as the Devil's handiwork. I spat three times, as she had taught me to do, and gave her a *keyna horra* and a "poo, poo, poo" (Jewish for: "you may be stronger and more magical than me, O Demon Spirit, but here's a little human spit to put you in your place").

She split. The music resumed, everyone no worse for the interruption. My father blinked and, smiling, drew my mother close to him. Their son had played so well. It was a party. A wedding. So why be glum? They sashayed offstage together, giggling into the "wah-wah" of a horn blast and Stan's pow, pow, *kapow*. Hector, however, shivered. We shared a look of apprehension not so different from the one we experienced that one time he came over in the middle of the night and we thought we saw a ghost, then a fire. But what else could we do? It was a party. A wedding. Why be glum? We danced ourselves into a brutal sweat, ruining the dry-clean of our suits.

———

Afterward, the entire family did its best to forget the wedding. We detected a funny aftertaste after the wedding cake and subsequent antacids. My mother's only extended commentary: "The *goyim* sure know how to throw a party. What was in that lemon spritzer is all I'd like to know." So we moved on. We threw ourselves into Stan's dinner.

Problem: my mother was a terrible cook; her rule of thumb was quantity, not quality. My father was the one with the creative touch. He'd fry bacon on Sunday mornings when my mother went window-shopping on Fifth Avenue with her on-a-budget girlfriends. He'd serve the crispy Christian sacraments to us on narrow strips of waxed paper and afterward spray the kitchen with Lemon Pledge. He'd plop bacon bits secretly on iceberg salad. He diced cloves of garlic in store-bought Italian salad dressing. He'd fold chunks of McIntosh apples and slices of overripe bananas into pancakes. He'd mix chives up in Philadelphia cream cheese when we had bagels. My mother considered him a regular pest in "her" kitchen, and blamed her mini-ulcer on the times he fried fish instead of baking it to death as she did or the instances he steamed fresh snow peas to a delicate crispness, instead of boiling canned peas into the consistency of mud-green pudding.

But, on this one occasion, she ceded control over the kingdom of Teflon and Pyrex, her minions of Minute Rice and powdered garlic. In a rare act of partnership, they planned the dinner menu together. My father drove all the way to White Plains Road to buy fresh Romano and Parmesan cheese, which he proceeded to grate with the knife that he used to skin fresh fish. He spent his own money on cashews and peanut brittle, fattening food my mother prohibited. The last of his dollars he spent on roses and lilacs, which my mother saw as throwing good money down the toilet.

"Trust me, dearie," he said. "*Most* ladies like flowers."

"Most *ladies* don't *finagle* with the budget I do."

"For once, live a little."

"When we move to Long Island, then I'll live a little."

"It's Stan, for chrissake," my father said. "You want to drive him away for good?"

For once, my mother listened to Willie. She paid attention to his admonitions "not to bake another dried-to-smithereens chicken with burnt potatoes," and was convinced into buying chicken cutlets instead. He taught her how to pound them to make them tender. He pointed out places in the cookbook where it gave suggestions about steaming—not boiling—broccoli. He used the green water beneath the steamer for soup stock. He rolled slices of chicken in flour and then sautéed them quickly in olive oil. Exhorting my mother to buy "romaine," not "iceberg," he showed her how to make Caesar salad with anchovies.

"A raw egg in lettuce?" she complained. "I wouldn't eat such poison if you paid me."

But she did admit that the kitchen smelled marvelous. Delegated to setting the table, my mother was about to throw dried parsley on the salad. My father screamed. He had bought four varieties of fresh herbs for the salad, peppermint-smelling green leaves he had read about in M.F.K. Fisher's *The Art of Eating*.

Stan, enchanted by the fragrance, wrote down the name of his favorite: *basil*.

When my father wasn't looking, my mother picked the "basil schmasil" out from the salad. In its place, she poured dry oregano from the A&P.

I had been impressed by the lack of formality my mother and father placed over this dinner, even with all the preparations that consumed them. Relatives as far west as Oakland heard that Helen was making her Kaplan debut. My mother phoned each like a politician, warning them not to dare drop by, promising them something pork barrel in return. "She's not a Jewish girl," was all she could manage by way of an explanation. "If there's another dinner, or God forbid a *shiddoch*, you'll be the first to know. No . . . I haven't met the *makhateyneste*" (in-laws). To fill in the static on the line, my mother added: "Stan, as you and I well know, needs someone." My parents knew the dinner was a test for them more than it was for Helen. They had to pass.

Helen was complex, upper-class, underdog and evasive. Like Stan, her face fronted a mask of shyness; beneath that, reddish eyes blinked from confusion to anger to angry confusion. My mother decided to fight her own hard-bitten impulses and paint a smile on her lipsticked lips. That was a mistake. The minute my mother opened the door, smiling like a saleslady from B. Altman, I saw what Helen needed: a no-nonsense mirror, for she was indeed more like my mother than my mother could know. That is why Stan worshiped the ground she walked on.

Helen handed my mother roses.

"You shouldn't have wasted money on these," my mother said.

"I'm not poor, Mrs. Kaplan."

"Even the rich shouldn't waste their pennies."

"I suppose you have a point, Mrs. Kaplan."

"Call me Linda."

The five of us stood by the front-door threshold.

"Come in," my mother said. But Linda didn't move a foot to the right or left to let her guest in.

I gripped my mother by her tense arm, and guided her a few steps to the side, so Helen could pass. The foyer was our family museum, filled with diplomas, trophies, graduation pictures — never mind a dozen framed photos of Frieda's children and grandchildren getting married over the last thirty years. My mother shivered at the gallery of white daughters and white daughters-in-law in white bridal wear.

My father emerged from the steaming kitchen, animated from his three afternoon beers. "What a pretty colored girl," he murmured to himself.

Helen laughed.

"What's so funny?" my father asked, laughing a bit, too.

Helen covered her mouth and shook her head.

Everyone knows it's a mistake to invite musicians to the house for dinner talk. We would have been better off had we asked Stan and Helen to play us some jazz. But that was not the Kaplan way of doing things. One ate; one talked; one bragged; one argued; one had gas. My mother's vision of a good wife suggested a woman who would stand by her man and in weak moments, which grew more numerous the more the marriage progressed, boss him into efficiency. My brother chose a cranky soulmate.

"One Stan in the world is enough," my mother whispered to me as she threw the roses in a jug of water.

As we sat down to dinner, I saw Helen regard the place settings: two gallon bottles of Pepsi (one diet, one regular), fluorescent-green paper napkins (left over from the going-away party my mother threw for her Irish ex-boss), plastic flowers (my mother compromised in that fight with my father), chipped Passover china (on which faded painted matzos could still be seen); and coffee mugs (on which each person's name was emblazoned, including Helen's). Helen wore blue flannel slacks and a black silk shirt. Her face was oval, like Stan's, but softer, as if she had been taught how to apply expensive face creams. More than her skin color, it was her class I deemed confrontational. Over her blouse, she wore a ridiculous necklace of pearls. My mother touched them without permission.

"Are they real?"

"Mrs. Kaplan?"

Like many Bronx family women, my mother liked the fact that she had no class, especially if it got in the way of her more-pressing need for direct and constant human connection. What class she had, she wore on her blue collars with pride. You want to take on a union woman, one who became a delegate to the United Federation of Teachers and rode a city bus to work? I don't think so. My mother scurried to her room and returned with her own string of pearls.

"See?" she said, placing the necklace on Helen's dinner plate. "Eleven ninety-nine."

"Linda!" my father admonished. "Not on the dinner plate." He handed Helen a clean dish.

"I'll have to pick up that necklace," Helen said, picking at her Caesar salad.

"Macy's bargain basement," my mother said. "Not a pearl left. But you can have these."

"Mrs. Kaplan. I already have mine."

"So, you'll have two."

Helen took the necklace from the plate; the shadow of suspicion lifted from her face and half-closed eyes. She set the fake pearls by her eyeglass case. My mother wanted a smile of affiliation, and she got it. Stan said nothing. He ate his food as if it were the last home-cooked meal he'd ever stuff down.

Afterward, there were glorious attempts at conversation — mostly my mother's. There was the story of Stan's first drum lesson: "The drum teacher said he was better than Buddy Hackett," to which Stan barked, "You mean Buddy Rich." She regaled Helen with the time Span spent a whole year cutting class. "You know what he was doing? I'll tell you. He was going to the public library to listen to records. Tchaikovsky. Beethoven. What's-his-name? — Mozart. Can you believe?" Stan grunted and looked away. Helen rubbed his hand and laughed. My mother spoke of her black boss: "One snazzy lady. She runs that school like you wouldn't believe, and believe you me, it's hard for a black gal to get up in the world these days." Stan snorted some snot in his nose. Helen touched his hairy forearm and nodded. My mother expressed eagerness for grandchildren, "Your life is empty without them," and then caught herself: "But some people's lives are meant to be empty." Stan rolled his eyes. Helen collected a piece of chicken that dropped from Stan's plate. She wrapped it up tidily in a napkin.

My mother rattled on about her husband the cook; "*Oy*, you should see the way he puts the herbs here, the vegetables here. Sometimes I wonder if he's not the wife and I'm not the husband." And she revealed a secret part of herself: "I want better for myself, but I don't know what to do to get it. So I just hope my boys succeed in a way I never did." There was the icing on the cake: "Marriage isn't for everyone. Sometimes it's better to make sure you're making the right choice, see other people, shop around, if you know what I mean, before you get yourself mixed up in something you might regret."

I coughed. "Did you know that Helen is an English major at Barnard?"

"You don't say?" my father said. "Who's your favorite author?"

"What are you going to do with an English major?" my mother interrupted. "Teach?"

"No, actually. I intend to be a percussionist. Like Stan. My parents would rather I teach."

My mother smiled. "Can you blame them?"

Helen smiled back. She saw it: no harm intended. She let out a giggle.

"What's so funny?"

Their eyes met and they nodded a private nod, a prayer, of sorts. Still, it was not safe. Helen scratched her head, fought yawns, complimented the meal. My mother chatted, scratched her head, and glanced at Stan.

"Does it trouble you that I am black?" Helen asked.

The room grew still; my father burped. Stan grinned. My

mother was in her element now: debate, ethnic torture, opinions, fears.

"Yes," Linda said. Her little-girl voice mitigated the pain of the truth. "But you seem to love Stan very much. For that, God willing, I am grateful."

Stan fidgeted.

"Will you get used to us?" Helen asked.

"In time—I believe."

Stan pushed his plate aside. "Right," he said.

"Stannie-boy," Helen hissed.

I couldn't tell what shocked my mother more: Stan's outburst or Helen's use of the Stan diminutive—the same as my mother's.

"You've always hated blacks—"

"What the hell!—" my father barked.

"Stan!"

"I think you've hated a lot of things."

"We made a nice meal for you."

"Stan!"

"It's okay now. The dessert—"

"Stan!"

A plate fell to the floor. A can of soda got knocked over. A fork dropped on a crystal cream pitcher, shattering its lip.

"C'mon, Helen, we're not welcome here."

"Stan!"

"I should have never dragged you into this mess. Assholes—"

"Who?"

"The pound cake. Fresh from . . . Stan!"

Helen and my mother stood next to Stan.

"Stan, get a—"

"Stan, we're—"

The women kept my father and Stan separated and cornered by my body. Together they understood.

"Stan, it's okay. The food was wonderful, Mrs. Kaplan."

"Don't 'Stan' me. Don't you ever again 'Stan' me, you goddamn bitch!"

We froze. Stan went for the door, stalking. He repeated the offending words over and over again. Helen grabbed her raincoat and straw hat, still damp from the Bronx rain. She looked at my mother, stunned. Indecision. Pausing, she thought better of her vow to Stan. We saw her stop.

From the corridor, I heard the elevator door open and then close with Stan inside it.

"Oh, my . . . "

"Go," my mother said. "Follow him."

My mother handed Helen the pearls. Helen took them, shoved them in her pants pocket, fumbled and then made her way, as if to Stan. One heard trains in the distance. Helen hesitated with all this knowledge, still in herself, but looking now outward, toward my mother and father, in an expanse of confusion, her mouth open, all so wide now.

"Go to him, Helen," my mother screamed. *"Now!"*

And with that Helen fled—out of the living room, then out of the foyer, to the front door, ajar. Out of the house.

———

My father turned to my mother.

"He's not my son."

"Willie."

They would have fought, but my mother's gallbladder acted up. My father made the Alka-Seltzer. The clear glass fizzled in her two hands. They shook. She retired to the living-room couch. She drank half; belched. She lay down, desperate for sleep. I held her tiny hand.

"You okay, mom?"

"I'm fine," she said. Then she made a brushing-away motion with her wrist that said: *I'm fine, but leave me alone. I'm out.* In a second, she called me back. I helped her rise from the couch. "I'm fine," she repeated. I walked her to the bathroom. I heard her retch.

My father knocked lightly on the bathroom door: "You okay, Linda?"

In a moment, she emerged, her face drenched in sweat, less pale, holding an empty bottle of Listerine, murmuring, "I'm fine. Just fine."

We watched an episode of *The Jeffersons*. My father reclined
in his La-Z-Boy. My mother curled up in a ball on the couch,
the only light from the TV. They dozed together to the sounds
of a family showing its love through quarrels.

Two hours later, my mother got up from the couch to tackle
the dishes. But after scouring one bowl, she turned off the water.
She stood at the sink, both hands on the faucets, steadying. She
burped up. "Basil-schmasil," she said. A breath or two. Then
moving around, dully. She found a pack of Salems she smoked
on occasion, and leaned on the living-room windowsill; it looked
out onto the Bronx projects below us. The sill had faced Frieda's
apartment when she was alive. My mother never lingered there
for fear her mother would pester her, waving, wanting: *I could use
some milk, company, nu?* Since Frieda died, the ledge had become
a place to sit, to think.

Linda sat immobile. At one point, my father approached shyly
and whispered in her ear. She never budged.

Stan returned home — at midnight. My mother didn't turn to
see him. "Hello, dear," she said. He retreated into the bedroom.
He threw himself into his bed. I said Helen was pretty. Stan
smiled, knowing I was half-lying. My father entered the room.
No knocking.

"Your mother's upset."

"Yeah, yeah. I know all about it."

"You selfish sonafa—" my father said, his voice thick with
drink.

"Take it out on me, old man. C'mon—"

I leaped up. My father swung his fist right in Stan's face.

In our family, there had been rare instances of violence. Stan
beat me up daily when I turned eleven. I fought back; we called
a truce. The one time my father tried to strike my mother, he was
so drunk he missed her and broke a bone on his fist from contact
with the concrete wall.

Carrying congas made Stan's arms thick with fat and muscle.
A right to my father's jaw.

My father had taught him. Although he was weaker, he was
smarter. Jabs to Stan's stomach: one, two, three. Stan gulps air

and then pushes. Willie almost falls to the floor. He grabs Stan's shoulders and shakes.

Me screaming: "Hey, cut it out!"

"Ya little goddamn creep."

"Old man."

I tried to pull them apart. A jab at my rib—winded. Just then, my mother, sobbing with choked cries, appeared.

"You are killing me!" she cried.

Stan and my father stopped. Blood trailed down the left side of my father's face. Stan's right hand looked bruised.

My mother looked at them. She covered her face in her hands. She hit her head. She pulled her hair.

I came over to her and held her, her hands. She was shaking like a little girl, coughing up. "I hate it," she cried quietly. And then a guttural caterwauling: "I hate myself." The mantra went on. My father walked to her, but she shook her head: no. We stood there, and waited for the Dark Angel to pass.

I walked Linda to the bathroom; she said she had to go. She asked to be left alone. I wouldn't leave her. My father stood by, helpless, his face scratched. My mother wet a washcloth in a daze, handing it to me, me handing it to him. I closed the door on him. My mother pulled down her panties. She peed. *Psssshhhh!* She sat there when it was over. Twice she reverted—a muffled wailing, pulling her hair. I stopped her; a touch to the back. Hold it in, but let it go. "Valium," she said. "In the stocking drawer." I left her. I found the bottle and doled out three. Two for her, one for me. My father: a shadow there, lurking. A clue? None, dad. I entered the bathroom. I closed the door. I had the water. She drank some and took the pills.

When she looked sleepy or past the business, I escorted her to her bedroom. "Sleep," she said. I opened the window to hear the storm. "Rain," she said. She was out. My father was pacing in the kitchen. I walked over to him and waved. He didn't see me.

My own bedroom was dark. Stan snored. I thought to wake him up and talk. I meant to do so. But in a moment, I was asleep.

I awoke. Three A.M. flashing on the new clock radio. Still in my clothes, parched. I knew it. Sheets and smells, but that's all. There was a note on the empty bed: "I can't live in this family. I'm gone." Then a separate note to me: "Mikey, you're okay. Don't let anyone tell you otherwise."

I tore the notes up in a hundred pieces.

———

Graduation came and went. That summer Hector's parents planned a trip to Puerto Rico and invited him to come along.

"I'm going to stay in the Bronx," he announced.

They left on a Friday afternoon. Hector invited me over the following Saturday night. "For dinner and entertainment," he said. I tried calling that afternoon, but he was so busy cleaning the house and buying candles and groceries, he couldn't talk.

"Get out of this house," my mother said, when she heard I'd sleep over Hector's. "I wish *I* could."

She picked out a black cotton shirt for me, and a pair of freshly washed blue jeans.

"Are you fellows going to meet some pretty girls?" she asked.

I nodded, but she wasn't paying attention.

"Mikey. You were always the one I knew would come through."

She hugged me.

I pried away from the embrace and made way for Hector's.

The streets were crowded with people doing their best to escape the thick heat indoors. I was now an only child. I saw Mr. McPhee and Mr. Candelario playing cards together on a wooden card table. "How's the Jewish mambo king?" Mr. Candelario called out. Mr. McPhee added, "He's going to make it, huh?" I walked away, needing Hector in a way that made my voice hoarse with shame.

———

Hector rearranged his parents' house. He made the living room into a bordello. Red curtains and black drapes covering the vinyl furniture, TV and sewing machine. A dozen votive candles burned. They were spaced equidistant from each other on the wooden floor. The place was immaculate, scented with Mr. Clean, incense, and island cooking.

Hector played a Patti Smith album. On the kitchen table lay a florid-looking meal of *plátanos*, chicken, reddish rice and red wine.

"You up for food?" he asked, like he was on a blind date.

He walked me into the bathroom, where the tub had been filled. He soaked me with a mammalian red sponge he said his mother used. "Just lay back and enjoy the Hollywood treatment," he said. He drenched my head in warm water, and then patted my cheeks. He sponged my back and armpits.

"All the basketball playing has paid off," he said. "Nice *Sports Illustrated* lats." He dried me off, hesitating longer by my crotch area. He laughed in his cornball way: "Hee-hee-hee." He escorted me into the bedroom. He lay me down onto the bed, front up, like he said they do in massage parlors.

His lips made an impatient trail down my body. When he got to my stomach, he turned me over and kissed each cheek. I felt a finger by my opening and gripped, but he eased my worries by placing his tongue there. I had never felt the sensation before and understood, in a way, why women liked to be kissed below so much. "You have a hot one," he said, confirming my suspicion about the whole affair.

"Gee, thanks."

"You know, pal-oh-mine, we don't got to go through with this." He looked at me, smirking, just like the old Hector.

"I think it's time, Hector."

We had tried it before, but to no avail. "All those gallbladder balls," Hector used to say, turning over, defeated, on his back. So we gave up. But since Stan left, I found myself craving what it scared me to crave.

Today, it would take about two hours. Really, he was taking me on a trip, using my fear as a road map for a jet plane or a helicopter or a magic carpet or power drill—whatever it was.

He aroused with words. "Look how wet you are," he said. And "You've been dying for the PR dick for months." He slid a finger up slowly, and with each fraction of an inch, he breathed a defamatory remark: "You Jewboys are all cunts." By the time he had three fingers in my ass, he fired off entire sentences, linked to my anatomy through metaphor. "Little fag gets real open . . . I'm going to open you up so much, it's past crying . . . you're going to cry into that big black hole. . . . I'm going to come in your little Jew hole . . . holy shit."

So that is how we lubricated our way into the promise of love. We were speaking over each other's voices, in each other's voices, our bodies so sweaty they seemed glued together by diluting words.

"Suck up my dick like it's love. . . . "

" . . . and I'll love you tonight."

His arms curved, his body over my chest. It hurt, and then the hurt turned into a stinging that made me giggle in between gasps for air. He was slapping, caressing. I could no longer contain the pleasure and the pain, and I grunted, "Hector." Likewise he was saying, "Mickey." I knew how much I wanted to say it, but I was frightened of pushing the pleasure of the moment into a demand. He was less worried. A second before he came inside me, he whispered the secret of love in my ear. I didn't need much prodding. I whispered back the same secret. As he released, in torrents of breath, his whisper turned into a statement. Our orgasm was one big declaration. And as he collapsed on me — in me — he implied with his breath, and his touch, and his eyes, that it was forever no more a secret.

———

I fell asleep — but not for long. Like a drunkard, I found myself waking many times, stunned at the raw sensation inside, awed by the new charge.

Hector was the only man I have ever known who found it impossible to fall asleep, if he were sleeping with another man, if the two bodies weren't touching. Sleeping with Hector was an exercise in how fucking can continue once the fucking is over — the need and obsession to merge, with the power plays still intact, continuing into the oblivion of the night. Hector liked holding me from behind as we slept, whispering unintelligible things in my ear. He liked it when I lay on top of him—it was his favorite way to dream. But since it was a little distracting for me, he made do with the face-to-face method.

That's why it startled me so to sense him gone. In a shift of focus that I thought I understood as a nightmare of abandonment and astonishment, I awoke.

Where was Hector?

The house was dark, no light coming from the bathroom or the refrigerator.

I got out of bed. I knew not to call his name. I chose the bathroom; I had to pee. I had certain fears that I never admitted to myself. I knew Hector could drink; he smoked dope now and then, and sometimes cigarettes. I hadn't spent the entire night with him in a while and worried what I'd find out.

I opened the door to the bathroom.

There he was, sitting like a curled-up animal on the cold black-and-white tile floor—naked and lit by the crescent moon. He held his arms around his body. He shook from the cold. He knew I was there, but didn't look up. I crouched like an insect to embrace him. I felt his body allow the touch, but he didn't return it. I took him by the chin, as my mother would do to me when I was consumed by a fit of rebellion. His eyes began to swim in his head. I let him be.

I went back to bed. I curved myself up in the sheets. In a moment or two, Hector padded in. He got in bed. Then he came to my side and tentatively placed his wiry arms around my body. I let him hold me. I touched his hands, fingering the veins that popped from his webbed fingers.

"Now you know me for who I really am."

I hadn't a clue.

There was some silence. He continued to hold on.

We listened to the sounds of the alarm clock ticking.

"Hector," I asked. "Are you a junkie?"

"Yeah," he said, recovering. "A love junkie."

———

The phone rang in the middle of the night. I bolted out of a dream and ran into the kitchen, reaching for the receiver.

"Meet me downstairs in five."

"Hector."

"Don't ask me no questions."

"Hector."

"Bring a jacket and all the money you can get your hands on. Corner of Jerome and 170th. Be there, *hombre*."

He hung up. I looked at the receiver. My mother and father stood in the dark.

"What's going on?" my mother asked. She sounded meek.

"Hector got locked out of his apartment. He's going to sleep in his car, but he needs some things."

"Tell him he can sleep here."

I gathered my coat, a few photos, five dollars. I asked my mother to lend me twenty. She handed me five twenties.

"Bring him here," she said.

My father shuffled into his slippers: "I'll go with you."

"No!" I grabbed my keys. I gave both a kiss and left. I didn't bother waiting for the elevator, for fear they would think twice and nab me, but ran down the seventeen flights of stairs.

———

I knew where I was going. In the privacy of our most intimate dreams and blasphemous moans, Hector and I had made our plans. True, it was a pact we never solidified for fear of making it profane with stupid-ass promises. But it was a pact all the same. I knew who Hector was. And, if there were any doubt, Frieda, dressed to the hilt in her black gabardines, came back from the dead to tell me. She was calling me: calling me to live the true human life. For too long, though, I dallied. Now it was time.

Hector had changed the definition of love as I understood it. He looked me in the eyes whenever he kissed me. He never let himself come in silence. (Silent orgasms, I believe, are indications of militaristic tendencies in young men.) He was not absorbed with membranes (his own or others'), yet he could approach sex as a masculine endeavor, replete with impromptu slaps, crude verbal exchanges, and fascinations with shoulder and biceps musculature; the more subtle, the more enticing.

Hector taught this: one's differences from another—and one-self—give love its blessing and curse. "You're a fucking alien," he'd say when his mother cooked me a ham for my birthday and I ran to the bathroom to puke. He clung to my nose, as if he were a rock climber, somehow turned on and amused by the Harpo Marx look. He found my confidence around homework enviable and watched the way I wrote an essay, not for words and ideas—he was actually more deep—but for speed and transition. "I like that 'subsequently' word," he commented once, and subsequently used it a little too much. He looked at my instinct toward self-deprecation as both something to envy and to disparage. "Of course you can do it, man," he said when teaching me how to take a deep toke on a joint, and then follow it up with sips of air. "It's just so funny"—sip, sip, sip—"to watch you think you fucking can't." Exhale.

I mimicked him. I scratched my crotch in public, for no particular reason. I stood in the street, with all my weight balanced on one leg. I stopped feeling so clumsy all the time. Hector had heard my father call me "a goddamn klutz" just about once a day. The one time he heard me refer to myself that way, he smacked me on the face and, with a pointed finger, admonished, "Don't you fucking dare." I developed the confidence to treat him similarly when he and I did homework together. "Stoop! If I see you bunch up a piece of paper one more time!" I threatened, removing a balled-up white sheet from the wastepaper basket. I unraveled it. "This is fucking genius," I said. "Hand this in and you'll get an A." I was right, and the bastard never let me live it down.

I began to eat like Hector. He once rifled through my parents' fridge and junked the ice cream, mayonnaise and sour cream my family raised me on. "No disrespect," he'd say. "But that's Totie Fields food." To my parents' horror, I began eating tuna directly from the can. "Let me put some milk and mayo in that," my father implored. "It's murder that way." But I resisted the temptation and lost ten pounds.

"You are getting as thin as me," Hector would say, touching my ribs. "Just watch that Jewish baby fat melt away."

There was the time he spent two weeks drilling me on basketball. We dribbled; spent an entire day executing lay-ups, another shooting hoops. "It's all in the concentration," he said. Never once did he smirk. He did have to smack my hand a couple of times when I dribbled the ball with a flat palm. "Curve your hand, man," he said, "like you're touching my ass." Afterward, I felt more at home on a court, even though I fled the area the moment I saw Hector approach with his old buddies.

It was this essential education — that we were the same apart from the differences in skin color, language and life's expectations — that was the real interstitial tissue that made up the dream for our future. It was an illusion. But being with Hector taught me that love, which is *not* an illusion, cannot exist without the bad breath and bad jokes and bad faith that come when you get into another person. When that person leaves, he takes his bad things with him. And in his place is an emptiness so huge that your soul cries out for its demons like you wouldn't believe.

———

Hector was waiting at the corner of Jerome and 170th. The sun was beginning its climb up toward the east. The sky was dark blue, not black. His back was toward me.

As he turned, I saw that he had been hit — a black eye.

"Hector!"

"My old man was going through my things and he found some junk in my drawer. Old stuff."

I grew stiff. "I thought you said you weren't no junkie."

"I lied."

"You're lying now."

What had really happened? Perhaps his father found a copy of *Playgirl* in his drawer and humiliated him in front of the whole family. Perhaps Hector got accepted to an expensive college — he was on the waiting list — and worried he couldn't pay for it. Perhaps he saw that his affair with Dottie and mine with Judy corrupted our future more than either of us suspected. Did he see that life was ending for us here in the Bronx?

"Hector." I touched him — brushing his neck with my dry morning lips.

"Shit, man. Someone could see."

I thought I saw him cry a little.

"What a pussy!"

"Hector. . . . don't!"

He looked up at the sky. He had a mission in mind, a secret he even didn't get.

"You can stay at my house," I said.

I was afraid his father would cruise by in the sedan and lynch us. From outside a window not far from us, I heard Billie Holiday sing, "Good Morning, Heartache."

"Are you coming home or what?"

"I can't stay at your place forever, Mike."

"True."

This was the Hector I first met, feet planted in the concrete, head swimming in the smog above the tenements like pigeons, soul ready to jet. He spoke. But just then a train rumbled by over the elevated train tracks. I couldn't hear what he said, and Hector was not one to repeat himself. I imagined I heard "Amtrak" and "Grand Central."

The Bronx grew quiet again. And with that, we stood still for a moment. The sun rose. I knew where Hector was pushing me, and I saw that he knew I knew.

I saw in Frieda's crystal ball the convincing proof. Years later, there we'd be: waking up in an Albuquerque hotel. I'll never forget how Hector might have looked in those dirty cotton sheets, bare arms and neck encased in a white comforter, hair splashed over the two white pillows. His twenties have been good to him. Indecision and boasting replaced by greater sensuality and a businessman's eyes. He appears so pliant and billowy, yet boyishly hard underneath the yawns—the way men look in movies after they've fucked the female lead. "G'morning, Mike," he says, making a kissing motion with his lips from afar, too sleepy to move his face to mine. I feel glad for the drawn-out morning weariness, for the way it throws into relief the gestures of love men can make for each other on the sly. *It's all here,* the gesture says: restraint and love—as much as you can summon up, as much as you can dare ask for. Equal parts suffering and bliss. The lips say with proud declaration: *These are the sacred lips of the Bronx.*

There is another vision: years afterward. A bungalow in another part of the Southwest. Los Angeles? His foibles have grown on me. The farts at night, the crankiness in the morning, the sullenness he develops around meals, his need to get high or drunk at least once a week, the fascination with books that out-reaches my own. All this destroys the image of perfection I mounted around him during the nights we had slept apart as teenagers. I see now that I could live with him for another ten years. He's sitting in the living room, reading *TV Guide.* He throws the book to the floor and dozes off, but not before dangling his arm from the bed, snapping his fingers, demanding that I hold his pinkie until the first crumb of a snore drops from his body.

The vision retreats. I shake my head. Now it's just us and the elevated train tracks a block away.

"Okay," I say. "Let's go. Let's get the fuck outta here."

———

I walked a little with Hector. Toward the subway—saying little. I wished we were already on the subway; I worried that one of my aunts would see me out so early and question me. I had never felt glamorous before. Now to live with another guy. To make a decision to leave everything behind. To kiss. To roll up marijuana cigarettes. To put my own body in his body and then talk about it afterward. To say to the world: this is what I do.

The closer we got to the elevated train tracks, the more the contract revealed itself. I felt the brass ring of the merry-go-round—and the nausea. It was Hector's hand I was touching. In a moment he was riffing in Spanish: *He's nervous, but he's coming. I'm so fucking fucked up. How fast can you get us to Greyhound?* I muttered. "I brought my poems and a hundred dollars?" and "Do you know anyone in Albuquerque besides your sister?" But it made no sense. I wanted answers, but I also knew how precarious it was to talk before coffee.

Hector was smiling nervously. A train was coming. By the rumble, I could tell it was a few blocks away.

"Let's run," I said.

Grabbing our bags, we climbed the two hundred stairs, taking two or three at a time.

We heard the train doors screech open.

"Fuck, wait for us!" Hector yelled, out of breath.

The train did — miraculously.

Hector rushed to the car door, winded. He fell onto a seat, catching his breath. Laughing! He was ahead of me. Seeing the inside of the car — empty — stirred a sensation in my calves. A pulled muscle? A cramping? Giggling, he got up and made way to push me in.

"I need a minute," I said.

Hector glanced at the conductor and said something in Spanish. The man said, *"Claro que sí,"* but of course. Hector stood in the doorway. He'd keep the doors from shimmying closed forever, if he had to.

"You okay?" Hector asked.

I began to stand up. The throbbing left.

"Better."

"Cool. Let's go."

"I need a minute," I said again.

The color left Hector's face. He bit his lip: "Ooh, it's like that." He looked at his Timex watch, which I had given him for his eighteenth birthday last month.

"Okay. One minute."

I stood on the platform. Hector stood in the doorway of the subway car, staring at the face on his watch, bracing his arms against the rubber flap of the doors. I swayed in place, not able to think, desperate to think. I wanted Hector to hold me and think this through with me.

"Minute's up, man."

I said nothing.

Then, with a quick wave of his hand, he gave a signal to the conductor. He ducked into the subway car and, clutching the silver bar, swung himself down into a seat. The doors slid closed. They jiggled open, briefly, then not so briefly, and jiggled shut again. The train began to move, chug off. I tried to look at Hector, to see something, a sign: a good-bye, a gesture about what was to come. Nothing. He sat in the car, looking at the dried Dentyne on the floor, skinnier than I had ever seen him. He sat alone in that graffiti-speckled car.

The train began to buckle and shove, beginning its hour-long or so ride downtown, stop by local stop, to Grand Central Station. With a jolt, it picked up speed quickly. Then the train left the 170th Street station.

I stood alone on the platform, watching the train grow smaller and smaller, until it retreated from sight for good.

All That

Jazz

———

ahar tosses off the covers. Flapping, the sheets make a sound, mini-thunder. The wrought-iron headboard knocks against the wall, shaking the chrome, pre-AIDS photo of Mark Ruffino hung above Tahar's bed. Tahar glances at the black-and-white image of his dead lover. He shakes his head.

Tahar goes for the red silk bathrobe lying at the foot of his bed. With the silk slipped on, he's transformed, back to some Kansas City time and place, where Mark was from; they traveled to Mark's ancestral home twice a year. I recognize the blankly fearful Midwest look, like the robe is magic, a charged-up version of the ruby slippers, taking Tahar back to dismal suburbia and tract homes. Mark wore the wrap during hospital stays. He'd murmur, "I wanna go home, I wanna go home." Now the contrast of the scarlet red in Tahar's stark white bedroom hits me. Stop. A house is going to fall on one of us.

"You okay?" I ask.

"I'm trying to take this in."

I sit up in Tahar's fluffy king-sized bed. "I was just doing what you told me to do," I say, feeling like I've gone too far. "You created a Frankenstein. You goaded me on."

"I didn't goad you on to leave a kid on a subway track."

Tahar goes to light a jay. He inhales so deeply he has no

choice but to stifle a cough, then cough. It's a side of him I've not seen — taut, holding everything in so much you can see a lot. Maybe he isn't Robert's antithesis at all.

"Why haven't you told me about Hector before now?"

"I never trusted anyone enough to hear this story without judging me . . . "

"Calling you a racist . . . "

"Tahar . . . "

"Well, you won't catch me calling you a racist."

"I knew I could depend on you."

He passes me the joint. "Now inhale in the fucker," he mutters, holding the smoke deep in his lungs. "I mean *really* inhale, or else you're just wasting it."

He sounds like Hector. I don't tell him that.

"Oh, you probably think I sound like Hector now."

"You're being presumptuous," I add, whispering in between tokes.

"Oh, am I? Why haven't you told this saga to Robbie-boy?"

"He'd be jealous."

"And I'm not supposed to be jealous?"

"I thought you would feel more connected to Hector than jealous of him. I guess I was wrong."

"Oh, I see, it's like that, the People of Color club. I'm afraid one of us doesn't exactly qualify. Or have you Jews decided to call yourselves 'of color' when you're around *schvartzes?*"

"Tahar, chill."

"Chill?"

"If I can't say 'chill' anymore," I declare, looking about for a roach clip, "then you can't say '*mishugeh*,' okay?"

"It's a deal," he huffs, digging into a small drawer in his mahogany night table. He tosses the clip on the bed. "I don't like how I see myself," he insists. "Like your friendship with me is compensation for your fuck-up with Hector. Like I'm taking his place, or some shit like that."

"In all fairness, Tahar, no one could take Hector's place."

He stands up, opens the door to the bedroom and strides out with loud, firm steps toward the kitchen. Lights and shadows flicker in the hallway to the bedroom as he marches through corridors, bathrooms, bedrooms, turning on the house.

"Isn't it time for you to get your little olive-skin butt home to your Wonder Boy?" he bellows out from the kitchen, where I hear water running, a kettle whistling. "So you can be the happiest white boys who ever lived, spurning your family, your race, never mind all us poor people o' color who didn't fit into your neat little plan."

"You're being unfair," I say, hollering so he can hear.

He marches in with thick clump-clump steps; he's dressed in black jeans and Mark's old brown construction boots. No shirt yet. Feeling exposed, he wraps Mark's ruby robe around his shoulders.

"Unfair?" His voice peaks in restrained bursts as he slips his arms into the robe's sleeves. "Unfair? You tell me what unfair is? That I buried my lover six months ago, that my T cells dropped by five hundred since then, that my father won't return my calls because I take dicks up my butt? That I lost my fucking day job from HIV? That a man tells the story for a couple of fucking hours about his fear of taking a chance of a lifetime with a brown-skinned man who loved his ass, and he expects me not to worry he'll do the same to me? That my friend Robert hates me because he thinks that I'm trying to steal his boyfriend when I'm just trying to make a fucking wimp into a man? That you're going to walk out of this door, after I let you fuck my ass for the first time ever, to your lover who you're thinking of leaving but never will leave because you're too chicken-shit white ass to do anything meaningful in your petty, pitiful, half-formed life? That you're going to leave me sleeping alone in this big bed, which is just as well because I sweat so much at night from this fucking HIV I'd have to wake you up at least once in the middle of the night to change the fucking sheets? This is all happening *and you have the fucking balls to tell me,* in your whiny little New York Jewish Prince faggy voice, that I'm being, well, 'unfair'?"

Tahar stands still in his bedroom. With all his arm waving and tensing, the red robe has slid off his body. His eyes glower at the hardwood panels in his floor.

"Tahar," I ask, "are you done? I mean, is the vent over?"

I see eyes peek up. Sheepishly: "Yeah, I'm done."

"I didn't tell you the Hector story to make you feel my regret. I mean, don't feel my grief, man. Let me."

He lies in the bed, pulling his white cover up close. How much like Robert he looks when chastised.

"But are you feeling your grief?" he asks, his voice quiet. "Or are you just going from one guy to another, pushing the sadness down like all us other fags do until death makes us crazy with sorrow. I mean, I don't want to be another fix for you."

I restrain myself from bursting out in giggles over Tahar's twelve-step approach to love. Instead, I decide to push forward: "There's more to my Bronx story."

"Oh, no."

"Oh, yes. But this next part isn't so much a story as it is a dream."

"A dream? Now, if that doesn't sound promising."

"Okay," I say, whispering, approaching his face with my face, fast and monsterlike. "But don't be *frightened!*"

He feigns an eye-popping, terrified look.

"But before I continue," I say, pushing myself off from the bed and stampeding toward his living room, "I have to see if you have any Miles Davis."

"I'm black. That's like asking a fag if he has *Color Me Barbra.*"

I find the Streisand CD. Right below it: a Miles Davis recording with John Coltrane.

———

One day, a few weeks after Hector's departure, I heard a telling knock at the door. I remember actually saying to myself, "Open, sesame." There she stood—a little hunched over, in her navy blue and off-white housedress and her long-abandoned gray wool winter coat.

"*Nu,* long time no see," the old woman sighed, digging a finger in her Brillo-like white-gray hair for a scratch. After dusting off the dandruff flakes, she handed me the furry, leaden coat. Then Frieda walked in small, lurching steps through the threshold as if two years of mourning had not passed through our apartment like one of Pharaoh's plagues. She wore her jet-black, thick leather shoes; the soles left dotlike traces on the black-and-white kitchen linoleum. I stood around, numb with fright. She sat herself down on her old antique dining-room chair, the only piece of furniture not covered in slipcovers. "So," she groused. "God forbid, you could get your old grandma a little tea."

I remember boiling the water in the Pyrex kettle like a good boy, shaking uncontrollably as if an early-winter hailstorm had bypassed the September humidity and cauterized our Bronx apartment with a few freezing gusts. It suprised me that Frieda didn't notice my panic. Or maybe she herself was orienting?

"And don't, God forbid, try to pass off that decaffeinated *chazeray* on me," she carped. "I've been dead so long a little pick-me-up, God forbid, wouldn't kill me."

"Sure thing, Gramma," I said. "Sure thing. A *bissl* milk, too?"

"Milk, half-'n'-half, skim, whatever mommie has in the fridge will do. *Vos iz dir chillek*, what difference does it make? But now that you mention it, a little cookie wouldn't be so bad."

"We got mandel bread. I remember how much you liked mandel bread."

"God bless you, Mikala, for remembering. Me, I forget. But tell you the truth, I'm dying from hunger."

At first, Frieda's stark return drove me back—sickened me, in a way, like the apparition did when I last saw her holographic form at Elena's wedding. But no, right now she was no apparition. I'm telling you, she was real. Qualities that bothered me in life—her stale milk smell, her Vaseline hair, her old, tattered housedresses, her benign tumors near her creaky joints—were magnified tenfold. The same with her nice parts, such as acute empathy, soothing caresses and a refusal to get hurt easily. An insipid smile poured into your aorta like plasma, or a case of Southern Comfort, threatening to poison a system not used to so much feeling.

"*Nu, kind*," she said, as she sipped her steaming cup of tea. "The cries at night? They're loud enough to wake the dead."

"I miss him."

"Why didn't you go already with him? He was, I am not mistaken, a nice boy?"

"You mean I should have split, *zay gezundt*, like that?" I asked, talking a little like her, throwing a few Yiddish words in for good measure. "Deserted my *elteren*"—*elteren* being Yiddish for "parents"—"and your eldest daughter?"

"They are my children, God bless them. Not yours."

She smiled so sweetly it gave me stomach cramps. Imagine a warm-blooded person who bore the delicate halo of an angel and hummed all the time like a microwave. Imagine a macabre nightmare that shocks you awake at 4:00 A.M. in a cold sweat, only to continue once you're wide awake and eating cornflakes with skim milk. Imagine a mushroom trip that turns on and off, and good and not-so-good, every few seconds. Imagine those layer-cake realities, and you'll have a pretty good idea of how I felt when Frieda came back into my life.

Later, when I retired to my bed at 11:00 P.M. to jerk off in peace, I heard her form creaking around Stan's bed. Could she have rendered herself invisible? I closed the porn magazine shut and shoved it in between my mattress and box spring, infuriated. "Frieda? You there?" I heard no answer. "*Bubbe,*" I whispered. "What's with the snooping?" She materialized vaguely—not unlike figures on "Star Trek" when they are being transported from one starship to another.

"Mikey," she said. "Please, not in between the mattresses. That's where *mamaleh* checks—I mean, cleans. Don't be so predictable." I took out the *Blue Boy* and slipped it into my private file cabinet—the one with a lock and key.

"Better."

"Thanks for the tip."

"Don't mention it. One good turn deserves another. It's the least I can do." (Frieda was always a little heavy-handed with the clichés.)

Okay, she grew on me, because most of the time she appeared in her role as kindly grandma. Sometimes, though, she was just too much. If you looked closely at her deathbed gaze, which she wore when nodding off, her face took on odd, droopy changes. She resembled at once the Virgin Mary, a Rubens painting, Betty Grable and, in the most hard-to-figure incarnation, Bessie Smith.

"Gramma. What is this with the skin color? What are you doing, playing games?"

"*Vos? Vos?*" she asked, having no idea what I was asking of her. "Don't be a mental case. I'm your gramma."

"Are you?"

"Who else could I be? God forbid the Pope?"

"Nah. You're definitely not the Pope."

"I rest already my case. And so does the Father, Son and Holy Ghost."

"Huh?"

"Ignore me my English. If I had taught you better Yiddish when I was alive, then could we talk! *Si helft via toytn bankes!*" (Loosely translated: "This is like applying leeches to a dead person!")

I saw how difficult it was for her to make small talk, especially in the ridiculous idiom of Bronx pidgin English. I stopped trying to milk her for data, since she was so ultimately short on the kind I was after.

Actually, the element that confused me the most had less to do with whom she resembled and what she had to say than where, in fact, Frieda lived. I might not have fretted so much had she identified herself as a wayfaring spirit from the other world. (I had been indoctrinated by her fables and the short stories of Isaac Bashevis Singer.) But I became convinced that she wasn't an outside manifestation at all, but rather lived inside me — *was* me, or at least a version therein. Yet, for the most part, I *saw* her. The paradox spooked me. Sometimes just the knowledge of her complex, transmogrifying presence sent me into a crying jag; I restrained the wimpy sobs as best I could because I knew the tears alarmed her. The more distressed she got, the closer she approached, the more flustered I felt — and so on. I tried not to think about the implications. At her most lucid, she implied she had an entourage. Great. Once, when I felt freaked, nearly deranged, by her implied references as to what she was really doing here, I picked a nervous conversation with her, to take my mind off my irrational phobias, to convince myself she was "outside" after all, like the rest of the world (ha-ha), and not a living, breathing, ravenous entity inside my own boyish skin and bones.

"So, *bubbe?*" I asked, resorting to more Yiddish to get on her good side. "*Nu, vos machst du?* How goes it?" My hands shook relentlessly as I carried her dinner plate from the kitchen to the living room where she sat most of the time, overlooking the family so as to give us some semblance of privacy. I nearly dropped half of her dinner of boiled chicken and boiled potatoes on the blue shag rug carpeting. (It was something about her half-dead, half-alive condition that required she eat the blandest of foods — no different from the tasteless platters she used to make when she was alive and kicking.) "What's up," I continued. "I mean, why aren't you in heaven, where you belong?"

She opened her wrinkled, fleshy mouth to answer for real. For some reason, she seemed unable to speak a clear, precise English when it came to expressing deep truths. (Not that she was ever a walking John Gielgud in life.) Each second she mouthed words through her peach-fuzz-lined lips, thousands of utterances piled out over each other, a compacted pudding of symbols and intentions. She clicked her false teeth for emphasis. The racket gave me a headache, then a migraine.

"Speak a little slower, *a bissl* slower, Frieda."

She only spoke faster. The more briskly she spoke, the more melodic the din got. And the less I tried to make linear sense out of her garbled exegesis, the more like bebop she sounded. The pain in my skull began to ease up as I let the music in.

I understood what Stan must have felt. I stopped grilling Frieda.

———

Spike won't stay. It takes Robert, the vet and me to keep the dog from leaping off the consultation table. Dr. Gibson holds him by his stomach, folded layers of pink doggy skin. The muzzle's leather straps bisect Spike's face in squares. I suggest that the doctor put Spike out.

"To take his temperature?" Dr. Gibson asks.

Dr. Gibson rubs Spike's back, massaging the skin-and-bones knob between his tail and back. "No, just lie back and enjoy it," Dr. Gibson tells Spike, shaking his thermometer. Dr. Gibson's blond hair hangs from the back of his white coat in a hip-hop ponytail. "I'm an awful top," he confides to Robert and me.

The thermometer grazes Spike's bottom. Spike yelps, scrambles off the counter, smeared in dog urine. He hits his nose on the door. *Daddy, protect me.*

"I think it is safe to say that Spike's temperature has not spiked," Dr. Gibson says.

The muzzle comes off. *I sorry, Daddy, but I was scared.* Dr. Gibson hands Spike a brown waffle-looking treat.

"Is he going to live, doctor?" asks Robert.

I look into Dr. Gibson's hazel-blue eyes, sparkled with pathos. Strange, for someone so handsome.

"I think he'll live out the day," Dr. Gibson insists, grinning at Spike, who's already fallen for the doctor despite the disgraceful behavior. "I really don't know what's wrong with him. You say he sleeps all the time? Doesn't eat?"

Robert gives his open-lipped signal. He wants information.

"I think I feel various masses near the armpits," the doctor mutters.

Spike nuzzles Robert's hand.

"Let's hold off funeral plans until the X rays come back — okay, boys?"

Robert looks down at the floor. "I told you we should have taken Spike to the vet earlier," he whispers to me. "Six months ago, I saw signs."

"Oh, great!" I say. "Let's make it better by blaming each other."

"Guys!" barks the doctor. "Hold your horses. You caught this early."

"Oh," Robert says. "So it is cancer then?"

"Robert, don't be a pig with the doctor."

"Yeah," says the doctor, smiling.

Spike gets up from the floor and walks over to a space between Robert and me. He slips down to the floor and into his floor sigh.

"Good ol' boy," Robert says.

"Good ol' boy," I add.

"Do you want to talk?" Dr. Gibson asks. "What's going on between — I mean . . . You guys doing okay?"

"Does it look like it?" I ask.

"Mikey!" Robert says.

"We're going through a period," I add. "We'll snap out of it."

"We're breaking up," Robert says.

"Really?" the doctor asks. "I thought you guys were the model couple. How long have I been seeing Spike? Six years? A healthy marriage, I always said, made for a happy pup . . . "

"You don't think Spike's sick because we're breaking up?"

"Robert," I say. "You're going ape shit."

Dr. Gibson picks up Spike's chart and turns the blue forms on the clipboard. Spike rolls on his back for scratches.

"Does he relate to one of you more than the other?"

"He listens more to Mike."

"He prefers Robert."

Dr. Gibson laughs. Spike yawns.

"If you can hold off on the moving plans until we talk next — is that too much to ask?" Dr. Gibson squints. "Unless it's unbearable, of course."

"Of course."

"Of course."

———

Our house would soon sing with jazz.

You see, there had been the question of what to do with Stan's cassette tapes; hundreds cluttered the house. At night, tone-deaf ghosts escaped from the serials of magnetic loops, releasing bad dreams in their quiet orchestra of recrimination. My mother left the Miles Davis and Stan Getz arrangements where they had last been seen: on the piano, in a kitchen cabinet, under the sink; they collected dust as did Stan's drum gear, *Down Beat* magazines and all the striped polyester pants and flowered shirts that still remained hung in the closet we shared. All these belongings he had accumulated since his youth, when he first began listening to Thelonious Monk on his headphones.

"I never knew there was so much music in my house," my mother announced, wielding her Lemon Pledge like bug spray, trying to figure out how to clean around the musical collection.

There was nothing to do but collect the music in one pile; the next step, of course, was to dispose of—or investigate—it. One day my mother popped a tape lying near the *Fiddler on the Roof* ashtray into the ghetto blaster Stan left behind. "Outta curiosity," she said. Instead of making her forlorn, which is what I had expected, the careering horns and frenetic cymbals raised her spirits like a quick browse through B. Altman. From her, it seemed, my father enjoyed his first contact high.

"Linda," he said, "I didn't know you had an ear."

"Me neither," she said, staring at the chrome tape player, scratching her chin suspiciously. "Last I knew, Johnny Mathis was in there."

Jazz now pumped through our Bronx two-bedroom almost twenty-four hours a day. It was almost like a sickbed conversion. My mother: "Where is that '52 recording of Davis's 'Someday My Prince Will Come'? I can't quit smoking without it."

My father: "The horns give me the chills—better than sex."

My mother: "How would *you* know?"

I'd come home from college, and my father would be blasting Tito Puente's Latin beat so loud that he didn't hear me come in. For five minutes, I watched his bent, solid figure dance the mambo with a silent partner. Trumpets blasted; saxes trilled; congas pounded. (I reentered the house, so as not to humiliate him with my voyeurism, clearing my throat so loud he jolted and then panicked: "Ya got pneumonia, kid?") My thrifty mother bought a brand-new chrome tape player at Crazy Eddie's, costing one hundred dollars. It made an impression, the way she shelled out the tens and twenties like they were tarot cards. The reading said: dance. But the tape player alone would not play the music—the tape turned inside the contraption, but no music emanated. My father slumped in the couch, despondent, his cigarette ash dropping into the little human dish he made with his hand. So I took my father's Dodge Dart and drove the two to fancy department stores located in Westchester where we purchased the proper receiver. "Grief will break my bank," I heard my mother whisper to herself when she gave the clerk her VISA card. "It's already done a number on my heart." Afterward classic jazz from the '50s and '60s pumped through the house ten hours a day, as if we had become the best music outlet in the Bronx.

We made our mall excursions into weekend rituals. We bought cassette holders, a turntable and three-foot-tall speakers for our new sound system. We also purchased a home entertainment center, a love seat on which to sit and listen to the music and two dozen jazz recordings. As we drove, I'd play the radio. Once we heard the thumping of the bass fiddle; the DJ played John Coltrane. "Turn it up," my mother said from the backseat. My father regarded her as if she were a new woman.

They enjoyed the New Rochelle mall. Sometimes they bought items that would have cheered them up in their previous life: coasters, orange-juice cups, plastic place mats. Now, however, the Musak of the mall unhinged them. They couldn't wait to withdraw into the sounds of the car or a West Village music store, where they'd browse through the jazz section like Stan used to, thumbing through old records only to buy none.

I found the emphasis on early '60s jazz a little obsessive and tried to divert their attention. I organized picnics to the Bronx Botanical Gardens; my parents wandered aimlessly through the fern dell, picking roses and getting yelled at by the guards. I suggested we go to the movies, but they chain-ate popcorn and talked in loud voices about what they didn't understand. All they wanted to do was go home and play the music they knew Stan loved more than he loved them.

"God bless you, Mikey," my mother said. "Without you, we'd be dead."

"The music has calmed you."

"Yeah, like it does the savage beast."

———

Dr. Myron sits up in his seat, fascinated. His white T-shirt bears an image of a transsexual Native American medicine person, reprinted from a black-and-white photo taken more than a hundred years ago. Has he lost all trace of professionalism?

"Jungians call this Frieda figure the anima," he says, jotting his insight down in his green steno pad. "A figure for the soul."

"Anima, schmanima. I was eighteen years old. I wasn't in therapy then."

"Oh, so you think this really happened?"

"Myron, I'm telling you this really happened. She came to me, okay?"

"She came to you. And it's taken you, let's see, fifteen years to remember it?"

"So I repressed it. Are you familiar with that notion, repression? Don't you guys have to take tests or something?"

"Tell me about your headache."

"It was getting better, until you reminded me of it," I say, rubbing my temples.

"It got better in the Hector section."

"Yeah, because I was talking sex. Sex always puts me in a good mood. But Myron, man. You have to believe me. I need someone to believe me. I feel like I'm about to go crazy."

"Of course I believe you. I believe you pretty deeply. So deeply I'm feeling her presence. And that's why I challenge you. Because I think she's still here."

"Get outta here!"

"You're talking like Hector again."

"So I'm regressing. Don't you guys know about regression?"

I rub my head; it's killing me.

"Go take the HIV test, Mike."

"You think I have it in my brain? I hear it passes through the nervous system into the brain. Then you get that dementia, and forget about it."

"There's a garbage heap on your head. You need to relieve the pressure. That's what she's helping you do. Unfortunately, she's both the headache and the antidote, but so cloistered underneath the pile you can't attend to it."

"Now you're starting to sound like Frieda, what with her analogies," I tell him.

"I told you she was here. A soul figure. What did I tell you? This is what it feels like to be coming out inside —"

"Myron!" I scream. "Would you please cut the New Age psychobabble? Soul figure! I've never heard anything like . . . If anyone's the fucking soul figure, it's Hector —"

"Now we're cooking with gas," he says, clapping his hands so loud he shuts both of us up. We experience a moment of silence, then tedious nodding.

"Now I'm confused," I sigh. "If Frieda's not a soul figure, who the hell is she?"

"A-ha!" Myron exclaims, triumphant. "All of a sudden we're so interested in psychological theories, aren't we?"

"Hardly. I'm just trying to follow your line of thinking. So far, I'm having a hard time."

He holds his knuckles to his stubbly chin. "Maybe Frieda's not Frieda at all."

"Myron, please!"

He opens and closes his fingers, displaying the two sapphire rings he wears on his right hand. "Maybe she's another part of your personality," he conjectures, "like the ancient part. Like there's Personality Number One and Personality Number Two. And you just projected the Number Two guy onto an old lady."

"This is sick. You're telling me I imagined the whole thing? Like it's one big myth or something?"

The smile is over. "I'm sorry, but our time is up."

"Myron, can't you be more original than that?"

———

Still, all was not *glatt* kosher. My mother began picking up the crazy pieces. Everywhere she turned, she found one of Stan's old Miles Davis or Stan Getz cassettes. She knew her eldest son's budget; alone he could not have afforded to buy all this music. Besides, as Linda would be the first to tell you, Stan was one helluva cheapo.

She looked up toward the sky. "I'm putting one and one together," she told me, a tear falling down her face. "And it does not equal two. Any ideas?"

I shook my head.

She knew a liar when she saw one. The music was an invitation into that part of us we couldn't figure. I remember the first time Hector saw me after Stan's departure. He was crowing like a tough-guy-in-training, talking about a girl in his typing class he planned to fuck, if she would acknowledge him when he called her name. When he took a more studied look at me, his countenance shifted and he grabbed me. "You know," he said, "they got those family-support groups. Like, my dad, he goes to AA. I know if you call up those Jew temples, your family can get something for free."

That was just like Hector, expecting the best from people. But all my parents wanted to do was forget. They wanted not so much to forget about Helen and Stan, but how they felt about them. It was as if the irreversible monster that had been tearing Stan apart was now revealed in the wormlike cry of my mother: "I hate myself." An unspoken truth followed with the tears: "And I blame you for it." It was hard to brush your teeth with Crest or drink a can of Tab and not hear that refrain echoed in the cracking plaster of the hollow walls. It was next to impossible to jerk off in the sudden quiet of the 1:00 A.M. Bronx, fiddling quietly under the sheets in case one parent or the other happened to walk in the room to grab a Spiderman comic book that was not theirs to begin with, and not hear the rhythm of sobs just as the body was racking into its final throes of numb ecstasy. It was the accepted wisdom of our shrunken family to expect to hear the leitmotif every time one asked one's mother for the "exact time, please," or one's father to go easy on the Hellman's.

The refrain echoed in my ears like the sound of mortar in a soldier's dreams.

Frieda would come to me in my dreams and whisper, *"Night*

hate . . . *night* hate." In case I doubted it was she who came to me, an ancient sky-blue handkerchief that soaked up my tears remained on my flat polyester pillow in the early morning. And now here Frieda was, in living color, to bring the volume up full throttle. I worried we were all so tone-deaf, we wouldn't let the music improvise its way from jazz to R&B to soul.

On Saturday mornings, when there was no class, my father would barge into my room at what he considered a late hour — 9.00 A.M. — without knocking, an unfiltered cigarette blazing from his dry lips, to serve me a cup of hot instant coffee. "What are we going to do today?" he'd ask, his free, hairy arm filled with old maps of upstate New York. In the background, I heard the sad voice of Billie Holiday and my mother's tone-deaf voice echoing the lyrics to "Good Morning, Heartache." The commotion eased me. I forgave my father his morning habits. How could I not, and still care for him? Oh, sure, I could recite a litany. When I was smaller, he ridiculed me for throwing like a girl. When I was fifteen, I got up the courage not to join Little League for another tortured year. "Faggy boy," he muttered as we passed each other in the hallway leading to the kitchen on our way to meals. At my bar mitzvah, the rabbi congratulated my father for "having such a good Jew for a son." My father approached me to congratulate me on my "soprano's voice." When I was a kid, he force-fed me mashed potatoes, thinking the starch-and-butter regime would "toughen me." I puked at the table. I did so nightly for an entire week.

Finally Frieda, who invited herself over one evening only to witness this drama, smacked him on the head. "Are you Himmler or what?" she asked.

I wondered: are these complaints not standard among kids who grew up in a world that had passed the WWII veterans by? The crisis of manhood; we've heard it all before.

"How 'bout a game of golf?" I asked.

From the hallway, I heard my mother cry: "You can't bring the ghetto blaster on the golf course."

"True," I said. "A museum?"

"Yick," my father moaned.

Frieda was intent on getting me out of the house to hang out at the college gay club with new friends. "You're being codependent," she implied, long before the word became so in.

"They're your children. Leave off."

She had taken to praying in the lamenting scales that bonded us together like yin and yang before I met Hector. The somber number, "Our Father, Our King"—"*Avinu Malkaynu*"—always proved a tearjerker, making you fish for your handkerchief like you were at the movies watching *Gone With the Wind*. And then there was the "*Kaddish*," which, with its ghostly Aramaic, let you know that someone had died. So this was the other side of the Jazz. Ancient stuff stuffed down, foretelling an Exodus. I bought earplugs. A headache kept me up at night until I extracted the wax from my poor ears and let the Red Sea part.

———

Tahar drives slow and easy, like beautiful people do on TV commercials for beautiful Saturns or Ford Escorts. His Jeep Cherokee, known for smooth handling, allows him to keep one hand on the wheel, the other in my lap.

"So what is this going to prove?" he asks.

"That I could do it without him?"

"And if you turn out to be positive?"

"I haven't gotten that far, Tahar."

"What is it about relationships?" he asks. "Why do they stop working, like an old person stops working?"

"I don't know," I offer. "You stop seeing your lover as a separate person?"

Tahar smirks. He has his own theory: "Or you stop seeing yourself as a separate person."

I blink hard, mimicking the way Data processes human truths that seem scientifically implausible on "Star Trek: The Next Generation."

Tahar has had it with my cynicism: "So you think the same thing's not going to happen to us? That we won't take each other for granted?"

"Tahar," I say, sighing. "We'll at least go to Myron. We'll

talk it out. We'll know there's stuff we don't know, which, lemme tell you, is a big thing. I don't know. We'll make a place for what your friend Dr. Myron calls 'the shadow,' so we don't have to put it in a dog. What am I saying? Robert and I did our best. How can you deal with your shit if everyone around you is dropping dead?"

"Talk about a loaded question?"

"Sometimes a question is just a question."

"People are dropping dead from their shit," Tahar says, his voice sounding strained.

"You don't really believe that?" I ask.

He downshifts. "Nah, not really."

Tahar drives in silence, picking up speed to get through a yellow light at Fountain. He looks at me.

"Stop rolling your eyes," he says, laughing.

"Remind me not to move in with you until you outgrow the New Age."

"Speaking of holding your breath, you keep threatening to stay the night."

Tahar turns right on Santa Monica Boulevard. Looking into his rearview mirror, he lights a jay. He offers me some while holding the smoke down.

"What are you doing getting so romantic?" I ask, turning down the pot. "You said you weren't even going to consider any of that until I resolved the Robert thing."

"You seem a little nervous," he says, taking a long, deep toke. "I'm trying to get your mind off your impending mortality."

We pull up to the clinic.

"I'm not nervous," I argue.

"Okay."

"I'm not."

"I believe you."

"Good."

I open the car door and puke up the breakfast Tahar made me this morning. The eggs scrambled with cilantro and rye toast buttered with homemade apricot preserves make a gourmet puddle in front of the AIDS testing site.

One night, I woke up at 4:00 in the morning to see my mother lying in a corner of the living room, talking to an invisible form in the far northwest corner, where the floor-length curtains met the big front window.

"I would have moved if you hadn't died so suddenly."

Silence. A lot of chin scratching and sighing on my mother's part.

"We split your inheritance up equally among the brothers and sisters. The poor got the same as the rich. Which meant I didn't have enough to move to a white ghetto. *Bubkes* I got."

"But you have enough to move," the voice from the corner said. It sounded just like Frieda, sad and understanding—to a point. "But enough already. Stop being such a *kvetch*. Is that how I raised you? In your savings, you have enough for a good start."

"How the hell do you know what I have, Ma? Have you been snooping?"

I cried out: "Mom."

She jolted, then stood up, trembling a little in the night. Passing buses cast shadows into our house from the venetian blinds.

"I don't want to hear it, Mikey," she said. "I don't want to hear it."

"We should go to see a psychiatrist—all of us. I'm serious. I—for one—could use a little Thorazine."

"What do you know?" she asked. With eye rolling and finger circles, Linda blew me off. "What are you now, an expert or something?" I stared her down. She averted her sagging eyes from mine. I put my hand on her shoulder.

"This too shall pass," she said.

"No," I answered, hearing Dinah Washington's "Look to the Rainbow," from where it seemed my father was rousing. "I don't think it will. I think it won't pass. I think it runs in the family. In all families, maybe . . . "

"*What*, may I ask, is it exactly that runs in our family?"

"You know, Linda."

"Like hell I do. Like hell."

Linda walked to a fake bronze table not far from where Stan used to sit to space out after dinner.

"I really don't know what's happening to our family," she said, rummaging in a stack of cassettes for Stan's tape of Ella Fitzgerald singing the George and Ira Gershwin songbook. "I really don't."

I thought about what my mother said: were we all a little kooky? Now that I think of it, it seemed Frieda did begin to go a little crazy after Isaac died, at least as far as the observance of Jewish law was concerned. But that's only if you didn't know her well or hadn't paid close attention to the behind-closed-door whisperings of the "other world" which she conducted with her husband of over fifty years.

We didn't see the nuances back then, probably because the charade of piety struck us grandchildren as archaic, and if you will, a bit off the wall. Isaac and Frieda might as well have been Martians by the black wool suits and long black dresses they wore respectively when in brighter moods. They closed their eyes shut to see you after an operation. They laughed to themselves when a cousin miscarried, or my father lost his winning Lotto ticket on the way to claim his $2,000 in cold cash. They sang psalms when TV commercials came on and everyone else raced into the kitchen to grab thawing Good Humor ice cream sandwiches.

Okay, a little crazy they might have been at times. But impious they were not.

God forbid you didn't go to the sardine can of a shul (in other words, the synagogue, the Yiddish hothouse for prayer) to commune with God at least now and then (and ruin your dry cleaning with profuse sweating from such close contact with a hundred elderly men and women senile from the heat). God forbid you sipped a little milk before the meat you had eaten four hours ago had fully digested. God forbid you said the Lord's name in vain when you stubbed your toe. (My father's "Jesus Christ almightys" forced Isaac into paroxysms of whisker scratching while Frieda spat away the Evil Eye. But don't get me wrong: my grandparents worshiped the ground my father walked on. He had, after all, married my mother, their daughter, and according to them, such a *"shiddoch,"* or match, was no bargain.)

Truth be told, there were hundreds of prohibitions you had to watch out for.

God forbid you mispronounced a Hebrew word during the Saturday-morning prayers; you'd be corrected over and over again by each and every congregant, as if your life depended on the proper enunciation of the ancient guttural letters you needed bifocals to read in the first place. (The old men even screamed at the rabbi if, because of blindness, he mistook the Hebrew letter "sh" for "s." Hector, who knew something about the nuances of sound on which ethnic people rely, explained this difference by way of illustrating the discrepancy between "Sit down" and "Shit down.") God forbid you didn't tell the story of "the Four Sons" during the Passover seder, or went so far — as the feminists among us did — to amend it to "the Four Daughters." God forbid you didn't say "Grace after Meals" after meals. God forbid you didn't "lay *tefillin,*" or phylacteries, every morning before meals, your arms and head wrapped in black ribbonlike bows like you were some demonic Christmas present or something. God forbid you forgot to send each of your fifty-five grandchildren birthday, anniversary and graduation cards a day or two before the big day. God forbid you didn't donate a few dollars a month to help a tree grow in Israel. God forbid you didn't hear the rabbi "blow shofar" at the final dusk-colored moments of Yom Kippur, the Day of Atonement. God forbid Frieda heard the cracks we made about "blowing the chauffeur." God forbid you forgot to say, "God forbid" at least twenty times a day.

God forbid you didn't pay attention to the spirits of the dead, especially when they came back from the other world to inform you of the changes you might make, if you would but listen up, God forbid, for a change.

———

The AIDS clinic is located next door to the Gay and Lesbian Center. Tahar holds the metal door open. An unlikely gathering

of men, women and transsexuals loiter in the thin corridor leading
to the clinic. Tahar leads me into the fluorescent-lit waiting room.
I see hustlers, hookers, West Hollywood beefcakes, and lonely,
straight-looking guys paging through *People, The National Enquirer*
and *The Advocate*.

"You didn't have to come with me," I say to Tahar.

"Something told me it was important to come."

The receptionist, a thin man in his early forties, his face dotted
with lesions, flashes a smile. "Got your number?"

"No one can get *his* number," Tahar says.

"Oh," the receptionist says. "A joker. This place is full of
them."

"Why are so many straight people here?" I whisper to the
man.

"Don't you read *The Angeleno*?" he barks at me. "AIDS is *not*
a gay disease. Besides, we're the most efficient clinic in town."
He bends down to whisper, blowing some AZT breath in my
face: "These breeders think they won't bump into anyone they
know."

"Breeders!" Tahar spits out.

"Excuse me," I say, leaning in, ignoring Tahar's political cor-
rectness, "but do you really think HIV is the cause?"

He puts his lips tight together. "I can only repeat for you the
prevailing community folklore."

I lean closer in. "Shoot."

"If you're positive," the receptionist continues, flashing Tahar
an even more pursed look, "it's not the cause. If you're negative,
it is."

Tahar laughs.

I walk off. "Hey," the receptionist calls. "Give us five or ten.
We'll call you."

Tahar guides me to a white plastic folding chair. From across
the way, I see a cluster of street hustlers, some in mohawks and
skintight Calvin Kleins, cluster around an older man.

"Hey, ain't you with Madonna?" I hear one asking.

"Nah."

"Yes, you is. I saw you on TV last night."

"Nah, man."

I look toward the group. I see the man from the distance, balding. He wears Rapper's clothes: bulky, black shorts, Converse sneakers and an overgrown T-shirt.

"See something?" Tahar asks.

The receptionist calls out: "You, over there in the corner. One, one, two, four."

So much for anonymity.

Now that Hector and Stan were gone, I began reminiscing over the little Jewish dramas I had begun to put behind me. For example, I recalled how one day my grandmother Frieda decided to show me the contents of her much-gossiped-over secret closet. "Brace yourself," she warned. She must have seen the demon of love in my brown eyes, or evidence of semen on my lips. I had never quizzed Frieda about the dark oak closet and its ominous padlock. I feared drowning under a shower of spittle as she cast the Evil Eye from my interfering lips. Now we stood in her bedroom, in front of a latched door, which she shook as a casino dealer shakes a cup of dice. *"Oy-yoi-yoi,"* she sang. "Master of the Universe — argggh . . ." Frieda opened the closet door with a sudden exhalation. *"Farges nisht vos Ikh hob dir ongezogt,"* she said. In other words, "Don't forget what I have told you."

Inside: a mausoleum of the Eastern European Jew and his tragic fate in America. I saw dozens of prayer shawls, some blue, others black — all frayed. I saw my grandfather Isaac's phylacteries, the leather straps he wore on his forehead and forearms each morning before breakfast to show his devotion to God. The upper shelves to the closet were lined with books: daily prayer books, prayer books for High Holy Days, Passover Haggadahs, tractates from the Talmud, Haftorahs, books on the Mishnah and other black books, bound in leather with hard-to-make-out titles. One said *Magic Numbers*. Another said *The Angel of Death*. I spotted my mother's wedding dress (worn by all her four sisters during their weddings); Frieda's marriage certificate in Hebrew; another in Yiddish; the English textbooks she bought when she first came

262 / Sacred Lips of the Bronx

to this country and then abandoned; Yiddish dailies announcing the first news of Hitler's butcheries; Passover dishes.

I couldn't fathom how such a tiny broom closet contained so many artifacts from the past. *"Ikh bin gekumen dir tsu lernen,"* she said. *I have come to teach you.*

I was remembering myself at sixteen again. I had necked with strangers—all men, all porn-house aficionados. The fire of the Lord burned in my groin and Frieda, being intuitive, saw that I had stopped wearing underwear. What else did she see? The hard black dicks I smelled but didn't dare kiss? The Latin men whose hands I held long after we had come? The boys who ran in the streets with me once the movies started to repeat themselves and no new faces showed up? The lonely subway rides home? The lies to my parents, who hated my trips to Manhattan almost as much as they hated my excursions to Frieda's?

No. Frieda saw the reality behind those lustful images. To her, the thunder in my skull was the same thunder she saw in her own when she cried for her beloved mother, may she rest in peace, left to die alone in Poland, or when she recalled her fifty odd years spent sleeping alongside a snoring Isaac, may he rest in peace. This was the thunder she wanted to share. But the aching roar was *not* to be found in the closet. Ever look in a porn magazine to find the man or woman of your dreams, only to find out that he or she isn't to be found in a single shot, but rather in the twinge you have in your heart once you close the periodical? Frieda wanted to show me the spirit of her Creator; but this God is invisible. So look instead to the artifacts of your experience; maybe there you will find, if not the world soul, then your own. In Yiddish she said, "In grief, we find God's calling card." She sighed: *"Ikh bin a yunge meydl un mayn harts tut mir vey."* ("I'm a young girl and my heart hurts.")

She patted my head and laughed at her own foolishness. The world soul? Calling cards? Please. What she felt was guilt. Hadn't she jeopardized her heritage during the ship's passage across the Atlantic? Her own children worked on the Sabbath to make a dollar; they were ashamed by Frieda's insistence on "talking Jewish at the goddamn bank." Hadn't she closed the door on her own precious secrets to open the door on a new life in America?

I remember Frieda closing the closet, walking me back to the kitchen where the business of a boiled chicken dinner and a few hours of talk in mixed Yiddish and English on world events would keep us occupied. I was remembering all this at the age of nineteen (and now thirty-three)? And for what purpose?

I soon had my answer. The flashback of the living Frieda was over. Now the dead Frieda pointed outside the kitchen, to the hallway leading to our living room.

That's when I saw that our family was in for it all over again. My father was stumbling, holding his weight dizzily against the wall. He looked toward me like a frightened doe. He opened his dry mouth. Words stuck in his throat; I saw the phlegm in his mouth, like drying glue. I jumped up in a panic. He had been complaining of a cold two days ago, a headache yesterday and the flu today. Now I saw he had trouble breathing. I helped him to a kitchen chair, nearby Frieda.

"Dad!"

"Where's your mother?" Willie asked hoarsely. "She's never around when I need her."

"She's shopping downtown. What's wrong, Dad?"

"Call an ambulance, Mikey."

———

I emerge from the consulting room. I grab onto a railing above a wheelchair ramp and sit down.

"So?" Tahar asks.

I give him both thumbs up. "Unbelievable," I say. "So much fear for so long. Fucking negative. I don't fucking believe it."

"I never doubted it for a moment," Tahar says, himself sitting down.

I cross myself.

"Stop crossing yourself," he yells. "That's sacrilege!"

"If only I had known earlier. I could kick myself for not finding out. Can you believe this? I'm feeling guilty."

"Well, if you want to keep feeling glum, remember what the receptionist said."

"Gee, thanks, Tahar."

"Always here to help." His voice sounds tweaked, worried. "Nah. You should feel relieved. At least one of us will survive this. At least I'll have a friend who won't be too sick to nurse me."

"What's wrong, Tahar?" I stare at his face, his lips dry, his face tight and twitchy. "You look like you've seen a ghost."

He swallows.

"That guy, the one who you were staring at," he says, stammering.

"Yeah? So what?"

"It was — I can't believe this. It was Stan."

"Whoa?"

"I know. I know. But lookit. I was nervous about your results. All of a sudden I got real nervous and shit — I started pacing. And I saw him. I saw him sitting, getting dissed by the homies for looking so dope. I thought I saw the family resemblance. Then, when he was alone, I approached, real tentative-like. I got up the courage and said, 'Stan?' He freaked. 'How the fuck you know my name, brother?' "

"What are you saying?" I'm almost screaming.

"He was on tour, a worldwide gig. When I started talking, saying you were here, man, was he upset! He wanted to see you, real bad. But fuck, he didn't want you to have to deal with your results and him at the same time. It was very confusing for him, like he was balancing some real heavy shit."

"You found all that out in fifteen minutes?"

Tahar's words pour out in a torrent: "I think he thought I was your boyfriend or something. 'Birds of a feather,' he said. He said he takes the test now and then, usually before going home to Helen and the kids."

Tahar hands me a card. It says: STAN KAPLAN, CONGERO.

"He told you to call," Tahar continues. "He said you should call the Bronx, too."

"He's back in touch with them?"

"I don't know. He didn't say. He just left his calling card. He just said to call. Call *soon*."

"I wonder if something's wrong."

"He didn't say."

———

Back then, the ambulances in the Bronx had a reputation for taking a year and a day. I quickly convinced my ailing dad that I knew how to drive even though I lacked a license. After all, Hector had given me a day-long crash course, and afterward I drove Hector in the Rodriguez sedan to Rockland County and Jones Beach on a regular basis. The tale took my father's mind off his broken heart. "You sneak," he said, overjoyed. I spirited him to Bronx Veterans Administration hospital. He slumped in the passenger seat, giving quiet directions. "God, could I use a cigarette," he said. But Frieda had nabbed them when he was shaving. (My father was a man of impeccable cleanliness. "You're having a goddamn coronary, Dad," I said, glowering at the razor. "I got to look presentable for the cardiologist," he said, turning slightly blue.)

A young rabbi with drag-strip sideburns met Willie at the hospital emergency room. "How are you feeling?" the ardent rabbi asked. The ex-hippie chaplain bothered my father, who waved him on: "I ain't dead yet." That's when I saw Linda huffing and puffing out from a cab, tossing dollar bills at the driver. When she passed the blazer-wearing rabbi, she spat on the ground to chase away the Evil Eye: "Poo. Poo. Poo."

"God bless you," he said.

"God bless *you*," she said, walking fast.

What did our family know from heritage? Not a single soul in our family hung around the temple when Frieda and Isaac's congregation began the twenty-minute-long standing prayer, called the *"Amidah."* My parents rolled their eyes at the hundred or so laws for koshering food. The floral-patterned plates you used for steak you kept as far away as possible from the Melmac you used for bananas and sour cream! The eggs you checked for blood! The meat you rolled in salt until it turned from a healthy blood-rich sponge to an anemic grey-looking rock. God forbid you tried to give that patty some longed-for flavor with a piece of Camembert melted on top just so: God Himself would emerge from the shriveled meat to repudiate your soulless cravings with a curse on all your appetites, including the one for Him!

But that fantasy—that the Master of the Universe reigned above as some kind of Hitlerian nutritionist—had no basis in Frieda's philosophy. Frieda had four sons and four daughters, all of whom kept *glatt* kosher for one reason and one reason only: so that Frieda could, God forbid, eat in peace at their houses. But Frieda could have cared less about eating a piece of *"traif"* — or *"unclean"*—food at any house besides hers. She kept kosher out of an obligation not so much to Law, but to Faith; not as a burden to inflict on others, but as a binding between her sense of duty and the Almighty's seeming indifference to it.

Slowly, though, her idea of the Maker of All Things changed, especially as she got older and older. It was no longer "an idea," but a fact of life, which changed from an old man like her grouchy father up in the sky to something inside her. Go figure. The more she became an ally with this terrifying hidden source of life, the more she laughed at her old-fangled orthodoxies.

Still, she never abandoned her Jewish rituals completely, which meant that Frieda had no choice but to be subjected to allegations of hypocrisy from her children. Once Frieda's youngest daughter, my aunt Eileen, found out that Frieda drank copious amounts of unkosher wine at my mother's house on a regular basis because, as Frieda said, "The Chardonnay tastes better than that cheap Manischewitz you buy." Eileen rained a lifetime of indignation on the old, enfeebled woman. "For years I followed these stupid rules for your sake," Eileen screamed. "I separated dishes, *fleishich* for meat, *milkhik* for milk, the china for the week of Passover. I spent extra buying kosher pullets, kosher brisket, kosher turkey, kosher franks, kosher salami, kosher wine, cake without lard, fish because it was parve, God forbid no shellfish, forget oysters, never mind prime ribs, special cheeses, special pots, margarine not butter, etcetera, etcetera, etcetera!"

Nonplussed, Frieda interrupted. *"Sha,"* she said. (Never has one syllable been able to indicate so much: "Cut the crap," "Do you know who you're talking to?" and "The Master of the Universe is with us, so watch how you torture me.") Frieda wanted to explain her life to Eileen. But by then Eileen had run out of the house, cursing Deuteronomy in childish sobs. That was the beginning of the end. When Frieda died, so did the old ways. No one saw each other anymore.

Tragedy brought us all together. Now all the relatives descended from the four corners of American suburbia into The Bronx to watch Willie die. My father's lips were cracked, his eyes glazed over with the boredom of numbed pain. Frieda sat at his bedside and folded a napkin in quarters only to refold it until it fell apart in tatters—her one nervous habit. (You always knew Frieda was around by the paper trails she left in her wake; in later years, it began to symbolize to me the part of her that doubted everything—an inverted version of the rosary.) A dozen people stood around Willie's bed; he could barely talk.

"Willie," bellowed Uncle Milton. "How ya feeling?"

A CPA, Milt was the first of Frieda's progeny to become really comfortable. (Milt's favorite joke: Two Jewish men cross the street. One gets hit by a car. The other rests a pillow under the hurt man's head. "Are you comfortable?" he asks his injured friend. "I make a living," the dying man answers.) Milt told jokes a mile a minute to pass the nervous time in the intensive care unit.

"*Sha,*" my mother hissed. I saw her bosoms cave into her chest, a sure sign of oncoming depression, a state of mind Linda fought like a guard dog fights a more powerful intruder. I touched her shoulder; it was thick like a quarterback's. What was she so upset over? The prospect of losing Willie? Of watching him die without hearing the final words. No: her eyes told a different story. She saw Frieda, and it scared the living daylights out of her, too.

In Yiddish, I heard Linda say to Uncle Milt but for Frieda's benefit: "My husband is dying, dummy. Do you have to scream in my ear?"

And still Uncle Milt raised his voice: "What, Linda? I

couldn't make it out. You know me: I don't talk Jewish. What's with Willie? He gonna make it or not?"

She shook her head. "Who knows?" Linda responded to her oldest brother the way you shake your head at an imbecile when he asks whether or not he is an imbecile.

But Milt wouldn't let up. "Is that a yes or a no, Linda? A yes or a no?"

"A man needs to have a *bissl* quiet," Linda said. *"Sha."* Her voice sounded so loud in Willie's ear, it forced him to shout back his own *"sha!"* at her.

And then Milt shot back at Linda for good measure: *"Sha."*

And then the whole room erupted in an opera of *"sha, sha! SHA!"* Frieda, stunned at the chain reaction Linda had caused, added her own final and musical *"SHA."*

The room of people froze in awe. What breeze was that? A breeze with a flatted ninth?

Frieda put her face in her hands. She cried tears of pity that only I (and I think Linda, who was also crying) could see. "Look, Mikey," Frieda told me, whispering in my ear. "We moved here to America to save the children from needless suffering. But who knows? Without suffering, maybe you suffer worse." She didn't really believe that. She didn't know what she believed anymore.

"I can offer you I think a way," she said. "To you? A little advice, *eppes?"* (*Eppes*: an untranslatable word you put at the end of sentences to show a touch of doubt in the face of your enormous skill as an advice giver.)

"What?" I asked quietly, keeping my jaws clenched like an angry ventriloquist so my relatives wouldn't think I had begun talking to myself.

"Let me, God forbid, inquire first. You are a —*oy vey iz mir* how to say? —a homosexual, a *fegeleh*, am I right?"

"I am not," I said, offended, jaws even more clenched.

"Excuse me!" she huffed. "I should, God forbid, go back to the dead and mind my own business. I didn't, thank God, come back from the dead to deal already with young hypocrites."

"Wait a minute, Grandma. All right already. Tell me what you have in mind."

But she wouldn't give me the time of day. And Willie started to moan all over again.

———————

Robert kneels in the garden, planting two rows of petite winter squash. The baby plants have already flowered in their green plastic containers. Robert turns his head and smiles to see me. He forgets what he should be remembering: that we don't smile at each other anymore. He resumes planting, digging discrete holes with his pointer finger.

"Robert. Why are you planting? We won't be living here by the time these vegetables produce fruit."

He doesn't divert his head from his enterprise.

"Is that the only reason to plant something? So you can eat it?"

"Touché!"

"No. Not touché. We tend to our gardens, be they what they may, even if they are no longer our gardens."

"You're becoming wise through all this."

"Not wise, just practical."

An earthworm virtually four inches long crawls on Robert's right hand. He sets it quietly down in the earth.

"What's wrong with being wise?" I ask.

"Nothing. Just that I gave you my wisdom."

A breeze comes in from the ocean, cool and over with in a flash. Sensing its departure, Spike wanders out to the garden and lies down in the grass, chomping at the tallest strands. He dislikes sea breezes now that he's ailing.

"And now you want your wisdom back?"

Robert stops planting. "Yes," he says. "Yes, I'd like it back very much, if you don't mind."

"It's yours."

The ground is too cold and hard for Robert's finger approach. Robert reaches for an old silver spoon, digging like a dog digs — fast and messy, but efficient. He finds Spike's old bones, some dried shit, old cigarette butts. Pizza? Nothing distracts now, not even his filthy fingers or the sweat pouring down the patch of back revealed by the faded-black sweatshirt he wears for gardening.

"What did I give you?" I ask. "Besides guilt, that is."

"You didn't give me all that much guilt," Robert says, a little guilt in his voice. He stares into the muddy earth, then wagers an answer. "Art?"

"I thought you were going to say 'beauty.' "

"Splitting hairs."

"Robert, I found out I was negative."

He puts his tools down, staring at the dirt. His hand shakes a little. His body caves in slowly, like a deflating balloon.

"Robbie, you okay?"

In all the time I've known Robert, this is the first I've seen him cry long enough to produce more than tears, but a sob.

"I'm negative, too," he says.

"What?"

"I found out last week."

"And you didn't tell?"

He doesn't budge.

"It's like everything that kept us together is falling away," he says.

I bend down to help wipe the tears.

———

Frieda couldn't bear another moment of the chattering at Willie's sickbed in the Intensive Care Unit at the VA. One aunt-in-law groused about her anxious preparation for the bar exam. "The best diet plan so far. When I—God willing—pass, I'll have to sew my lips shut." Another expressed rage at having to drive through a Bronx ringing with gunfire to sit vigil at Willie's bed. "One day I'm going to get a flat in the Mercedes. And then how will Linda and Willie feel when the blacks blow my brains out for my car?" One uncle complained to another about the problems of running an automotive store in Scarsdale, where everyone bought new. "Spare parts these rich Jews need like they need a hole in the head."

"My husband is dying," Linda said in Yiddish. "Have you no

respect?" Frieda, herself a little pissed off, barked for good measure: *"Gey avek,"* which, translated into English, means "Go away." No one paid her any mind; so much chatter reigned in their skulls, they could not hear, let alone comprehend. Instead, they rubbed their heads and collectively reached in their pockets and pocketbooks for some Excedrin. By accident, the ghetto blaster my mother had brought for my father began playing "I've Got You Under My Skin" so loudly that it seemed only to exacerbate everyone's pain in the neck. In a moment, all of my aunts and uncles, as well as my mother, filed out of the room.

I followed suit to leave Frieda alone with Willie, who was by now somewhat more stabilized.

"Mikey," Frieda said, gesturing to me, without getting up from her Formica hospital chair, her lavender cotton housedress exposing some of the benign lumps that grew every few years from her elbows. "Stay with me for a while and read to me the Yiddish paper."

"Okay, Grandma," I said, pulling up a chair.

My father roused from his Demerol-induced sleep. Heart machines buzzed and bucked on both sides of his bed.

"Mikey?" he asked. "You see her, too?"

"Sha," Frieda said to my father. She dipped a dark blue washcloth in a basin; she wrung out the water. She lay the cloth over Willie's forehead. "God willing, Willie, rest," she said. She returned to her vinyl seat.

"Will he make it?" I asked.

"Yes," she said. "With flying colors. You will all soon return home. One happy family."

I was stunned: "You can see into the future?" I asked.

Frieda shot me a tight-lipped frown, suggesting I better watch my Ps and Qs. *"Luz mir aleyn,"* she added. ("Leave me alone.")

I wasn't ready to give up so easily. "Can you really see how things are going to work out. If—"

"Tataleh," she said, a nervous look crisscrossing her face. "I can see a little bit here, a little bit there."

A potent thought occurred to me: "Can you tell me if I'm going to see Hector again?"

She looked worried, offended. *"Kin∂,"* she said. "These are secrets. Not for you."

"Please," I say. "I miss him. There are certain things I need to know."

Her frown faded away. She turned to Willie. When she turned back to me, I saw she had changed. In the hollow of her sockets I thought I saw images, scenarios — like an inner movie or something was playing in her retina.

"I'll let you in on a little," she whispered, conspiratorially. "Maybe. But, *eppes*, on one condition . . . "

———

We're watching CNN: "Larry King Live," "Crossfire," "World Report." A new president has been elected. I have made some California short-grained brown rice and steamed a pound of broccoli and carrots. We eat on the bed together, passing the tamari.

"Back on the diet, huh?" Robert asks.

I ignore him.

"I thought you said John liked you meaty."

I take the dishes to the sink and rinse them before the tamari draws our ant army out from under the bungalow. Robert retires to his room. I hear him fiddle with the wooden frame of his futon. At night, the contraption pulls out into a bed.

"Robbie," I say.

"Yeah."

He wanders into the kitchen. Barefoot and shirtless, he looks like the kid I fell in love with. Shamelessly cute and not aware that he is shameless and cute. He is one of the few people I know who can just *be*.

"I think it's dumb for us to sleep in separate rooms," I say. "I mean, just because we're breaking up doesn't mean we have to make ourselves miserable."

"You have a point."

I turn the lights out in the kitchen. We read in bed together, our feet touching up against each other's beneath the blanket like nothing has happened, propping up our books on our pajama-clad chests. In the past, we'd always find the book the other

person was reading more appealing. We'd fight over Howard Zinn's *The People's History of the United States* (Robert's purchase) or *Women Who Love Too Much* (my purchase). Now we read the same books, in this case, *Iron John* (or, as Robert says, *Iron Dick*). Our bookshelves are filled with two of everything. It's one of the wasteful household habits we agreed on when we thought we figured out how not to fight.

Spike lays next to our bed on his own cedar-stuffed blue mattress that fits his body like a glove. He sighs heavily, his signal that he's ready to sleep the night. Poor skinny mutt.

"Robert," I say.

"Yeah."

"We may not be able to move away for months, what with the dog and everything."

"Months? Yeah, I guess you're right. Who knows, though?"

"You're right, who knows?"

More reading.

"I think that we can invite our friends over."

"Friends?"

"You can put quotation marks around the word if you want."

"Oh, you mean 'friends'?"

"Right."

"Special 'friends.' "

"Like."

"Like . . . Marty and Tahar, right?"

"Now you're cooking with gas."

"For dinner?"

"And for dessert."

"And appetizers?"

"And cocktails."

"I don't drink."

"Then we'll make you Shirley Temples. I'm sure Marty can whip one up for you."

"While Tahar whips up something else."

"Yes," I drawl, taking my eyes out of my book and looking down toward Robert's buttocks. "I know something that could use a little whipping."

"Well," Robert says, turning serious. "We'll have to make schedules. I don't think I could handle the sounds in my house."

"Don't worry. Tahar's too romantically involved to be a good top now. Ah, the good ol' days."

Robert continues to pretend that he's reading. It occurs to me that he has not turned a page in the last five minutes.

"This book sucks," he says, sighing.

"Do you miss Marty?" I ask.

He frowns into his book. "Of course not," he says.

"You don't think about him all the time?"

"No, of course not."

He shakes his head, then adds: "No."

I make myself read a line by Robert Bly.

"It's not like I'm obsessed or anything, Mickey. He's just a kid."

"A kid who loves you. A kid with a chest of death."

Robert laughs. "He does have a nice chest. So smooth."

I immediately feel hairy.

"Of course, I have nothing against hairy chests," Robert adds.

"Of course not. Iron John, now, he was hairy."

"On second thought."

We read for another five minutes. We turn pages.

"This book sucks," he says. "I mean, what am I supposed to do, buy a drum and dance around naked or something?"

"Robert," I say. "If Marty loves you, I can't see any reason why I shouldn't want the best for him and you."

"You're becoming wise through all this," Robert says, underlining a section from his book that deals with the "deflated king."

"Not wise," I answer. "Just practical."

———

I pulled away from Frieda's eyes, having seen a bit more than I was prepared for. "On second thought," I admitted, "I'm not so sure I want to go through with this."

"Then don't," she said. "It's not necessary, not healthy. Be practical, Mikey. Don't go looking into the business of the dead. Right? Of course, right."

Frieda's
Last Laugh

———

"You know, Gramma. You're absolutely right."

"Of course, I'm usually right, especially since I've been dead, *oy*, I sometimes even amaze myself with how right I can be."

I thought long and hard. She was right. This was none of my business.

"Good," she said, reading my mind.

I changed it.

"I need to know about Hector," I said, pressing.

She bit her lips, an annoying habit of hers when she fought tears. "I can't show you, *tataleh*, the future, per se. Because, well just because. How to explain? I can show you options, the ones already existing in you. There is no such thing as one future. Yet there is only one outcome. Many options, *oy vey iz mir*."

"Do they entail Hector?"

"Mikala —"

"Do they entail Hector?"

"You're giving me a headache with God forbid these questions."

"Just answer this one simple one. Do I get to see Hector again anytime soon?"

"*Oy*."

"You can say that again."

"*Oy*."

"Very funny."

"I will show you what I can show you, but only if you agree . . ."

"Agree?"

"Mikey! You have to decide what to do with this *chazzeray*. With the options? Since when do you get something for nothing?"

"You're my gramma. You always gave me things."

"Sure. Sure I expected in return, too."

"Like what?"

"Like what? Like you know what. *Eppes* phone calls, visits every now and then. Even that was expecting too much."

"Hey, *bubbe*. I stopped by your house *every* day."

"Every *other* day."

"Who's counting?"

"My point, *yingeleh*, is that—all right. I will tell you. But you must go along with your part of the deal."

"*Pfh*. My part of the deal. I feel like I'm making a pact with the Devil."

"Pshhh. A preview such as this, everyone, believe me, gets. But people, they are such *mishugehs*, they forget."

I look into Frieda's eyes. They have mutated into little human triplexes.

———————

I saw that I was twenty-four. I've invited my parents out for a Friday-night dinner in Manhattan. "Come home for dinner," Linda implores. The last time I visited the Bronx, the elevator had a puddle of piss in it. An old Jewish man paced the lobby beating his chest. The elevator peeled to expose graffiti. I insist now that my parents and I meet on the Upper East Side. I'm frightened of being seduced by the charms of the old neighborhood.

My parents show up first, loitering in the posh foyer in their winter parkas.

"We schlepped for an hour and a half to get here before you?" my mother asks.

"Mom," I say, whispering. "This is a French restaurant."

"Schlep is good French, isn't it?"

Our waiter, a bald, wiry man, escorts us to our table. We are handed menus.

"It's all in French," my mother cackles.

"Linda," my father says. "The kid's got class."

"And a student loan. What is so important that you have to drag us down to Manhattan to eat food we can't understand?"

The waiter arrives, bowing to my mother.

"I'll have a salad," she says.

"Which kind, madame?"

"I don't care."

"As for myself, *monsieur*," my father declares, "I'll start with the escargots. *Est-ce que magnifique, non?*"

"You will not," my mother interrupts. To the waiter, she whispers: "Give my husband a salad, too. His gallbladder . . . "

I order a bottle of Chardonnay, pointing to my mother that her veto is being vetoed.

There is no recourse but to tell them in Morse code. My heart thumping. I say I met a "cool guy" and we're in love. I add that "I had always been that way" and that "his name happens to be Robert."

"Are you trying to tell us you're gay?" my mother asks.

"Yes," I stammer.

"Well, then, spit it out," she says.

"You sound angry."

"I'm not angry. I always knew."

My father clears his throat. "So what else is new with you? School — "

My mother: "Did you hear that your aunt is having an affair? Oy, is she in love — "

"That Murray was a bum," my father adds.

"May he rest in peace."

We eat our salads. The wine is brought. My mother prohibits more than one-half glass per person. "I've witnessed too many drunken family-dinner fights," she says.

Only once do I ask my mother: "So, don't you have anything to say?" She answers, "What's to say? It's your life."

When the waiter inquires about our entrées, my mother insists, "We already had them. Check, please."

I walk them to 68th Street and Lex to catch the Bronx-bound bus. Winter winds tousle my mother's hair. My father tugs a scarf around his neck. My mother talks about her job, my aunt, the fact that she corresponds secretly with Stan's Helen, that they have two boys "brown as hot chocolate." I hear about Stan. He plays with Harry Connick, Jr., Billy Idol and Lionel Hampton — maybe Madonna. My mother sends Helen money, writing her, "This is for drumsticks, the kind you eat."

My father throws his two cents in, such as, "Kids today, they got no respect." She argues how old-fashioned he is, that he didn't

understand young people, never did. The bus comes. My mother lunges for a hug, during which she stuffs some crumpled, sharp bills in my hand. "Next time you want to tell me something, come home." I watch them wave from the bus.

―――――

"What a weird and awful scenario," I said, rubbing my eyes as Frieda rubbed hers. "I almost didn't recognize myself, so fat."

"Maybe we should stop while we're ahead," Frieda advised. "So you ate like a normal person for a change. *Nu*, that was so terrible? But enough for now. These things, they make a person crazy, yes?"

"Show me the rest, Gramma."

"*Luz mir aleyn.*"

"Show me the rest."

"Didn't you get enough already?"

"I wanted to see Hector. Instead you showed me breaking my mother's heart . . ."

"What? *Vos*? You were being honest . . ."

" . . . Selfish."

"*Feh*. You were being true to yourself."

"*Feh!*"

"Don't *feh* me."

"*Feh!*"

"Suit yourself."

"Gramma!"

"I'm going back to the dead."

"Show me Hector!"

"I said I'm going back."

"I want to see Hector!"

"*Sha!* You're giving me a headache already with your wants and needs."

―――――

There's a savage knock on the door. Spike barks. "It's just me, Spike, dude," goes the voice. I recognize the Valley intonations. He's early. The sun has just set over Venice; it's barely night. A

shade of orange and red clouds shines in our living room as I open the door.

"Well," I say. "If it isn't Marty."

"How postmodern," he says, looking postsurfer. "As for myself, I'm more for family values."

"Did you bring your toothbrush?"

"Yes, Dad."

"No. Robbie's your dad, remember?"

Marty laughs. "You should know better than that," Marty says, making a fucking signal by sliding his right forefinger through a tight hole he makes with the left forefinger and thumb. "We're both bottoms. It's hell."

"Sounds like heaven to me," I muse.

"Well, we could use you," he says, conspiringly.

Robert approaches and smacks him on the head. "Get in the room," Robert yells.

"Yes, Daddy," Marty whines. He retires to Robert's room, but not before winking at me.

"The young." I sigh.

Robert has something to say to me. "Um, Mike. With Marty, well, I'm not a bottom. I'm not."

"I believe you."

"I swear I'm not."

"Robert," I say, biting my lip. "I believe you."

"Are you sure this is going to work?" he asks. By the same token, I can see by the flush on his face that all he can think about is lying on top of Marty.

I point to my earplugs. "A boy always comes prepared," I say.

"I was asking a philosophical question, not a logistical one," Robert says. "Besides, we won't be loud."

"I'd prefer it if you were loud, I hate to think you are having sex with someone as quiet as yourself."

I live to regret my words. Robert has made Marty into a little fuck-toy; Robert grunts and groans from 1:00 A.M. to 2:00 A.M. — totally unlike him. Just as I am about to fall asleep, Marty starts speaking in tongues: "I'm close, close. No. I'm close." I hear Robert say, "You little fuck-toy." I've taught him well. Then he adds,

"You *like* being a little fuck-toy, don't you?" I've taught him *too* well.

I boil a cup of skim milk. I hear the door to Robert's room creak open. Marty walks out. He is naked. Only when he's naked and his little tough-boy muscles stand out from his taut skin like seashells do I understand precisely what the appeal is. With his skimpy surfer clothes, he had looked scrawny. Now I see he's not.

"Got any beer?" he asks.

I smile to reveal a mustache of white milk. I feel like his grandma.

"When you get old," I say, "you need help falling asleep."

Marty looks at me in the pathetic way I notice that Robert has begun to mimic. He opens the fridge and helps himself to my skim milk rather than Robert's more fatty stuff.

"Do you think you should be walking around naked. I mean, what would Robert say?"

"I fucked him senseless," Marty says. "An atom bomb wouldn't wake him."

"I've always found Robert to be a rather light sleeper."

"When I'm done with him, he's brain dead. I'm telling you, Mike, you and I could be fucking ourselves to death on the couch and he wouldn't hear. If you don't believe me, you should check it out."

"I believe you."

Marty rifles through the refrigerator. "There's some tofu and rice in the Tupperware," I say. "I made it."

"Gross."

"You know, Marty, where I come from, we have words for people like you. *Mensch* is not one of them."

He doesn't know what I'm talking about. Or maybe he does. He drinks the milk from the container. His rudeness: that's how he gets attention. Now he has mine.

"Ugh," he says, spitting the milk out from his mouth into the kitchen sink. He rummages through the fridge again, this time finding another Bud in the back of the icebox. "I want to thank you," he murmurs, twisting off the bottle cap. "I'm just learning

about love and everything. I mean, you've made this a lot easier. I feel supported by you."

"Don't mention it."

"No, really," he says, standing his ground. "I think you're really amazing. If I met you first, before Robert—"

"Marty, *please.*"

He takes a sip of beer, then puts the bottle back in the ice box, sans cap. I stare. "I'll drink it tomorrow, Dad," he says. The icebox closes. He bends down and gives me a kiss on the lips, discreet and warm. "Thanks," he says again. He pads off to Robert.

I take my Robert Bly book to the living room couch. Moments later, I hear the door open. Marty comes back.

"What's up, Marty?"

He sits down. I see his eyes are red. Why hadn't I noticed that before?

"I got my test results today," he says.

"What?"

"You guys inspired me, so I went to do the blood thing."

"You hadn't gotten tested before." *A little Pop-Tart like you?*

"Nah," he says, with a defensive little sniffle. "But neither had you, right?"

"Fucking shit," I say.

He collapses into my chest. He sobs like a little baby, choking on his phlegm, keeping his voice down so as not to wake Robert, but really letting it out. I want him to stop, but find myself saying, "It's okay, you can let go."

He gets a grip. I get him a Kleenex.

"Have you told Robert yet?" I ask.

"Mmmm."

"You should."

"I'm afraid he'll leave me."

"Marty."

"He's the only guy who's ever been nice to me. I'm twenty-seven fucking years old."

I hold him for a long time. He falls asleep, dribbling a little on my T-shirt. I have to get him up and back to Robert. His body

is curved up in a little ball. I caress his arms, shoulders. He sleeps deeply, snoring just like Robert, in polite little harumphs.

———

With Marty sleeping in my arms, I dream that Spike is rushed to the hospital with an AIDS-like opportunistic infection. I see the back of a man in a white lab coat whom I identify as Spike's specialist, speaking with great authority about the dog's condition.

"Thass fucked," he says. "The blood, man, filled with yucky corpuscles an' shit. Damn, his goose is cooked!"

"I thought Spike was HIV negative," I protest.

"Man-oh-Manischewitz," the doctor says. "What's wit you guys? You know that what's wrong is bigger than AIDS."

The doctor turns around to face me. He grins, wide-eyed — filled with the flavorful smacking of teeth on tongue and lips.

"Hector?"

"Miguel, my main man."

"You're Spike's vet?"

Hector's mother, assisting as head nurse, chimes in: "My son, the doctor."

Spike rests on the blue Formica table in a ball. His ribs show through. His eyes, wet with fever, open. *Thanks, Daddy.* He falls asleep.

"The chemo made him so nauseous," I say.

"We've never known Spike not to eat," Robert adds. "It was such a shock, all of a sudden."

Hector shakes his head. "The chemo can be hard on dogs."

"On people, too," Robert adds.

"On people, too," Hector adds. "But man, he doesn't seem to be suffering too much right now."

"Oh, doctor," Robert says. "He was crying all last night. We didn't sleep a wink. He went to the bathroom in his bed, which is right near our bed. He was too weak to go outside. Doctor, you had to be there."

I touch Robert. He pulls away.

The doctor asks if we're ready. Tears pour down Robert's

face. I feel numb. We hold Spike's belly, his head. His eyes open.
Hi, guys, how ya doing? I just had the wildest dream . . .
The doctor gives Spike the shot.
I just felt something.
Robert bites his lip.
Oh, it's just you and me, guys. Thanks. I like Dr. Hector, but he is so sappy sometimes. And I hate his dog biscuits.
"Robert," I say.
"Yes, Mike?"
Robert bites his lip harder. The tears pour down.
Daddy, why crying?
Spike's eyelids close, just like they always do when Spike senses us close.
Daddy! What's happening?
Then a sharp whine, like someone stepped on his toe.
"Oh, shit. Mikey, what's happening?"
"It's okay, Robbie."
Another whine.
Daddy!
"Do you think he knows?"
"It's okay, Robbie. Don't freak out the dog."
"It's our Spikey."
A retch.
Hector takes out his stethoscope. Robert takes a breath in. He lets out a howl. It's a quiet howl, like the ones he and Spike would make together. Then Robert takes a deeper breath, and, with a face upturned toward the ceiling, he lets out a howl loud enough to startle the doctor. Then there's another. Spike's body grows cold.

Hector waits for Robert to finish. I want to feel grief, like Robert, but instead I'm feeling rage, a big billowing vision of blackness that's rising up in me, all directed at Robert. I stifle it.

Robert turns on me. "Why don't you join in with me?" he asks.

"I can't," I say to Robert.

Hector tries to leave the room, backing out.

"Don't you fucking leave," Robert flashes at him. "I want you to witness this. I've lived with a man ten years, and he can't even join me in a howl. All he can do is obsess on you. And I'm sick of it."

"Robert!" I scream.

"Don't you scream at me! You're always screaming at me." Robert's eyes fill with water.

Robert runs out of the Pet Medical Center. I panic. I go to follow him, running, too. Outside, on Lincoln Boulevard, I see Robert running like a mad dog across the street, fast. He's racing in and out of cars, speeding down Lincoln Boulevard.

"Robert!" I scream.

A truck, turning out of a Chevron station, collides into a VW. The Bug swerves and hits Robert. Robert falls down. I can't see him.

Hector stumbles out of the Pet Medical Center. "What the fuck is going on with you two?" he asks.

Cars honk. A crowd gathers. Sirens drown out the screams.

"Call a fucking ambulance," Hector roars at the nurse, standing by the open front door. *"Now!"*

———

In the morning, I wake up alone. I hear the phone ring in Robert's room.

Marty: "Let the machine pick it up."

Robert: "The doctor said he'd call."

Marty: "Okay. But don't move so fast. I want you to keep it in me as you talk."

Robert: "Okay, okay."

Some tousling.

Robert: "Good morning!"

Silence.

Robert: "Oh. Wait a minute, Dr. Gibson." In a whisper: "I gotta pull out, goddammit."

Marty: "No way, Jose!"

Robert: "Marty, you little jerk. I'm sorry, Dr. Gibson. Let me get up. I mean, let me write it down. Hold on a second. Marty,

stop crying. Dr. Gibson, you still there? I'm listening, Dr. Gibson."

———

I was amazed by the variety of options Frieda's eyes provided me, little coming attractions — movies of destiny — that, in most ways, I was not ready to view or digest in any healthy way. I saw parts of myself I didn't recognize. I saw an angry, bitter man shouting vicious recriminations at his poor, aging parents. I had taken a public stand on TV. They didn't approve. So what? They didn't understand what they had done wrong. Was it so terrible to want grandchildren? How could they live without grandchildren? I saw a two-by-four hitting Mike's head and blood pouring out on a dark, deserted street in the meatpacking district of Manahttan. (A funny maybe-this-could-have-happened spin on that tragedy: Mike dead. Stan arriving home for the funeral and making peace with Willie and Linda.) I saw Mike on his knees in two bathhouses. I saw Mike chasing a man whom he had no business chasing, Robert's career the only partner Robert said he cared to share his life with. I saw that man break Mikey's heart: "I don't love you and never will," the man said, trying to be honest, being honest. I saw Mike drop out of college. I saw a funny cloud over Mike's head, then over all of Manhattan, like a plague, no, not *like* a plague. I saw the man who said he didn't love Mike fuck him even as the nighttime news gave it to them straight about STDs.

I saw Mike afraid, calling up Judy for coffee, later on making love to her in the Bronx where she still lived, but now alone. I saw the two moving for a time to Hackensack. (There's a funny maybe-this-could-happen gloss to that incident. I see relatives arriving at a reception, some stuffing envelopes in the pocket to Mike's suit jacket. Judy indulges in a little salsa step-ball-chain she recalls from Elena's wedding.) I saw Mike moving to L.A. to get away (to get away from Judy? to get away from Robert?) only to meet Robert's ex in Hollywood. Mike and Marvin-the-ex clicked, right off. I saw that when Marvin came down with AIDS, Mike moved him into his Hollywood Boulevard studio. Mike fed

him baby food. I saw Marvin suffering headaches; they were from toxoplasmosis. I saw Mike fighting to get Marvin a bed at a county hospital. I saw that Robert visited the two toward the end. (A funny maybe-this-could happen gloss on that scenario: Robert gets real famous: international tours and all. Marvin grows blind, loses his hair. Robert cuts short the make-it-or-break-it tour; he plants a vegetable garden for Marvin.) I saw that, by the end, Robert's famous pasta primavera was all Marvin will eat.

———

I stop mid-story.

"Wait a sec," Dr. Myron says, a bit confused by this chapter. "She showed you the future? I don't understand. I really don't. Different versions of the future? How could she do something like that?"

"I asked to see Hector. She showed what she could."

"But she never showed you Hector."

"A cagey one, that Frieda, huh?"

"Yet I find it interesting that all of these versions center around your decision to live or not live life fully as a gay person. I wonder why, as an Orthodox Jewish woman, your homosexuality was so important to her?"

"Good question."

"Have any ideas?"

"No, not really. Frieda always wanted me to be a *mensch*. She wanted to show me the cards that were dealt to me. She just wanted me to make a strong play. She did not feel the cards themselves were a problem."

"I'm surprised she showed you only those options then."

"Oh, no. Myron. There were many, many more."

"There were?"

"Yes. The movie kept rolling. It was actually quite infinite, filled with more stories than all the books in all the libraries through history put together."

"You don't say!" he says, writing fast.

"Yep."

"And each story came from her, entailed her?"

"Yeah, I guess."

The doctor stares me down: "You guess?"

I swallow hard. "Yeah. No. I mean, yeah. Each one. Yeah, right. I guess you could say she was in each one, more as a phantom or a feeling than anything else."

"You guess?"

"Yeah. What's wrong with guessing?"

Dr. Myron puts his pad down. "I don't get it. No Hector? Hmmm. So she gave you these stories, these options, whatever they are, and she asked you to choose between them?"

"Well, sort of. I mean, right. No, not really."

"Well, then. What did you choose?"

"What did I chose?" I ask. "What do you think?"

"I mean, was it as clear as all that?" Dr. Myron asks, zeroing in. "Was she on target?"

"Yeah," I say, nodding. "Pretty much, give or take a detail here or there. I mean, the guy's name wasn't Marvin, but Martin. And he never had toxoplasmosis. He had pneumocystis. But why split hairs? And Judy and I didn't move to Hackensack, we moved to Teaneck."

Myron shakes his head. "I'm awfully confused. I mean, what did you end up doing? It's not at all clear to me. What's going on, Mike? What are you struggling with? What *did* you struggle with?"

What was going on? Frieda saw what was going on. I saw what was going on. So she stopped. She ended the movies with a brisk blink of her cataract eye. Enough was enough.

I looked closely at Frieda—her pale face, creased in a hundred places just like it was in life, her whiskered jowls tucked in her neck like sacs holding food for the young. I gathered up the courage to do what had so far been too terrifying to do. I touched her. My hands traced the pliant lines in her face, her whiskers, her grey-black hair. I sucked in a sharp breath. She was as real as life, ripe with tears—yet, what? I saw then that the movies she showed me were just a ploy, a diversion, a mere sleight of

288 / Sacred Lips of the Bronx

hand by someone who couldn't really be bothered with cornball, bar mitzvah–style magic.

Something was wrong. She saw that every breath she took, so sad and poignant in its simplicity, broke me down to certain elements: I couldn't bear those elements, too many conjunctions of truth. Too bad how empathy could mock. For it was then, at the moment of greatest feeling, that I saw her for who she really was. Her face changed. Into that of Hector? Or rather the memory I had of Hector in his most idealized fashion? My breath swelled into a climax of feeling and longing—a homosexual's Beatrice, no? The face smiled benignly, though. The face spoke silent truths: It belonged to both Hector and Frieda—and to neither. The images I saw were clearly constructed and fluid, but the *feelings* the images called up were real and even absolute. This was, then, the soul? The voice of Frieda came through loud and clear even though it was Hector's face shimmering in sparkly neon colors before (or in?) my eyes. The Angel of Death was also the Angel of Life—wed together in the soul, and by the memories of Frieda and Hector? That's when I heard the music in my skull fade down into the near-silent whoosh of a breeze.

I was being given several choices.

To live with all this jazz?

Or to live without it all and go on like before?

It would be up to me. If I couldn't bear the weight of so much love and rage, Pandora's box would shut tight again, for a time. But it was clear what "she" preferred: *Choose me! Ikh bina yunge meydl un mayn harts tut mir vey.* I am a young girl and my heart hurts. *Ikh bin gekumen dir tsu lernen.* I have come to teach you. *Farges nisht vos Ikh hob dir ongezogt.* Don't forget what I have told you.

I had to forget. I could not bear to do otherwise. She made my own heart hurt too much. I spat her away like she was the Evil Eye. *Pfh. Pfh. Pfh.* "Go away," I shouted. "*Gey avek*, whoever you are."

She—whoever she was—wept. She would not be consoled; parting words meant nothing. She turned in on herself; she convoluted. She diminished. The smoke rose from her dissipated

body and her spirit vanished into thin air. By the time my father awoke, she-who-came-as-Frieda had gone. So had her music. So had her distracting coming attractions. She wasn't even a memory at that point. Neither were my memories of her.

———

I slump in the chair, looking around at Dr. Myron's office, filled with odd-looking sculptures and ancient forms. Just a few minutes ago, these little gold-and-red beings seemed so animated; now stone quiet. I'm sweating. My heart settles down. Dr. Myron rests in his seat. The room returns to normal.

"You turned her offer down, heh?"

"Sherlock Holmes you're not."

"Mike —"

"Wouldn't you have done the same?"

No answer.

"Now," he says, exhaling, smiling a little in relief, "we can get to work."

———

Spike rests on the blue Formica table in a ball. His ribs show through. His eyes, glazed with fever, open. *Thanks, Daddy.* He falls asleep.

"The chemo made him so nauseous," I say.

"We've never known Spike not to eat," Robert says. "It was such a shock, all of a sudden."

Dr. Gibson shakes his head. "The chemo can be hard on dogs."

"On people, too," Robert adds.

"On people, too," Dr. Gibson agrees. "He doesn't seem to be suffering too much right now."

"Oh, Doctor," Robert says. "He was crying all last night. We didn't sleep a wink. He went to the bathroom in his bed, which is right near our bed. He was too weak to go outside. Doctor, you had to be there."

The doctor asks if we're ready. We hold Spike's belly, his

head. His eyes open. *Hi, guys, how ya doing? I just had the wildest dream . . .*

The doctor gives Spike a shot.

I just felt something.

Robert bites his lip.

Oh, it's just you and me, guys. Thanks. I like Dr. Gibson, but he is so sappy sometimes. And I hate his dog biscuits.

"Robert," I say.

"Yes, Mike?"

Spike's eyelids close, just like they always do when Spike senses us close.

Daddy! What's happening?

Then a sharp whine, like someone stepped on his toe.

"Oh, shit! Mikey, what's happening?"

"It's okay, Robbie."

"It's quite okay," the good doctor says. "Just a little ol' distemper shot. Okay, we can let him down."

We carry Spike off the table and set him on his feet. Dr. Gibson hands Spike a munchie, which he gobbles up without chewing.

"This is the last treat I hope to give you in a long while, ol' pup," Dr. Gibson says, giddy. Spike slumps by our legs to nap, licking the place where he gets his distemper shot.

Dr. Gibson is beaming: "Look at the X rays, boys. I haven't seen a remission like this in years. Your dog's going to be okay. Do you hear that? Okay."

Robert grabs my hand. He takes in a deep breath. I anticipate a howl. Instead, Robert lets out a little cry mixed with hesitant laughter.

ike a practical joke, the American Airlines 747 circled above the old Bronx neighborhood — my own apartment building, can you believe? — before nose-diving into John F. Kennedy Airport. Once at the airport, the mania of refugees rushing into near-forgotten arms and vacationers pacing guiltily over their trips pressed into my heart like memories I never remembered having. The old terminal exuded cigarette smells, body odor and more unknown languages than the streets of Hollywood, California. Dark-haired ex-Soviets looked at me as if I were a returning exile. I took two Bufferin. A gypsy cab-driver spirited me to the Bronx for twenty bucks.

I had read stories in newspapers about my abandoned Bronx — bombed-out streets, alleys overrun with gang posses, vans crowded with crack babies, exploding mini-discos. But the morning elevated train felt as lazy and melancholic as ever. My rubbish-stuffed subway car was half-filled with men and women getting off night shifts. The *Daily News* sagged under their eyes like premature pillows. I got off at Yankee Stadium.

I circled the hot-dog stands. I felt like a teenager again, only now my Spanish was better. I nodded to overgrown kids my own age; some nodded back. I walked up toward the Grand Concourse and then veered west toward Jerome Avenue. I smelled the Hudson River, its chemical corrosion. I saw the top lights of the George Washington Bridge. I saw the blue-grey eight-story building, now burnt around the glassless windows, in which Hector's friends had given a get-high dance party, and the femmy teenagers merengued to golden oldies, such as "It's My Party and I'll Cry If I Want To" and Petula Clark's "Downtown." I remembered: when no one was looking, Hector shoved me into the porcelain-white bathroom to kiss me once or twice like he was doing me some favor. Now I squinted: what floor had we been on? Were we that high? That night I had seen a kid my own age shoot up for the first time. He was that surly guitar player with the tight blue veins and bad Patti Smith imitation. In his junkie's eyes I saw destinies of pleasure and pain laid out before us like an infinite smorgasbord. The trick was not to approach the appetizers like either a monk or a pig.

I saw the Jewish bakery, now a *Clínica Para Mujeres,* where the sugar-flaked, skinny owner gave me and Hector marzipan samples on a regular basis. I saw the Fordham Road movie theater, now a brightly lit porn theater, where Hector and I necked during matinees in the back and in secret while *The Exorcist* played over and over again for days, then weeks, until we memorized the line: *Your mother sucks cock in Hell.*

For the life of me, I could not find the Jerome Avenue shul.

I asked everyone I saw a question: "Excuse me, but do you know where the shul, the one-story, triangular, compact brown-bricked building had gone to? *Recuerde vd?*" One young girl from Cuba empathized; as far as she was concerned, the Jews had kept Cuba alive during Castro. She was trying to be helpful. I criticized myself for not remembering the jagged block Frieda and I had walked to nearly every day seventeen years ago. I searched out metropolitan landmarks: Hector's gated basketball courts; Mr. McPhee's Tide-sprinkled laundromat; the smell of Hebrew Nationals wafting from the now-defunct kosher deli two blocks away; the rumba of the approaching elevated train. I could not align a single one of these signposts with the concrete Bronx spread out before me. I felt transparencies, but no matched set.

I found an emblem from childhood, a fish market that had changed ownership from "Spiegel's" to "Cisnero's" but still looked the same, the ice and sawdust creating puddles and foul-smelling rivulets on the floor. Still: Where was the Jerome Avenue shul? I wouldn't rest until I located the house of worship in which Frieda had instructed me in the language of her heart: the Creator epiphanizes himself to us in the form of what we love.

No trace of the shul could be found in the Bronx I had just now stepped foot in.

I walked to the Grand Concourse. I trudged northbound, passing stoops and cornice-lined apartments that now showed shards of broken glass near the fire escapes and charred window-panes. I passed dark, narrow alleys that I knew by heart. There was the alley in which I had hid from Hector when we fought about "my time and space problem" (I expected fifteen-minute grace periods; he was punctual to a fault). There was the alley in which I had written "Fuck you, Moses" as my first — and last — attempt at antiheritage Bronx graffiti. (Little did I know that Moses was the name of the local coke dealer. I nearly got iced.) I passed my favorite subway entrances: the Grand Concourse station I had ducked into when I saw a cadre of uncles looking for a useless teenager to pick on; the Bainbridge IND I took with Hector when both of us had Times Square peep shows on our minds. I passed by the Catholic Church I had scowled at like the ghetto Jews do in *Fiddler on the Roof*. Eventually, my bigotry against Christ melted with Hector who felt he had a lot to teach me about the Holy Ghost. (Especially when Hector would go home to his own house after making love to me in mine; in his sharp absence I'd feel my friend more real than ever.)

I thought about all that now — the subway, the Holy Ghost, *Fiddler*. I had had expectations about meeting someone unimaginable during this walk down the memory lane of projects and poverty. Maybe an old adversary of the family or an old friend of Hector's family would emerge from one subway stop or other and wave hello. Maybe not Elena, Hector's sister, but someone who was tight with Elena. A second cousin? A long-lost neighbor who watched over Elena's and Carlos's babies like a hawk during the fire that nearly destroyed Hector's sister's home? There could be small talk, then some justifiable tears. I craved the smell of yucca, matzo balls, fried chicken, melting ice-cream sandwiches, tobacco, asphalt, burning coke. I craved odors that might waft to me from open windows, corroded apartment lobbies, and small cracks in car windows. I craved someone who would remember those smells with me, this bouquet of lapsed life where the flowering and wilting is all in your head. I half-fantasized seeing old Jewish men around fold-out tables shaking dice, dominoes, packs of cards, then, of course, their heads. Maybe one or two remembered Frieda through their dementia. Maybe one remembered the rabbi or, better yet, the rabbi's son.

I was so busy dreaming of what I might remember in the Bronx of my dreams that I managed to bypass my own apartment building. Hard to believe, but some imbecile had painted the six-story apartment complex fire-engine red. It now looked as distinct as a mini-mall. The ancient copper-green fountains that had once proudly spouted rusted water had been pulled out like a root. In its place, management had plopped down a security office. Freshly painted black gates guarded windows, doors and entranceways. The building cringed from nakedness. What had they done without all the fire escapes? What about the little plots of grass and flowers here and there? A security guard asked what business I had in "Bronx Gardens." I told him that I had once lived in this dump, long before they yanked out the flowers and shrubbery so they could name the place "Bronx Gardens."

I walked to Hector's old home. I needed to know about the whereabouts of the Rodriguezes: Elena, Hector, Maria, Roderigo. Maybe Hector had the peculiar luck to return home the same day as I did. Maybe we might bump into each other unawares. I prayed hard for that magical reunion as I walked past the hints of Bronx striving lamely toward renovation: a new high-rise, a demolished tenement and a fancy parking lot with just-painted white lines for the Geo Metros. That's when I realized that my fantasy was dead. The parking lot was located where Hector's house used to be.

I sat on a stoop across the street. An early fall rain came, more like mist than a downpour. The lot took on a woolly and wet odor; damp leaves fell on my leather jacket. I remembered:

Hector's building was reputed to be menacing due to an excess of dark corners and broken stairway lights. I don't remember feeling danger there, but you had to be on your toes. Now those corridors had disappeared. More leaves fell.

I took the bus to Jamaica, Queens; I walked five blocks to a quiet, tree-lined street on which a three-story cottage curtsied into the sky. The woman who opened the door wore a green blouse; I think it was silk or crepe or linen, I couldn't tell which. She touched herself by her breast, then her cleavage, like her skin told stories only she could decipher. She had grown slightly more gray, less plump—stately, I guess. We had written each other and spoken on the phone. We had met once or twice in Saks Fifth Avenue on a lark, for we both loved window-shopping. Now she held me like she was my sister. She dropped tears on my neck, which was not inappropriate, but not really expected.

The tiny three-bedroom house was chock full of toys—and two young boys, Ralph and Jacinth. Their boyish shouts— "Daddy, Daddy, he looks funny, like you"—were expected. The dozen congas were not. You couldn't walk without tripping over timbalis, maracas, vibraharps and a million sticks and half as many brushes. I realized that these accessories belonged to Helen and the boys as much as Stan. What a headache when everyone was at home! Stan had gotten stockier, but not fatter. In voice and eye contact, he felt lighter. We stood speechless before each other on the black shag carpeting.

"You haven't changed a bit," I said.

"Yeah, right."

As children, Stan and I had been abnormally affectionate. When our parents fought like mad dogs, chasing each other's tails when their insomnia hit hard, Stan and I held each other puppylike in the dark. Even though he was older, sometimes he'd droop his bumpy head on the faded jeans of my lap and I'd stroke his gnarly, Brylcreem hair into fitful sleep. Before puberty, Stan and I laid together on his narrow cot swapping stories about yappy aunts and uncles, mimicking their Slovak-Jewish accents while trading baseball cards. (Stan and I played terrible practical jokes on poor Aunt Chana. When she waltzed into our Bronx door for the High Holy

Day feasts, we'd greet her in her very own intonations: "*Nu*, Tante Chana, *Chelo, chelo*, how's by you, dahling?" Never once did she catch on.) As I grew more aware of my more sexual leanings, I did pull back from Stan's touch, allowing just legs over legs while watching "Saturday Night Live." He tried going for the more head-on-lap maneuvers, but I wouldn't have it.

The memories of closeness shamed me now that the bald, stocky man lurched like an adult before me. He refused to stand on ceremony. We talked. He alternately held my hand and patted my back — a little forced, if you ask me, but sunny and consoling all the same.

Jacinth and Ralph benefited, too, from his touch, which Stan provided to his boys easily in lieu of easy communication: pitter-pattering on shoulders, foreheads and kneecaps with knuckles and fingertips and the back of his palms. These kids boasted more spontaneous, jerky smiles than Stan or I could ever have worn. Their skin color shifted from olive to brown moment to moment. Ralph jumped on my arm like he knew me. He called his father "Gates." (Stan explained that "Gates" was jazz talk for someone whose music "swings.") Jacinth, of course, affected a more retiring pose. They had Jewish noses but Helen's soft brown skin and head tilt. Thank God I had had the presence of mind to purchase gifts: L.A.-styled space-age doodads such as Geo stones, Star Trek phasers, and a paint-by-number set of Joshua Tree. The kids giggled into paroxysms of unbelieving contentment while holding the stones up to the light. How had they remained so well adjusted in view of Stan's pathological silences? The boys themselves were not chatterers, but not overly serious either. "Uncle Mike," Ralph said to me, "anyone ever tell you, you got Brillo for hair?" Jacinth went star crazy over the map of the galaxies. Their mother, the measure of this family, set the scales. Helen spoke Stan's will to his sons, as in, "Get your little butt over here, Ralph-Ralph, and give Uncle Mikey a kiss thank you," or "Now that's a nice pattern on the vibraharps, Jacinth, but don't you think it's time to clean up the gift wrap?" Ralph was wiry and extroverted and, at ten years old, ready to explain every observation regarding his gifts to onlookers. Jacinth set the gifts quietly aside and just watched Stan and me try and talk. Jacinth was stick thin, a geometry whiz at the age of twelve. He seemed ready to have an uncle magically appear at his doorstep with a not-so-cheap paint-by-number set and stack of fresh comic books and a funny way of sitting quietly with the father that Jacinth must have picked up, too, in the years that kept father and sons apart during Stan's gigs with Lionel Hampton, Wynton Marsalis, and Madonna.

———

Since our Bronx days, Stan and I had seen each other and spoken by phone, but, truth be told, this extended afternoon was our first real intimate time together in many years. So Stan managed more words than usual, a flood of catch-up information, with the ellipses filled in delicately by Helen. Although Stan and Helen shielded me from the specifics, I understood immediately that somehow the family had grown quite close to Linda and Willie, who apparently had recovered just fine from his one-and-only heart attack. For a second, I felt gypped out of the peace treaty. "It was the children," Helen protested. "We wanted them to feel the love of grandparents—the rest, it could all be forgotten for the boys' sake." I saw pictures of the kids and my parents at Fort Lauderdale. (They looked only somewhat older, if a little less overweight and a little less gray.) I saw pictures of Ralph in Willie's arms; I saw pictures of Linda diapering Jacinth, a smile the size of Shea Stadium across her peach-fuzzy lips.

"What exactly happened?" I asked Stan. I understood: or thought I did, or something. It felt a blur, the exodus from The Bronx, the angry letters, the person-to-person phone calls that Linda and Willie placed and I never took. Now nothing seemed so upsetting. I tried to rationalize my rage; or, more to the point, I tried to rationalize my frozen anger that had never thawed into rage. I couldn't. There were times I had been on TV, written articles, spoken about the dying. Willie and Linda couldn't be proud on cue—AIDS had terrified—and I couldn't bear with them, hold their hands. Had Stan, behind my back, made a separate peace?

Helen counseled me not to worry. Linda and Willie had long ago forgotten. Now they wished everyone well. Perhaps all this family meddling and cracking and mending was a blessing in disguise. For they, too, had decided to get on with their lives. They were not recognizable to me, by Helen's description. My mother was reputed to be a delegate for the Democratic party; she had won a lottery; she took in foster children. My father was said to have opened a hardware business of his own. They had a fax machine, a computer, friends. "We've all mellowed," Helen said, sounding so much like Linda.

At some point, Helen took the kids in the van to pick up pizza and Diet Cokes, fighting-for-fun over whether to go for plain cheese or pepperoni. "Not very kosher," Ralph said, "the meat, the cheese," and then he added, in Frieda's tongue, being tongue-in-cheek, "God forbid, a *shanda*." I was stunned. Helen explained that although she had been raised a Catholic and had long ago abandoned confession and the rest, she felt it necessary to raise the boys as both Catholic and Jewish — "and what-have-you." The boys laughed at the Hebrew school teachers they hired in Queens — "Such *nebbishes*, Uncle Mike!" — but understood God as an under-the-table kind of thing. "They're under no impression that God cares whether you're Jewish or Muslim or this or that," Helen said to me. Like you hold up a net and you catch what's in the air. To Helen, the net was the human heart. I took a look around at all the drums in the house and understood.

Alone, Stan and I discussed Frieda's presence without naming names. It was our way to make sense of our history. "We felt like aliens, didn't we?" he asked me. He had theories: that maybe our past enabled us to bear the full weight of our futures. "Perhaps," he wagered, "if I hadn't been so angry, I wouldn't have drummed like my life depended on it." He prided himself on a new attitude, one he attributed to his life as jazzer — that the past was set in place so the future could have a chance to improvise its fate. "You need a little dissonance to get the groove going," he said. He called this "groove" his guiding ghost.

"Dig," he said. "They'd be happy to hear from you."

I slid a picture of my mother and father out from Helen's

narrow black photo album. Linda held Ralph's hand. Willie held Jacinth's. The kids smiled ice-cream-sandwich smiles; in the background, a roller-coaster ride soared down into its steep drop.

"And what about Hector?" Stan asked. Just then I heard the kids yelping, "Pizza, schmizza, pizza, schmizza."

"Boy, am I starved," I said.

Stan pressed on: "You ever hear from him?"

"Hector?" I asked. "I let him go a long time ago."

Stan had something to say, but Helen doled out the paper plates and Italian red pepper. Before we knew it, all of us were picking goops of cheese off our laps, slurping the grease down with cold drinks and the kinds of stories kids tell about the origin of pizza and cardboard boxes, and why it's good luck to eat the crust first as opposed to the triangular tip.

A taxi spirits me from LAX to Venice Beach, where a thick layer of marine mist welcomes me home. I resist an impulse to kiss the ground or the Palestinian taxi driver. A huge stretch of swamplike nothingness separates the airport from Marina del Rey and other beach communities. The openness beckons to me with the grace of expansive redemption that has always lured exhausted Europeans and New Yorkers westward.

At home, Tahar announces almost too soon that Robert has called in my absence. I try not to shiver. Tahar has been looking after Spike and house sitting, and taking daily walks to the ocean ("to chill out those Ts"). Now it's awkward, with me home. I see that Tahar wants a lot: to hear about the trip; to touch me; to see if I want him to stay the night. I watch him like he's a guru, or a master telephone operator. He puts all of his wants on hold. I decide to let him leave me for now, so I can digest the news about Robert. He hands me my keys, saying, "Welcome home." Pointing to Spike, he adds, "We missed you." I return the keys to him, saying, "They're yours."

I unpack my bags and feed Spike. I call Robert. I brace myself for his bravado: tall tales of a trip to Australia, news about how Marty was taking his HIV status, whether or not the two had decided to move in together or wait it out. Instead, his voice sounds shaky. He says he missed me.

"Can we meet for dinner?" he asks. "Tonight?"

We hang up and I think, "out of the frying pan . . . "

It's midafternoon. I can't think of what to do till dinner. I lift Spike's leash like it's a lasso. For the first time in six months, he leaps into the air, barking like a puppy.

You take Western Avenue a mile or two north from Hollywood Boulevard to get away. It's the desert, sagebrush. Boulders covered in green-and-yellow lichen. Wild daisies, white and dark purple. The city's exhaust; dry dust. Snakeskins. Men cruise in the bushes. The sounds of modern cowboy boots on the hills they made old cowboy movies on. There's an ecosystem: a brook; mestizo uncles with blanca nieces; Guatemalan donas; Valley boys with cigarettes and Malcolm X hats. Robert and I had picnicked here when we first moved to L.A. Spike ran around our blanket. Robert discussed plans. I nodded off. He held my hands under the blanket.

Today the fern dell feels overrun with winter growth. There are plateaus of moss, cradled into stones and black dirt. Spike, almost himself, charts the path a few steps ahead, always protecting, always on the lookout.

I see Spike stop in his dusty tracks. He spots something important. Then I do, too. Or rather I feel it, like the way you sense the phone call in the middle of the night (how it will change your life!) a moment before the phone rings. The smog inside lifts.

"Hector!"

Spike barks.

"It's okay, Spikey," I say, hearing my voice crack. "I see. It's an old friend."

The man turns around, sharp—anxious. Was I wrong? He stands on the other side of the lake, twenty or thirty feet away. The body is lean. A short-sleeved black silk shirt blows in the wind. The silk clings to his ribs, cut into precision as far as I could tell. The lips look paper thin; the hair jet black; the eyes darkened inside sockets so oval I think they're eggs. The wind comes. Suddenly it is spring. I smell the lake, polluted with cig-arettes and beer. The man's hair rattles in the wind.

"Oh, shit!" he says.

We laugh, our mouths opening in fits of surprise and comedic appreciation. Spike throws his head hard and fast against my leg. *Who is it, Daddy?*

Spike and I watch the man walk to my side of the water, laughing in little starts, secret starts. He shakes his head this way and that. The walk takes its sweet time. And with the walk, a certain aperture into history that is both a rapture and a lament.

"Hector? I don't believe my fucking eyes."

The man stops, looking at me hard. He smiles, but not just sweet. "Oh," he says. "That one." Spike sniffs around. "Hey, pooch," he says, holding his hand out to Spike's face. Spike's whiskers twitch. Then he licks the man's hand.

I look more closely. "Huh?"

"Is that your pick-up line or something?" he asks. "Like, you act like you know somebody and then, oops, realize you've made a mistake?"

"Huh?"

" 'Hector,' " he says, holding the name up in quotations. "I like that. Has character."

I shake my head. The man extends his hand. "The name's Lewis. Or, if you prefer, Luis?"

"Luis. Lewis. I'm sorry. I confused you with someone else."

"I bet." A snort. "You guys are all the same."

In a moment, Luis and I stand mere inches apart. Loud laugh-ter between us. People looking. Spike breathing with his tongue out, salivating. *What's so funny, guys?*

"I know you won't believe this," I mutter, "but you bear an amazing resemblance to a man I once knew. The first great love of my life, as a matter of fact."

"Great line, *hombre.*"

"It's not a line."

"Right."

"Right."

A few additional creases by the forehead, maybe. The eyes sagging at nuanced creases. His hair dangles long, speckled with grey. He's tightly thin, pumped up in a gymlike way. A silver cross hangs from his neck. An open button by his shirt exposes skin. A scar above his left cheek. The same rain-forest eyes; the same studied introversion. But not the same person.

"It looks like you're processing a mile a minute," he says.

"Hey," I offer. "Sounds like you're a therapist or something."

"I am."

"Cool."

"But I don't go in for any of that depth-psychoanalytic, shrink-shit. You got a problem, let's fix it. I mean, get a life. Know what I mean?"

"Yeah. Sure."

We sit down on a bench. Spike collapses in a neat pile on the cool forest floor, nodding out now that he's gotten some real human company.

"So what you do?" Luis asks.

"I'm a writer."

Another snort. "I might have guessed. What with your wild imagination and all."

It is hard to talk. I feel the heat from his body, near his silk shirt. I am conscious of my arm brushing up against his, sensing the warmth that comes, it seems, from a place on his arm. My heart kicks in with simple lust; it hadn't in so long. His breath smells of coffee and cigarettes and milk. His hair hasn't been washed today.

Luis resorts to facts. He works as a counselor in Barstow, California. He's driven into L.A. to be interviewed for a job to head a foundation that works with street youth in the Pico Union area. He says he is a post-Chicano. His meeting is to take place an hour from now. He had been married. He has a five-year-old boy.

I say, "A day hasn't gone by when I haven't thought of this guy Hector. And then here you are, but you're not him. But in a way . . . I don't know."

"Man," he whispers, putting his finger to his lips. "Shhh."

We sit still, for as long as ten minutes. I wonder why the silence doesn't feel unbearable. I close my eyes.

In the dark spaces, I see my departed grandmother, as if sitting on her easy chair. We had seen the basketball players together. We had moved our fingers together along the lines of prayer books. We had spared each other loneliness. Now, no more. Until death. Good-bye.

I must have said the word out loud, because Luis heard me.

"Yes," he says, "time to be going. I don't want to be running late."

"No."

"Mike," Luis says, protesting.

"No."

He gets impatient, picking up his leather briefcase, riffling inside. Spike perks up his ears. "Look, here's my card. I'll be in L.A. next month. And if I get this job—"

I kiss the guy, lightly, quickly—in the middle of the fern dell, in broad daylight. His lips taste of salt, soft.

"Man, watch your fucking back. This is a public place, you know?"

"Right."

"Right."

I watch him walk off. Spike bounces up and follows Luis for a few paces. He turns back; so does Luis. "Don't lose the fucking card," he tells me.

Before I can say, "I won't," he's on his way again. In a moment, gone. And the fern dell is empty of people. And the sun begins to set. I attach the leash to Spike and we walk away.

———

Robert sits in a corner of the Thai restaurant, near a fake bronze statue of Buddha. He sees me come in. He waves. It seems as if a dozen just-served heavy-metal types in black miniskirts and too-tight leather jackets get up from their tables, keeping me from making my way to Robert. I wind my way to the back, where Robert is. I scoot into his booth. The red vinyl seat is cracked, sticky with curry.

"You're smiling," he says.

"It's good to see you."

"I don't remember you this happy."

"I'll say it again: I am happy to see you."

"Me, too."

He grows quiet. "Wow," he says. "It's been so long."

"A few months."

"Three."

"A long time for us."

"A real long time."

"Spike's in the car?"

"Resting peacefully. Missing you terribly. Boy, is he in for a treat!"

"I'm so glad he didn't fucking die, Mikey-Moo."

The waitress comes. Robert orders vegetable curry and brown rice. I go with a chicken dish. I want to know about a recent trip to Australia, if he took Marty along. I wonder who's cooking Robert his meals. He brushes it all away in a sip of hot tea. "A gig," he says, blowing into the steaming teacup.

He goes for a gulp. "Mikey-Moo."

"Robert!" I say. I reach for his hand. It's there. "Robert, the most amazing thing happened to me today."

"What?"

I pause. "I had a rendezvous—"

"Really!"

"In a fern dell."

"Really? Who with?"

I smile and blow it off. He rubs his head.

"You still got that headache?" I ask.

"It was bad, real bad after the move," he says, our meals arriving. "Now it just kinda ebbs and flows. Hey, I hear from Tahar that you took a trip to the Bronx. How'd it go?"

I dig into my food. "Robert," I say. "Whew. I went and, well, it was this very simple trip. I mean, you wouldn't believe how simple it was. But that's a whole other story. Hey, I hear you got a new place. Tahar tells me it's fucking palatial."

"It's no mansion, Mikey-Moo. I mean, the roof leaks and everything. And I hate living with someone who doesn't read."

————

We split the check, our first time doing so in many years, maybe ten years. The waitress takes the money. She goes. We don't get up. The whole time Robert holds my hand. Our meal is just getting going. He presses his lips together. A waiter takes an order next to us, looking at us. It gets dark outside. The palm trees brace against the wind, shaking a bit on top. Robert holds my hand. We look. Sitting quietly into the meal, as it digests in us, the fears about how we would leave the restaurant, and the sense that we would leave it, but only for now. We sit quietly. The house in Venice near the ocean is emptied of dog barks, meals. The books divided up. The voices, placated. Now just us. There was a visit. Now the man who had never spoken to me of visits is sitting here, visiting. His hand on mine, in the now-empty restaurant. We sit still, hands clasped and lips silent. The words will come. Not now, but soon. Through the lips. Like a kiss. Like a breath. Like a wish. Like a riot. Like a voice from another world. Like who knows anymore. *Farges nisht vos Ikh hob dir ongezogt....*